He began to kiss her more passionately and she couldn't find the strength to push him away – perhaps the truth was she didn't want to find it. She wished she weren't so sensible, so religious, so cautious, that she could find the courage to live with him openly and not give a damn about being respectable and what anyone thought. Or that she were harder, like John, able to leave the people she loved behind without a second thought.

But she was none of these things. She was Alice Lacey, who had four children, who lived in Amber Street, Bootle and owned her own hairdressers'. Somehow Alice knew she would never escape these simple facts, because deep down in her heart she didn't want to. She was her own jailer, bound by conventions she would never break. Even her love for Neil, which was far greater than she had ever admitted either to him or to herself, wasn't enough to change her.

He was carrying her into the bedroom and she didn't protest.

'We didn't know last night we would never make love again,' he whispered, 'and I'd like the last time to be special. Promise you'll never forget me, Alice.'

Maureen Lee was born in Bootle and now lives in Colchester, Essex. *Stepping Stones*, *Liverpool Annie*, *Dancing in the Dark*, *The Girl from Barefoot House*, *The House by Princes Park*, *Lime Street Blues*, *Queen of the Mersey*, *The Old House on the Corner*, *The September Girls*, *The Leaving of Liverpool*, *Mother of Pearl*, and the three novels in the Pearl Street series, *Lights Out Liverpool*, *Put Out the Fires* and *Through the Storm* are all available in Orion paperback. Her novel *Dancing in the Dark* won the 2000 Parker Romantic Novel of the Year Award. Visit her website at www.maureenlee.co.uk.

Have you read them all?
Curl up with a

Maureen Lee

STEPPING STONES

Lizzie O'Brien escapes her dark Liverpool childhood when she runs away to London – towards freedom and a new life. But the past is catching up with her, threatening to destroy her dreams . . .

LIGHTS OUT LIVERPOOL

There's a party on Pearl Street, but a shadow hangs over the festivities: Britain is on the brink of war. The community must face hardship and heartbreak with courage and humour.

PUT OUT THE FIRES

1940 – the cruellest year of war for Britain's civilians. In Pearl Street, near Liverpool's docks, families struggle to cope the best they can.

THROUGH THE STORM

War has taken a terrible toll on Pearl Street, and changed the lives of all who live there. The German bombers have left rubble in their wake and everyone pulls together to come to terms with the loss of loved ones.

LIVERPOOL ANNIE

Just as Annie Harrison settles down to marriage and motherhood, fate deals an unexpected blow. As she struggles to cope, a chance meeting leads to events she has no control over. Could this be Annie's shot at happiness?

DANCING IN THE DARK

When Millie Cameron is asked to sort through her late aunt's possessions, she finds buried among the photographs, letters and newspaper clippings, a shocking secret . . .

THE GIRL FROM BAREFOOT HOUSE

War tears Josie Flynn from all she knows. Life takes her to Barefoot House as the companion of an elderly woman, and to New York with a new love. But she's soon back in Liverpool, and embarks upon an unlikely career . . .

LACEYS OF LIVERPOOL

Sisters-in-law Alice and Cora Lacey both give birth to boys on one chaotic night in 1940. But Cora's jealousy and resentment prompt her to commit a terrible act with devastating consequences . . .

THE HOUSE BY PRINCES PARK

Ruby O'Hagan's life is transformed when she's asked to look after a large house. It becomes a refuge – not just for Ruby and her family, but for many others, as loves, triumphs, sorrows and friendships are played out.

LIME STREET BLUES

1960s' Liverpool, and three families are linked by music. The girls form a successful group, only to split up soon after: Rita to find success as a singer; Marcia to become a mother; and Jeannie to deceive her husband, with far-reaching consequences . . .

QUEEN OF THE MERSEY

Queenie Todd is evacuated to a small town on the Welsh coast with two others when the war begins. At first, the girls have a wonderful time until something happens, so terrifying, that it will haunt them for the rest of their lives . . .

THE OLD HOUSE ON THE CORNER

Victoria lives in the old house on the corner. When the land is sold, she finds herself surrounded by new properties. Soon Victoria is drawn into the lives of her neighbours – their loves, lies and secrets.

THE SEPTEMBER GIRLS

Cara and Sybil are both born in the same house on one rainy September night. Years later, at the outbreak of war, they are thrown together when they enlist and are stationed in Malta. It's a time of live-changing repercussions for them both . . .

KITTY AND HER SISTERS

Kitty McCarthy wants a life less ordinary – she doesn't want to get married and raise children in Liverpool like her sisters. An impetuous decision and a chance meeting twenty years later are to have momentous repercussions that will stay with her for ever . . .

THE LEAVING OF LIVERPOOL

Escaping their abusive home in Ireland, sisters Mollie and Annemarie head to Liverpool – and a ship bound for New York. But fate deals a cruel blow and they are separated. Soon, World War II looms – with surprising consequences for the sisters.

MOTHER OF PEARL

Amy Curran was sent to prison for killing her husband. Twenty years later, she's released and reunited with her daughter, Pearl. But Amy is hiding a terrible secret – a tragedy that could tear the family apart . . .

Laceys of Liverpool

MAUREEN LEE

An Orion paperback

First published in Great Britain in 2001
by Orion
This paperback edition published in 2001
by Orion Books Ltd,
Orion House, 5 Upper St Martin's Lane,
London WC2H 9EA

An Hachette UK company

9 10 8

Reissued 2009

A CIP catalogue record for this book
is available from the British Library.

ISBN 978-0-7528-4403-9

Printed and bound in Great Britain by
Clays Ltd, St Ives plc

The Orion Publishing Group's policy is to use papers that
are natural, renewable and recyclable products and
made from wood grown in sustainable forests. The logging
and manufacturing processes are expected to conform to
the environmental regulations of the country of origin.

www.orionbooks.co.uk

For Paul,
May the force always be with you.

Prologue
CHRISTMAS 1940

The woman lay listening to the rain as it beat against the hospital windows. She and Alice hadn't picked a good night to have their babies. As had become the custom in Bootle over the last few months, there'd been an air raid, a bad one, and they'd all been moved down to the cellar. Alice's lad had been born only minutes after the All Clear, at a quarter past eleven. Her own son had arrived almost three hours later, so they'd have different birthdays. Later, there'd been an emergency. Some woman had been found in the rubble of her house about to drop her baby. Since then, things had quietened down.

In a bed opposite, her sister-in-law was fast asleep, dead to the world, like the other six women in the ward. 'Why can't *I* sleep like that?' the woman murmured fretfully. 'I can never sleep.' Her mind was always too full of plans for the future, schemes: how to get this, how to do that. How to make twenty-five bob last the whole week, including paying the rent and buying the food. Oh, how she'd love new curtains for the parlour! But new curtains, new anything, were an impossible dream.

Unless she stole something, pawned it, bought curtains with the money. She'd stolen before, her heart in her mouth, sweat trickling down the insides of her arms. The first time it was only a string of beads that looked like pearls. The price ticket said a guinea. The pawnbroker had offered a florin, which she'd accepted gratefully and bought four nice cups and saucers in Paddy's Market.

One day she'd walked all the way into town and nicked a cut-glass vase from George Henry Lee's, which she kept on the mantelpiece, though she was the only one who knew it was cut glass. Billy thought it was just a cheap old thing. The silver candlestick she'd robbed from Henderson's had paid for a nice mat in front of the parlour fireplace. Some things she kept, some she pawned. She'd become quite skilled at shoplifting. The trick was to stay calm, not rush, smile, make your way slowly to the door. Stepping outside was the worst part. If spotted, it was the time you'd be nabbed. But she'd got away with it so far.

The woman didn't care how she looked as long as it was respectable, or what she ate, but she liked pretty things for the house: curtains, crockery, cutlery, furniture. Furniture most of all. She'd give anything for a new three-piece: velveteen, dark green or plum-coloured. She licked her lips and thought about brocade cushions with fringes, one at each end of the settee, on each of the chairs.

Most of all, she'd like a nice big house to put the lovely things in. She was sick to death of living in a two-up, two-down in O'Connell Street. But if curtains were an impossible dream, then a big house was – well, out of the question. Being married to a no-hoper like Billy Lacey, she was just as likely to fly to the moon.

She shoved herself to a sitting position. The red light on the ceiling cast a sinister glow over the ward, over the prone bodies beneath the faded cotton counterpanes. 'It looks like a morgue,' she thought. Paper chains crisscrossed the room and she remembered it was Christmas Eve. 'Everyone's dead except me and that fat bitch in the corner snoring her head off.'

The clock over the door showed a quarter past four. A cup of tea should arrive soon. Alice, who already had three kids, all girls, and knew about such things, said the tea trolley came early, around five o'clock, which seemed an unearthly time to wake anyone up. In the meantime she'd go for a walk. If she lay in bed till kingdom come, she'd never go asleep.

The rain was lashing down, making the windows rattle in their frames. It drummed on the roof and she hoped Billy would keep an eye on the loose slates over the lavatory. She'd been at him to fix them for ages, but would probably end up fixing them herself. She fixed most things around the house. Her lips twisted bitterly when she thought about Billy. His brother, John, had stayed in the ozzie with Alice until an hour before their lad was born. He'd only left because the girls were being looked after by a neighbour who was scared of the raids. But Billy had left *her* on the steps outside the ozzie when she was about to have their first-born child. Off to the pub, as usual. He didn't know yet if she'd had a boy or a girl.

There was a nurse in the glass cubicle at the end of the ward where a sprig of mistletoe hung over the door. She was at a desk, head bent, writing. The new mothers were expected to remain confined to their beds for seven whole days, not even allowed to go to the lavatory, but the woman slid from under the bedclothes and crept past, opening one half of the swing doors just enough to allow her through. The nurse didn't look up.

The dimly lit corridor was empty, silent. Her bare feet made no sound on the cold floor. She crept round corners, through more doors, dodged into the lavatories when she heard footsteps coming towards her. The footsteps passed, faded, and she looked both ways before coming out, hoping it wasn't someone on their way to

3

her ward who'd notice the empty bed, though it was unlikely. The hospital was understaffed. Some nurses had joined the Forces, or gone into better-paid jobs. There were a lot of part-timers and older nurses who'd retired and come back to do their bit.

She arrived at the place that had been her destination all along: the nursery. Five rows of babies, tightly wrapped in sheets, like little mummies in their wooden cots. Most were asleep, a few grizzled, some had their eyes wide open. Like her, they couldn't sleep.

Her own baby had been whisked away because of the emergency and she'd barely seen him. Now she did, she saw he was a pale little thing. He looked sickly, she thought. There was yellow stuff in his eyes. As she stared at her sleeping child, she felt nothing. She was twenty-seven, older than Alice, and had been married longer. But she hadn't wanted a baby. The sponge soaked in vinegar she'd inserted every night, which Billy knew nothing about, hadn't worked for once.

The child couldn't possibly have come at a worse time. Just when she'd worn Billy down, ranted at him mercilessly for month after month, until he'd conceded that letting his missus get a job wasn't a sore reflection on his masculine pride. Not with a war on and women all over the country working in ways they'd never done before. Why, there were women in the Army, on the trams, delivering the post, in factories doing men's jobs.

It was a job in a factory on which the woman had set her eye, making munitions. You could earn as much as four quid a week, three times as much as Billy. And as she said to him, 'Any minute now, you'll be called up. What am I supposed to do then? Sit at home, twiddling me thumbs, living on the pittance I'll get from the Army?'

His face had paled. He was a coward, not like his

brother John, who'd volunteered when war broke out, but had been turned down because he was in a reserved occupation. John was a centre lathe turner, Billy a labourer. There was nothing essential about *his* menial job. John, anxious to make a contribution towards the war, had become a fire-watcher. Billy carried on as usual and haunted the pubs waiting for his call-up papers from the Army to land on the mat.

She'd only been in the munitions factory a fortnight, packing shells. It was hard work, but she liked it. If she felt tired, she thought about the pay packet she'd get on Friday, about the things she'd buy, and soon perked up. Then she discovered she was up the stick, pregnant and, stupid idiot that she was, she told the woman who worked beside her and next minute everyone knew, including the foreman, and she'd got the push.

'This is not the sort of job suitable for a woman in the family way,' the foreman said.

The woman glared through the glass at her baby. She hadn't thought what to call him. She wasn't interested. Billy wanted Maurice for some reason if they had a boy, but she had no idea if Maurice was a saint's name. Catholics were expected to call their kids after saints. Alice's girls had funny Irish names and she didn't know if they were saints either. The new kid would be called Cormac. 'No "k" at the end,' John had said, smiling. He humoured his silly, dreamy wife something rotten.

Where was Cormac? There were cards pinned to the foot of each cot with drawing pins. 'LACEY (1)' it said on the cot directly in front of her. Her own baby was 'LACEY (2)'. Alice had yet to see her little son. It had been a difficult birth and she'd been in agony the whole way through. John had been close to tears when he'd had to go home. Afterwards, with seven stitches and blind with pain, Alice had been given something to make her sleep.

Her own confinement had been painless – she wouldn't have dreamt of making a fuss had it been otherwise. She hadn't needed a single stitch. Her belly still felt slightly swollen and she hurt a bit between the legs, that was all.

Even though she didn't give a damn about babies, the woman had to admit Cormac was a bonny lad. He had dark curly hair like his dad, and he wasn't all red and shrivelled like the other babies. His big brown eyes were wide open and she could have sworn he was looking straight at her. She pressed her palms against the glass and something dead peculiar happened in her belly, a slow, curling shiver of anger. It wasn't fair: Alice had the best Lacey, now she had the best son.

From deep within the bowels of the hospital, she heard the rattle of dishes. Tea was being made, the trolley was being set. Any minute now, someone would come.

The woman opened the door of the nursery and went in.

Chapter 1
CHRISTMAS 1945

Alice Lacey sang to herself as she swept a cloud of Florrie Piper's hair into the corner of the salon. 'Away in a manger, no crib for a bed . . .' She brushed the hair on to a shovel and took it into the yard to empty in the dustbin.

'They say you can sell hair like that for a small fortune in the West End of London,' Mrs Piper yelled from under the dryer when Alice came back.

'Who to?'

'Wig makers. They're always on the lookout for a good head of hair.'

'Really,' Alice said doubtfully. The hair she'd just thrown away was more suitable for a bird's nest: dry as dust, over-permed, full of split ends and dyed the colour of soot.

'You can comb Mrs Piper out now, Alice,' Myrtle said in a slurred voice.

'About time too,' Florrie Piper said, tight-lipped. 'These curlers are giving me gyp.'

'I don't know how you stand it to be honest.' Alice switched off the dryer, and Mrs Piper heaved her large body out of the chair and went to sit in front of a pink-tinted mirror.

'We can't all have naturally wavy hair, Alice Lacey, not like you.' Florrie Piper chose to take offence. She

7

sniffed audibly. 'You shouldn't work in a hairdresser's if you can't take what's done to the customers.'

Alice removed the net and yelped when her fingers touched a red-hot metal curler. It must be torture, sitting for half an hour with bits of burning metal pressed against your scalp. 'I'll take them out in a minute,' she muttered. 'Would you like a mince pie?'

'Well, I wouldn't say no,' Mrs Piper said graciously. She'd already had three. Food wasn't usually provided in Myrtle's Hairdressing Salon, but it was Christmas Eve. Some rather tired decorations festoòned the walls and a bent tinsel star hung in the steam-covered window. There'd been sherry earlier, but the proprietor had finished off the lot by dinner time. Myrtle was as tipsy as a lord and had made a terrible mess of Mrs Fowler with the curling tongues. The waves were dead uneven. Fortunately, Mrs Fowler's sight wasn't all it should be and she refused to wear glasses. Hopefully, she wouldn't notice.

Mrs Piper had recovered her good humour. 'What are you doing for Christmas, luv?' she enquired when Alice began to remove the curlers. Her ears were a startling crimson.

'Nothing much.' Alice wrinkled her nose. 'John's mam's coming to Christmas dinner, along with his brother Billy and his wife. They've got a little boy, Maurice, exactly the same age as our Cormac. Me dad usually comes, but he's off to Ireland tonight to spend Christmas with his sister. She's not been well.'

'Your Cormac will be starting school soon, I expect.'

'In January. He was five only yesterday.'

'And how are your girls? You know, I can never remember their names.'

'Fionnuala, Orla and Maeve,' Alice said for the thousandth time in her life. 'They're at a party this avvy in St James's church hall. Something to do with Sunday School. I made them a cake to take. I managed to get some dates.'

Mrs Piper eyed the remainder of the mince pies. 'Would you like another?' Alice enquired.

'I wouldn't say no,' Mrs Piper repeated. 'It would be a shame if they went to waste. You're closing early today, aren't you? I must be one of your last customers.'

'We've got a couple of trims, that's all. Here's one of 'em now.' The bell on the door gave its rather muted ring – it probably needed oiling – and Bernadette Moynihan came in. She was a vivacious young woman with an unusually voluptuous figure for someone so small. Alice smiled warmly at her best friend. 'Help yourself to a mince pie, Bernie.'

'I thought we were having sherry an' all,' Bernadette cried. 'I've been looking forward to it all day.'

'I'm afraid it's gone.' Alice glanced at Myrtle who seemed to have given up altogether on hairdressing and was staring drunkenly at her reflection in the pink mirror.

Bernadette grinned. 'She looks like a ghoul,' she whispered.

Myrtle was a tad too old for so much lipstick, eyeshadow, mascara and rouge. Now, everything was smudged and she looked like a sad, elderly clown. Her grey roots were showing and the rest of her hair had been peroxided to a yellow frizz. She made a poor advertisement for a hairdressing salon.

'Don't comb it out too much, luv,' Mrs Piper said when the curlers were removed. 'I like it left tight. It lasts longer.'

Alice loosened the curls slightly with her fingers and Mrs Piper said, 'How much is that, luv?'

'Half a crown.'

'And worth every penny!' She left, tipping Alice threepence, with her head resembling the inside of an Eccles cake.

The door closed and Alice looked from Bernadette to Myrtle who was slowly falling asleep, then back again. 'I'm not supposed to give trims, not official, like.' She usually went to Bernadette's to trim her hair, or Bernadette came to hers.

'Well, if you don't cut me hair, it doesn't look like anyone else will.' Bernadette seized a gown and tied it around her neck. 'I just want an inch off. Anyroad, Al, you've got the knack. You couldn't do it better if you were properly trained. I only came 'cos it's Christmas and I was expecting mince pies and a glass of sherry. To be sadly disappointed,' she added in a loud voice in Myrtle's direction, 'in regard to the sherry.'

Alice giggled. 'Sit down, luv. An inch you said?'

'One inch. A fraction shorter, a fraction longer, and I'll complain to the management.'

'You'll be lucky.' Alice attacked Bernadette's smooth fair hair, draped over one eye like Veronica Lake, with the scissors. 'Are you looking forward to tonight?'

Bernadette grinned. 'Ever so much. I've always liked Roy McBride. He works in Accounts. I was thrilled to pieces when he asked me out – and to a dinner dance on Christmas Eve!'

'I hope you have a lovely time.' Alice placed her hands on her friend's shoulders and they stared at each other in the mirror. 'Don't be too disappointed if he turns out like some of the others, will you, luv?'

'Like *most* of the others, you mean. All *I* want is company, all *they* want is . . . well, I can't think of a polite word for it. Men seem to think a young widow is game for anything.' Her usually cheerful face grew sober. 'Oh, Al, I don't half wish Bob hadn't been killed. I feel guilty going out with other men. I get so lonely, but not lonely enough to jump into bed with every man I meet. If only we'd had kids. At least they'd make me feel wanted.'

'I know, luv,' Alice said gently.

'We kept putting them off, kids, until we got a house. We didn't want to start a family while we were still in rooms. Then the war started, Bob was killed, and it's been horrible ever since. And I'm still living in the same rooms.'

Alice squeezed her shoulders. 'Don't forget, you're welcome round ours tomorrer if you feel like a jangle. Don't be put off 'cos it's Christmas Day.'

'I'm going to me mam's, Al, but thanks all the same.' Bernadette reached up and touched Alice's hand. 'I'm sorry, luv, for being such a moan. You've got enough problems of your own these days, what with John the way he is. It's just that you're the only person I've got to talk to.'

'Don't you dare apologise, Bernadette Moynihan. You're the only person I've told about John. Today was your turn for a moan. Next time it'll be mine.'

The final customer of the day arrived; Mrs O'Leary, with her ten-year-old daughter, Daisy, who was in Maeve's class at school and whose long, auburn ringlets were in need of a good trim. By now, Myrtle was fast asleep and snoring.

'Would you like me to do it?' an embarrassed Alice offered. 'I won't be long with Bernie.'

'Well, I haven't got much choice, have I?' Mrs O'Leary laughed. 'At least you'll probably cut it level both sides. Myrtle's usually well out. I sometimes wonder why we come. I suppose it's because it's so convenient, right at the end of the street, but I think I'll give that place in Marsh Lane a try. Each time we come

Myrtle's worse than the time before. And it's not just the drink. She's every bit as useless if she's sober. If it weren't for you, Alice, this place would have closed down years ago.'

'Hear, hear,' cried Bernadette. 'It's Al who keeps it going.'

Alice blushed, but she had a feeling of dread. If Myrtle's closed, what would she do? She'd started four years ago, just giving a hand: sweeping up, wiping down, putting women under the dryers, taking them out again, washing hair, fetching towels, putting on gowns. Lately, with Myrtle going seriously downhill in more ways than one, she'd been taking on more and more responsibility. It was impossible to work in a hairdresser's for so long without learning how it was done. Alice was quite capable of giving a shampoo and set, a Marcel or Eugene wave, a perm – the new method was so much simpler than having to plug in every curler separately, a procedure that took all of four hours – and she seemed to have a knack with scissors. It was just a question of holding them right.

She only lived in the next street. It was easy to pop home when business was slack to make the girls their tea, keep an eye on them during the holidays. She usually brought Cormac with her. An angel of a child, he'd been quite happy to lie in his pram in the kitchen, play on the pavement outside when he got older, or sit in the corner, drawing, on the days it rained. But it wasn't just the convenience, or the extra money, useful though it was. Nowadays the hairdresser's provided an escape from the tragedy her life had become since last May. For most people the end of the worst war the world had ever known was a joyful occasion, a reason to celebrate. For the Laceys it had been a nightmare.

Myrtle's was an entirely different world: a bright, cosy,

highly dramatic little world behind thick lace curtains and steamed-up windows, quite separate from the one outside. There was always something to laugh about, always a choice piece of gossip doing the rounds. The women had sorted out the war between them – it would probably have ended sooner had Winston Churchill been privy to the sound advice of Myrtle Rimmer's customers.

Most women were willing, even anxious, to open up their hearts to their hairdresser. There were some very respectable men in Bootle who'd have a fit if they knew the things Alice had been told about them. She never repeated anything, not even to Bernie.

Bernadette waited until Alice had cut Daisy O'Leary's ringlets so they were level both sides and Mrs O'Leary pronounced herself satisfied. She wished them Merry Christmas and departed.

Alice locked the door, turned the 'Open' sign to 'Closed' and between them the two women half carried, half dragged the proprietor to her flat upstairs and laid her on the bed.

'Jaysus,' Bernadette gasped. 'It don't half pong in here. She's not fit to live on her own, Al, let alone run a hairdresser's.'

The bed was unmade, the curtains still drawn. Alice covered her employer with several dirty blankets and regarded her worriedly. 'I'll pop round tomorrer after dinner, like. See if she's all right. She said something about going to a friend's for tea.'

'Has she got any relatives?' Bernadette asked.

'There's a daughter somewhere. Southampton, I think. Myrtle's husband died ages ago.' She heard someone try the salon door, but ignored it. There was a notice announcing they closed at four.

They returned downstairs. After Bernadette had gone,

Alice brushed the floor again, gave it a cursory going over with a wet mop, wiped surfaces, polished mirrors, straightened chairs, arranged the three dryers at the same angle and tied the dirty towels in a bundle ready to go to the laundry when the salon reopened after Christmas. She glanced around to see if there was anything she'd missed. Well, the lace curtain could do with mending, not to mention a good wash, the walls were badly in need of a lick of paint, and the oilcloth should be replaced before a customer caught her heel in one of the numerous frayed holes and went flying. Otherwise, everywhere looked OK. She could go home.

Instead, Alice switched off the light and sat under a dryer. Go home for what? she asked herself. The girls weren't due till five. Her dad had taken Cormac to the grotto in Stanley Road. John was finishing work at three. He'd be home by now. Alice shuddered. She didn't want to be alone with her husband.

John Lacey regarded what was left of his face in the chrome mirror over the mantelpiece. It had been a handsome face once. He wasn't a conceited man, but he'd always known that he and his brother Billy weren't at the back of the queue when the Lord handed out good looks. Both were tall, going on six feet. John's dark-brown hair was curly, Billy's straight. They had the same rich-brown eyes, the same straight nose, the same wide brow. His mam, never one to consider anyone's feelings, used to say John was the handsomer of the two. He had a firmer mouth, there was something determined about his chin. Billy's chin was weak.

Mam didn't say that now, not since her elder son had turned into a monster. John stroked the melted skin on his right cheek, touched the corner of the unnaturally angled slit of an eye. If only he hadn't gone to the aid of the seaman trapped in the hold when the boiler had exploded on that merchant ship. The hold had become a furnace, the man was screaming, his overalls on fire. He emerged from the flames, a blazing phantom, hair burning, screaming for help.

The irony was he hadn't managed to save the chap. He had died within minutes, writhing in agony on the deck, everyone too terrified to touch him. Everyone except that dickhead, John Lacey, who'd dragged him out, burnt his own hands, burnt his face. The hands had mended, but not the face.

A further irony was that the war was virtually over and the accident had had nothing to do with the conflict. The firefighters were on duty at Gladstone Dock, as they had been every night over the past five years, when the boiler had gone up. They'd come through the war unscathed, all his family, his brother's family, his mam, his father-in-law. Amber Street itself hadn't been touched, not even a broken window, while numerous other streets in Bootle had been reduced to rubble. Then, in the very last week, John had lost half his face.

He stared at the grotesque reflection in the mirror. 'Fool!' he spat through crooked lips.

Where were his children – his three girls, his little son? More important, where was his wife? He remembered the girls had gone to a party. His father-in-law had Cormac. But there was no explanation for why Alice wasn't home.

'She don't fancy you no more,' he told his reflection. 'She's with another fella. He's giving her one right now, sticking it up her in the place that used to be yours.'

John groaned and turned away from the mirror. He'd never used to think like that, so coarsely, lewdly. Making love to Alice used to be the sweetest thing on earth, but now he couldn't bring himself to touch her, imagining her shrinking inside, hating it.

The back door opened and his wife came in. Until last May, until a few days before the war ended, until his accident, he would have lifted her up, kissed her rosy face, stared into her misty blue eyes, told her how much he'd missed her, how much he loved her. They might have taken the opportunity, the kids being out, of going upstairs for a blissful half-hour in bed. Instead, John scowled and said gruffly, 'I tried Myrtle's door on the way home, but it were locked. That was more than half an hour ago. Where have you been, eh? With your fancy man?'

She looked at him reproachfully. 'I haven't got a fancy man, John.'

Oh, she was so lovely! She was thirty-one, though she didn't look it: tall, gawky like a schoolgirl, a bit too thin. He used to tell her she had too many elbows, she was always knocking things over. Her face was long and oval, the skin flawless, the eyes very large and very blue. They were innocent eyes, guileless. Deep within his soul, he knew she would never be unfaithful, but the new John, the John Lacey who now inhabited his body, found it just as hard to believe that such an attractive woman, a woman born to be loved, hadn't found someone else since her husband had become so repulsive.

'So, what have you been doing with yourself for the last half-hour?' he sneered.

'Tidying up. I remember hearing someone try the door when me and Bernadette were upstairs with Myrtle. She drank all the sherry and ended up incapable.' She sighed. 'I'll make some tea.'

He grabbed her shoulder when she turned to leave. 'I don't believe you.'

'There's nothing I can do about that.' She was about

to shrug his hand away. Instead, she bent her head and laid her face against it and he could feel the rich-brown hair fluttering on his fingers. The gesture touched his heart. 'I don't need a fancy man, luv,' she said softly. 'I've got you. Why don't we go upstairs for five minutes? I can get dressed in a jiffy if the latch goes.' Alice missed making love more than she could say. She didn't care about his face. For his sake, she would prefer it hadn't happened. But it *had* happened and she loved him just as much, if not more. Sadly, it was impossible to convince John of this. Anyroad, his face wasn't nearly as bad as he made out. The right side was a bit puckered, that was all. The burn had slightly affected his eye, the corner of his mouth, but he looked nothing like the monster he claimed. She reached up and stroked the puckered skin. 'I love you.'

If only he could believe her! He wanted to, so much. But he knew, he was certain, she was forcing herself to touch him. She was a good, kind woman and felt sorry for him. She was probably feeling sick inside. The tender, loving look on her face was all put on. He seized her wrist and pushed her hand away. 'I don't want your sympathy,' he said gruffly.

He truly hadn't meant to be quite so rough. He noticed her wince and rub her wrist when she went into the kitchen. Water ran, the gas was lit and John Lacey realised he had just hurt the person he loved most in the world. He looked at himself in the mirror. Sometimes he wondered if it would be better for all concerned if he did himself in.

Alice had borne three daughters within two and a half years of her marriage to John Lacey. Fionnuala was only two months old when she had fallen pregnant with Orla and Maeve had arrived when Orla was still on the breast.

Her husband realised something had to be done. Alice was barely twenty-one. At the rate they were going, they'd have a couple of dozen kids by the time she reached forty. Although strictly forbidden by the Catholic church, for the next five years, with Alice's approval, he took precautions. Then the war started and they decided to try for a son. Nine months later, Cormac was born. Four children was enough for anyone and John started to take precautions again. It was easier now, with French letters available over the counter at the chemist.

They were an exceptionally happy family. The girls were the image of their mam with the same brown hair and blue eyes. Cormac was a lovely lad, a bit pale, a bit small, rather quiet compared with his sisters. He had his mam's blue eyes, if a shade or two lighter. Apart from that, no one was quite sure whom he took after, with his straight blond hair and neatly proportioned features.

John didn't mind when his wife went to work in the hairdresser's in Opal Street. He earned enough to feed his family, keep them comfortable, but the girls were mad on clothes and it didn't seem fair that the eldest was the only one who had new things. Anyroad, Orla was a little madam and would have screamed blue murder at the idea of always having to wear her sister's hand-me-downs. Alice worked to dress her girls and she was happy at Myrtle's. And if Alice was happy, so was John.

At least that used to be the case. Now, it was the first war-free Christmas in six years. It should have been the best the Laceys had ever known, but it turned out to be the worst.

Orla had made a show of herself at the Sunday School party, Fionnuala claimed. She'd sung 'Strawberry Fair' and 'Greensleeves'. 'Though no one asked her. I felt dead embarrassed, if you must know.'

'Miss Geraghty asked who'd like to do a turn,' Orla said haughtily. 'I put me hand up, that's all.'

'Perhaps our Fionnuala didn't hear what Miss Geraghty had said,' suggested Maeve, the peacemaker.

On Christmas Day, after dinner, when everyone was in the parlour, Orla offered to sing again.

'That'd be nice, luv,' Alice said quickly, hoping a few songs might lighten the atmosphere. It had been a miserable meal and though she didn't like to admit it, not even to herself, it was all John's fault. He glowered at everyone from the head of the table, snapped at the children, was rude to his wife. Even Billy, his brother, normally the life and soul of the party, had been subdued. By the time the pudding stage was reached the conversation had dried up completely.

As soon as the food was eaten, Billy escaped to the pub. John wasn't a drinker, but he used to like the occasional pint, particularly at Christmas. This year, he'd churlishly refused. He rarely left the house, except for work, when he wore a trilby with the brim tipped to show as little as possible of his face. At Mass he sat at the back.

Cora was watching everything with a supercilious smile, as if she was enjoying seeing the Lacey family fall to pieces. Alice had never got on with her sister-in-law. Cora was so cold and reserved. She had made it obvious from the start that she didn't want to become friends. She had, possibly, softened a little since Maurice was born, but Maurice himself seemed the sole beneficiary of this slight improvement. Yet she was strict with the boy, too much so. Alice had seen the cane hanging on the wall in her sister-in-law's smart house off Merton Road, but had also witnessed the soft look in Cora's strange brown eyes, almost khaki, when they lighted on her handsome son.

Maurice was a Lacey to his bones. His gran doted on

him. Meg Lacey carried a photo in her handbag of John and Billy when they were little, and either one could have been Maurice they were so alike.

Meg had Maurice on her knee, stroking his chubby legs — she made it obvious she had no time for Cormac. 'Who's my favourite little boy in the whole world,' she cooed.

Cora didn't look too pleased. Her small, tight face was screwed in a scowl. Alice wondered what she would look like with her hair combed loose, instead of scraped back in a knot with such severity that it stretched the skin on her forehead. Except for the odd brown of her eyes, there wasn't a spot of colour in her face. Cora scorned make-up and nice clothes. Today, she wore the plain brown frock with a belt that had been her best since Alice could remember.

Orla sang 'Greensleeves' in a fine, strong voice. If there'd been the money, Alice would have sent her to singing lessons — Mrs O'Leary's Daisy went to tap-dancing classes — but then Fionnuala would have demanded lessons in something or other and it wouldn't have been fair to leave out Maeve, although her placid youngest daughter wouldn't have complained.

'Any requests?' Orla enquired pertly when she'd finished her repertoire.

'Yes, shurrup,' Fionnuala snapped. It was said so viciously that Alice was dismayed. The girls had always got on well with each other. Perhaps, because the house was so full of love, they hadn't found it necessary to compete. Lately, though, Fion, who Alice had to concede could be dead irritating at times, had become resentful of Orla, making unnecessarily spiteful remarks, like the one just now. It didn't help when Orla, eleven, started her periods and the older Fion showed no sign. Alice wondered if it was the change in atmosphere that had done it. The house may well have been full of love once, but it certainly wasn't now.

Oh, God! This was a *horrible* Christmas. Normally, she never let Cora bother her, nor the fact that John's mother made such a fuss of Maurice and entirely ignored her other grandson. Alice was fond of Maurice, but it would have been easy to get upset. Instead, she and John usually laughed about it. Other Christmases, John organised word games. He sometimes sang, usually carols, in a rather fine baritone voice. He made sure everyone had a glass of sherry and told them amusing things that had happened at work. In the past, John had even been known to make Cora laugh. Now, Alice wasn't sure what she wanted to do most, burst into tears, or scream, as two of her daughters squabbled, Maeve looked bored, Cora scowled, her mother-in-law cooed and John's face was like thunder. Only Cormac was his usual sunny self, playing quietly on the floor with a truck he'd got for Christmas. If only her dad were there! He'd see the funny side of things and they could wink at each other and make faces.

Suddenly, John grabbed Fion and Orla by the scruffs of their necks and flung them out of the room. 'If you're going to fight, then fight somewhere else,' he snarled.

Alice got up and left without a word. The girls were in the hall, holding hands, she noted approvingly, and looking shaken.

'I *hate* Dad,' Orla said spiritedly.

'Me, too,' echoed Fionnuala.

'We weren't exactly fighting.'

'It was more an argument.'

'Your dad gets easily narked these days.' She put her arms round both her girls, they were almost as tall as she was. 'You need to humour him.'

Orla sniffed. 'Can I go round Betty Mahon's house, Mam? She got Monopoly for Christmas.'

'If you want, luv.'

'Can I come?' Fionnuala said eagerly.

Orla hesitated. Why couldn't Fion find friends of her own? Not only was she getting dead fat, but she was a terrible hanger-on. She remembered her sister had also been unfairly treated by their dad. 'OK,' she said.

Alice sighed with relief when the girls left; two less people to worry about. She opened the parlour door. 'Maeve, would you like to help me make some tea, luv?'

'I *hate* Christmas,' Maeve declared in the kitchen. 'It used to be nice, but now it's awful. Will Dad ever be in a good mood again?'

'Of course, luv. He's still getting over the accident.'

'But Mam, it wasn't *our* fault he had the accident. Why is he taking it out on us?'

Alice had no idea. Maeve had inherited her mother's easygoing nature. It wasn't like her to complain. John was gradually alienating every member of his family. Only Cormac seemed sweetly oblivious to the change in his dad.

She made tea and Spam sandwiches, spread a plate with biscuits, took them into the parlour, told Maeve that, yes, it would be all right if she stayed in the back and read her new Enid Blyton book, then excused herself from the company, saying she had to go round to Myrtle's and make sure she was all right.

The acrid grey fog that had enveloped Bootle earlier in the day was beginning to fall again. On the nearby River Mersey, ships' foghorns hooted eerily. The pavements glistened with damp, reflecting the street lights in glittering yellow blurs. It was lovely to see the lights on again after five years of blackout.

Hardly anyone in Amber Street had closed their parlour curtains. Alice passed house after house where parties were going on. She had been born only a few streets away, in Garnet Street, in another cramped terrace house that opened on to the pavement, and had known most of these people all her life. They felt like family. The Fowlers were having a riotous time, doing the 'Hokey Cokey'. Their two lads had returned unharmed after years spent in the Navy. Emmie Norris had all her family there, including the twelve grandchildren. The Martins were playing cards, a whole crowd of them in paper hats, laughing their heads off.

Everywhere Alice looked people were having the time of their lives. The strains of 'Bless 'Em All' came from the Murphys', 'We'll Meet Again' from the Smiths'.

Apart from Orla, no one had sung at the Laceys'. They had pulled crackers, but hadn't bothered with the paper hats, not even the children. It just didn't seem right for some reason. For the first time Alice felt like a stranger in the street that was as familiar to her as the back of her hand, as if she no longer belonged, as if her life was no longer on the same keel as those of her friends and neighbours.

She sighed as she went through the entry into Opal Street. Myrtle's was in darkness, upstairs and down. She remembered being at school with the girl who had lived there when it had been an ordinary house. It was more than twenty years since Myrtle had moved in and it had become a hairdresser's. The wall between the parlour and the living room had been knocked down and turned into one room. Mam had taken her there to have her hair cut. Myrtle had seemed old then, going on sixty. She claimed to have worked for some posh place in London doing rich people's hair.

'Debutantes,' she boasted, 'titled personages.' No one had believed her.

Alice unlocked the door. 'Myrtle,' she shouted. There was no reply. She went up to the bedroom, where the bed was empty, still unmade. Myrtle must have gone to tea with her friend, which was a relief.

Downstairs again, she sat under the same dryer as she'd done the night before, the middle one. She was even more miserable now than she'd been then. What was to become of her, of John, of their children? How was she to convince John that she loved him? Would she continue to love him if he remained the angry, glowering, suspicious person, nothing like the man he used to be? Could you love someone who made your children unhappy? Did he love her? What had happened was awful, but as Maeve had wisely said, he had no right to take it out on his family.

'White Christmas' was being sung not far away. 'Just like the ones we used to know . . .' Not any more, we don't, Alice thought bleakly. This Christmas has been nothing like the ones we used to know. The first after Mam died had been bad enough. Dad was gutted, but he'd done his best to brighten things up for his daughter. He'd bought her a new frock, taken her to the pantomime on Boxing Day. She was eight, an only child.

Alice knew she wasn't a clever person. She hadn't a single talent she could think of. She was often tongue-tied, stuck for something to say, slow-witted. She had achieved just five things in her life: she had married John Lacey, whom all the girls at Johnson's Dye Factory had been mad about, and she'd had four beautiful children.

But if she was to get through the years to come and stay sane, she needed to do something else. Time passed so quickly. Pretty soon the girls would start getting married. There'd only be Cormac left and what if John was still the same? Things at home were unbearable now and they'd be even more unbearable with the girls gone.

Yes, she had to *do* something. But what? At the moment, even her job was on the line and it wouldn't be easy getting another, not with servicemen coming home, wanting back their jobs in the factories, and women all over the place being given the sack – women used to earning a wage and unwilling to return to being housewives. Bernadette said there'd been forty-two applications when the Gas Board where she worked had advertised for a wages clerk. Most were from women who'd been in the Forces, but it was a man who'd got the job. Not that Alice was fit to be a clerk of any sort, she couldn't even add up.

'We'll not go round our John's next Christmas if things there don't improve,' Billy Lacey said as he walked home through the fog with his family. 'I'm glad you said we were having someone round to tea, luv, even if it were a lie. I couldn't have stood another minute in that house.'

'It wasn't a lie,' Cora said coolly. 'Mr Flynn's coming to tea.'

'Mr Flynn, the landlord!'

'The very same.'

Billy grimaced at the idea of another meal accompanied by stilted conversation. They were passing O'Connell Street where they used to live and which Billy much preferred to where they lived now. 'I think I'll drop in on Foxy Jones. I haven't seen him since he came out the Army. I'll be home in time for tea, luv.'

'Like hell you will,' Cora muttered as her husband, hands in pockets, whistling tunelessly, made off down the street. She wouldn't see him again until the pubs closed. Not that she cared. The less she saw of Billy the better.

'Dad!' Maurice called plaintively, but his dad ignored him.

Cora gave her son a little shake, annoyed he wanted his dad when he had her. 'I've got a bone to pick with you.'

Maurice took the words literally. 'A bone, Mam?'

'How many times have I told you not to sit on your Grannie Lacey's knee? I can't stand to see her maul you.'

The little boy felt confused. Gran had sat him on her knee. He'd had no choice in the matter. 'I'm sorry, Mam.' He apologised to his mother a hundred times a day. He was always getting things wrong, though was often mystified as to what they were.

'You will be sorry when you get home.'

His stomach curled. He knew what the words meant and could tell by the way Mam walked, very quickly, shoulders back, lips pursed, that she was going to hit him with the cane. For the rest of the way home he did his best not to cry, but the minute the front door closed he started to bawl. 'Don't hit me, Mam. Please don't hit me.'

His mother ignored his cries. 'In here,' she said imperiously, opening the door to the living room. 'Come on!' She tapped her foot impatiently.

Maurice walked slowly into the room, dragging his feet. What had he done wrong? He never knew what he'd done wrong. He was shaking with fear as his mam told him to bend over a chair and the cane swished three times against his bottom. It hurt badly. The little boy sobbed helplessly, knowing his bottom would sting for ages. He could understand being beaten if he broke windows, did something really bad, but although he tried very hard to be on his best behaviour, somehow he always managed to make Mam angry.

'You can get to bed now.'

It was too early. He hadn't had any tea. Still crying, the child made his way upstairs. In the living room his mother listened to the faltering steps. There was something very touching about the way he climbed, drawing his feet together on each stair. Her heart turned over as she imagined the sturdy little figure clutching the banister. She heard him reach the top, go into his room, then flew after him. He was sitting on the bed, knuckles pressed into his eyes.

'Maurice!' She fell on her knees, clutched him against her breast. 'Don't cry. Oh, don't cry, luv. Your mammy loves you. She loves you more than anyone in the whole wide world.'

He felt hot, his small body shuddered in her arms, his heart thumped loudly against her own. Two small arms curled around her neck. Cora held him closely as wave after wave of raw, savage emotion coursed through her veins. There was nothing, absolutely nothing on earth comparable to the love she felt for the child sobbing in her arms, clinging to her, and it was made even sweeter by the knowledge that he loved her back, unquestioningly, wholeheartedly, because she was his mother.

'Do you love your mam, son?'

'Oh, yes.'

'Shall we go down and have some tea?'

Maurice hiccuped. 'Please, Mam.'

'Would you like some Christmas cake?'

He nodded. 'Yes.'

'Let Mam carry you.' She picked him up, laughed and said, 'Lord, you're a weight. Pretty soon you'll be carrying me.'

She carried him downstairs like a baby. Maurice, more confused than ever, wondered what it was he'd done right.

★

It was three years since Cora and her family had moved from O'Connell Street to Garibaldi Road. The new house was a great improvement on the old: semi-detached, with three good bedrooms, a proper hall, small gardens front and back. There was a bathroom and separate lavatory upstairs. Even Billy, who hadn't wanted to move, appreciated having a lavvy inside.

'But we'll never be able to afford the rent on a place like that,' Billy protested. He was home on leave from the Army where he appeared to be having a whale of a time.

'It's twelve and six a week, half a crown more than we pay now.' Cora was no longer prepared to be dictated to by her husband. If Billy wanted, he could stay in O'Connell Street on his own.

'Only twelve and a tanner for a house in Garibaldi Road!'

'According to the landlord, yes.'

Billy looked dubious. 'I don't want us to move, then have that Flynn geezer shove up the rent.'

'He won't,' Cora assured him. 'I work for him, don't I? I told you. He calls himself Flynn Properties. I keep the books.'

She'd been badgering Horace Flynn for a better house for years. They couldn't afford it, but she'd take in washing, she'd do anything to get out of O'Connell Street. Then, he'd owned just over thirty properties. Now there were forty. Every few months he bought another house.

'We're good tenants, aren't we?' she'd reasoned years ago. 'We're never late with the rent.'

'No and I don't know how you manage it, not with your husband in the Army. I've had to give notice to quit to half a dozen of me tenants since their hubbies were called up. What is it you get; a shilling a day, and twenty-five bob a week allowance?'

'I'm good at managing with money.'

Mr Flynn glanced around the neat parlour of O'Connell Street. He was small and tubby, shaped like a ball, with exceptionally short arms and legs. A fringe of greying hair went from ear to ear at the back of his otherwise bald head, which was covered with brown blotches, like over-large freckles. From what she could gather, he wasn't married.

'I must say you keep the place nice.' He shook his head. 'But no, Mrs Lacey. I'm not prepared to move tenants up a notch until I feel assured they're in a position to pay the increased rent.' He smiled a touch sarcastically. 'Perhaps one day, when the war's over and your husband's in a well-paid job.'

If she had to wait for Billy to get a well-paid job, she'd be in O'Connell Street until the day she died. Cora gnawed her bottom lip. She was still shoplifting. It was easier with a baby in a pram, then a toddler in a pushchair. Like before, some things she kept, some she pawned. Once, when it was winter, she'd taken a fur coat from C & A Modes, not an expensive one, it being C & A, though she'd got five quid for it from the pawn shop. But she couldn't very well tell Mr Flynn *that*.

Maurice was two, and she'd already bought the cane, hung it on the wall and had used it a few times, when once again she had a go at Horace Flynn about a house. There was a lovely one going in Garibaldi Road and she knew it was one of his because she'd seen him collect the rent. The previous tenants were two old maids in their fifties who'd gone to live in America. She asked him into the parlour to remind him how nicely it was kept.

'I've got a job,' she lied, 'serving in a shop.'

'Which shop?'

Cora thought quickly. 'Mercer's the newsagent's in Marsh Lane.'

'I'd like to see some proof; a wage slip, a letter from the manager, if you don't mind, so I'll know you can afford the rent.'

'I'll ask the manager for a letter. I don't get wage slips.' She didn't want to admit she'd lied. Next week, she'd just pay the rent and keep her gob shut. If he mentioned Mercer's she'd say she'd left.

There was silence. Mr Flynn was staring fixedly at the wall at the cane. 'What's that for?'

'Me little boy. I'm a firm believer in discipline.'

He licked his lips. 'So am I.'

Cora saw a gleam of perspiration on the round bald head, a craving in the round wet eyes. She also saw something else: a way of getting the house in Garibaldi Road. It was the way she was to use to get the lovely furniture that went in it, the reason why it was many years before she shoplifted again.

She smoothed back her hair, curled her lip disapprovingly, said sternly, 'Have you been naughty, Mr Flynn?'

He nodded eagerly. Saliva oozed from his mouth. 'Very naughty, Mrs Lacey.'

'Then we shall have to do something about it.' She unhooked the cane from the wall.

Chapter 2

For more than a month, Alice virtually ran Myrtle's on her own. The girls took turns to give a hand on Saturdays and after school. Orla complained loudly that it was dead boring and the smells made her sick, particularly the ammonia, but sixpence a week was too good to miss. Fionnuala loved it. She would have done it for nothing, because it made her feel important. Maeve didn't care what she did as long as she was left to do it in peace.

Only occasionally did Myrtle put in an appearance. She looked terrible, usually wearing tatty carpet slippers, her face grey and mottled. Once she came down in her dressing gown, a filthy plaid thing without a belt. Alice turned her round and sent her back upstairs.

'She's lost her mind,' one of the customers at the time pronounced. 'I reckon it's 'cos the war's over. It was the war that kept her going. Remember when we had to bring our own towels?'

Alice smiled. 'And we made shampoo by grating soap and boiling it in water. I was reduced to using Lux soap flakes on the customers once.'

'I remember you setting me hair with sugar and water when you'd run out of setting lotion. Myrtle used to open dead early or dead late, even on Sundays, to accommodate the women working in factories, otherwise there'd never have been time for them to get their hair done. She never charged extra.' The woman sighed. 'We all pulled together then. I wouldn't want the war back, not for anything, but there was a nice friendly spirit around. People put themselves out, like Myrtle.' She jerked her head towards the stairs. 'Is anyone seeing to her, like?'

'I usually make her a bite to eat for breakfast and dinner, and her friend, Mrs Glaister, comes round every day to make her tea and put her to bed. She's written to Myrtle's daughter in Southampton to say she needs looking after permanent.'

'You'll soon be out of a job, then?'

'Looks like it.'

Olive Cousins, Myrtle's daughter, took her time coming from Southampton. It was over four weeks later, at the beginning of February, that she turned up; a sharp-faced woman in her fifties, wearing too much pink face powder and a beaver lamb coat that smelt of mothballs. Even then, she didn't go straight upstairs. Alice was in the middle of a perm and was forced to listen while she explained in a dead posh voice, that occasionally lapsed into broad Scouse, that Christmas had been so hectic she was fair worn out and had needed time to recuperate. Her son had been home from university, her daughter had not long married a doctor and his parents had come to stay – she emphasised 'university' and 'doctor', in the obvious hope Alice would be impressed. Alice was, but decided not to show it. She disliked Olive Cousins on the spot.

'Where is mother?' Olive enquired, glancing around the salon as if expecting mother to pop up from beneath a chair.

'Upstairs, in bed,' Alice replied briefly.

'Well, I don't like the look of *her*,' the recipient of the perm announced as Olive Cousins's high heels clattered up the lino-covered stairs.

She stayed for three days, eating and sleeping in a bed and breakfast place on Marsh Lane, not that anyone blamed her for that, considering the state of upstairs. On the second day she came into the salon and announced that next morning she was taking mother back with her to Southampton.

'That's nice of you,' Alice remarked, revising her opinion of the woman, but not for long. Myrtle would be going into an old people's home in a strange part of the country where none of her friends and neighbours could visit. It was, however, more convenient for her daughter.

'She couldn't possibly live with us, there isn't the room, and I can't be doing with travelling halfway across the country every time something goes wrong.'

'You'll let us have the address, won't you? Of the home, that is, so we can write to her.'

'Of course. It'll be nice for her to get letters, but I doubt if she'll be up to reading them,' Olive said brightly, as if they were discussing the weather not her mother's health. 'Now, about the salon. I'd been expecting to sell it as a going concern, but' – her lip curled – 'no one would give tuppence for a dump like this, so I've written to the company that owns the premises. The salon will close today.'

'Today!' Alice's mouth dropped open. She probably looked dead stupid. The thing was, the appointment book was full for weeks ahead, and quite a few women had booked months in advance for weddings and the like. There was a sinking feeling in her belly. She'd have to put a notice on the door.

'Today,' Olive Cousins repeated firmly. 'I don't doubt

you'd have liked more notice, but you must have seen this coming for a long time.'

'I suppose I have.'

'Of course, you could always take the place over, assuming you could afford the lease.'

'What's a lease?' Alice felt even more stupid.

'Like rent, only more long term,' Olive explained brusquely, obviously realising that if someone didn't know what a lease was it was unlikely they could afford it. 'Mother appears to have signed a new seven-year lease only last year and it still has six years to run. There was a letter upstairs from the property company asking for this year's payment and complaining about the state of the place. Me mam, I mean mother, hasn't kept it properly maintained.' She sniffed derisively. 'Instead, she's let it go to rack and ruin.'

'She hasn't exactly been well,' Alice said. 'How much is the lease?'

'A hundred and seventy-five pounds for seven years. That's cheap at the price. My hubbie's in business, so I should know. Mam, mother, paid at the rate of twenty-five pounds a year.'

Twenty-five pounds! Alice had never even *seen* twenty-five pounds. She glanced around the shabby room and imagined the walls repainted – mauve would look nice – new curtains on the windows, new oilcloth on the floor. The chairs needed upholstering, but could be patched up for now, and the dryers looked as if they'd come out of the ark, but a good polishing would bring them up a treat. She wasn't sure what came over her when she said to Olive Cousins, 'Have you posted the letter yet to the property company?'

'It's in me, *my* bag, to post as soon as I go outside.'

'Would you mind leaving it till morning? If I'm not round by nine o'clock, post it then.'

★

The wireless was on in the living room of number eight Garnet Street. Geraldo and his orchestra were playing a selection of Cole Porter songs.

'Night and day,' Danny Mitchell hummed as he ironed his favourite shirt: blue and white striped with pearl buttons. He grinned as he thought about the evening ahead. In an hour's time he would call for Phyllis Henderson, a widow in her forties. They would go to the pub, have a few drinks, Phyllis would play hard to get, but end up inviting him back to her house for a mug of cocoa and thence into her bed.

Danny had a well-deserved reputation as a ladies' man. During the ten years he'd been married to his beloved Renee and the ten years after Renee's death, when he'd had a daughter to bring up, Danny had never given another woman a second glance, but then Alice had got married and he began to sow his wild oats, if rather late.

He was fifty-one, an electrician on the docks, and as lean and fit as a man half his age, with a full head of wavy hair the same colour as his daughter's. There was nothing particularly handsome about his face, but he had a quirky smile that people found attractive and a look in his blue eyes that made women go weak at the knees. There were numerous widows and spinsters in Bootle whose main aim in life was to tie the knot with Danny Mitchell.

'Night and Day' ended. 'You were never lovelier,' Danny sang under his breath. He was thinking of Phyllis in her black satin nightie when the back door opened and his daughter came in. All thoughts of Phyllis and the evening ahead fled from his mind and he looked anxiously at the face of his only child. He was relieved to see her eyes were brighter than they'd been in a long while. Perhaps things had started to improve between her and John.

'I've brought a couple of mince pies, Dad. There was

mincemeat in a jar left over from Christmas.' She put a paper bag on the table. 'They're still warm.'

'Ta, luv. I'll have them in a minute. There's tea in the pot if you fancy a cup. Pour one for me, if you don't mind. I've only got the cuffs of this to do.' He turned the cuffs back, ready for the studs, and hung the shirt behind the door. Then he folded the badly singed blanket he used to iron on, put it away and took the iron into the yard where he left it on the step to cool, by which time Alice had poured the tea. They sat opposite each other across the table, Alice in the place where her mother used to sit.

'How's Cormac getting on at school?' Danny asked the same question every day since his grandson had started, mainly because he liked hearing the answer.

'As I said before, Dad, he's taken to reading like a duck takes to water. The teacher's ever so pleased. He was sitting up in bed looking at a book when I left.'

'Good.' He smacked his lips with satisfaction. His grandson had always lived in the shadow of his cousin, Maurice, and it was nice to know Cormac was better at something for a change. From what he could gather Maurice was only average at school.

'Our Orla wants to see you to ask about the Great War. It's something they're doing at school.'

'Tell her to come round Saturday. I'll get some cakes in.' He would never have admitted it to a soul but Orla, with her enthusiasms and quick temper, was his favourite of the girls. He was already looking forward to Saturday.

'You'll do no such thing,' Alice remonstrated. 'If you want cakes I'll make 'em for you. I'll send some round with Orla.'

At the mention of cakes, Danny remembered the mince pies. He removed one from the bag, ate it with obvious enjoyment and quickly demolished the other.

36

Alice regarded him suspiciously. 'Have you had anything to eat since you came home from work?'

''Course, luv,' he assured her. He could only be bothered with making himself a Piccalilli sarnie.

'I wish you'd come round to ours for your meals.'

'You've enough to do, luv, without having another mouth to feed. And I'm always there for me dinner on Sundays, aren't I?'

She reached across the table for his hand. The eyes that had seemed so bright when she came in had dulled. 'I'd sooner you were there all the time.' There was a catch in her voice. John was apt to mind his tongue in the presence of his father-in-law and it was nice to have someone on her side, someone who would never turn against her, no matter what happened.

'It wouldn't be right, Alice,' Danny said gruffly. He knew why she wanted him, as a buffer between her and her husband, but the situation in Amber Street had to be worked out between the main participants. Lately, though, he felt increasingly tempted to give John Lacey a piece of his mind. It wasn't right, him taking things out on the folks who loved him most, particularly when the folks concerned were his dearly beloved daughter and his grandchildren.

Within the space of months, Danny had seen Alice turn from a happy, tranquil young woman into a sad, listless creature who rarely smiled. Lord knew how she'd feel when the hairdressing job went, which was likely to happen any minute. At least it provided some respite from the atmosphere at home. If only he could *do* something to put things right.

Alice released his hand. 'Anyroad, Dad. I'm here on the cadge.'

'Just say the word, luv. What's mine's yours, you

know that.' He would have given his life for her and her children.

'I need some money.'

Danny didn't show his surprise, though he knew John earned reasonable wages and had never kept her short. He dug into his pocket. 'How much?'

'I need more than you'll be carrying in your pocket, Dad.'

'Me wallet's upstairs.' He got up. 'I'll fetch it.'

To his horror, she put her head in her hands and burst into tears. 'I must be daft,' she sobbed. 'I must need me head examining. I told the woman to leave the letter till tomorrer, but I couldn't get twenty-five pounds together in a month of Sundays, let alone a few hours.'

He felt himself go pale. 'Twenty-five pounds, luv? It'd take me all me time to scrape together five, and then I'd have to wait till tomorrer when I get paid. What the hell d'you need all that much for?'

'For Myrtle's. The salon's closing, it already has, but I can take over the lease if I want. It costs twenty-five pounds. Oh, Dad!' She turned and put her arms round his waist, pressing her face against his rough working shirt. 'I'd give *anything* if Myrtle's could be mine. I'm good at hairdressing, everyone ses. I'd've hated to leave, anyroad, but now, with the way things are at home . . .'

'I know, luv,' Danny said gently. His mind rapidly assessed his few possessions. What could he pawn? Nothing worth anything much, he realised. There was only the furniture, the bedding, oddments of crockery and cutlery, a few ornaments, his books. He felt guilty for having so many shirts, for not having put away a few bob a week for a rainy day. But he was a man who liked a good time, a man free with his money. His hand was always first in his pocket when it came to a round of drinks. He enjoyed buying presents for his grandchildren. He liked feminine company, perhaps a bit too much, and the various lady friends he'd had over the years hadn't come cheap. There was a ten-shilling note in his wallet upstairs. At that minute he was worth about twelve and a tanner.

'It's so horrible at night, Dad.' Alice's hands tightened round him. 'The girls go out, not that I blame them. I encourage them to. I put Cormac to bed as early as possible. He doesn't mind if I leave the light on, so there's just me and John downstairs. He won't even have the wireless on nowadays. It's as if he can't stand anything cheerful. I stay in the back kitchen as much as possible, but there's a limit to how long you can wash dishes and do a bit of baking for tomorrer, so I try to get on with some sewing. It's hopeless trying to read. I can't concentrate, knowing John's glaring at me. Oh, Dad!' she cried. 'He accuses me of having affairs. He's got this thing in his head that I'm having it off with other men. As if I would! He's the only man I've ever wanted. Now Myrtle's has gone,' she groaned. 'At least it was something to look forward to. I loved it there. It was like a fairy-tale world, all bright and shiny.'

'There, there, luv.' Dan stroked her hair. He'd definitely be having a word with John Lacey. He'd never known his daughter in such a state, as if she were at the end of her tether. He furiously tried to think of a way of getting twenty-five pounds and wondered if there was a bank he could rob and get away with it. He thought of a possible solution and his nose wrinkled with distaste. 'What about asking that Cora woman?' he said. He couldn't abide Cora Lacey.

'Cora!' Alice stopped crying and looked at him. 'It didn't cross me mind. We're not exactly friends.'

'She's never been exactly friends with anyone,' Danny

said curtly. 'But she never seems short of a few bob, though Christ knows where it comes from. Billy earns a pittance clearing bomb sites. There's no way he could afford to pay for a house in Garibaldi Road.'

'She works for the landlord, Horace Flynn,' Alice explained. 'She does his books, whatever that involves. I suppose he let her have the house as a favour.' Horace Flynn was one of the most notorious landlords in Bootle, who chucked people on to the streets without so much as the blink of a fat eyelid.

'I reckon it involves more than doing his books.'

'Oh, Dad!' She sounded shocked. 'You've got a dirty mind. I've never known anyone so strait-laced as Cora.' She put a finger thoughtfully to her chin. 'I might go round and ask her. It won't do any harm. All she can do is say no.'

'And she might say yes. Would you like me to come with you?' He entirely forgot about Phyllis Henderson.

'No, ta, Dad. It would be best if I went on me own.'

'You'd better get a move on. It's almost half past seven. Does John know where you are?'

'I said I was coming round to yours with the mince pies.' She laughed bitterly. 'He probably thinks they're for one of me secret lovers. I'll be cross-examined when I get back, particularly if I'm late.'

'Does he know about the twenty-five pounds?'

She shook her head. 'No, he might have stopped me coming if he had. John doesn't like me working no more. He wants me safely at home where I can't get up to mischief.'

Danny Mitchell swallowed an expletive. He hadn't realised things were quite so bad. 'He won't be all that pleased if Cora comes up with the cash and you start the hairdressing on your own,' he said cautiously, worried that Alice was getting into a situation that would only make things worse.

'I don't care, Dad.' Her face tightened in a way he'd never seen before. 'I'm entitled to something out of life and I'm not getting it now. I wish with all my heart John had never had the accident. I love him, I always will, but I've given up trying to make him believe it. He's impossible to live with, so I'll just have to make a life for meself outside the house.'

Danny hadn't thought his normally timid daughter capable of such determination. He nodded approvingly. 'Right thing too, luv.'

Come in,' Cora said in surprise when she opened the door and found her sister-in-law on the step.

Alice rarely came to Garibaldi Road, mainly because she was rarely asked and Cora wasn't the sort of person you dropped in on uninvited for a jangle.

'What can I do for you?' Cora asked when they were seated in the nicely furnished living room, as if she realised it wasn't a social visit and Alice had only come for a purpose for which an explanation was due.

'Where's Billy?' She didn't want John's brother blundering in.

'At the pub, where else?' Cora sneered.

Alice nodded. 'Right. I want to borrow some money,' she said bluntly. She wasn't prepared to beat about the bush, engage in chit-chat to pass the time, then tactfully come up with a request for a loan.

'Really!' Cora laughed. It must be for something of very great importance. Under normal circumstances, Alice wouldn't have asked her for the time of day, let alone money. 'What for?'

In a cool voice Alice explained about Myrtle's. 'I'll pay

you back the twenty-five pounds as soon as possible with a fee on top, for borrowing it, like.'

'You mean interest?'

'Do I?' Alice said, confused.

'Interest is what you pay for borrowing money.'

'Then I'll pay interest.'

'At what rate?' Cora asked, in order to confuse her sister-in-law more.

But Alice understood what Cora was up to. 'At whatever rate you say,' she replied, cool again.

The older woman smiled unpleasantly. 'Why should I loan you a penny?'

'Because you'll make a penny in return.'

Cora smiled again. Then her voice became hard. 'It would have to be a business arrangement.'

'That's all right by me,' Alice said nonchalantly. Inwardly, she was desperately trying to keep her wits about her. She didn't trust Cora Lacey as far as she could throw her and wished she had taken up Dad's offer to come with her. What on earth was a business arrangement?

'I'll lend you the twenty-five quid, but I'll draw up an agreement and we'll both sign to say we'll share the profits till the loan's paid back.'

'*Share* the profits!' Alice exlaimed. She wanted Myrtle's more than anything on earth, but sharing the profits seemed a bit rich. 'You mean half each? That hardly seems fair. It's me who'll be doing all the work.'

'OK, you have two-thirds, I'll take a third.' Cora had known Alice, dim as a Toc H lamp though she was, would be unlikely to agree to half. A third was what she'd wanted all along. It was the easiest way she'd ever come across of making money. 'I'll just go in the parlour and write it down. I won't be long.'

Alice waited on the edge of her chair. She'd done it!

Tomorrow morning Myrtle's would be hers, but she wished it hadn't been necessary to involve Cora Lacey. It left a nasty taste in the mouth. A third of the profits! She held out her hands to warm them in front of the small coke fire. It was cold in here. She shivered. The fire gave off scarcely any heat. Cora surrounded herself with nice things, but had no regard for creature comforts. No wonder Billy took himself to the pub night after night.

She knew nothing about her sister-in-law other than that her maiden name was Barraclough, her mother had died when she was born and she'd been brought up in Orrell Park by two spinster aunts, both long dead. Nothing was ever said about a father.

It was a constant wonder what she and Billy had seen in each other. Billy was hardly ever in, Cora rarely went out. In company they ignored each other. Billy seemed nervous in the presence of his cold-eyed wife, Cora contemptuous of her childish, good-natured husband.

Her legs were numb with cold. Alice got up and walked around the room to bring them back to life. She picked up a glass vase off the mantelpiece. It shone like diamonds as she turned it back and forth in the dim light. She flicked it with her fingernail and it gave off a sharp, tinkling sound, like a bell. Cut glass! How on earth could Cora afford such a thing? Where had she got the twenty-five pounds from, come to that? Off Horace Flynn?

'I reckon she does more than keep his books,' Dad had said, or something like it. Alice shivered again at the thought of fat, greasy Horace Flynn coming within a yard of her, let alone doing his books – or far more intimate things if Dad was right.

There was a child's book on the table; a colourful cardboard alphabet book with an animal beside each letter. A for Antelope. She turned to the back page: Z for Zebra. A piece of paper fell out on which had been written several simple sums: 1 + 1, 2 + 2, 2 + 1. The answers had been filled in by a clumsy, childish hand. Cora must have written the sums, Maurice had filled in the answers. She must be teaching him at home.

For some reason Alice glanced at the wall where the cane usually hung. It wasn't there. She noticed it propped against the green tiled fireplace. Her stomach turned. Was Cora whipping her little boy to make him learn?

Alice suddenly longed to get away from this lovely, cold room with its expensive ornaments and return to her own comfy, warm house, where there wasn't a single ornament costing more than sixpence, but which was far preferable to here. Hang Myrtle's. Cora could keep her money and her business arrangement.

She made for the door – and remembered John who would be sitting in the chair under the window waiting for her, glowering, wanting to know where she'd been, how many men she'd allowed to touch her. The accusations were getting wilder and wilder, more and more offensive. She couldn't bring herself to tell Dad some of the things John had said. How many men had she serviced? Did they stand in line? How much had she made? Terrible accusations from the man she had thought would love her for ever. Alice suppressed a sob, just as Cora came into the room with a piece of paper torn from a writing pad.

'Sorry I was so long, but it had to be worded carefully. Just sign here where I've drawn a line of dots. I've brought the ink with me and a pen.'

'I'd like to read it first.'

'Of course,' Cora said smoothly. 'You should never put your signature to anything you've not read first.'

'I, Alice Lacey,' Alice read aloud, 'acknowledge receipt of the sum of twenty-five pounds from Cora

Lacey, entitling the said Cora Lacey to a third share in perpetuity of the business presently known as Myrtle's Hairdressing Salon.' She frowned. 'What does "in perpetuity" mean?'

'Till the money's paid back.'

'That's all right, then.' It wasn't often she put her signature to anything. She sat down and carefully wrote 'Alice M. Lacey' on the dotted line.

'What's the M. for?' Cora enquired.

'Mavoureen. It was me mam's name. Me dad called her Renee.'

Cora nodded. 'Well, here's your money.' She held out a small piece of paper.

Alice regarded it vacantly. 'What's that?'

'It's a cheque for twenty-five pounds.'

'But I need the money, not a cheque!' She'd only vaguely heard of cheques and had never seen one before.

'A cheque's the same as money,' Cora said with a superior smile. 'Just give it to Myrtle's daughter. She'll know what to do with it.'

Alice wanted to protest, but it would only show her ignorance. She took the cheque, thanked Cora and said she had to be getting home.

Outside the house she paused. She felt uneasy. How could a piece of paper be worth the same as twenty-five pound notes? Oh, if only she could ask John! He seemed to know everything worth knowing. Alice sighed. But the days were long gone when they could discuss things – should they have a day out in New Brighton on Sunday if the weather was fine, for instance? Or perhaps Southport, easier to get to on the electric trains that ran from Marsh Lane Station? Was it possible to squeeze another bed into the girls' room now that they were getting older? Orla constantly complained about sleeping three to a bed.

The cheque thing was bothering her. She would have gone back to Dad's, but he'd be out by now, probably with Phyllis Henderson, his latest woman. But Bernadette would know. Unlike Alice, she was clever. Although they'd started St James's Junior and Infants together, Bernadette had passed the scholarship at eleven and gone to Seafield Convent. She lived no distance away in rooms in Irlam Road. Hopefully, Bernadette would set her mind at rest. It would make her late home, but she was already late and by now John was probably doing his nut.

'Oh, well! I may as well be hung for a sheep as for a lamb.'

'Of course a cheque's all right, silly.' Bernadette laughed. She was already in her dressing gown ready for bed although it was only half past eight. Since Christmas she'd been feeling low. Roy McBride had turned out like all the other men she'd known, except for Bob, and had tried to get his hand up her skirt in the taxi on the way home from the dance on Christmas Eve. She had decided to give up on men altogether and rely on books for company.

'We get loads of cheques in the Gas Board. What's it for, anyroad?'

For the third time that night, Alice explained about Myrtle's, then described her meeting with Cora. 'She made me sign an agreement of some sort – and she wants a third of the profits, but never mind. As from tomorrow Myrtle's will be mine, that's all that matters.'

'Oh, Alice!' Bernadette looked dismayed. 'I wish you'd asked me first. I would have loaned you the money and you wouldn't have had to sign anything. I wouldn't have demanded a share of the profits, either. Just the money back when you could afford it, that's all.'

Alice regarded her friend, equally dismayed. 'It never entered me head you were so flush, Bernie.'

Bernadette shrugged. 'It's why Bob and I never had kids, isn't it? I stayed at work so we could save up for furniture for our house. Since he was killed I couldn't bring meself to touch a penny. It didn't seem right, buying clothes and stuff, so the money's been lying in the Post Office for years. There must be going on for forty pounds by now. You could have had the lot and used some to do up Myrtle's place a bit. It certainly needs it.'

'Oh, Bernie! I wish I'd known.'

'Tell Cora to stuff her cheque and I'll arrange to draw the money out tomorrow.'

'I can't, can I? I told you I signed an agreement.'

Bernadette looked at her doubtfully. 'What did it say?'

'I can't remember.'

'You're too trusting by a mile, do you know that, Alice Lacey? Anyroad, how about a cup of tea? Better still, a glass of sherry to toast your new business venture.'

'You make it sound very grand.' Alice smiled.

'It *is* very grand. I feel dead proud that you're my friend. Hold on, I'll just get some glasses from the kitchen.'

While she was gone, Alice glanced around the big, rather gloomy room that was at least warm. A big fire burnt in the massive fireplace. The book Bernadette had been reading was lying face down on the floor alongside an empty cup that had obviously contained cocoa. She wouldn't have wanted to be in Bernie's shoes, not for a moment, but just then she felt a certain amount of envy for her friend for being able to do as she pleased – go to bed when she liked, stay out as long as she cared to without someone breathing down her neck wanting to check up on her every single moment. She squirmed guiltily when she considered how much nicer life would be without John.

Oh, Lord! Alice felt sick. According to the sideboard clock it was ten to nine. But, she reasoned, if John was worried it was his own fault. She couldn't confide in him any more, tell him about Myrtle's. Even when she got back she could tell him where she'd been, but not *why*. He would be quite likely to tear up the cheque, say he didn't want her working. Best to leave telling him till Myrtle's was actually *hers*.

'Hey! I've just thought of something.' Bernadette returned with the glasses. 'How did Cora know who to make the cheque out to?'

'I've no idea.' Alice took the cheque out of her bag and read it properly for the first time. 'It ses "Pay Flynn Properties".' She read it again, frowning. '*Flynn Properties*'?

Bernadette shrieked, 'The bitch! Myrtle's belongs to Horace Flynn. *He's* the owner of the property company that awful daughter was on about. Oh, Al! Right now, I bet Cora Lacey's laughing up her sleeve.'

Myrtle came into the salon wearing a slightly bald astrakhan coat with a brown fur collar, a dusty black hat shaped like a turban and fleece-lined ankle boots. The lace on one of the boots was undone. Alice made her sit under a dryer while she tied it. 'In case you trip over, like.' She stroked the creased, bewildered face. 'Take care, Myrtle, luv. Look after yourself, won't you? We're not half going to miss you.'

'Here, here,' echoed Florrie Piper who had just arrived for her weekly shampoo and set.

A taxi drew up outside and Olive Cousins came downstairs dragging a large, shabby suitcase. 'Gerra move on, Mam,' she snapped. She went pink. 'I mean, do

48

hurry, Mother.' She turned to Alice. 'Good luck with the salon,' she said shortly. 'I hope you do better with the place than Mother did. I must say you could have knocked me down with a feather when you turned up this morning with that cheque.'

Mrs Glaister, Myrtle's friend, appeared. 'You forgot your handbag, luv,' she said gently. 'I've put a clean hankie inside and a quarter of mint imperials, your favourite.'

'Ta.' Myrtle smiled tremulously at everyone. 'Can I have a cup of tea?'

'No, you can't, Mother. The taxi's waiting. Say goodbye to your friends.' Olive roughly dragged the old woman to her feet. She glanced sneeringly around the room. 'It won't exactly break my heart not to see *this* place again.'

The door closed and Myrtle Rimmer left Opal Street for ever. Mrs Glaister burst into tears. 'It won't exactly break my heart not to see *her* again either. Expecting to find Myrtle had saved thousands of pounds, she was, when all she'd saved was hundreds. Mind you, she's taken every penny.'

'It wouldn't be a bad idea to make that cup of tea, Alice,' Florrie Piper said. 'Forget about me and me hair for the minute, though I wouldn't mind a cuppa meself.'

Alice hurried into the dingy back kitchen to put the kettle on, remembering that Olive Cousins had emptied the till last night, but hadn't thought to pay her. She'd worked four days for nothing. But never mind, from now on she would be paying herself. The sadness she felt for Myrtle was mixed with jubilation. She didn't care what underhand things Cora might have got up to with the cheque, nor did it matter that Horace Flynn owned the building. *She*, Alice Lacey, was now the proprietor of a hairdressing salon. Apart from her wedding day and the times she'd had the children, this was the proudest day of her life.

'That's a nasty bruise you've got on your cheek, luv,' Florrie Piper remarked when Alice came back.

Alice touched the bruise as if she had forgotten it was there. 'I walked into a door,' she explained.

'You should be more careful.' Had it been anyone else, Florrie would have taken for granted that the bruise had been administered by her feller, but everyone knew that John Lacey would never lay a finger on his wife.

He hadn't meant to hit her. He never meant to hurt her, either by word or deed. But she was out such a long time and by the time she got back he was genuinely worried and as mad as hell.

One by one the girls came in. He didn't see much of them nowadays. They seemed to spend a lot of time in other people's houses. As soon as they realised their mother wasn't there they went straight to bed. He could hear them chattering away upstairs, laughing and giggling, and he felt excluded, knowing they were avoiding him, knowing *he* was the reason why they were out so much and never brought friends home as they used to. It was the same reason why Alice put Cormac to bed so early – so the lad wouldn't witness the way his dad spoke to his mam.

John went to the bottom of the stairs and listened to his daughters fight over who would sleep in the middle, knowing Maeve would be the loser, always wanting to please. What was needed was an extra bed. It could be squeezed in somehow. A chap at work had told him you could get bunk beds and John wondered if he could make a set, or a pair, or whatever they were called. He liked working with wood, so much more natural than metal. There'd be fights over who'd sleep on top, which was reached by means of a small ladder, but he'd organise a rota. He'd talk it over with Alice.

No, he wouldn't! With a sound that was almost a sob, John Lacey sat on the bottom of the stairs and buried his monstrous face in his hands. He had forgotten, but he and Alice didn't talk any more, and it was his fault, not hers. John felt as if he'd lost control of his brain. His brain made him say things, do things, that the real John found despicable and wouldn't let him do the things he knew were right.

The clock on the sideboard chimed eight, which meant Alice had been away an hour. But she'd said she was only going round Garnet Street to see her dad! John's lip curled and hot anger welled up in his chest. He'd like to bet she was up against a wall in a back entry with some feller. In fact, he'd go round Garnet Street and check, prove beyond doubt that he'd been right in his suspicions.

'I'm just going out a minute,' he shouted upstairs.

Only Maeve deigned to answer. 'All right, Dad,' she called.

John grabbed his coat and hurried out into the gaslit streets. It took just a few minutes to reach Garnet Street and even less to establish that there was no one in Danny Mitchell's house. To make sure, he went round the back and let himself in, but the house was as dark as it was empty.

Afterwards John was never quite sure what happened to his head. There was a glorious feeling of triumph, a quickening of his heart and a shiver ran through his bones at the realisation that he'd been right all along. Now he had a genuine reason to hate her.

He returned home, sat in the chair under the window, tapping his fingers on the wooden arm, waiting for Alice, his slut of a wife, to come home.

★

It was half past nine when she arrived and by then he was beginning to worry that she'd left him, though common sense told him she would never leave the children – certainly not with him.

He had rarely seen her look so lovely. Any man would be suspicious if his wife came in all starry-eyed and pink-cheeked, as if she'd just won a few hundred quid on the pools. It was the way she used to look when they made love. Something must have happened to make her eyes shine like that. Whatever it was, it was nothing to do with her husband.

'I'm sorry, luv,' she said in a rush, 'but after I'd been to me dad's I decided to drop in on Bernadette because she's been feeling dead low since Christmas. We had a drop of sherry each and I seemed to lose track of the time.'

'You've been gone two and a half hours,' John said icily.

'I know, luv. As I said, I'm sorry.'

'You've been with a feller, I can tell by your face.' Why, oh why, did he so much want this to be true? It was as if he wanted to wallow in his misery, make it worse.

She sighed. 'Oh, don't be silly, John. Go round and ask Bernadette if you don't believe me.'

'Do you think I'm daft enough not to know you've fixed a story up between you?'

'Think what you like,' she said tiredly and went into the kitchen where she put the kettle on. 'Did the girls have drinks when they came in? I can still hear them talking upstairs. Perhaps they'd like a cup of cocoa.'

Had he been the sensible man that he used to be this would be the time to mention the bunk beds. Instead, the man he had become followed his wife into the kitchen and grabbed her arm. 'I want to know where

52

you've been. I want to know why you've got that look on your face. How much did you make? How much have you got in your purse?' He released her arm. She had hung her handbag on the knob of the kitchen door. It was one of those shoulder things that had become popular during the war. He undid the zip and turned it upside down. A gold enamelled compact smashed on to the tiled floor, followed by her purse, a little comb, two neatly ironed hankies, the stub of a pencil, a couple of tram tickets and a scrap of paper.

'John! Me dad bought me that compact for me twenty-first. Oh, look, the mirror's broke.' She was close to tears, kneeling down, picking up the broken bits of glass. 'That's seven years bad luck.'

'I'll get it fixed.' Jaysus! He looked like a monster – and he acted like one. Kneeling beside her, he began to put the things back in the bag. Their shoulders touched and he longed to take her in his arms, dry her tears. Dammit, he *would*. It was now or never. Things couldn't possibly go on like this. He would just have to take the risk of seeing the disgust on her face. He said humbly, 'I don't know what gets into me some . . . what's this?'

'It's a cheque,' Alice said in an odd voice. She snatched it away before he could see who it was from and all John's suspicions returned with a vengeance he could scarcely contain.

'So, you get paid by cheque, eh? It must be some posh geezer you do it with? Let's see.'

'No!' She stubbornly put the cheque behind her back. 'It's nothing to do with you.'

'Oh, so me wife can sleep around all over the place and it's nothing to do with me!' He laughed coarsely. 'Let me see that fuckin' cheque.'

Alice shuddered. He'd never sworn in the house before, not so much as a 'bloody'. She suddenly felt sick and knew it was no use keeping the cheque from him. He was stronger than she was and could easily take it off her. 'It's from Cora Lacey,' she said. 'She's loaned me twenty-five pounds for Myrtle's salon. As from tomorrer it'll be mine.'

A year ago John would have been delighted. A year ago he would have borrowed the money for her. A mate of his had borrowed from a bank to set up his own small engineering company. But now, a year later, John felt only blinding rage, accompanied by tremendous fear. He didn't want her independent, having her own business, no longer reliant on him for money. Lately he'd even resented the few bob she earned at Myrtle's. He wanted her at home. If he could, he'd have stopped her going to the shops. He raised his hand and struck her across the face, so hard that she stumbled and almost fell. She screamed, then stopped the scream abruptly, her hand over her mouth, worried the children would hear. The cheque dropped to the floor and he grabbed it.

'Are you all right, Mam?' Orla called.

'I'm fine, luv. Just knocked meself on the kitchen cupboard, that's all.' She looked at her husband. 'If you tear that up,' she said in a grating voice, 'I'll only ask Cora for another. You're not me keeper. And as from tonight, I'll not think of you as me husband either. Go on, hit me again,' she said tauntingly when he raised his fist a second time. 'Hit me all night long, but you won't stop me from having Myrtle's.'

It was the first time she had answered back and, staring at her flushed, angry face, John Lacey realised that he'd lost her. With a groan that seemed to come from the furthest depths of his being, for the second time that night he buried his face in his hands. 'I don't know what's got into me, Alice,' he whispered.

Had Alice's cheek not been hurting so badly she might

have felt sorry for him, but for ten months she'd been treading on eggshells, trying to get through to him, putting up with his rages, his moods and, worst of all, his insults, all because she loved him. Perhaps she still loved him, she didn't know, but he had gone too far. Hitting her had been the last straw. He had frightened her girls away so they were hardly ever in. Only Cormac had been spared his bitter anger. She took the cheque and left the room.

Seconds later she was back. She felt extremely powerful, as if it was her, not him, who was in control. 'I'd sooner sleep on me own from now on,' she said curtly. 'I'll kip in the parlour. You can have the bed to yourself.'

Chapter 3

On Sunday, after early Mass, Alice and the children changed into their oldest clothes. Armed with several paintbrushes, a large tin of mauve distemper, a smaller tin of white, silver polish, rags, and various cleaning fluids and powders, and leaving behind a silent, brooding John, they made their way to Myrtle's.

Even Orla, not usually willing to lend a hand, found it very exciting. 'The girls at school will be dead envious when I tell them we own a hairdresser's,' she said boastfully.

'We don't exactly own it, luv. I only lease the place,' Alice told her.

'Oh, Mam, it's just the same.'

Bernadette Moynihan arrived just as Alice was unlocking the door. She wore old slacks and her long fair hair was tucked inside a georgette scarf. She grinned. 'Just in time.'

Alice grinned back. 'Thanks for helping, Bernie.'

'I wouldn't have missed it for worlds. What shall I do first?'

'Can I start painting the walls, Mam?' Fionnuala pleaded.

'Not yet, luv. Let's get the place cleaned first including the kitchen. There's years of dirt out there and I daren't look at the lavvy in the yard. I used to feel ashamed when customers asked if they could use it. Meself, I went home and used ours whenever I felt the urge.'

Bernadette offered to clean the lavatory. 'You can't very well ask one of the girls and you need to stay here and keep an eye on things.'

'Ta, Bernie. You're a mate. There's bleach somewhere.' Alice handed out various tasks. 'Fion and Orla, you wash the walls, Maeve, clean the sinks, there's a luv. Cormac . . .' She tried to think of something suitable for a five-year-old to do. Cormac looked at her expectantly, his small face puckered earnestly, his blue eyes very large. He was such an adorable little boy. Unable to resist, she picked him up and gave him a hug. 'You can wipe the leather chairs for your mammy.' The chairs weren't leather but leatherette and she was going to make enquiries about having them re-covered.

Everyone sang happily as they worked, all the old war songs: 'Run Rabbit Run', 'We'll Meet Again', 'We're Going to Hang Out the Washing on the Siegfried Line' . . .

At half past eleven they stopped for lemonade and meat paste butties. By one o'clock Maeve, who tired easily, had begun to wilt and Orla complained she was fed up to the teeth with cleaning. Cormac was kneeling on a chair playing with the big old-fashioned till that Alice had always thought entirely unnecessary in a hairdresser's. Fion was scrubbing away in the kitchen, longing to get her hands on a paintbrush. Having finished the lavatory, Bernadette was now brushing the yard. Alice had polished the dryers until they sparkled, though there was little she could do about the paint chipped off the hoods.

'When are we having our dinner?' Orla wanted to know.

'Four o'clock. I told you before it would be late today.

Go home if you want. You too, Maeve. Your grandad will be here in a minute to distemper the ceiling.'

'Oh, Mam!' Fion cried from the other room. 'I wanted to do the ceiling.'

'You can do the walls, luv. A ceiling needs an expert hand. I did our kitchen ceiling once and I ended up covered in distemper and looking like a ghost.'

Maeve went home to read a book, but Orla decided to stay when she realised Grandad was coming. They stopped and finished off the sandwiches, and Alice made tea in the amazingly clean kitchen. 'You've done a wonderful job with this stove,' she told Fion. 'It looks like new.'

'Can I do the walls now?'

'Not yet, luv,' Alice said patiently. 'But I tell you what you can do, go upstairs and look for some old sheets to spread around while the ceiling's being done. We don't want paint spilling everywhere.'

'What are you going to do about upstairs, Ally?' Bernadette enquired.

'What d'you mean?' Alice looked at her vacantly.

'Well, it's a flat, isn't it, soft girl. You can let it, make a few extra bob a week. Once it's cleaned up it'd be nice and cosy up there. It might . . .' She paused.

'It might what?'

Bernadette glanced sidelong at Fion and waited until the girl had left the room before continuing. 'It might do for the person who give you *that*!' She nodded at the bruise on her friend's cheek that was gradually turning from purple to yellow.

'Bernie!' Alice gasped, shocked to the core.

'I loved my Bob to bits, but he'd have been out the door like a shot if he'd so much as laid a finger on me.' Bernadette folded her arms and regarded her sternly. 'Say he hits you again or lashes out at one of the kids?'

'He'd never hit the kids!'

'This time last year would it have crossed your mind he'd hit you?'

'Well, no,' Alice said soberly.

'It's not right, Alice. No woman should be expected to put up with violence from her husband.'

Alice was trying to think of what to say in reply when the bell on the door gave its rusty ring and her dad came in. He climbed into a pair of greasy overalls and proceeded to paint the drab ceiling a lovely sparkling white.

Bernadette had turned bright pink and seemed to have lost the power of speech, Alice noticed with amusement – she'd had a crush on Danny Mitchell since she was eight.

At last Fion got her hands on a paintbrush and started on the walls. Alice began to rip up the tatty linoleum, aided by Cormac and Orla – a man was coming at eight o'clock in the morning to fit the lino she'd bought on tick yesterday in Stanley Road: black, with a faint cream marble effect, the sort she wouldn't have wanted in her house, but that was perfect for a hairdressers.

She'd got a length of white lace curtaining and two lampshades at the same time, which she'd put up when the distemper was dry. She felt a tingle of excitement. Everywhere was going to look dead smart when it was finished.

Bernadette and Danny came back to Amber Street for their dinner. For once, John's glowering face wasn't allowed to dampen the atmosphere during the meal. Everyone was too full of the hairdresser's and what they had achieved.

'What are you going to call it, Mam?' Maeve enquired.

'Why Myrtle's, luv. I wasn't thinking of changing the name.'

'I think you should,' said Bernadette.

Danny nodded. 'So do I.'

'Why don't you call it Alice's,' suggested Orla.

Alice thought that sounded a bit clumsy and wondered how anyone could be as stupid as she was; fancy not thinking about a new name and not realising the upstairs flat was included in the lease! 'You're as thick as two short planks, Alice Lacey,' she told herself.

'You could call it Lacey's,' said Fion.

'That has a nice ring to it.' Bernadette nodded her approval.

Danny said it sounded classy, Maeve thought it perfect, Cormac remarked it would go with the lacy curtains, Alice looked pleased, John merely scowled and Orla pulled a face, cross that Fionnuala's suggestion had been taken up, not hers.

And Fion glowed. She had actually christened a hairdresser's and felt very proud of herself.

After the table had been cleared and the dishes washed, Bernadette announced she was going home. Danny offered to walk with her as far as Irlam Road.

'There's no need.' Bernadette went all pink again. She never knew what to say to Danny Mitchell.

'Actually, there's something I wanted to ask you,' Danny said when they were outside. 'Where did that bruise come from on our Alice's face? She claimed to have walked into a door, but I'm not sure if I believe her.'

'John did it.' Bernadette had no intention of protecting John Lacey from his father-in-law's wrath. She was slightly disappointed that Danny was only walking her home because he'd wanted to ask about Alice. 'It was on

Thursday night, when Alice came back with the cheque.'

Danny swore under his breath. 'I'll be after having a word with him as soon as I get the opportunity.' Later that night, maybe. Alice had said something about going back to the hairdresser's to put up the curtains so there was a good chance John would be alone.

Thinking she was being helpful, Bernadette told him about the flat over Myrtle's. 'I said it would do for John, but Alice wouldn't hear of it.'

'Quite right, too.' He sounded even more shocked by the idea than his daughter had. 'You can't chuck a man out of his own home, no matter what he's done,' he said, outraged.

'Huh! No matter if he'd put your Alice in hospital or done the same to one of the kids?' She forgot her awe of him and lost her temper. Men! The world would be a far better place without them. There'd only been one good one and he'd been killed in the war.

'It's not the way things are done,' Danny said testily. He was beginning to wish he hadn't offered to take her home. He'd always thought her a rather quiet little thing. He wasn't used to women arguing with him. They usually agreed with his every word.

'Well, it's about time it was. Are you suggesting women are born to be punchbags?'

He was flummoxed. What could he say to that? 'I'm suggesting nothing of the kind.'

'Yes, you are. You're saying a woman can be knocked to bits and nothing should be done about it.'

'She can always leave.' He regretted the words as soon as they'd left his mouth, because the quiet little thing burst into sarcastic laughter.

'In that case, if John hits your Alice again, I'll suggest she ups with the four kids and parks herself on you.'

Both seething, they walked the rest of the way to Irlam Road in silence.

Alice finished hanging the white lace curtains and imagined the reaction of the customers tomorrow when they saw the changes that had been made to Myrtle's – she corrected herself – *Lacey's*. She must get a signwriter to change the name over the window and pushed to the back of her mind the knowledge that there'd been a time when John would willingly have done it.

There were other things she must do – buy new towels, for instance, mauve if you could get them. And she needed a clock, a little cheap one – how on earth had Myrtle managed without a clock for all those years? And she'd have price lists printed on little cards, like wedding invitations.

She rubbed her hands together excitedly. She'd have to engage an assistant, someone to do the same things she'd been taken on for herself. A woman with school-aged kids would be ideal because Fionnuala was only too willing to come and help when she finished school, as well as on Saturdays.

All the pictures of the beautiful, dead smart coiffures that Myrtle couldn't have managed in a month of Sundays had been removed from the wall so it could be painted. Alice began to put them back with the drawing pins she'd saved, along with the adverts for various shampoos, setting lotions and hairdressings – she liked the one for Rowland's Macassar Oil the best. Her arms were aching. But it wasn't just the hard work she'd put in today, but that she'd been sleeping on the settee in the parlour since Thursday and it was extremely uncomfortable, much too short and much too hard.

Things couldn't continue at home the way they were, but once again Alice refused to think about them.

Instead, she sat under the dryer and regarded Myrtle's –
Lacey's – with satisfaction. Tomorrow it would look even
nicer with the lino laid.

Across the street, well away from the street lamp, a dark
figure stood watching the woman at her various tasks. He
saw her sit in the centre of the three dryers, saw the way
her face glowed when she glanced around the salon,
which he had to concede had improved out of all
proportion for the better.

John Lacey felt sick with love for the woman who was
his wife, along with stirrings of anger and jealousy, never
far away these days. The bloody salon had taken *his* place
in Alice's heart, but then he only had himself to blame
for that.

For the first time in his life he felt the urge to get
drunk, to get totally inebriated, forget everything. He'd
only been that drunk once before – at a mate's wedding
when he was eighteen. It hadn't been a very pleasant
experience, but right now the idea of forgetting everything was infinitely appealing.

Where to go to achieve this agreeable state of mind?
Not a pub where he was known, or a quiet, respectable
place where they'd stare at his face. One of those rowdy
ale houses on the Dock Road would be ideal. They were
usually packed to the gills with foreign seamen and
prostitutes. No one would take a blind bit of notice of
him.

John took a final look at Alice, turned up the collar of
his coat, pulled his hat down over his scarred face and
hurried in the direction of the Docky.

Hours later Danny Mitchell, on his way to have a stern
word with his son-in-law, was still seething over the
conversation he'd had with Bernadette. If she were

older, she'd probably have been one of them damned, stupid suffragettes, chaining herself to railings so women could have the vote.

A little worm of reason penetrated his stubborn brain. It wasn't exactly fair that women *shouldn't* have the vote. After all, whatever those fools of politicians got up to affected them just as much as it did men. And they'd been worth their weight in gold during the war. And if a man knocked a woman about, was she supposed just to stand there and let him?

Danny squirmed uncomfortably. It niggled him that the little girl who'd been his daughter's best friend for as long as he could remember had caused him to have such disturbing thoughts. He felt like a traitor to his sex and tried to concentrate on his meeting later with Phyllis Henderson. Phyllis would butter him up no end, restore his equilibrium, as it were.

To his surprise, when he entered his daughter's house the light was on, but it appeared to be empty. 'Is anyone home?' he called.

'Only me, Grandad,' Cormac shouted from upstairs.

'Surely you haven't been left all on your own!' Danny exclaimed on his way up to the boxroom where his grandson slept.

'Dad said Mam or the girls'd be back soon.' Cormac was sitting up in bed, his slightly too big wincyette pyjamas buttoned neatly to the neck. He put down the book he was reading when his grandad came in.

'Your mam'll be dead cross if she finds you all by yourself. I'll stay till someone comes.' Danny sat on the edge of the narrow bed. 'What's that you're reading, son?'

'I'm not 'xactly *reading* it, Grandad,' Cormac explained gravely. 'I'm trying to do the sums.'

Danny gaped. The lad, only five years old, was

actually studying an *arithmetic* book. His heart swelled with pride. Wait till he told Phyllis and his mates in the pub! 'Need any help, son?' he enquired, though beyond the twelve times table he needed help himself.

'What's that word?' Cormac turned the page and pointed to the heading.

'Multiplication. It means . . .'

'I know what it means, Grandad. It means "times". I didn't know how it was said. The next page is "long" something. I don't know how that's said either.'

'Long division, son.' He was beginning to think his grandson was a genius. 'Can you do all these things – the long division and the times?'

'Only with little figures,' Cormac confessed sadly.

'Can the whole class do them?' Danny asked.

Cormac shook his fair head. 'Acshully, Grandad, school's a bit fed-upping. I wish it weren't so dead easy.'

He should be moved up to a higher class, Danny thought indignantly. He'd have a word with Alice when she came in.

Not far away in Irlam Road, Bernadette Moynihan also felt indignant. To think that all these years she'd been sweet on such a rampant misogynist! Even when she'd been married to her darling Bob she had continued to find Danny Mitchell slightly disturbing.

It had started when his wife died and Danny had appeared so devastated. She was eight, same as Alice, and had resolved to marry him, take care of him, when she grew up. He was only twenty-nine and, as Bernadette grew older – became twelve, sixteen, twenty – in her eyes Danny remained the same. One of these days she'd catch up with him, he'd notice her and ask for her hand in marriage. She had spent many happy hours imagining what it would be like being Danny Mitchell's wife. This was one of the few dreams she hadn't confided to Alice, who might not care to have her best friend as a stepmother.

Then Bernadette had met Bob Moynihan and all thoughts of Danny Mitchell had fled from her mind – except when she met him in the flesh, when her knees were still inclined to grow weak and her cheeks to turn pink. She used to pray Bob wouldn't notice and he never had.

But now! Now she had completely gone off him. 'You can't chuck a man out of his own home no matter what he's done,' he'd actually said. Oh, really! She'd have flattened John Lacey with a frying pan if she'd been in Alice's shoes, then dragged him outside and had the locks changed so he couldn't get back in.

She hated men, every single one of them, and she hated Danny Mitchell the most.

At the next table a black man had pulled a girl on to his knee and was touching her breasts beneath her green jumper.

The girl laughed and pulled away. Her face was orange with powder and her mouth a vivid scarlet. She had a green bead as big as a marble dangling from each ear. 'Eh, mate. I don't usually let fellas do that for free.'

The man leered, showing large, very white teeth. 'How much you charge?'

'Five bob and I'm all yours for half an hour.'

'Where we go?'

'Outside, I'll show you where, but give us the five bob first.'

The couple left and John Lacey felt something stir in the pit of his stomach. After ten chaste months and half a dozen pints of ale, he was badly in need of a woman. In the past the idea of using a prostitute would have disgusted him, but right now perhaps it was the drink that made him consider the idea not all that repugnant.

Jaysus! Did he really intend to sink so low? Well, why not? To have set foot inside this den of iniquity wasn't the act of a man who cared how low he sank. There'd already been a fight – two men had produced knives and gone for each other. They'd been thrown out, leaving behind quite a lot of blood. The fight had been over a woman, a gaunt young woman with hollow cheeks and vacant eyes who had followed them outside.

The place was called the Arcadia and when he'd first set foot inside the large, square room with its worm-eaten pillars, the low ceiling blackened by age and smoke, it had made him think of a scene from hell. The wooden floor was scattered with sawdust, the tables long, full of stains and cigarette burns, with benches either side. It was packed, as he had expected. Noise assaulted his ears, hurt them. Men and women shouted at each other in order to be heard above the din – the women's shrill voices seemed the louder. Directly in front of him a man with a black patch over his eye swept his arm across a table and dozens of empty glasses smashed to the floor. There was the pungent odour of dirt, unwashed bodies, cheap scent. The smoke that hung in the air smelt musky and sweet – it wasn't just tobacco.

His first instinct had been to turn on his heel and leave, but he remembered he'd wanted a place where no one would know him. What did it matter where he got plastered? Two hours later he knew his first instinct had been right. He was only half drunk, he had forgotten nothing and the ale had made him feel even more depressed. The tragedy that was now his life seemed worse, more insoluble, even less bearable, than ever. In such alien surroundings he found it hard to believe he was a married man with a lovely wife and four equally lovely children.

Another thing, sex had been furthest from his mind when he came in, but now he could think of little else. He had tried to, but couldn't, take his eyes off the grotesquely painted women in their tight frocks and short skirts. He imagined doing things with them that he had never done with Alice. He thought about what the black man was doing with the girl in the green jumper and felt himself swell.

A woman slid on to the bench opposite. 'Like a spot of company, luv?' she asked in a coarse, gruff voice. She was twice his age, with hair dyed an unnatural red, almost purple, and a gaudily painted face. John's eyes were drawn to the breasts that swelled over the top of her black blouse, the nipples prominent through the thin, gauzy material. She was wearing nothing underneath.

He shook his head, though his heart was pounding and he longed to reach out and touch the bulging breasts. 'No, thank you.'

'Just come for a gander, have you?' she sneered and went away, muttering, 'Filthy bugger.'

All it needed was courage. Men and women kept disappearing and reappearing half an hour, an hour, later. All he had to do was approach a woman – he didn't even have to say anything, just show the money and nod towards the door. But he was terrified that even these women, the lowest of the low, would turn him down because of his face. Even worse, they might take his money with the same expression of distaste on their faces that he'd seen on Alice's, though she flatly denied it.

Someone older might be less choosy. He regretted

sending away the woman who'd asked if he wanted company – clearly, his face didn't bother *her*. He wondered where she'd gone so he could say he'd changed his mind. His eyes searched the packed room for her red head, but she was nowhere to be seen.

Then he saw the girl. She was two tables away, sitting demurely with her hands clasped on her lap, head bent, as if she was closely studying something on the table. Her hair was long and straight, and so fair it was almost white. Even from this distance John could see the long, pale lashes surrounding a pair of large grey eyes. The girl raised her head, as if aware she was being watched, and through the crowds their faces met – the faces of the man with the melted skin and the girl who would have been pretty if it hadn't been for the ugly hare lip.

Her name was Clare he learnt after they had made love. She'd written it down because he couldn't understand the strange, gutteral sounds that came from her mouth. She had a cleft palate, no roof to her mouth. She gestured a lot, her face fierce with concentration, pointing to herself, to him. When he asked her age, she wrote 'twenty' in the air with her finger.

John liked her. He liked the fact that she never smiled, because he himself hadn't felt much like smiling in a long time. He sensed that she found life as burdensome as he did. He admired her for not painting her face or wearing revealing clothes – she had on a plain black frock and flat black shoes, no jewellery. She was very clean and her room, on the top floor of a narrow three-storey house just round the corner from the Arcadia, was neat and tidy.

He hadn't done the disgusting things he'd imagined with the other women. He made love to her as he would have done to his wife – gently, with some passion, quite satisfyingly. Other than wrapping her legs around his waist, she didn't respond, but nor did she give the impression she found the act objectionable.

When they had finished he felt as if a great load had been lifted from his shoulders. For the first time since he'd been fire-watching and that damned ship had gone up in flames, he was able to relax. He lay beside her on the bed, watching the cold moon shining through the small window. Stars twinkled in the dark sky.

'Do you want to go back to the Arcadia?' he asked after she had answered his questions as best she could and they had lain there for a while. He was stopping her from earning her living.

She shook her head and pointed to the door, indicating that he could go if he liked.

'D'you mind if I stay? I feel dead tired.'

Closing her eyes, she gave a tiny sigh, which he understood to mean she was tired too.

John reached out and touched her twisted lips with his finger. 'You're very pretty.'

There was surprise in the intelligent grey eyes when she turned towards him. She seemed to hesitate, then lifted her hand and stroked his melted cheek. He decided he could quickly get used to her painful pronunciation when she said in her awkward way, 'You're very handsome.'

Alice had been cross the night before when she came home and discovered that, unusually for him, John had gone out, which she didn't mind, but he shouldn't have left Cormac on his own.

Her dad thought he'd almost certainly gone for a drink. 'Do him good, if you ask me.'

'Yes, but he might have *said*.'

Danny left, rather late, to meet his lady friend. The

girls came home. Alice made cocoa and several rounds of toast, and they sat round the fire, giggling helplessly, telling each other silly jokes. They made so much noise that Cormac came down to see what was going on and told the unfunniest joke of all: 'Why did the chicken cross the road?'

'To get to the other side!' everyone screamed.

'Oh,' gasped Maeve, bent double with laughter. 'It's a pity Dad isn't out more often. It's much better fun without him.' She went very red and everyone fell silent as they contemplated the truth of this remark.

'Well,' Alice said eventually, 'I think it's time we went to bed. I'm fair whacked and I need to be up early tomorrer to let the man into Myrtle's with the lino.' There didn't seem much point waiting up for John. Since last Thursday they'd hardly exchanged a word.

'Lacey's,' Fionnuala reminded her.

'Oh, yes, Lacey's.'

Alice fell asleep immediately on the uncomfortable settee and was woken by the sound of clinking bottles. The milkman had arrived. She went into the living room in her nightie and felt cross again when she discovered John hadn't lit the fire as he normally did before going to work – he'd used to wake her up with a cup of tea, but those days were long gone.

She lit the fire herself, made tea, woke Cormac, then the girls. 'I'll have to be going in a minute,' she told the three sleepy faces. I'll trust you to make sure your brother eats his cornflakes and that he's properly dressed for school. He's inclined to forget his vest if you don't watch him.'

'OK, Mam,' they chorused, and she thought what lovely children they were and how nice and cheerful last night had been without their father's brooding presence.

Perhaps he'd go for a drink more often, she thought hopefully.

The linoleum had been dead cheap and the man cut it into shape in no time. 'It's not going to last all that long,' he warned, 'not in a hairdresser's with so much traffic.'

'It's only temporary,' Alice assured him, 'just to make the place look respectable until I can buy some of that inlaid stuff.'

He wished her luck, promised to recommend Lacey's to his missus and Alice tipped him sixpence.

'You've worked a miracle, Alice,' the first customer gasped when she arrived for her nine o'clock appointment. 'Mauve, white and black go together perfect.' Throughout the day, customers continued to express their astonishment at the transformation that had taken place in Myrtle's – now called Lacey's, Alice informed them. She didn't feel the least embarrassed when a few asked to use the lavatory. At least it was clean and as soon as she could she'd paint the walls.

Late in the afternoon Mrs O'Leary popped her head round the door to ask if their Daisy could possibly be squeezed in for a trim. She regarded the salon with amazement. 'It looks lovely and bright, like a grotto. After Christmas Eve, I swore I'd never set foot in here again, but now I'm glad Gloria's in Marsh Lane were too busy to take us. Our Daisy's got a concert tomorrer night and she needs a trim dead urgent.'

Daisy tossed her auburn curls. 'I'm an elf,' she announced.

'I'm afraid you'll have to wait a bit.' Alice was halfway through a perm, and there was a customer under a dryer who would shortly need combing out. She was doing the work of two women and felt worn out.

'You look puffed,' Mrs O'Leary remarked as she sat down. 'What you need is an assistant.'

'I know. I keep meaning to put a notice in the winder, but I've been too busy all day to write it out.'

'I'd apply meself, but our Kevin's only five – he started school with your Cormac – and I'm not prepared to let him and Daisy wander the streets until you close, and on Saturdays an' all. Me neighbour's got Kevin at the moment, but I couldn't ask her every day.' She pulled a face. 'I could do with the money. The cost of Daisy's dancing class went up in January and her costumes cost a mint. Me husband claims we can't afford it and keeps threatening to make her stop. The thing is, the dancing teacher ses she's got talent.' She chucked Daisy under the chin. 'You want to go on the stage when you grow up, don't you, luv?'

'Oh, *yes*, Mam,' Daisy concurred.

'Mmm,' Alice said thoughtfully. Mrs O'Leary was always nicely dressed, and she had a warm smile and a pleasant manner. She used to get on Myrtle's nerves, boasting incessantly about Daisy and her dancing, but Alice could do much worse for an assistant. She said, 'Actually, the job would only be during school hours. Our Fion's helping out the rest of the time. In fact, she should be here any minute. Ah, here she is now.'

Fionnuala burst into the salon, eager to start work properly as a hairdresser. She pouted when her mother told her to sweep the floor. 'Oh, *Mam*!'

'Just get on with it, luv. You're not ready to give a perm just yet.' She turned to Mrs O'Leary. 'What do you say, about the job, that is?'

'I'd *luv* it,' the woman said breathlessly. 'When can I start?'

'Tomorrer wouldn't be too soon.'

'Tomorrer it is. Me name's Patsy, by the way. You

can't very well call me Mrs O'Leary and me call you Alice.'

I might as well be invisible, John Lacey thought sardonically when he arrived home from work and realised no one had noticed he'd been out all night. As far as his family were concerned he didn't exist.

He'd spent the night with Clare, feeling guilty, but at the same time hoping Alice would worry herself sick – he'd worried himself enough over her. He had concocted a story – he'd met a mate, drunk too much, gone back to his house and fallen asleep. But the story wasn't necessary. All Alice did was rattle on and on about hairdressing and the marvellous day she'd had, and you'd think Fionnuala had given Queen Elizabeth herself a shampoo and set from the way she spoke, when all she'd done was wash some woman's hair.

'I'm going out,' he said in a surly voice after he'd finished his tea.

'Have a nice time, luv,' Alice said brightly.

John saw Orla wink joyfully at her sisters as he left the room and longed to turn round, tell his family how much he loved them, make everything better. But it was too late. They hated him. He'd passed the point of no return.

Cormac had followed him into the hall and John wondered if the divil now possessed his soul. How could he have thought his little lad could hate anyone, let alone his father?

'Got ten out of ten for me sums today, Dad. I've brought the book home to show you.'

Tears stung his eyes as he sat on the stairs and lifted Cormac on to his knee. 'Let's have a dekko, son.'

'They're add up and take away.'

'So I see. Gosh, that's dead neat writing.'

'The teacher said it's the best in the class.'

He stroked Cormac's soft cheek. 'I bet she did, son.'

Alice poked her head round the door. 'I was wondering if you'd gone or not. I didn't hear the door slam.'

John put Cormac down and reached for his coat. 'I'm going now. By the way,' he said gruffly, 'you have the bed from now on. I'll use the settee.'

The Docky was always busy. The offices of the shipping merchants, the importers and exporters, were closed and there was less traffic than during the day. But at seven o'clock the pavements were still full of seamen and sailors of myriad nationalities. Behind the high walls of the docks activity could be heard – the shouts and thuds as ships that could have come from anywhere in the world were being loaded or offloaded in the bright glare of floodlights.

Particles of ice were being blown crazily about, this way and that, by the bitter wind that blew in from the Mersey. John could hear the water slushing noisily against the walls of the docks. He drew up his scarf around his neck.

He arrived at the Arcadia, where two small children, a boy and a girl, were cuddled against each other on the steps outside, shivering in their thin clothes. He gave them a penny each.

'Thanks, mister,' the boy said with remarkable cheerfulness.

Clare was sitting at the same table as the night before, her back to him. John's heart lifted and he began to push his way through the crowded room. He'd been looking forward to this moment all day, a day when he'd felt at ease with himself for the first time in months. He slid on to the bench beside her. 'Hello, there.'

She frowned. At first he thought she was annoyed with him for coming until he recognised the frown was one of disbelief. Her cheeks went pink and he realised she was pleased and flattered that he was back.

She nodded furiously. 'Hello.' She hesitated, as she had done the night before, then reached for his hand. 'Glad,' she whispered. 'Glad you're here.' And then she smiled and the smile made her look almost beautiful.

John smiled back and thought what a miracle it was that he had met a woman who was as damaged as himself and that they could make each other smile.

Cora Lacey came into the salon at the end of Alice's first week. The hairdresser's was just about to close. Fionnuala was cleaning the sinks and Cormac was kneeling on a chair in front of the big till ringing up numbers.

'Had a busy week?' Cora enquired.

'I've been run off me feet if you must know.' Alice collapsed under a dryer. 'Thank the Lord it's Sat'day. I've just sent our Orla and Maeve round for fish and chips. I haven't the strength to make the tea.'

'Good,' Cora said with satisfaction. It meant the takings must be considerable. 'Shove over, son.' She gave Cormac a little nudge with her hip and he reluctantly climbed off the chair. 'Is this all there is?' She glanced suspiciously at her sister-in-law. 'Not a single note?'

'The notes are at home,' Alice explained. 'I empty the till each night, don't I? And I hardly ever take notes, anyroad, except for perms and I didn't do one today.'

'Then I'll come back to the house with you to collect me share.'

Fionnuala had stopped work to listen. She glared at her aunt whom she had never liked. 'What's she on about, Mam?'

'It's none of your business, luv.'

76

'Why is she taking money out the till? It's *our* salon.'

'Your Auntie Cora put money into the business,' Alice explained patiently. Her eldest daughter usually managed to test her patience sorely. 'She's entitled to some of the profit.'

'But there won't be profit for weeks and weeks, Mam,' Fion exclaimed. 'You said so only the other day, what with the price of paint and everything.'

'Yes, but . . .' Alice paused. Fion was right. The cost of improvements shouldn't just be borne by her, but shared with Cora, too. And the wages – she wondered if she was entitled to claim a wage for herself? Oh, Lord! She must be the stupidest woman in the world for not having grasped the blatantly obvious.

She swallowed hard – Cora always made her feel dead nervous – and said in a firm voice, 'I'm afraid you can't just come in and help yourself. I need to work things out first, what comes in and what goes out, like.'

'And what exactly goes out apart from the price of a few tins of paint?' Cora wanted to know. She had been expecting to go home with a few quid in her pocket and was annoyed at being thwarted.

Alice was about to reel off the things she'd bought and those she intended buying, when Fionnuala said aggressively, 'She said she'd write them down, didn't she? It's *our* hairdresser's. We don't have to answer to you for everything we buy.'

'Shush, luv.' Alice squeezed her daughter's arm.

The door opened and Orla and Maeve came in, each carrying a parcel of fish and chips wrapped in greasy newspaper.

'Shall we take them home and put them in the oven, Mam?' Maeve enquired.

'Please, luv. We'll be there in a minute.'

Orla's bright, curious eyes went from her mother to

her aunt, then to her sister's red, angry face. 'What's going on?'

'There's nothing going on, luv. Just get them fish and chips home before they turn cold.'

'We'll wait for you.' Orla and Maeve came into the salon and stood alongside their mother. Cormac bent his head against his mam's hip and Alice idly began to stroke the soft fair hair.

Faced with the girls' hostile eyes, it dawned on Cora that she wasn't going to find their gormless mother the easy touch she'd expected. She also felt disturbed at being presented with such a united front, conscious she had no one on her side. She wished she'd brought Maurice so she could stroke his hair the way Alice was stroking Cormac's and she wouldn't look so very much alone.

'I'll be in Monday for a statement,' she muttered.

'It might not be ready by then.' Fionnuala smirked. She was thoroughly enjoying protecting Mam from the horrible Cora. It was *her* who had reminded Mam the hairdresser's wouldn't show a profit for ages, *she* who had given it its name. She felt annoyed and very unappreciated when Mam tugged her sleeve and told her again to 'shush'.

'I'll have the statement ready for Monday,' Alice promised.

She had been born, Clare informed him, when her mother was forty-seven. By then her three brothers were in their twenties; all married, all living in different parts of the country. They rarely came home. Her parents' marriage had broken down years before. John was astonished to learn her father had been, possibly still was, a solicitor's clerk.

'My mother said she only had me because he raped

her. She hated me right from the start.' She conveyed this in a mixture of gestures, facial expressions, sounds and the pad on which she wrote. Her full name was Clare Frances Carlson. 'They were ashamed of people knowing I was their daughter.'

She'd been sent to a special boarding school, returning home at fourteen when her education was complete. Within months she had run away – she came from Widnes – but couldn't think of a job someone like her could do apart from cleaning. Even then, 'People don't like this.' She pointed to her mouth, then wrote, 'They think I'm an imbecile.'

'You're anything but.' John took her hands in his. She was a very clever young woman – he wouldn't have known how to spell imbecile. There were books on the sideboard, pencil drawings on the walls that he was surprised to learn she'd done herself. They were mostly of the Dock Road, which could be seen from the window – the traffic, the teeming pavements, the funnels of ships protruding from behind the dock walls. A few were sketches of the crowded interior of the Arcadia that she'd done from memory.

Her short life story was told without a shred of self-pity. She hadn't drifted into prostitution, no one had coerced her. She just heard it went on and it seemed a good way for someone like her to make a living. She didn't like it, but she didn't hate it either.

'Surely there were other things that you could have done,' John said, conscious of a note of reproof in his voice.

'What would you have done if you'd been born with your face like that?' she scribbled, underlining the 'born'.

For some reason he seized the pencil. 'Hidden from the world,' he wrote.

'That's what I'm doing in my way,' she wrote back.

'You deserve better,' he wrote in turn. He'd never been greedy for money. A few extra bob a week wouldn't have come amiss for the odd luxury, but as a skilled tradesman he earned slightly more than the average man. There'd always been enough to keep his family comfortably warm and fed, and the bit Alice got from hairdressing was merely the icing on the cake. But he longed to take Clare away from this run-down house full of tarts, find her somewhere respectable to live, support her, so that she could come off the game and belong to him alone.

But without money none of these things was possible. It gnawed at his gut, knowing that before he came, or after he'd gone, she was in the Arcadia touting for customers, yet he had no right to ask her to stop. He couldn't have afforded to see her more than once or twice a week, had she not refused to let him pay after the first night.

'I said you're different. We're friends,' she wrote, turning away the five shillings he offered. She was a curious mixture of hardness and innocence.

He thought 'friends' described their relationship perfectly. They were friends drawn together by adversity and loneliness. At the back of his mind there was always the awareness that a year ago he wouldn't have dreamt of going near the Arcadia or sleeping with a prostitute. He had told Clare he was married, but still worried that he was using her. Having broken through her hard shell, he was taking advantage of the soft, generous woman inside. He worried that he might hurt her, let her down, that she would become too dependent on him. If things ever improved between him and Alice, for instance . . . But – he sighed – things never would, particularly now that she was so deeply involved with that damned hairdresser's.

★

The nightly visits to the pub were doing John the world of good. Alice only wished he'd gone before. He was nicer to the girls, and after tea he'd put Cormac on his knee and discuss the things he'd done that day at school. He'd even deigned to speak to his wife in a civil manner, suggesting he build bunk beds for the middle bedroom.

'The girls are getting too big for three in a bed,' he said and actually smiled.

Alice opened her mouth to say that Maeve had been sleeping with her since she'd occupied the double bed, but quickly closed it. 'Them bunk beds sound the gear, luv,' she said warmly. 'The girls will be dead pleased.'

'I'll get the wood this weekend.'

'John!' She laid her hand on his arm and was dismayed when he quickly moved away as if disgusted by her touch. She regarded him sadly, thinking how much she'd once loved him, then felt even more dismayed at the realisation she didn't love him now. He had spurned her too often. He had driven her away.

'What?'

Alice sighed. 'Oh, nothing.'

Chapter 4
CHRISTMAS 1951

'Who'd like another mince pie?' Alice cried.

'Me!'

'Apart from you, Fionnuala Lacey. I thought it was your intention to lose a few pounds. Any minute now and you'll need a bigger overall.' The overalls were lilac nylon – 'lilac' sounded so much nicer than 'mauve', Alice thought, more tasteful.

'Oh, *Mam*!'

Alice virtually danced across the room to pass the plate beneath the noses of the three women under the dryers. They each took one.

'You look happy, luv,' Mrs Curran remarked. 'Did you make these yourself?'

'I was up till midnight baking,' Alice said cheerfully. 'It's home-made mincemeat too. I managed to get a pound of sultanas in Costigan's. I think it's disgusting. The war's been over six whole years and the country's still on rations. Do you fancy a drop of sherry with the pie?'

'Ta all the same, luv, but no. Drink plays havoc with me gallstones. I wouldn't mind a cup of tea, though.'

'Fion, make Mrs Curran a cup of tea, please.'

'On the Empire, she was,' Patsy O'Leary was saying as she combed out Mrs Glaister's wet hair ready for Alice to set. 'All the dancing schools in Liverpool took part, but our Daisy was the star of the show. Wasn't she, Alice?'

'Oh, yes,' Alice dutifully lied.

Fionnuala looked at her mother and winked. Alice must have been asked the same question a hundred times since the concert last week. Daisy had been good, but a few other girls and one or two boys had been better.

'Poor Myrtle, she wouldn't recognise this place if she saw it now,' Mrs Glaister said sadly.

'Do you ever hear from her, luv?'

'No. I always send a Christmas card, but I haven't had one back for years. I still miss her, even after all this time. She was a good friend, Myrtle.' Mrs Glaister's old eyes grew watery. 'I reckon she must have passed on.' She crossed herself.

'It happens to us all,' Patsy O'Leary commented.

'Fion,' Alice called, 'put a gown on Mrs Evans. I'll be ready for her soon.'

'Come on, Mrs Evans, luv,' Fionnuala said in a sickly, sugary voice, and proceeded to help the woman, who was barely fifty and as fit as a fiddle, to her feet, and shove her arms inside the sleeves of the lilac gown as if she hadn't the strength to lift the arms herself.

'I can manage on me own, thanks,' Mrs Evans snapped.

It was Alice's turn to wink at Patsy. Fionnuala persisted in treating anyone over forty as if they had one foot in the grave. She would help women down to the lavatory in the yard, wait for them outside and help them back again. Even when asked by one woman, admittedly elderly, but resentful at being fussed over, if she was waiting to wipe her arse, it hadn't prevented Fionnuala from assuming that most of her mother's customers were helpless invalids. Still, Alice thought, her heart was in the right place.

Alice went over to a chair facing the mirror and laid

her hands on Mrs Evans's shoulders. 'What is it you want, luv? Explain to me again.'

'Frosting. Just the tips of me hair bleached. I would have thought you'd have heard of frosting, Mrs Lacey,' the woman said sniffily, 'you being a hairdresser, like.'

'Of course I've heard of frosting. I get *Vogue* every month to keep up with the latest styles and products, don't I? I just wasn't sure if you knew what it was.' Bleached ends wouldn't suit someone as dark as Edna Evans. But then, the customer was always right and if she wanted to end up looking dead stupid it was up to her.

'I wouldn't have asked for it if I didn't know what it was.'

'Just making sure, luv,' Alice said serenely. Some customers could be really difficult.

'You're obviously very busy,' Edna Evans said grudgingly.

'I've had to turn customers away. We've been booked solid for weeks, but then Christmas Eve is always busy. Patsy's only helping today as a special favour.'

The door opened, the bell chimed sweetly and Bernadette Moynihan came in. 'Oh, it's like a little oasis in here,' she sang. 'It's dead gloomy outside. The lights in the window look the gear, Al. Lovely and bright.'

'They actually spell "Lacey's". It took me ages to do. Patsy,' she called, 'would you comb out Mrs Curran, then put a gown on Bernie and wet her hair.'

'I'm here for a Peter Pan cut, Al. It doesn't need wetting.'

'I read the other day that hair cuts better if it's wet. I thought I'd experiment on you.'

'Oh, ta! Friendship can have its limits, Alice Lacey. If you spoil me hair, I'll never speak to you again.'

The dryers gradually emptied. Edna Evans went away looking as if she'd been sprinkled with icing sugar, tipping Alice sixpence, so *she* must be pleased. Mrs Glaister seemed reluctant to leave the warm, brightly lit salon with its silver decorations and coloured lights. Feeling sorry for the old woman, knowing that after five years she still missed Myrtle, Alice suggested she stay and have another glass of sherry. The salon would be closing in half an hour.

'And there's still a few mince pies left, luv. Help yourself. Fion, start cleaning the sinks, there's a good girl. Patsy, you can go if you want. Thanks for coming.'

Patsy O'Leary wished everyone Merry Christmas and went home. Mrs Glaister realised her time was up when Alice turned the 'Open' sign to 'Closed'. Fionnuala went to tidy the kitchen and Bernadette examined the Peter Pan cut in the mirror. It was a big step, going from very long to very short in the space of a few minutes. Her neck felt cold, she complained. Alice gave her a towel to keep it warm.

There were footsteps on the stairs and a stocky young woman with a vivid, smiling face entered the salon. She wore a warm tweed coat and a knitted mohair tam-o'-shanter. 'I'm off now, Mrs Lacey.'

'Miss Caddick!' Alice kissed the woman on the cheek. 'Have a lovely Christmas and I hope the wedding goes really well. Good luck for the future.'

'Same to you, Mrs Lacey. I couldn't have wished for a nicer landlady. I've just given upstairs a good clean, ready for the new tenant.'

'Ta, luv. I wish you were getting married in Bootle. I'd have come to the church for a look.'

'If I was getting married in Bootle, you'd have been invited, Mrs Lacey, but Durham's a long way to ask someone to come.' She shouted, ''Bye, Fionnuala,' bestowed a glittering smile on Bernadette and left.

'So, you've got to find a new tenant for upstairs,' Bernie said.

'I've already got one. The teacher taking over Miss Caddick's class at St James's is taking over the flat as well. Nell Greene, her name is, with an "e" on the end. I take it she's a "miss". She comes from London.'

'What's she like?'

'Dunno, I haven't seen her. It was all arranged by letter.'

Bernadette worriedly regarded her hair. 'Does this look too boyish? And I don't like the look of me ears.'

'Peter Pan was a boy, so it's bound to. As for your ears, I'll give them a trim if you like.'

'You say the nicest things. Albert'll have a fit tonight when he sees it. We're going to Reece's to a dance.'

'Albert Eley hasn't got the strength to have a fit. And I'm surprised he can dance, if you must know.'

Bernadette pretended to look angry, then her face collapsed in a loud sigh. 'He'll probably not even notice me hair or me new dress. He's a good dancer, though. He had lessons in some place in Spellow Lane.'

'Tap-dancing? Like Daisy O'Leary?'

''Course not, idiot.' She giggled. 'Ballroom dancing. He went with his mam.'

'I don't know what you see in him,' Alice said bluntly. Albert Eley was a bachelor of forty who lived in Byron Street with his mother. He was the most uninteresting man she had ever known.

Bernie shrugged. 'He's company. At least he's never tried anything on.'

'Only because he wouldn't know how. Seriously, Bernie. You're only thirty-seven, you're still dead pretty. There must be loads of men out there who'd be an improvement on Albert Eley.'

'Until I met Albert, I never came across a single one

who didn't want to jump into bed with me within the first five minutes. He's easy to be with, very polite, free with his money. The only thing that gets me down is him going on and on about his bloody mother. It's mam this and mam that until I could scream.' Bernie giggled. 'Anyroad, *you're* only thirty-seven and still dead pretty. There's a few men around who'd be an improvement on John Lacey.'

'Shush!' Alice put her finger to her lips and nodded towards the kitchen where her daughter could be heard washing dishes. 'Me and John get on fine nowadays.'

'Not all that fine,' Bernie said in a hoarse whisper. 'He still sleeps in the parlour. The kids must have guessed there's something up by now.'

'They think it's his back, he ricked it and he has to sleep on his own.'

'A likely story!'

'It *is* a story, Bernie, and as long as the kids believe it, that's all that matters. Anyroad, it doesn't bother me, not much. I've got used to it by now.' She gave her friend a little shove. 'Stop trying to make me miserable. I love having me own salon. I'm dead happy, even if things aren't exactly perfect at home. Now shove off and make yourself beautiful for Albert. Oh, and by the way, when you come to Christmas dinner tomorrer, try not to rile me dad. All you two ever do is argue.'

Bernadette opened the door. 'Tell him not to rile me,' she said pertly before closing it.

'Phew!' Alice locked the door and collapsed in a chair. 'It's been a day and a half, today has. Have you nearly finished, Fion?' she called. 'It's time us two went home.'

'I've only got to dry the dishes, Mam.'

'Just leave them on the draining board to dry themselves.'

Someone tried the door. 'We're closed,' Alice

shouted, but the person banged on the glass. 'Oh, Lord,' she groaned. 'It's only your Auntie Cora.'

'Tell her to sod off, Mam.'

'Don't be silly, luv.'

'I've just come to wish you Merry Christmas and discuss the lease,' Cora said when Alice reluctantly let her in. Her light skin was becoming sallow and her colourless hair was scraped back in its usual sparse bun. She wore an unflattering camel coat.

'Merry Christmas, Cora,' Alice said coldly. 'What about the lease?' The seven-year lease expired at the end of the month and was due to be renewed. No doubt Cora had come on Horace Flynn's behalf to announce the cost of a new one.

'It's going up,' Cora said.

'I expected it would.' It seemed only fair.

'A new seven-year lease will be fourteen hundred pounds.' The small eyes gleamed with pleasure. She clearly enjoyed being the purveyor of such grim news.

'Fourteen hundred!' Alice gasped. 'I can't afford that much, Cora! The rates went up earlier this year and the last electricity bill made me eyes pop.'

'You'll just have to cut down on expenses,' Cora said. 'Get rid of that assistant, for one.'

'Not our Fion!'

'No, the other one. That Patsy woman. You haven't needed her since Fionnuala's been full-time.'

'I couldn't possibly. She needs the money. Her husband's dead mean and she's desperate for their Daisy to go on the stage.'

'There's no room for sentiment in business, Alice.'

'There is in mine,' Alice cried. 'There's no way I'd get rid of Patsy. Anyroad, we're often in need of three pairs of hands.'

Cora shrugged her narrow shoulders. 'Take it or leave it — the lease, that is.'

'We'll leave it, thanks all the same,' said a voice. Fionnuala came in from the kitchen. Cora shrank back. She wouldn't have come if she'd known the girl was there. While she could wrap her gutless wonder of a mother around her little finger, she was nervous of Fionnuala who somehow always seemed to get the better of her. It was Fionnuala who, years ago, had demanded a copy of the agreement that her stupid mam had signed and pointed out Cora was only entitled to a third share of 'the business presently known as Myrtle's Hairdressing Salon', so wasn't due a penny from the upstairs flat: it was Fionnuala who made sure Cora bore her share of every single expense incurred by Lacey's, down to things like lavatory paper and hairpins and even the tea the customers drank. Fionnuala had laughed like a drain when Cora tried to suggest that tips were part of the takings.

However, even Fionnuala couldn't claim that 'in perpetuity' didn't mean just that. In perpetuity. For all time. For ever.

'But I asked you at the time, and you said "till the money's paid back",' a shocked Alice had said, years ago, when she thought she had repaid the twenty-five pounds with interest.

'I did no such thing.' Cora had contrived to look indignant. 'I assumed anyone in their right mind would know what "in perpetuity" meant. I didn't just give you a loan. I invested in the business. A third of it's mine. It ses so on the agreement.'

'You're not half an idiot, Mam,' Fionnuala had groaned and Cora couldn't help but silently agree.

Now, Fionnuala looked contemptuously away from her aunt towards her mother. 'Mam, someone said the other day that Gloria's in Marsh Lane is closing down. That agreement you signed was for Myrtle's. If we moved somewhere else it would be null and void.'

Null and void! Alice wondered where her daughter had got such a grand phrase from. 'That's right,' she said to Cora.

Cora's lip curled. Fionnuala wasn't quite as clever as she thought. 'That's funny,' she said. 'Mr Flynn holds the freehold of Gloria's and he's never mentioned anything about it closing down.'

Fionnuala was only momentarily taken aback. Her eyes flickered slightly. 'Then maybe I heard wrong, but we could still move somewhere else.'

'What, and lose all your custom?' Cora sneered. 'Don't forget, if you upped and left, this place could still be let to another hairdresser. It doesn't have to close down.'

'Oh, no!' Alice flung her arms around a dryer. 'I wouldn't want anyone else to have Lacey's.'

'Well, there you are, then.' Cora smacked her lips. 'As I said, you'll just have to cut down on expenses. It's much too warm in here, fr'instance, and you don't need so many lights on, not now you're closed. Get rid of that Patsy woman and stop being so free with the cups of tea.' She eyed the single mince pie left on a plate and the remains of the sherry. 'I bet women don't get given stuff like that when they get their hair done in Mayfair.'

Fionnuala almost exploded with rage. 'How dare you tell us how to run our business?'

'Shush, luv. Goodnight, Cora,' Alice said with false brightness. 'I'll tell you after Christmas whether I'll take up the new lease or not. It needs some deciding, like.'

'Honestly, Mam,' Fion groaned after her aunt had gone. 'You were dead stupid signing that bloody agreement.'

'Horace Flynn could still put up the lease whether I'd signed the agreement or not.'

'Yes, but we could *afford* it if we didn't have to give Cora such a big chunk of what we earn.'

'Hmm,' Alice said thoughtfully. Her dad still maintained Cora did more for the landlord than keep his books. Alice wouldn't have touched him with a bargepole, but there were more ways than one to get round a man like Horace Flynn.

Next day all the Laceys, along with Bernadette Moynihan and Danny Mitchell, sat down to Christmas dinner in the parlour of the house in Amber Street. It was a happy, festive occasion, occasionally hilarious. Bernadette and Danny pretended to be nice to each other – they'd even bought each other presents – a loud check scarf and a frilly pinafore.

From the head of the table, John Lacey beamed proudly at his family. The girls, once so similar, had acquired their own, singular features as they approached adulthood. Orla was dead pretty, the spitting image of her mother. A real heartbreaker, she already had a steady boyfriend of whom John disapproved. She'd got herself a job with the *Crosby Star*. At first, all she'd done was run messages and the like while she learnt shorthand and typing at night school. Now she was taking letters and had her own desk and typewriter. She was going to be a reporter one day, she said boastfully. 'With a big London paper.'

Maeve seemed to have stopped growing at the age of twelve. Small, dainty, quietly self-assured, she worked at Bootle General Hospital in Derby Road, just skivvying to be blunt, but with the intention of training to be a proper nurse when she was old enough.

He sometimes worried about his eldest daughter,

Fionnuala, who, at only eighteen, had become matronly stout and didn't appear to have a friend in the world. She was an awkward, graceless girl, tactless – always saying the wrong thing – and over-effusive when there was no need. Perhaps it wasn't good for her to work with her mother, mixing with women two, three, four times her age and not a lad in sight.

And Cormac! John beamed most proudly of all upon his son, eleven the day before yesterday and certain to pass the scholarship next year and go to St Mary's grammar school. He used to worry that his lad, so quiet and studious, his head always buried in a book, would be bullied at school, particularly when he'd been moved up a class and put with children a year his senior. But Cormac, with his sweet smile and gentle face, never made a show of his cleverness, never bragged. And he was good at games, not so much footie, but his slight, fragile frame could move like the wind. If the school played rugby he'd be a star.

'John, Bernie would like some more wine.' Alice smiled. 'You were in a little world of your own just then.'

'Sorry, Bernie.' John refilled her glass. 'Alice was right. I was miles away.'

Alice! His wife had ripened over the years. No longer gawky, her movements were confident, self-assured. And she was growing more and more confident by the day. He felt proud of Alice too. He hadn't thought she'd had it in her to run her own business. But, he thought drily, perhaps he'd driven her to it. She'd been given the choice of Myrtle's or staying at home and, like any sane, sensible person, she'd chosen Myrtle's. He watched her, flushed and lovely, blue eyes sparkling animatedly as she discussed hairstyles with Bernadette. She had her own hair in something called a French pleat, which he didn't like – it made her look sophisticated, a bit hard, he thought.

'Not so much, luv.' Alice put her hand on Fionnuala's arm as she was about to take a third helping of Christmas pudding.

Did he still love her? John wondered. Probably. Probably just as much as he'd ever done. But now he felt they belonged to two different worlds – the world of the damaged and the world of the perfectly formed. He smiled to himself. And ne'er the twain shall meet!

The meal finished, the table was cleared and they played cards – Cormac could wipe the floor with everyone at poker.

At four o'clock John announced he was going out. 'To the yard. I'd like to get a bit of painting done so it'll be dry by tomorrer. I've got this urgent order, see.'

'But it's Christmas Day, luv,' Alice wailed. 'And surely you're not working Boxing Day as well?'

'I can't let these people down, Alice. It's the first time I've actually had an order from a big shop.'

'And it's dark, John. You should have done it this morning if it's all that important. It's blowing a gale out there.'

'I didn't want to miss seeing the kids open their presents. I'll probably go for a drink later, so I'll be late home.'

She fussed around, tying his scarf round his neck, buttoning his coat, and he tried not to show his impatience. Across the room his father-in-law was eying him suspiciously. He was so used to clandestine assignations himself that he automatically assumed John was off on a similar mission.

Alice came with him to the door, bemoaning the fact that he had to go all the way to Seaforth. 'I'm surprised you couldn't have found a more suitable place much nearer home in Bootle.'

'I tried,' John said and closed the door.

When Alice returned to the parlour, Bernie and Danny were in the middle of an argument. Why had he bought her a pinny? Bernie wanted to know. Had he done it deliberately to emphasise a woman's place was in the kitchen?

Danny winked. 'I might have.'

'Well, it won't work. I'll never wear it.'

'I'll not wear that jazzy scarf. I don't know what made you think I had such dead awful taste.'

'You,' Bernadette said furiously, 'are the most maddening man in the whole world.'

'And you're the most abominatable woman.'

Bernadette wrinkled her nose haughtily. 'It's abominable, actually.'

Danny chuckled. 'Whatever it is, you're it, particularly with that hairstyle. It makes you look like a convict.'

The girls and Cormac were listening with interest to the inevitable squabble between Grandad and Mam's best friend. They found them highly entertaining. 'Why don't you two like each other?' Maeve wanted to know.

'It's a long story, luv.' Danny shook his head resignedly.

'They're only *pretending* not to like each other,' Cormac wisely said. 'They like each other really.'

'Don't be so ridiculous, luv.' Bernadette blushed beetroot red. Danny found something tremendously interesting on the back of his left thumb, and Alice stared at her father and her friend, flabbergasted.

'It's time for tea, Mam,' Fionnuala reminded her.

'Oh, yes.' Alice came down to earth. 'Mind everyone while I set the table.' They had guests coming – Orla's

94

boyfriend, Micky Lavin, and two girls from the hospital, friends of Maeve.

While she prepared the sarnies, Alice tried to discern how she would feel if Cormac, clever little chap, were right. She'd always known Bernie was keen on her dad – not that she'd ever mentioned it – but it hadn't crossed her mind the feeling was reciprocated. Danny was twenty-one years older than her friend, but still a vital, attractive man, a bit like Clark Gable, though not quite so tall and less broad – much preferable to the lacklustre Albert Eley. She'd not minded Danny's never-ending stream of women in the past, because she'd always known they weren't serious. But Bernie, only the same age as herself! Would she take her own place in her father's heart?

Oh, what did it matter? Alice laughed out loud. They were two of the people she loved most in the world and it would be the gear to see them happy together. She began to plan what she would wear for the wedding.

It must have been a ten-force gale. John had to battle his way through the streets on his way to Seaforth.

These days, Alice wasn't the only Lacey with her own business. Five years ago John had built bunk beds for his girls, which had become the subject of much interest. In an area of mainly small houses and generally large families, space was always at a premium. The Murphys down the street were the first to ask if John could spare the time to make them a set of bunk beds, or two sets if he had even more time.

John had obliged and the Murphys had insisted on paying, not only for the wood, but for his labour. Before long, orders for beds stretched ahead for months. Then he made a bed for himself in the parlour, because sleeping on the old settee was crucifying for a chap as tall as he was. It was a very simple design and he managed to upholster it himself – a settee, with a seat that pulled forward and a back that slid down to make a double bed.

With many a parlour used to accommodate growing children, ageing grandads and grannies, spinster aunts and lonely uncles, even married sons and daughters, John Lacey's folding beds quickly became as popular as the bunk beds.

Instead of months, he was deluged with orders that would have taken years to complete. It seemed only sensible to give up regular employment and concentrate on making furniture.

He had rented a yard, an old dairy, and there was more than one reason why he'd chosen Seaforth, so far away from Bootle. It wasn't only because he wanted to avoid the neighbours and his family dropping in for a chat, preventing him from getting on with his work.

The wind was less fierce within the shelter of the narrow streets of Seaforth. The yard was on the corner of Benton Street and Crozier Terrace, the latter a cul-de-sac. Next door was the shop that used to be the actual dairy where milk and eggs had been sold. It had been empty for years.

John undid the padlock on the double gates. There was no sign yet announcing the name of the company inside, but the heading on the order books and invoices he'd had printed was B.E.D.S. It had been Fionnuala's suggestion and he thought the capital letters and full stops gave the name a certain authority – much better than just 'Beds'.

There was another padlock on the two-storey building inside the yard that had once housed the dairyman's horse. John used the top floor as an office and kept the finished furniture downstairs. He climbed the ladder, turned on the light and removed a paper carrier bag from beneath the table he used as a desk. Then he locked the stable, locked the yard gates and hurried away. He had no intention of doing a mite of work on Christmas Day.

The bag in his hand, John walked quickly along Crozier Terrace, his eyes fixed on the end house where light gleamed through the flowered curtains. The houses were even smaller than those in Amber Street, with only two bedrooms and no hall — the front door opened straight from the parlour.

The key already in his hand, John inserted it in the lock and went inside. The aroma of roasting chicken greeted him and music, which he had heard from outside — something classical and very grand.

Clare immediately rose from the chair in front of a roaring fire. The other chair was empty, waiting for him. She held a tiny baby in her arms. Another child, about two, with white-blond hair like his mother, was playing with bricks on the floor. He leapt to his feet.

'Dad!' He flung his arms round John's legs.

John's eyes met smiling grey ones across the room. 'Merry Christmas, Mrs Lacey.' He held up the bag. 'Prezzies.'

Meg Lacey had been round for her Christmas dinner. Billy had gone missing the minute the meal was over and Cora did her utmost to encourage his mother to follow suit — Mrs Lacey still insisted on mauling Maurice, something which made Cora's stomach curl.

'I think I'll pop round and see me friend, Ena. Her husband only died last July, so it's her first Christmas on her own. You don't mind, do you, luv?' Meg seemed as anxious to escape as Cora was to see her go. 'I'd call round our John's, but that Danny Mitchell will be there. I can't stand that man, forever making eyes at me.'

You'll be lucky, Cora thought cynically. Danny

Mitchell liked his women glamorous – he wouldn't be seen dead with a plump, grey-haired sixty-year-old like Meg Lacey. For women interested in such things, she supposed Danny Mitchell was dead attractive.

Only one man interested Cora and it wasn't Danny Mitchell. It wasn't her husband either. Not long after Maurice was born she'd begun putting Billy off: pretending to be asleep, claiming a headache, not going to bed until he was snoring fit to bust. She'd always had trouble sleeping, was usually awake at the crack of dawn, and up by the time Billy stirred himself and got ideas. She could only assume he paid for it if he needed it, or had a girlfriend. Either way, she didn't care as long as he left her alone.

His brother, John, though, was a different kettle of fish. She'd always considered him the best of the Lacey brothers and would have much preferred him to Billy, but since the accident, she'd felt even more drawn to the man with the destroyed face. She visualised touching the puckered red skin, being kissed by the twisted mouth, when she'd always thought kissing disgusting and the thing that was done in bed beyond the pale. But now, when she imagined doing it with John Lacey, there was a fluttery feeling in her belly that she'd never had before.

She didn't see much of him these days, only the times he came to visit Billy. He would nod at her curtly and not say a word. Cora was no longer welcome in Amber Street, hadn't been for years, not even at Christmas.

It's not fair, she thought. Alice was desperate for that twenty-five pounds. If it weren't for me, she'd never have got that bloody hairdresser's. Why should *I* take the blame just because she was too thick to understand a perfectly straightforward business agreement?

Cora was never usually in need of company. She enjoyed being alone, plotting and planning, thinking of things she'd like for the house. But it was Christmas Day, Billy was out, Meg had gone, Maurice was in his bedroom, where he'd been sent to avoid his grandma's mauling hands, and the house seemed much too quiet. It didn't seem right that it should be so itchily silent, not on Christmas Day. Horace Flynn was coming to tea, and she remembered what would inevitably happen afterwards once Maurice was in bed and gave an involuntary shudder, though she didn't usually let it bother her.

In Amber Street they'd probably be playing cards by now, or them parlour games she'd always considered stupid. But she wouldn't have minded being there right now, part of the noise and bustle.

There *was* something she could do to become part of it. She could go round Amber Street with the paper Alice had signed and tear it up, throw it on the fire, redeem herself in everyone's eyes, even Fionnuala's, whose loathing for her aunt was palpable.

Cora felt an odd, unexpected pang at the thought of Alice's warm smile welcoming her back into the fold. She fetched the agreement from the elegant bureau in the parlour. The words 'in perpetuity' seemed to stand out from the rest. She *had* told Alice a lie, misled her. But Alice was too trusting by a mile. Anyone with half a brain would have double-checked before putting their signature to a legal document.

Why should I tear it up? she asked herself. Why should I give up a regular income just because the house is a bit quiet? It'll be all right tomorrer. Sod the Laceys, I don't give a damn whether they like me or not. A little voice insisted she did, but Cora ignored it.

She went to the bottom of the stairs and called Maurice. 'Would you like to go for a walk?' she asked when he appeared, such a handsome, strong lad, at the top of the stairs.

'OK,' he said dully. Slowly he plodded down towards his mother.

'How are you getting on with the Meccano set you got for Christmas?'

'I'm still wondering what to make, like.' Maurice couldn't understand the instructions. He had no idea what bolt went where. What he would have liked was to take the kit round to his cousin, Cormac, and ask him. Cormac would no doubt knock up a crane or a lorry in no time. But it was more than Maurice's life was worth to ask if he could go to Amber Street on Christmas Day.

'When we get back, we'll do sums together till teatime,' Cora said.

'Yes, Mam.' Maurice sighed. He dreaded to think what would happen if he didn't pass the scholarship with Cormac. He reached the hall, glanced through the door of the living room, saw the cane hanging on the wall and decided if he didn't pass he'd run away. 'Can we go down the Docky?' he asked hopefully.

Cora was about to refuse – she would have preferred Merton Road with its big, posh houses. But it was Christmas Day and Maurice looked a bit downcast. 'All right,' she said charitably. 'We'll go down the Docky.'

At half past seven Danny Mitchell went to meet his latest woman, Verna Logan, in the King's Arms, with a rather bewildered glance at Bernadette on his way out. Orla disappeared into the parlour with Micky Lavin and stern instructions from her mother to 'leave the door open, if you don't mind'.

Maeve and her friends went up to the bedroom to discuss their future nursing careers and Cormac's head was buried in the encyclopaedia he'd got for Christmas. Every now and then he would lift his head and announce some astounding fact. Toboggan was another name for a sledge; that the proper name for salt was sodium chloride; and Guy Fawkes really had existed.

'Everyone knows that,' Fionnuala said tartly in response to the last.

'*I* didn't,' said her mother.

Bernie shook her head. 'Nor me.'

Fionnuala wondered why everything that came out of her mouth sounded wrong, either the words or the way she said them. She could have said, 'Everyone knows that' and laughed, and it would have sounded quite different. Instead, it appeared as if she was belittling Cormac, something she hadn't intended. She couldn't communicate like normal people, she thought tragically. It was the reason no one liked her, why people preferred Maeve or Orla – particularly Orla, who was everyone's favourite, including Dad and Grandad, with the gift of saying the cheekiest, most outrageous things and everyone adored her. On the occasions Orla came into the salon the customers' eyes would brighten and they'd be dead flattered if she so much as remembered their names. Yet Fionnuala, who was as nice as pie, had the horrible feeling she got on their nerves.

'This is nice,' Alice remarked pouring out a fifth, or it might have been sixth, glass of sherry. 'D'you want filling up, Bernie?'

'No, ta. I'll never find me way home at the rate I'm going.'

'I'll make some tea and sarnies in a minute.'

Bernie didn't answer. Instead, she stared into the fire. 'They're only *pretending* not to like each other,' Cormac had said earlier. 'They like each other really.'

Was it possible, was it truly possible, that she was still attracted to Danny Mitchell after he'd revealed himself as such an out-and-out misogynist? Was it possible that Cormac was right and Danny was attracted to *her*?

Well, he had another think coming if he thought she'd have anything to do with a man who'd give a woman a pinny for Christmas because he considered her place was in the kitchen. Oh, Lord! She'd had too much to drink, because all of a sudden she was imagining herself *in* Danny's kitchen, wearing the bloody pinny, making his bloody tea. Jaysus! *She was wearing nothing BUT the pinny*, and Danny was stroking her bottom and telling her she was beautiful. Bernadette moaned with delight.

'Are you all right, luv?' a concerned Alice enquired. 'I hope you're not going to be sick.'

'I'm fine,' Bernie replied in a choked voice.

In the parlour, Micky Lavin was trying to force his hand up Orla's jumper.

'No,' Orla said firmly. He could touch her breasts outside the jumper, but not in.

'Oh, come on,' Micky said coaxingly. He was nineteen, dead gorgeous, with jet-black curly hair, wickedly dirty eyes and a sexy mouth. Had the door not been open, Orla might easily have succumbed.

Micky transferred his hand to her knee and it began to creep up her skirt.

'Stop it.' She slapped the hand away. 'Why can't you just kiss me like a normal man?'

'Normal!' Micky laughed. He had lovely teeth, large and very white. 'You don't know the meaning of normal.'

'I'm not sure I want to if it means all this silly fumbling about.'

'Silly!' He laughed again.

'If you're just going to echo every word I say, then you can go home,' Orla snapped, knowing he wouldn't.

'All right, then. I'll just kiss you.'

At the touch of his lips, Orla's head began to swim and she couldn't bring herself to stop him when his hand returned to her breasts, *inside* her jumper, because it was so incredibly nice.

'Let's get married,' Micky said hoarsely when they came up for air. 'I know you're only seventeen, but your dad'll let you, won't he?'

'That's something you'll never know, Micky Lavin, because I've no intention of asking me dad any such thing. I don't want to get married, not yet. Ask me again in another ten years.' It wasn't the first time he'd proposed. He was never put off by her repeated refusal, but would ask again a few weeks later. Perhaps he was trying to wear her down, which could be easily done if he kissed her and stroked her breasts for much longer. Orla pushed him away and jumped to her feet. 'I think I can hear me mam making tea.'

She had the horrible feeling she was in love with Micky Lavin with his wicked eyes and sexy mouth. If so, she was determined to resist it. Only the other day at work the editor, Bertie Craig, had said she had an aptitude for writing racy little news items and thinking up suitable headlines. He had complimented her on her shortand and suggested that, in the very near future, she might be sent to cover council meetings.

Orla badly wanted to be a reporter like Rosalind Russell in *His Girl Friday*. She longed to leave the narrow confines of Amber Street, of Bootle, and move to London. She would live in a smart little flat somewhere dead posh and report on big criminal trials – even murders – or be sent to interview royalty and famous film stars.

Micky Lavin, who was an apprentice something or other in a foundry in Hawthorn Road, didn't feature anywhere in the plans Orla had for this exciting and fascinating future.

★

On Boxing Day, Alice put on the cornflower-blue frock she'd bought especially for Christmas. It had a satin bow at the neck and a long, straight skirt. She buckled the stiff wide belt as tight as it would go. Yesterday's gale had lessened, but it was still cold. Even so, Alice decided to wear a navy-blue boxy jacket rather than her winter coat and high-heeled shoes instead of boots. She carefully made up her face and coiled her hair into a French pleat.

'Where are you going all dolled up to the nines?' Fionnuala enquired when her mother came downstairs.

'Never you mind.'

'Can I come with you?'

'Sorry, luv, but this is something I've got to do on me own. What are you doing here, anyroad? You should have gone to the pantomime with Grandad and our Cormac.'

'The seats were already booked, weren't they?' Grandad had asked weeks ago if she'd like to go to the pantomime, but Fionnuala thought it a drippy thing for a girl of eighteen to do on Boxing Day. She had imagined something far more interesting would turn up. Except it hadn't and now she was about to be left all on her own – Maeve had gone with her friends to see Joan Fontaine in *From This Day Forward*, Dad was working and Orla was out somewhere with Micky Lavin. This last fact caused Fionnuala considerable heartache. She had always envied Orla – her slim figure and her confident manner – but nothing like as much as she envied her having Micky Lavin for a boyfriend. Fionnuala desperately wanted a boyfriend, any boyfriend, but to have someone as handsome and desirable as Micky Lavin panting after her seemed little short of heaven.

The rotund figure of Horace Flynn came to the door wearing a crumpled shirt without a collar and baggy trousers supported by a pair of frayed braces. He didn't look well, his face a sickly grey and slightly moist. He regarded the visitor with shrewd, hostile eyes.

'Hello, there,' Alice said in her sweetest voice and with her sweetest smile. 'I wanted to see you about something. I'm Alice Lacey, from the hairdresser's in Opal Street,' she went on when the landlord looked at her vacantly, which wasn't surprising, as they'd never spoken before and she only knew him by sight. He stood to one side and nodded down the hallway, which she took as a signal to come in, though she had the feeling that if it hadn't been so cold he would have left her to have her say at the door.

The large house in Stanley Road was more comfortably furnished than she would have expected from a man living on his own. He led her into a room at the back overlooking a white-painted yard. A fire burnt brightly in the black-leaded grate, in front of which two plush upholstered armchairs were set at an angle either side. The black wooden dresser was full of hand-painted plates, various items of brassware, an assortment of china vases and pretty figurines. A wireless was on, not very loud, and Nelson Eddy was singing 'September Song'.

'D'you mind if I sit down?' As she was nodded towards a chair, Alice began to wonder if he'd lost his voice. He sat his corpulent frame in the chair opposite.

'Seeing as it's Christmas, I thought I'd bring you a few bits and bobs to eat, like, knowing you lived on your own.' She put two paper bags on the table. 'There's a few mince pies and a piece of Christmas cake there, as well as a steak and kidney pudding, which'll need a bit of warming up. I made them all meself.' Her voice faltered in the face of the man's still hostile expression. This was going to be harder than she'd thought. It was said that the way to a man's heart was through his stomach and, as

Horace Flynn's stomach was such a notable part of him, she had hoped to soften him up with food.

He spoke at last. 'What d'you want?' he grunted. People only came to see Horace Flynn if they wanted something. Although Alice didn't realise it, he was quite appreciative of the food. He'd been offered many things over the years in lieu of rent – women's bodies, expensive ornaments: most of the stuff on the dresser had come by way of hard-up tenants – but no one had ever thought to suggest a good meal.

And this woman wasn't the plaintive, wheedling sort of creature he usually came across. She was extremely attractive, well-dressed, with her own successful business. He was well aware how much the property in Opal Street had improved since she'd taken over the lease.

'It's hot in here. D'you mind if I take me coat off?'

He shook his head, furtively taking in her slim waist and the way her skirt rode up when she crossed her trim ankles.

'It's about the lease for the hairdresser's,' she said. 'To be blunt, I can't afford it. I expected it to go up, naturally, but not from a hundred and twenty-five pounds to fourteen hundred. The salon can't stand it. I mean, it's no good squeezing things till the pips squeak, if there's no pips left to squeeze.' Alice winced. That last bit sounded dead stupid.

Horace blinked. He was a greedy man, he was cruel and heartless, but he wasn't a fool. It wasn't good business to demand more than the market could stand. And, unlike a house which could go overnight, if a shop was vacated it could stand empty for months, if not years. He had told Cora to increase the lease to seven hundred pounds. Who did the little tart think she was, going against his wishes, demanding double! He recognised a family feud, remembering this woman was Cora's sister-in-law. Was Cora trying to put her out of business?

Apparently not, otherwise she'd be cutting off her nose to spite her face, because the woman said, 'I might, only might, be able to afford it,' she continued in her sweet, lilting voice, 'if me sister-in-law didn't take such a large share of the profits.' She rolled her eyes and laughed girlishly. 'Silly me! I was dead ignorant in those days. I signed this agreement I didn't understand and now I'm beholden to Cora.'

Horace had the uncomfortable and alarming feeling that he'd been done. He needed Cora, but he wouldn't have trusted her as far as he could throw her. She'd never mentioned she had a share in Lacey's hairdressing salon and he wondered if *he* would have seen the extra money she was asking off this rather nice woman who worked hard running her own business and had thought to bring him food. With her smiling face and sparkling eyes, she had brought a breath of fresh air into an otherwise dull and lonely Boxing Day.

On the wireless, Dooley Wilson began to sing 'As Time Goes By'. 'I love this song,' Alice cried. 'Did you see the picture, *Casablanca*? I went to see it with me husband. It was the last . . .' She paused. It was the last picture she and John had seen together before he'd had the accident. She remembered they'd walked home, hand in hand. 'You must remember this,' John had sung. It was rarely she thought about John now. She'd grown used to their loveless relationship. The fact that they were friends seemed enough, but the song had brought back tender memories and her eyes filled with tears.

'Oh, gosh, you must think me an idiot.' She jumped to her feet and struggled into her coat. 'I'm sorry, Mr Flynn, to have forced meself on you, right in the middle of Christmas too. It was thoughtless and rude. I'll go home and leave you in peace. Forget about the lease. I'll pay it somehow, even if it means sacking one of me staff. Thanks for your time.'

She was already in the hall when he called, 'Mrs Lacey!' She went back. He was still sitting in the chair, his back to her. 'A hundred pounds a year will do.'

'What?'

'A hundred pounds a year for seven years. I'll bring the papers round meself in the new year.'

She gasped with delight. 'Thank you very much, Mr Flynn. It's much appreciated. When you come, I'll make you a nice cup of tea.'

Outside, Alice undid the belt that was killing her and let out a long, slow breath. She'd done it! He'd halved the cost of the lease. She felt quite shameless, recalling the way she'd rolled her eyes, fluttered her lashes, even showed a bit of leg. She fished in her bag for a hankie and rubbed her wet cheeks. The tears, though, had been real.

Chapter 5

The door of the salon opened and a man's voice with a cut-glass accent said cheerfully, 'Hello, there!'

Men rarely set foot inside Lacey's. Occasionally one might come to make an appointment for his wife, usually scarpering pretty sharpish at the sight of so many strange-looking women, like characters out of a Buck Rogers science fiction picture.

'Good morning.' Alice went over to the appointment book.

'Are you Mrs Lacey?'

'I am.' She thought it wasn't fair that a man should have such lovely hair. It appeared to have been spun from pure gold and was in bountiful curls all over his head. He had warm brown eyes, a perfectly straight nose and pink lips that could only be described as pretty. He wore corduroy trousers and a thick hand-knitted jumper. A colourful striped scarf was thrown carelessly round his neck. He looked about twenty-five. Fionnuala was staring at him, mouth hanging open, as if any minute she'd start to drool. 'What can I do for you?' Alice asked.

'I'm Neil Greene. By tonight I hope to be living in your upstairs flat.'

'Neil!' Alice exclaimed, flustered. 'I thought your name was Nell. I was expecting a woman.'

'I'm so sorry, it's my frightful writing. I'm afraid you've got a man. I hope you don't mind. My car's outside, loaded to the gills with all my stuff. Is it all right to start bringing it in?' He beamed at the assembled customers who were regarding him, wide-eyed. 'How do you do, ladies?'

Embarrassed, the three women under the dryers patted the thick net-covered curlers as if trying to make them disappear. Mrs Slattery, in front of the sink with her head covered in blue paste, was trying to slide down the chair out of sight.

'Of course you can bring it in.' Alice nodded, still dazed.

Fionnuala darted forward. 'Would you like a hand?'

'How terribly kind.' He smiled angelically as he unwound the scarf to reveal a slender white neck. 'But only if you can be spared.'

'I can, can't I, Mam?' Fionnuala pleaded.

'Yes, luv, but not for long.'

'Well, isn't he a regular Prince Charming!' one woman remarked when the door closed.

'He looks like a right pansy to me,' said another, Mrs Nutting, whom Alice had never much liked.

'I wish my hair were that colour.' Mrs Slattery sighed. 'And doesn't he talk nice? Dead posh.'

'More like he's got a plum in his gob,' sneered Mrs Nutting.

'I thought he'd be a woman,' Alice gasped.

'I reckon he almost is.'

'What's he here for, Alice?'

'He'll be teaching at St James's, the infants.'

Fionnuala returned, carrying a box of gramophone records, Neil Greene behind with two large suitcases. 'Don't worry, I haven't brought the kitchen sink,' he sang.

'Can we have a gramophone, Mam?'

'Perhaps, one day.'

'Isn't it time this tint was washed off, Alice?' Mrs Slattery said.

'Oh, yes. Sorry, luv. I'm a bit taken aback, if you must know. It looked just like Nell on the letter.'

'I wonder if he's related to that film star, Richard Greene? He's dead handsome too, though he's dark, not fair. Have you ever seen him, Alice?'

'No. Me and John didn't get to the pictures much when the kids were little. Nowadays we both seem to be working all the hours God sends.' She had to pretend things were normal, that they would have gone to the pictures had they had the time.

'I suppose one day soon you'll decide Amber Street's not good enough and you'll be off somewhere more select. You could easily afford it with all the money that must be rolling in.'

'I wouldn't dream of it, Mrs Nutting,' Alice said stiffly. 'Amber Street is quite select enough, thank you. It's where I live and it's where I'll die. We're having the wash-house turned into a bathroom, so we won't have to go outside to the lavvy no more. That's enough for me.'

'Oh, well, it's nice to know the money for me shampoo and set is contributing towards an indoor lavvy for the Laceys. I'll sleep better tonight, knowing that.'

Alice was amazed that the horrible woman managed to sleep at all and that her nasty mind didn't keep her wide awake all night long. She kept the thought to herself, sometimes difficult with customers who were particularly unpleasant.

'He's so *handsome*,' Fionnuala said dreamily over tea. 'A bit like the Angel Gabriel. There's not a single film star who comes near him. And you'll never guess what he did when I finished helping him move in. He only *kissed me hand*!'

'Honest!' Maeve looked impressed, but Orla, at whom the words were directed, seemed miles away.

'He's got a gramophone,' Fionnuala continued, willing her sister to listen, 'loads of records and hundreds of books.'

It was Cormac's turn to look impressed. 'What about?'

'Oh, all sorts of things. Too many to remember. He said I can borrow them, though, whenever I like.'

'Would he let me borrow some too?'

'I'll ask him if you like.' Fion gave a superior smile. 'We're already friends. Aren't we, Mam?'

'Well, yes, luv. I suppose you are.' The new upstairs tenant seemed determined to be friends with everyone.

'He asked if he could call me "Fion" and I said yes, and when I called him Mr Greene he said to call him Neil, even though he's a teacher.'

Orla came to life. 'I should think so too,' she said indignantly. 'He's not *your* teacher, so you're equal. Why should he expect to be called mister by someone your age? You're not a child.'

'I call Mr Flynn Mr Flynn,' Fionnuala said lamely.

'Yes, but Mr Flynn's *old*. How old is this Neil?'

'Twenty-seven, he told me.'

'*There* then,' Orla said, as if this proved her point. 'And I don't like the name Neil.'

Fionnuala went red. 'Well, I don't like Micky.'

'I don't care.'

'Neither do I.'

'Girls!' Alice said tiredly. 'Please can we have our tea in peace?'

'Then tell our Orla to leave me alone,' Fionnuala said sulkily.

'Orla, stop being so sarcastic with your sister.'

'Was I being sarcastic?' Orla looked around the table with pretend innocence, but no one answered.

Once the meal was over and the table cleared, Cormac started on his homework. He seemed able to concentrate no matter how loud the noise around him. Fion washed the dishes and Maeve dried them. Alice started to make pastry for a mincemeat and onion pie for tomorrow.

Micky Lavin called for Orla. They were going for a walk, which Alice considered a mad thing to do in the depths of an icy winter, but then she and John had done the same sort of silly things when they were courting. Young people in love wanted only to be with each other. The weather, no matter how awful, didn't matter.

Alice rolled out the pastry and hoped things weren't serious between Orla and Micky. He was a nice lad, considering his background: the middle child of a family of nine, whose dad was hardly ever in work and whose mam could only be described as a slattern – never seen without a pinny, even at the shops. The eldest lad was currently in jail for thieving. Coming from such a family, Micky had done well for himself, somehow managing to become an apprentice welder.

Even so, Alice wanted someone better for her daughter – for all her daughters, come to that. She wondered if it was possible something might develop between Fion and Neil Greene, but thought it most unlikely. Once his presence became known, every young single woman in Bootle would be setting her cap at him, as well as some of the married ones.

She put the pastry in the meat safe to keep cool. Fion appeared in a tweed coat and a headscarf, and announced she was going to confession.

'You only went on Friday. What awful sins have you committed that you need to confess again so soon?'

'None, Mam. I just feel like going to church.'

'Don't stay out too long, luv. It's awful cold outside.' It seemed pathetic that all a girl of Fion's age had to do was go to church.

Maeve, who was on early shift at the hospital and had to be up at the crack of dawn, went to bed early with a book. Alice offered to bring her up a cup of cocoa shortly. Cormac finished his homework and also went to bed, in his case armed with an encyclopaedia.

At last Alice was left alone. She turned on the wireless – there was a play on soon. There'd be no sign of John till all hours. She was usually in bed by the time he came home. That horrible Mrs Nutting had been talking through her hat, going on about all the money rolling in. After allowing for the overheads, Alice took little more than she'd have done in a factory and John made a surprisingly small amount considering all the hours he put in. Still, he was generous with what he did get, witness the planned new bathroom.

Sometimes Alice felt guilty, sitting in a nice warm house with her feet up, listening to the wireless or reading, knowing John was hard at work in the yard. If only he'd got a place somewhere closer she'd have popped round evenings with a flask of tea and a nice warm pie. As it was, she hardly saw him. Her face grew sad. Their marriage had become a travesty, a joke. They treated each other with friendly politeness.

The play started and she turned up the sound. She'd sooner not think about John and the way things were now.

'I love you, Orla,' Micky whispered. 'When I'm at work, all I think about is you. I can't get you out me mind. It's driving me up the wall.'

And I love you, Orla wanted to say. I feel exactly the

same. I can't wait for you to kiss me. I think about you all the time.

However, Orla said none of these things. She didn't want him to know she found him so disturbing. Instead, she said, 'I don't like it in this entry, Micky. It's dark and dirty, and smells of wee-wee.'

'Where else can we go?' Micky said helplessly.

'Why can't we just walk?'

'I'm tired of walking. I'm desperate to kiss you. Would your mam let us use the parlour, do you think?'

'What for?' Orla asked tartly.

'You know what for.'

'I feel uncomfortable in our parlour, knowing me mam's just on the other side of the wall.'

'We could do harmless things like kiss.'

'I hope you're not suggesting we could do less harmless things elsewhere?'

Unexpectedly, Micky began to walk away. 'I wouldn't dream of it,' he said coldly.

She watched the boyish, not very tall figure recede along the entry. The lights from the rear of the houses either side shone on his black hair, his broad shoulders. Even from the back he looked dead handsome. She knew he was hurt because she refused to take him seriously. Something twisted in her heart and she found herself shaking, as strange sensations she had never felt before swept through her body.

'Micky!' she called when he was about to turn the corner. 'Oh, Micky!'

'Orla!'

They ran to meet each other. Micky swept her up in his arms, kissed her, swung her around, kissed her again, undid her coat, grabbed her waist. His hands pushed under her jumper and she could feel them hard on her ribs through the thin material of her petticoat.

'Micky,' she breathed rapturously when his thumbs touched her nipples. Somehow, straps were moved, her bra undone and Orla groaned in delight when her breasts were exposed to Micky's seeking hands.

Oh, my God, she was wetting herself! And Micky was pulling up her skirt, stroking the bare flesh at the top of her legs, feeling inside her pants.

Orla could never quite remember exactly what happened next, only that it was mind-shatteringly thrilling and quite wonderful. Afterwards they walked back to Amber Street, Micky's arm round her shoulders, hers round his waist. She was still shaking and felt extremely odd, as if she'd entered a different world from the one she used to live in. She'd left the house a girl and returned a woman.

At the door, Micky said huskily, 'We're made for each other, Orla. We've got to get married now.'

'Did you have a nice walk, luv?' Alice enquired when her daughter came in.

'OK,' Orla said in a bored voice. 'I think I'll make meself a cup of cocoa and take it to bed. I've got a busy day tomorrer.' She was being sent on her very first assignment – some person off the wireless, whom admittedly she'd never heard of, was coming to Waterloo to open a shop.

'Mind you don't disturb Maeve. She's got an even busier one.'

'I won't, Mam.' As Orla waited for the kettle to boil she made up her mind that, after tonight, she would never see Micky Lavin again. It was too dangerous.

It was Cora's birthday, not that anyone knew or cared except herself. Billy had forgotten, as usual. Alice used to send a pretty card – 'From John and Alice, the girls and Cormac' it always said. Cora missed the cards, but they'd stopped five years before, along with the invitations to Christmas dinner and other events, like birthday parties.

Since Christmas, Cora had been in a terrible state. For one thing, the least important as it happened, she was fed up with the house – there was a limit to how nice it could be made to look and she felt she'd reached it. What she would like more than anything was to start afresh in a different house, this time bigger – a detached one in a wider road with trees. She wouldn't mind moving as far afield as Waterloo or Crosby. Months ago, Horace Flynn had acquired a lovely bungalow right on the shore in Blundellsands. The elderly widower he'd bought it from was a penny short of a shilling and had let it go dead cheap. Horace was having the place done up before he let it.

Cora had intended demanding it for herself in return for services rendered and would have done if it hadn't been for her sister-in-law. Because of her, going behind her back, telling tales, she'd lost favour with the fat, greasy slob of a landlord. Cora's blood boiled when she thought about it. Her hands twitched, as if she'd like to get them round her sister-in-law's neck and squeeze. She'd only seen Horace once since Boxing Day and then he'd torn her off a strip.

'How dare you countermand my orders?' he'd demanded. She'd never seen him look so cross. 'Did you intend keeping the extra money for yourself?'

'Of course not,' Cora insisted, though she had been wondering if she could get away with it. It would have depended on whether Alice paid by cheque or with cash.

'Have you done anything like this before?' His little round eyes flashed angrily.

'I only did it the once,' she said humbly. 'Only because it was personal.'

'Ah, yes, that reminds me. Why didn't you tell me the hairdresser's partially belongs to you?'

'I didn't think it mattered, if you must know.'

'Of course it matters,' he snapped impatiently. 'It was clearly your intention to cause your sister-in-law some harm. You made the mistake of letting your emotions cloud your judgement.' He left, saying he intended going very carefully through the books to make sure he hadn't been done. It was a pity, but he didn't trust her any more.

Since then, he hadn't given her any more work, nor dropped in for a spot of titillation and to give her the five quid that always followed. Even worse, one day she'd seen him coming out of Lacey's hairdresser's, so had kept watch and seen him twice again.

It was a good job she had the money from the hairdresser's, because all of a sudden she found herself paying the full rent for Garibaldi Road, which she could never have afforded on the pitiful amount Billy earned.

It was vital she get back in with Horace Flynn. He wasn't particularly old, only in his fifties, but he was a sick man – you could tell by his unhealthy colour. There was something wrong with his heart. It didn't beat proper. She wouldn't be a bit surprised if he dropped dead any minute. In fact, she often hoped he would, because he hadn't a close relative in the world, just some far-off cousins in Ireland. They'd actually talked about it once.

'I don't like the idea of some person or persons I've never met benefiting from all my hard work when I pass on,' he'd said.

'Surely you know someone closer you could leave it to,' Cora had said innocently, knowing there was only her.

'Hmm.' He'd eyed her speculatively. 'In that case I would have to make a will.'

Since then, whenever she went to his house and he wasn't looking, she'd searched for a will, but if he'd made one it must have been left with his solicitor, because she never found it.

'I'm sorry, luv, but she's gone to the pictures,' Alice said to the distraught young man outside.

'Again!' Micky Lavin said wildly. He ran his fingers through his black hair, as if about to tear it out. 'She went to the pictures last night. I stood outside the Palace in Marsh Lane until the picture finished, but I didn't see her come out.'

'She didn't go to the Palace last night, she went to the Rio in Fazackerly with some girl from work. I'm not sure where she's gone tonight,' she added, in case Micky stood outside again.

'Can I come in and wait?' His bottom lip quivered like a child's.

'I was just about to go to bed, luv,' Alice lied. 'It's not really convenient.'

'I'll sit on the step, then, till she comes.'

'I'm not sure if she'll come in the back way or the front.'

'I'll do me best to keep an eye on both.'

Alice felt dreadful as she closed the door on his desperate, unhappy face. She went to the bottom of the stairs and called, 'Orla?'

'Yes, Mam?'

'That's the last lie I'm telling Micky Lavin on your behalf. He's a nice lad and he's obviously mad about you. If you don't want to see him again, then tell him so to his face. D'you hear me, our Orla?'

'Yes, Mam.' In the bedroom, Orla buried her face in

the pillow so no one would hear her cry. It had been awful listening to Micky's anguished voice. She tried not to imagine him walking down Amber Street, as miserable as sin — as miserable as she felt herself, if the truth be known. It was all she could do not to rush out of the house and call him back. But look what had happened when she'd called him back the other night! Jaysus! It had been out of this world, totally wonderful. She ached for it to happen again.

But, she reminded herself, she wasn't the sort of girl who made love in back entries. She was going to *be* someone one day, someone dead important. Why, only yesterday Bertie Craig had suggested she practise her shortand, make it faster, so that she could become a verbatim reporter.

'When you're interviewing a politician, say, it helps if you can take down every word. If he later denies he said a certain thing, you can flourish your notebook and prove he did.'

A politician! One of these days Orla Lacey might actually interview a politician, beside which marrying Micky Lavin came a very poor second.

Oh, but if only she could get him out of her mind!

'I didn't realise until yesterday that you were the mother of the genius,' said Neil Greene.

'Eh?' It was Saturday and the salon had just closed. Alice was transferring the takings to her handbag to tot up later.

Neil had obviously been shopping in town. He was carrying several Lewis's and Owen Owen's carrier bags. 'Cormac Lacey, he's your son, right?' He raised his perfect eyebrows.

Alice swelled with pride. She nodded. 'He is so.'

'Going to pass the scholarship with flying colours, so I

understand. They're always talking about him in the common room. I knew you had a son at St James's, but I thought it was the other Lacey, Maurice. He has the look of Fion.'

'Maurice is me nephew. We don't know who Cormac takes after.'

Fionnuala emerged from the back where she was washing cups, eager to bathe in some of her brother's reflected glory. Alice felt slightly irritated by the look on her face, like a sad little puppy waiting to be noticed by its lord and master. Fion was useless on Saturdays, on edge waiting for Neil to pop in and out.

'Ah, Fion!' Neil's smile was wonderful to behold. The customers claimed it made them go weak at the knees. 'I've bought you a present.' He rooted through one of the bags and took out a little red box.

Fionnuala almost collapsed with gratitude before she even knew what the present was. 'Oh, ta,' she gasped. She opened the box and took out a large silver brooch in the shape of an 'F'. 'It's lovely,' she breathed. 'Oh, and it's got a little diamond in.' She clasped the brooch against her chest. 'I'll treasure it all me life,' she said shakily.

'I'm afraid the diamond isn't real. It's called a zircon.' Neil beamed as he handed Alice a green box. 'And one for you. It's an "A".'

'Thank you very much.' Alice deliberately didn't look at her daughter's face, knowing that she would be shattered that Neil hadn't bought a present just for her.

'That's by way of an apology,' Neil said.

'Apology for what?'

'For not putting "Mister" on my letters, for inadvertently letting you think I was a woman. With the flat, situated as it is over a hairdresser's, you might have preferred having a female of the species upstairs. You showed admirable restraint when I turned out to be the wrong sex.' He grinned. 'Another person might have given me a good bollocking and told me to take my bags elsewhere. I just hope I don't disturb the customers too much when I come in and out.'

Alice assured him he was no bother and he went upstairs. 'That was nice of him, wasn't it?' she said warmly to Fion. 'And he must think a lot of you, buying you a brooch as well as me. I mean, if it's by way of apology like he ses, there was no need to include you, was there?'

Fionnuala's face brightened – she was very easily pleased, Alice thought sadly.

'Not really, Mam.' Fion couldn't wait to show the brooch to Orla who didn't have a boyfriend at the moment, having gone completely mad and ditched that gorgeous Micky Lavin.

She'd had to tell him to his face eventually. She'd taken him into the parlour because she didn't trust herself in a place where he could take her in his arms and touch her the way he'd done before. They'd only end up doing that crazy, wonderful thing again and she'd be lost.

Oh, his expression when she told him! She would never forget it – shocked, disbelieving, close to tears. His eyes were black with despair.

'But I love you,' he'd said, as if this were the end of the matter.

'Well, I don't love you,' Orla said spiritedly.

'You do! Of course you do. You know you do. I can tell. What we did together was magic. Wasn't it, Orla?' He shook her arm. 'Wasn't it?'

She looked straight into his eyes. 'No,' she said. 'It was all right, that's all. I quite enjoyed it.'

'You're lying. You thought it was magic, same as me.'

Orla shrugged and longed for him to go, get out of the house, out of her life, for ever. She folded her arms and wished him goodnight.

'And that's it, then?'

'That's it.'

'So it's tara?'

'Tara, Micky.'

'You've broken me heart,' he said in a cracked voice.

'It'll soon mend,' she said carelessly.

The front door slammed. Arms still folded, Orla began to rock backwards and forwards on the settee. Tears dropped on to her knees, her skirt, made wet patches on her shoes and the floor around them.

It was Cormac who found her, rocking like a maniac and flooding the parlour with her tears. 'Why have you told Micky to go away when you want him to stay?' he wanted to know, which only made Orla cry even more. Her alarmed mother came in, did her best to soothe her, then sent her to bed with cocoa and a couple of Aspro.

That was weeks and weeks ago, and Orla still couldn't forget Micky's face, though now she hated it. She hated every single thing about Micky Lavin.

His face was in front of her now, staring at her from the sheet of paper in the typewriter. She resisted the urge to pull the paper out, rip it to shreds, because the face would only appear again when she put more paper in.

Another woman worked with her in the small office, Edie Jones, Bertie Craig's secretary. Edie and Orla didn't get on. The older woman seemed to resent the younger one being such a favourite of her boss.

'What's the matter with you?' Edie asked as Orla sat scowling at the typewriter.

'There's nothing the matter with me,' Orla snapped.

'Then why do you look as if you've lost a pound and found a sixpence?'

'Perhaps I have, that's why.'

Edie shrugged. 'I was only asking.'

Orla wondered what her reaction would be if she shouted, 'I think I'm pregnant, *that's* what's the matter. I bloody well think I'm bloody pregnant. And I don't want to be. I don't want to be bloody pregnant more than anything in the world. I *hate* Micky Lavin. Men are supposed to take precautions, wear things. But Micky didn't and now I'm bloody well pregnant.'

'Are you sure you're all right, Orla?' Edie sounded worried. 'Now you look as if you're about to burst into tears.'

'Wouldn't you if you'd lost a pound and only found a sixpence in its place?'

'I'm only trying to help, dear.'

Perhaps it was the 'dear' that made Orla start to weep. 'I'm sorry for being rude,' she sobbed. 'There *is* something wrong, but I can't possibly tell you what it is.'

'Why don't you go home? I'll tell Bertie you weren't feeling well. He'll understand.'

'I think I will. Ta, Edie.'

She wandered along Liverpool Road towards Bootle. She'd missed two periods, which had never happened before. She was definitely up the stick, had a bun in the oven, as some people crudely put it. Approaching Seaforth, she passed a doctor's surgery and contemplated going inside and asking the doctor to examine her. But she looked so young and wasn't wearing a wedding ring. What would the doctor say?

Orla had never cared particularly what people thought, but having a baby without a husband was just about the most shocking thing a girl could do. There was a girl in Opal Street who'd done it. That was ten years ago and the girl was now a woman, but it was still talked about as if it were only yesterday. The baby had been sent to an orphanage.

'*Mine won't.*' Orla clutched her stomach. It was no use asking a doctor, because she knew in her bones that there was a tiny baby curled up in there waiting to be born. She also knew that she had to keep it, that to have it taken away would be wrong. And if she didn't want her baby growing up with the stigma of having an unmarried mother, the equivalent of having a sign saying 'bastard' hung round its neck, then she would have to marry Micky Lavin. Furthermore, she was only seventeen and needed her parents' permission, so she would have to tell Mam and Dad.

A young woman approached, pushing a large, shabby pram. The baby inside was shrieking, as if it was being severely tortured. 'Oh, for Christ's sake, shut your gob,' the woman said in a despairing voice as she passed by.

Orla turned and watched her walk away, bent and weary. 'That will be me in a year's time,' she thought with horror. 'I'd sooner be like them.'

She glanced across the road at two girls, slightly older than she was, strolling along arm in arm, talking animatedly. They were smartly dressed in tweed costumes and little felt hats. One carried a big grey lizard handbag that Orla badly coveted. The girls were everything that she had one day planned to be herself.

Horace Flynn had taken to dropping in at the hairdresser's at least once a week. 'Just to see how things are going, Mrs Lacey,' he would say.

'Things are going fine, Mr Flynn. Thanks for asking.'

'He's got a crush on you,' announced Fionnuala. 'What on earth did you do on Boxing Day when you went round to ask about the lease?'

'I just fluttered me eyelashes a bit, that's all,' Alice replied uneasily.

'If you'd fluttered them some more, we might have got the lease for nothing.'

'Oh, Fion, don't!' Alice squirmed. 'Anyroad, it's your fault he comes so often. There's no need to make quite such a desperate fuss of him, taking him into the kitchen, plying him with cups of tea.'

'I feel sorry for him. He's got sickly skin. He probably comes because we're the only people in the world who are nice to him. Everyone else hates his guts.'

'With good reason, luv. He's a horrible man.'

'Horrible or not, I prefer having him on our side rather than Auntie Cora's.'

'There's no need to talk about sides, Fion. There isn't a war on.'

'Oh, yes, there is,' Fionnuala said darkly. 'We're on one side, Cora's on the other. One of these days we're going to win.'

These days, John Lacey considered the world darn near perfect. He rarely thought about his face. It had happened, there was no going back. He felt no guilt about having two families. It had been a question of survival and Clare had given him the ability to live with himself.

At six o'clock he locked the yard and went down Crozier Terrace to the end house where he let himself in. Robby came running towards him from the kitchen, demanding to be picked up. John hoisted the little boy on to his shoulder.

'Been for walk in park, Dad,' he gurgled. 'Lisa cried all day. She's growing tooths. Did I cry when I was growing tooths?'

'All the time,' John assured him. 'Hello, luv.'

Clare emerged from the kitchen looking slightly harassed. She wore a gingham pinny over a plain brown frock. Her long fair hair was pinned back with a slide. She rolled her eyes towards the stairs and made a guttural sound, which John immediately understood. His daughter, Lisa, was upstairs, asleep for once.

'Been getting you down, luv?'

She made a face and nodded furiously, then suddenly smiled, folding both him and their son in her slim arms. 'But happy,' she said. 'Very happy. Tea ready.'

He had learnt to read the expressions on her face, translate the strangled sounds that came from her mouth into proper English. 'Good.' He smacked his lips. 'I'm starving, and I think I can smell liver and onions.'

She nodded again and he followed her into the tiny kitchen where the table was set for three. As they ate, John wondered if he had ever felt so blissfully contented during the first years with Alice and remembered that he had. The memory disturbed him. He was doing a terrible thing, betraying his wife and their four children with a woman who had once been a prostitute.

Clare lightly touched the back of his hand with her finger. 'You all right?'

'Yes.'

She seemed able to read his mind as easily as he understood her awkward speech and facial expressions. On the pad she always kept beside her she wrote, 'Conscience?' There were some words she didn't even attempt.

'I'm afraid so.'

'Go home early,' she wrote. 'See your family.' She shook her head. 'I don't mind.'

'You're a saint.'

Her eyes sparkled. 'I'm anything but.'

'I'll see how I feel.' He knew he wouldn't go home

early to the house where nowadays he felt like a stranger. Alice had adapted very easily to his absence, he thought cynically. She never reproached him for being being away so often. His girls showed no sign of missing him. Only Cormac seemed to mind his dad not being there, a fact that caused John some heartache.

Still, there was nothing to be done. It was a question of survival, he reminded himself for the umpteenth time. He glanced around the table, at Clare, at his white-blond other son. A small cry came from upstairs, and he and Clare smiled at each other. She went upstairs to fetch Lisa. In six months' time there would be another baby.

This was his family now. These were the people who accepted him for what he was, what he had become. One of these days he would abandon the other family altogether – once the girls were married and Cormac was old enough to understand. Alice would be all right. She had the hairdresser's to keep her busy.

It was midnight when John rose from the bed he shared with Clare, got dressed and returned to Amber Street. To his surprise, Alice came into the hall to meet him. He'd never known her stay up so late before.

'Something's happened,' she said.

He noticed her eyes were red with weeping. 'Are the kids all right?' he asked, alarmed.

'Sort of. Can we talk?'

'Of course.'

She led the way into the living room. There was a teapot with a striped cosy on the table, two cups and saucers, sugar in a bowl, milk. He felt slightly guilty. She must have been waiting a long time for him to come.

'What's up?' His heart was beating rapidly in his chest.

'It's our Orla, she's in the club.' She poured tea and handed him a cup.

'Pregnant?' The cup jerked in his hand and tea slopped into the saucer.

'Pregnant,' Alice confirmed.

'The little bitch! I'll bloody kill her . . .' He rose to go upstairs and drag his daughter out of bed, shake her till her teeth rattled.

'John! Leave her. You'll only wake Fion and Maeve, and they don't know yet. Orla only told me tonight.'

He hadn't realised people actually did see red when they were angry. 'Is it that Micky chap?'

'Yes, and it was only the once. She hasn't seen him in weeks.'

'It only needs the once,' John spat. 'You should have kept a closer eye on her.'

'Oh, so it's my fault!' Alice laughed incredulously. 'You're hardly ever here, but it's *my* fault if our daughter falls for a baby. What was I supposed to do, follow her and Micky wherever they went?'

He knew she was right, but wasn't prepared to admit it. 'Did she know the facts of life?' he growled.

'Yes, she did, as it happens. I told all three of them at the same time. I trust you'll do the same with Cormac,' she added pointedly. 'Assuming you can find the time. Look,' she said reasonably, 'why can't we discuss this like civilised people? Things have to be done, said.'

'Such as?'

'We have to go round the Lavins, all three of us; you, me and Orla, talk it over with Micky's family. He hasn't been told, but Orla's convinced he'll marry her. The thing is, he's only nineteen and an apprentice welder. He earns peanuts. What are they going to live on?'

'He should have thought about that before he poked my daughter.'

Alice winced at the coarse expression. '*Our* daughter,' she said firmly. 'And it's the present we have to deal with, not the past. Orla thinks he'll give up the apprenticeship and get a proper job – he's a decent lad, John, no matter what you think. That means he'll just end up a labourer like your Billy. They need supporting for the next couple of years until he's finished his training. I wondered, could we put them up in our parlour?' Putting aside the rather unfortunate circumstances, Alice quite fancied having a baby in the house.

He was completely taken aback. 'What!'

'Our parlour, John.'

'What about me?'

'You can sleep upstairs. I'll sleep with the girls. There'll be an empty bed.'

'I'll do no such thing,' he gasped, outraged. 'Why should we have to put ourselves out because Orla's behaved like a little whore?'

'John!' Her eyes widened in shock. 'That's a terrible thing to say.'

'It's a terrible thing she's done.' He couldn't adjust to the fact that the prettiest of his girls, his favourite, had actually let a man touch her in that way. It was disgusting. 'Where did it happen?' he asked, almost choking on the words.

'I don't know, do I? I didn't ask. But whatever she's done, John, she's still *ours*. We've got to stand by her. Now, about the parlour . . .'

'She's not having the parlour,' he said brutally. 'If this house had twice as many rooms, I wouldn't have her, or that Micky, under me roof. She's made her bed, let her lie on it.'

'I see.' Alice's voice was cold. 'You know, John, when that fire burnt your face, it burnt something else an' all. It sounds a bit daft to say it burnt your heart, but that's what it seems like. There's not a drop of charity left in your body. You're as hard as bloody nails. It's not fair. You've no right to behave like this with your family.'

His wife and daughters all seemed part of the accident. When his face had been destroyed, something had happened to the love he felt for the people in this house, even Cormac. It had been damaged, perverted in some way, riddled with suspicion. He had changed from Dr Jekyll into Mr Hyde.

He wanted shot of them. They were no longer his concern, more like an intrusion into his present happiness. He felt like fleeing Amber Street there and then. He longed for Crozier Terrace, for Clare and his other family with whom he felt completely at ease.

He stood abruptly. 'I'm going to bed.'

'Will you come with us to the Lavins tomorrer night?'

'No! I'll sign the necessary forms so she can get married and off me back, but Orla can rot in hell for all I care.' He couldn't believe he'd just said that. He stopped at the door, turned to say he hadn't meant it. He was confused. He always felt confused in Amber Street. But Alice had picked up the cups and was taking them into the kitchen, and he couldn't be bothered calling her back.

The following evening Orla went on her own to Micky's house in Chaucer Street to tell him he would shortly become a father. Alice followed an hour later, apprehensive and nervous, worried the Lavins would react as badly as John had and there'd be a scene. She was surprised to find Micky had already told his mam and dad and they were delighted at the news.

She was taken into the shabby parlour, which had obviously been given a quick dusting because there were still smears of dirt left on the sideboard. A broken orange box burnt in the grate. To her further surprise the room contained one of them new-fangled television things, which she later learnt had fallen off the back of a lorry – one of the Lavin lads just happened to be there at the time.

'They'll be wed with our blessing,' Mrs Lavin said grandly. 'Won't they, Ted? We can have the do afterwards in the Chaucer Arms – our Kathleen works there as a barmaid.'

'I doubt if Orla will want much of a do. Will you, luv?'

'No, Mam.' Orla was sitting as far away from Micky as she could in the small space provided by the parlour. She looked pale and subdued, as if they were planning her funeral rather than her wedding. Micky was watching her anxiously. He was crazy about her, Alice realised, and a lump came to her throat. Were two lives about to be destroyed by this marriage? Three, if you counted the unborn child. Last night she had suggested Orla forget about Micky and go away to have the baby.

'And what would happen to it?' Orla asked thinly.

'It would have to be adopted.'

Orla shook her head. 'No, Mam. That would be dead irresponsible. I'd feel terrible for the rest of me life.'

'So would I, if the truth be known. I couldn't stand the thought of me first grandchild being brought up by strangers.'

One of the younger Lavins was being despatched to buy a bottle of sherry so a toast could be drunk to the about-to-be-married couple. Mrs Lavin wondered aloud if it was too late to go round St James's church that night and post the bans: 'So they can get spliced at the earliest, like.'

Alice found herself warming to the good-natured, red-faced woman, with her kind, generous manner and her equally kind husband. She felt deeply touched when the subject of where the young couple would live was raised and Mr Lavin said instantly, 'They can sleep in the parlour. We don't want our Micky giving up his apprenticeship and we wouldn't ask a penny off him, would we, luv? Not when he's got a wife and a kiddy on the way.'

Mrs Lavin's plump, worn face creased into a broad smile. 'The good Lord always seems to provide sufficient food for the table. At least, so I've found.'

It was so different from John's attitude the night before. 'John and I will help out, of course,' Alice said, feeling obliged to include her husband in the offer.

'They'll get by,' Mrs Lavin said placidly.

Orla uttered a strangled cry and fled from the room.

They got married, Orla Lacey and Micky Lavin, on the first Monday in March. The Nuptial Mass was at ten o'clock. Although the bans had been called for the last three weeks, few onlookers turned up at the church at such an early hour. There were no wedding cars to attract attention, no bouquets or buttonholes, no brides-maids.

In place of the bride's father, who had unfortunately been struck down a few days before with a severe bout of flu – or so Alice told the extravagantly sympathetic Lavins – Danny Mitchell gave his granddaughter away. Lacey's hairdresser's was closed for the day. Maeve was on afternoon shift at the hospital, so had no need to ask for time off. Cormac, who found the whole situation completely baffling, stayed away from school. He'd thought people only got married because they made each other happy, but all Orla did was snap people's heads off every time they spoke, particularly Micky's.

Bernadette Moynihan took the morning off to be with her friend on such a stressful day.

'I'd imagined having a great big bash when the kids got married,' Alice confessed tearfully as she got ready. 'Y'know, picking the bride's and bridesmaids' dresses, ordering flowers and the cake, arranging a nice reception with a sit-down meal. But this is going to be awful and John not being there only makes it worse.'

'What's Orla doing about her job?' Bernie asked.

'She's given in her notice. She had no choice, did she? Any minute now she'll start to show.'

Orla looked like death in the simple blue suit her mother had bought. She held a white prayer book in her white-gloved hands. Throughout the ceremony, Micky couldn't take his troubled eyes away from her stony face.

'She's going to make his life hell.' Alice's heart sank. This was a nightmare of a wedding.

Chapter 6

'The letter came this morning to say he'd passed, which means he'll be off to St Mary's grammar school in September. You should see the list of things we've got to buy!' Alice laughed and made a face. 'He was a bit put out to find he's got to wear a cap, but he's going to keep it in his blazer pocket till he gets to school.' Blazer! She never dreamt she'd have a son who'd wear a blazer.

'I suppose it's nice to have some good news for a change,' said Mrs White who came once a month for a shampoo and set. 'Your Cormac passing the scholarship makes up a bit for Orla.'

'What exactly do you mean by that?' Alice enquired in an icy voice.

'Well . . .' Mrs White must have been put off by Alice's tone. 'Nothing, really.'

'We're all very happy for Orla, if you must know. Micky Lavin is a fine lad who'll make a good husband. And we're dead pleased about the baby.'

'Yes, but . . .'

'But what?'

'She's so young to be a mother,' Mrs White said lamely.

'She's seventeen. I was only a year older when I had our Fionnuala.'

'You're fastening the curlers too tight, Mrs Lacey.

Would you mind undoing the last two and rolling them up a bit looser.'

Alice sniffed. 'Sorry.'

'I understand you're about to expand.' Mrs White must have decided this was safer ground. Alice Lacey was a brilliant hairdresser, the best in Bootle, and it wouldn't do to annoy her. She was relieved to be rewarded with a smile.

'Yes, I'm taking on a trained assistant, if you can call that expanding: Doreen Morrison, only part-time. She used to work in this exclusive salon in town till she retired.'

'She's old, then?'

'Only fifty. She retired because of a heart complaint, but feels she can manage four afternoons a week and Sat'days. She only lives down Cowper Street, so she won't have that big journey into town.'

The salon was getting busier. Women were coming from further and further afield, and Alice was often booked solid for weeks ahead. As well as taking on an assistant, she had felt obliged to have a telephone installed.

She placed a net over Mrs White's curlers, tucking two large cotton wool pads inside to cover her ears, sat her under the dryer, then went into the kitchen to make herself a cup of tea, leaving Fion in charge. Though not for long – there was a trim arriving any minute, followed by a tint, and Mrs Nutting would shortly need combing out.

It was a lovely, hot August day. The schools had broken up a fortnight ago – Cormac had gone to Seaforth sands with his mates and stern instruction only to paddle, not swim. Alice took her tea into the backyard to drink, glad to escape from the salon for a few minutes and not just because it was so warm in there.

136

The trouble with Bootle, which she loved with all her heart, was that everybody knew everybody else's business. She was sick to the teeth with women making remarks about Orla, who'd only been married five months, but was already as big as a house. The baby was due at the end of next month and she wondered, grimly, what people would have to say *then*.

It was annoying that Mrs White had taken some of the sheen off Cormac's achievement – she must go round and tell Orla as soon as the salon closed. It might cheer her up a bit.

Only might! Alice sighed. Orla was behaving as if the world had ended, giving poor Micky a terrible time. His mam, whose patience seemed inexhaustible, was full of sympathy.

'I was out of sorts when I was having a couple of mine. She'll be all right by the time the baby comes.'

Somehow Alice doubted it. Being confined to the Lavins' cramped, noisy parlour with a baby to look after was likely to make Orla even worse. What was it that film star, Jimmy Durante always said? 'You ain't seen nothing yet!'

If only she could afford to rent them a little house! Hopefully, once Doreen Morrison started, the profits would go up and she'd ask Horace Flynn if he had a place going.

There were all sorts of 'if onlys'. If only John earned a bit more from the business. Instead, he gave her less housekeeping than when he'd been working as a turner. He was always vague when he handed over the money, muttering about needing new tools, more stock, increasing overheads. If it hadn't been for the hairdresser's, Alice wouldn't have been able to manage. She would, though, insist John contribute towards the cost of

Cormac's uniform and all the other stuff required – she remembered there was a tennis racquet on the list.

'When will I see Dad so I can tell him?' Cormac had asked that morning when the letter came.

Alice pursed her lips, angry that John was never there when something nice happened – or something bad, like that business with Orla, with whom he had cut off contact altogether. 'I dunno, luv. Not till Sat'day, probably.' It mightn't even be then. They seemed to be seeing less and less of him, even at weekends. 'I'll wait up late and give him the news,' she promised.

'Can I come down if I'm still awake?'

'Of course, luv.'

There was yet another 'if only'. If only she hadn't been so stupid as to sign away a third of the business to Cora! It was galling to think that the money her sister-in-law took every week would have been enough to pay the rent on three, or even four, small houses.

'Mam!' Fion yelled. 'Geraldine O'Brien's here for her trim.'

'Coming, luv.'

Maurice Lacey had had nothing to eat or drink all day, having been confined to his room ever since the letter had come to say he'd failed the scholarship. Now he reckoned it was nearly teatime, and he was starving hungry and aching for a drink.

'You're bloody thick, you are,' Mam had screeched. 'Get up to your room, I'll punish you later. I daren't do it now, else I might kill you I'm so bloody mad. I thought you'd be dead clever like your dad.'

This was a very strange remark, as Mam usually claimed his dad was as thick as two short planks. He wondered if Cormac had passed and would like to bet he had. He'd also like to bet that Auntie Alice wouldn't have made a huge big scene if Cormac had failed. He felt envious of Cormac, having Auntie Alice for a mam. She didn't hug him and squeeze him and kiss him, the way his own mam did, but nor did she hit him either – there was no sign of a cane in Amber Street.

For the first time in his eleven years, Maurice was struck with the thought that life wasn't fair. There'd been nearly forty children in his class, but only a few had been expected to pass the scholarship. Were all those others who'd failed shut in a dark bedroom with the threat of the cane hanging over their heads? They were more likely playing football in the street or in the park, or had gone to the shore, like Cormac. Why was he always treated differently from everyone else?

'It's not fair!' A ball of misery rose in his parched throat, where it stuck and he couldn't swallow. He badly wanted to cry because he felt so unhappy.

The front door slammed, indicating his mam had gone out. Maurice tried his own door, but it was locked from the outside. He glanced out of the window, where the sun was shining brightly enough to split the flags, and felt a longing for fresh air, the company of his mates from school. He was rarely allowed out on his own.

In a garden behind he could hear the sound of children playing and through the trees he spied a swing. They actually had a swing of their own!

His heart in his mouth, he slid open the window, climbed out on to the kitchen roof, then shinned down the drainpipe to the ground.

He was free! There'd be hell to pay when Mam got back and found him gone, but right now Maurice didn't care. He'd always done his best to be good. He was never naughty, never got into trouble, never answered

back. He'd tried with all his might to pass the scholarship. It wasn't his fault that the questions were too hard.
Anyroad, his brain had gone numb. He couldn't think.

Without any idea where he was going, Maurice began
to run. If he went to North Park he'd be sure to find
someone to play with. Instead, some ten minutes later,
he found himself outside Auntie Alice's hairdresser's. He
wanted to see her pretty, kind face light up in surprise
when he went in. She was fond of him, he could tell.
He'd only been in the hairdresser's a few times, but he
liked it very much. It was a cheerful place and everybody
there seemed happy.

He opened the door and a bell chimed. His cousin,
Fion, was brushing the floor and another lady was
washing another lady's hair. There was no sign of his
aunt.

'Hello, luv,' Fion exclaimed. 'Is your mam with you?'

Maurice shook his head. He liked Fion, who was
inclined to make a fuss of him, but it was her mam he
wanted.

'You look hot. Would you like a glass of cherryade?'
Fion enquired. 'We've got some in the kitchen.'

'Yes, *please!*'

'I'll get it you in a minute, as soon as I've finished this
floor. Me mam's in the yard, having a quick breather. It's
been like a Turkish bath in here today. Fortunately, we'll
be closing soon. Why don't you go and say hello.'

Maurice trotted down the salon, through the kitchen
and into the yard, where Auntie Alice was sitting on a
chair. Her face was a bit sad, he thought, but brightened
considerably when she saw him.

'Hello, Maurice, luv.' She beamed. 'Are you out on
your own? That makes a change.'

He had no idea what came over him, because all of a
sudden he'd thrown himself at his aunt and she'd dragged

him on to her knee, and he was sobbing his heart out, and she was stroking his face and saying, 'There, there, luv. Tell your Auntie Alice what's wrong.'

'I've failed the scholarship,' he bawled. 'Me mam shut me in me room and tonight she's going to kill me.'

'Oh, she is, is she!' his aunt said in an ominous voice.

'I didn't mean to fail. I tried dead hard, honest.'

'I'm sure you did, luv. The best anyone can do is try.'

'I'm dead stupid.' He sobbed.

'If everyone who failed the scholarship was stupid, then the world would grind to a halt,' his aunt said wisely. 'None of our girls passed, nor did I, nor your Uncle John. Neither did your mam, come to that. Anyroad, you're good at other things – footy, for instance. You're a much better player than our Cormac.'

'I suppose so,' Maurice conceded with a hiccup.

'And you're dead handsome.' She ran her fingers through his dark curls. 'I bet you'll break lots of hearts when you grow up, by which time you'll find yourself good at all sorts of things. Me, now, I used to think I was as daft as a brush, until I discovered I was good at doing women's hair.' She hugged him very tight. 'Now, don't you ever call yourself stupid again, do you hear?'

The bell went on the door and his aunt said, 'That's probably me final customer. All she wants is a trim. You can keep me company in the salon for a while, then I'll take you home.'

He pressed himself against her. 'I don't want to go home!'

'I'm afraid you'll have to, luv, otherwise your mam will call out the bobbies and I'll be charged with kidnapping.'

'I'm hungry, Auntie.'

'In that case I'll give you your tea, *then* I'll take you home.'

It's not right, Cora,' Alice said. 'To deprive an eleven-year-old of food and drink all day just because he didn't pass a silly exam . . . well, it's just not right.'

'It's none of your business,' Cora argued hotly. 'How I treat me son is nobody's affair but me own.'

'It *is* my affair when I become involved,' Alice replied just as hotly. 'The poor little lad was forced to come to mine for summat to eat. He drank a whole bottle of cherryade and I don't know how many glasses of water. His throat must have been as dry as a bone.'

Cora cast around for something to say in excuse, but could think of nothing. She'd thought about Maurice with mixed feelings while she'd been out at the shops. She was slightly uneasy that he hadn't been fed all day, but at the same time her blood was boiling because he'd let her down and failed the scholarship. If Cormac had passed, which seemed likely, it meant Alice Lacey had got one up on her again. She'd give Maurice a good thrashing when she got home, teach him a lesson. A little thrill ran through her when she thought about after-wards, after she had forgiven him. He would fling his arms around her neck, tell her how much he loved her and she would hold him close, so very, very close. Then they'd have a lovely tea.

She went into the greengrocer's and bought a pound of new potatoes and a pound of peas, then to Costigan's for four slices of boiled ham, but remembered she had a husband and increased the order to six. Finally she bought a large cream cake in Blackledge's, Maurice's favourite, with raspberry jam as well as cream.

She was at home, putting the things away, unaware that Maurice wasn't in his room, when there was a knock on the door and Alice Lacey was outside, looking very cross indeed and holding a sulky Maurice by the hand. Cora had always thought her sister-in-law wouldn't say boo to a goose and hadn't realised she had such a temper.

She stood in the parlour, angrily waving her arms. 'It's not right,' she kept saying. 'In fact, it's cruel.'

It was a good half-hour before a strangely inarticulate Cora got rid of her. She slammed the door and stood with her back against it, breathing deeply. With each breath her own anger mounted – anger that it was no use directing against Alice. Anyroad, it was Maurice who was the cause of her shame.

She advanced on the living room, where he'd been sent out of earshot of the shouting women, and found him standing by the window. Children were playing in the house behind and their cries carried sharply on the calm evening air, emphasising the stillness and quietness of their own house.

'Don't you dare go round that bloody hairdresser's again,' Cora said in a grating voice. 'And if I shut you in your room, you bloody stay there. Do you hear me, lad?'

'Yes,' Maurice said distantly.

'Yes, what?'

'Yes, Mam.'

'You made a right show of me today, going to see Alice, telling her you were hungry. What the hell must she think of me?'

Maurice shrugged. 'Don't know, Mam.'

She had never known him appear so indifferent to her words and it only made her more angry still. Her head throbbed and she felt dizzy with rage. Hadn't he realised what he'd *done*? Didn't he understand she had to feel better than everyone else? She *had* to. As a child, dirty and unkempt, always hungry, the continual butt of her two elderly aunts' brutality, she had vowed to herself that one day she would *be* someone. She'd hardly ever gone to school, though hadn't minded, because the other kids made fun of her ragged clothes and lack of shoes, the nits in her hair and the fact that she smelt and was useless at every single lesson.

'It won't always be like this,' she used to tell herself as she lay down to sleep in the bedroom that was bare of everything except a mattress and a few flea-ridden blankets. 'When I grow up I'll live in a palace.'

She'd seen off her aunts in the end, but the following years had been hard. She had slept on the streets for a while, because no one wanted to give a job to a girl who couldn't add up, couldn't read, who didn't even know how to behave proper.

Eventually she'd got a live-in job cleaning for a woman who owned half a dozen lodging houses.

'Did no one ever teach you how to use a knife and fork?' the woman asked on her first night – Cora was eating the food with her fingers.

She'd learnt how to use cutlery, when to say 'please' and 'thank you', to wipe her bum when she went to the lavatory, to change her clothes before they began to smell. She'd learnt also to read and write, do sums. The woman she worked for had helped. She said Cora had a quick brain. It was a shame she hadn't learnt all these things before. She would have done well at school.

When she was twenty she'd met Billy Lacey, very personable and far better-looking than the men who'd shown interest in her so far. By the time he proposed, Cora had already realised he was a loser. She far preferred his brother, John, who was the dead opposite, but apart from being polite, otherwise he showed no interest in his brother's fiancée. Still, if she married Billy she'd get her own house. For a while it didn't matter that it was in O'Connell Street.

It hadn't been long before wishy-washy Alice Mitchell appeared on the scene, hanging like a leech on to the arm of John Lacey. Apart from her aunts, Cora didn't think she'd ever hated anyone before as much as she hated Alice on the day she married John and changed her name from Mitchell to Lacey.

The urge to *be* someone, to have beautiful things, was just as strong, but stronger still was the need to be one up on Alice Lacey. Cora thought she had achieved this with her handsome, stolen son, with the house in Garibaldi Road, with the third share she had wangled in the hairdresser's, but somehow Alice always seemed to go one better.

Cora stared balefully at the son who'd let her down so badly. She reached for the cane and flexed it between her hands. Nodding towards a chair, she said curtly, 'Bend over.'

To her everlasting surprise, Maurice ignored her.

'Bend over,' Cora insisted, aware a note of hysteria had crept into her voice.

'No.' He stuffed his hands in the pockets of his grey shorts and looked at her stubbornly.

'In that case . . .' She raised the cane and whipped it against his shoulders. It must have hurt through the thin cotton of his shirt, but it was like rainwater off a duck's back as far as Maurice was concerned. Cora raised the cane again and was taken aback when he caught the end in his hand. For several awful seconds' they tussled over possession, but he was a big, strong lad for eleven, stronger than she was, and he easily won.

For a horrible moment, Cora half expected the cane to be turned on her. She cowered against the wall, arms raised protectively, but Maurice merely bent it till it broke in two. He threw the pieces on the table and stared at them for a long time, as if wondering why he'd never done it before.

'Huh!' he muttered and walked out of the room. She

assumed he was on his way upstairs to sulk in his bedroom. Instead, seconds later, the front door slammed. Cora flew down the hall and opened it.

'Where are you going?' she called shakily.

'To the park to play with me mates.'

She'd lost him! Her body froze with horror. He was the only person in the world she had ever loved, the only person who had loved her in return. She wanted him back, would do anything to get him back, but had a horrible, sickly feeling that it was too late.

And, as usual, it was all the fault of Alice Lacey.

She felt as if she'd been pregnant for ever. She could hardly walk she was so big. Maybe she was expecting quins like that woman in Canada. The bed creaked like mad every time she turned over and she turned over all night long, waking Micky, who was red-eyed with tiredness in the mornings.

But Orla didn't care. She didn't care if his eyes fell out or his head dropped off. All she cared about was herself and her predicament.

She hated Micky, whose fault it was that she was in this mess, and she hated her dad for not letting them have the parlour in Amber Street, a much nicer place to be. She hated her sisters: Fionnuala looked so superior, as if trying to say, '*I'd* never get in a mess like you,' which was probably true, as there wasn't a boy in Bootle who'd go near her, and you'd think Maeve had delivered hundreds of babies the way she kept offering advice, yet there wasn't a maternity ward in Bootle hospital.

Most of all, she hated the Lavins for . . . oh, for all sorts of reasons. There was always a row going on for one thing, or two or three rows, come to that, with people screaming at each other at the tops of their voices from rooms all over the house. She hated the way they came into the parlour to watch the bloody telly when she was trying to rest and instead she had Gilbert Harding or Barbara Kelly or Lady-stinking-Barnet bawling down her ear. She hated the fact that Mrs Lavin sent one of the kids every morning to pinch a bottle of milk off someone's step for the expectant mother, then sat, watching the same expectant mother while she drank every bloody drop, oozing bloody sympathy and acquainting her with the gory details of her own nine births.

It was horrible, sitting down to a nice meal of roast beef, or lamb chops, or chicken, to have Mr Lavin wink and say, 'You'll never guess where this came from!'

Orla had guessed months ago – well, who wouldn't! The food was stolen, it had 'fallen off the back of a lorry'. She imagined Mr Lavin running after a speeding lorry, picking up the joints of meat that were being scattered in its wake. All Mrs Lavin ever bought was vegetables. The other day there'd been a trifle, a huge thing in a fluted cardboard case.

'You'll never guess where that came from!' Mr Lavin winked.

How the hell had he managed to nick a *trifle*?

Orla groaned. If she were still working for the *Crosby Star*, she might be interviewing a politician right now, or have been sent to cover a murder.

The lovely chiming clock on the mantelpiece, which had no doubt come the same way as virtually everything else in the house, struck five o'clock. Mam would be back in Amber Street soon, and she'd go round and see her. It was the only place where she got any peace and Mam was the only person in the world whom she didn't hate. Oh, and their Cormac.

Alice was just unlocking the salon door on a drizzly morning in September when Micky Lavin skidded to a halt outside on a rusty bicycle. 'It's Orla,' he gasped. 'She's gone to the hospital. The pains started about an hour ago.'

'Oh, dear!' It meant the baby was going to be a fortnight early, or two and a half months early if people were expected to believe Orla had remained virtuous until her wedding night. People never would! She prayed the baby would be small so she could claim it was premature.

It was a terrible way to think when her daughter was about to give birth. Alice nudged the thought to one side and said anxiously to Micky, 'Is she all right?'

Micky rolled his eyes. 'Is Orla ever all right? She was screaming blue murder when I came to get you.'

'I'll look after the salon, Mam,' Fion offered. 'Patsy'll be along shortly and Doreen's in this avvy. We'll manage between us, don't worry.'

'Ta, luv.' There were times when Fion could be extremely capable. 'I'll try and ring from the nursing home, tell you what's happening, like.' To Micky she said, 'You get along back, luv. I'll catch a tram. I'll be there in no time.'

Orla was in a side ward still screaming blue murder, when her mother arrived, out of breath, excited and at the same time dreading the next few hours.

'It hurts,' Orla yelled. 'Oh, Mam, the pains hurt really, really bad.'

Alice's heart sank when she saw Mrs Lavin sitting in a chair next to the bed. She was holding Orla's hand and singing a lullaby for some reason. 'Rock-a-bye baby, on the tree top . . .'

No wonder Orla was screaming.

'Why don't you go home, Mam, and see to the brekkies,' Micky suggested, as if sensing the presence of his mother wasn't helping.

'. . . when the tree falls, the baby will stop,' Mrs Lavin crooned. 'Or is it drop? Hello, Mrs Lacey. She's having a wicked time, just like I did when I had quite a few of mine. Our Micky, though, he just popped out, like a pea from a pod.'

'*Mam!*' Orla screeched.

'I'll take over now, shall I, Mrs Lavin? You've got little 'uns to see to, not like me.'

'Well . . .' Mrs Lavin seemed reluctant to give up Orla's hand or her seat beside the bed.

'I think they only allow two visitors, Mam,' Micky said.

'Oh, I'll be off then.' Mrs Lavin left after making Micky promise to come and tell her the minute the baby arrived. 'I'll bring some flowers and a bunch of grapes,' she said generously.

'Only if she finds a lorry for them to drop off,' Orla said through clenched teeth when the door closed. 'I'm more likely to get a side of beef or a chicken already trussed.'

'Try not to talk, luv.' Micky tenderly stroked the brow of his young wife. 'Save your breath for the pains. They're called contractions,' he said to Alice as if she didn't already know. 'They get closer and closer as the time comes for the baby to be born. I read it in a book,' he said proudly, 'that I got out the library.'

Orla had got a bloke in a million, Alice thought. It would take time, he was only twenty, but if she stuck it out she'd do well with Micky Lavin.

'Shurrup, Micky,' Orla snapped. 'Oh, there's another pain coming! Oh, Mam!'

Alice became quite impatient with her daughter as the morning progressed and she continued to scream and yell. There were two other women having babies at the same time and between them they didn't make half the fuss that Orla did. Alice suspected the screams were directed at Micky in an attempt to make him feel guilty.

The labour lasted five and a half hours and Orla was whisked to the delivery ward the minute the midwife judged her ready to give birth.

Alice and Micky sat in the corridor outside and waited for the screams to start again. To their surprise, in no time at all, the door opened and the midwife appeared. 'It's a girl,' she said jubilantly. 'She's absolutely beautiful and a whole seven pounds, two ounces. I've never known such a swift and painless birth. Congratulations – Dad! Would you like to come and see your daughter?'

Micky looked wistfully at Alice. 'Now it's all over, I wonder if she'll be happy? Will she stop blaming me, do you think? I love her, Mrs Lacey. I love her more than anything on earth.'

'I know you do, luv.' Alice kissed him, but felt unable to offer a single hopeful promise for the future. Her wilful, strong-minded daughter apparently considered this rather decent young man had ruined her life for ever.

'I'll go and see her now.' Micky was scarcely gone a minute, when he came out again. 'She wants you,' he said. His eyes were bright with tears.

'Why don't you nip home and tell your mam?' Alice said.

'I'll do that.' He looked relieved to have something to do.

The midwife had been right! The new baby was beautiful, a perfectly formed little girl, not the least bit red or crumpled like some babies and already with a fine head of dark, curly hair. Her eyes were wide open and her tiny body wriggled impatiently against the tightly wrapped blanket.

'She's going to be a lively one,' her grandmother whispered. 'I suppose it's all right if I pick her up.'

As she nursed her first grandchild, Alice wished with all her heart that John were there, not the John of now, but the one she had married. This was a unique moment, the sort a woman should share with her husband. She sighed. *Her* husband seemed no longer interested in his family.

'Have you decided on a name yet?' she asked Orla. Names for the baby had been the only thing that had sparked her interest over the last months.

'Lulu,' Orla said listlessly.

Alice had never heard Lulu mentioned before and thought it awful, like a music hall turn or a silent film star. However, it seemed wise to keep her trap shut.

'Hello, Miss Lulu Lavin,' she whispered. The baby stirred in her arms and uttered a tiny cry. 'I think she might want a feed. Are you up to it, luv?'

'I'm not sure. I feel as if I've just been dragged through the mill and back again,' Orla said weakly.

'The midwife said she'd never known such a swift and painless birth.'

'How would she know?' Orla demanded in a voice that was suddenly weak no more.

Alice shrugged. 'Through experience, I guess. What was it you said to Micky to make him leave so quick?'

'I told him I didn't want to see him, that I wanted you. Frankly, I don't care if I ever see him or the Lavins again.'

'Then why did you marry the poor lad?'

Orla pouted. 'I didn't have much choice, did I?'

'You didn't have many choices,' Alice conceded, 'but you didn't *have* to marry him. Nor, I might remind you, did *he* have to marry *you*. Another chap might have run a mile, or claimed the baby wasn't his. But Micky did the honourable thing and you've made his life a misery ever since.' Oh, it was hard, speaking so sternly to her pretty, distressed daughter, who was probably expecting buckets of sympathy, not a lecture, off her mam. 'I take it the . . . er, the time you conceived, he didn't rape you, that you were just as much a willing partner as him?'

Orla blushed and didn't answer.

Alice was all set to continue with the lecture, but two nurses arrived to move the new mother to a ward and take the baby to the nursery, so she excused herself and went to look for a telephone. She rang Fion to let her know she was now an aunt.

'Nip home as soon as you've got a minute,' she said, 'and let our Maeve know. She'll be back from the General by now. She can tell Cormac when he gets home from school. Tonight, we'll all come together to visit Orla and the baby.'

Maeve wrinkled her pert little nose. 'It seems dead peculiar, having a sister who's a mother.'

'I know.' Fion nodded her head vigorously. 'Dead peculiar.'

'Have you ever done, you know, the thing Micky did with Orla to make her have the baby?'

'Lord, no!' Fion gasped. 'Have you?'

'What? And end up living in the Lavins' parlour with people sitting on the bed watching telly while you're trying to sleep? No, thanks, I wouldn't dream of it. You'd have to be mad.'

'Perhaps our Orla is mad!'

'Perhaps. Though I wouldn't mind kissing Micky Lavin,' Maeve said thoughtfully. 'He's a dish.'

'What's a dish?' enquired Fion, who wouldn't have minded kissing Micky Lavin either.

'Someone who's dead gorgeous. Montgomery Clift's dishy, and Frank Sinatra.'

'Neil Greene's dishier than both of them,' Fion said.

She fancied kissing Neil even more than she did Micky Lavin.

In mid-afternoon Mr and Mrs Lavin arrived at the hospital, laden with fruit and flowers, and accompanied by four of the children. Visiting time was almost over. Before a nurse could complain there were too many visitors around the bed Alice left, promising to return that night.

Outside, the morning's drizzle had become a steady downpour and she wished she'd brought an umbrella. She stood in the rain and wondered whether to go home or to the salon. She didn't feel like doing either. Her nerves were on edge after the conversation with Orla. It worried her that the girl would refuse to see sense and eventually Micky would snap. There was only so much a person could stand. So far, Micky had been dead patient. But he wasn't a saint.

If only she could talk to someone – her dad or Bernie, but they'd be at work for hours yet.

She could talk to John. He might not agree, but it was every bit as much *his* problem as it was hers. Anyroad, despite the way he'd acted with Orla, he had a right to know he'd become a grandfather. And she wouldn't wait till tonight. She'd do it now while she was in the mood, go round to the yard and see him. You never knew, his attitude might change if he could be persuaded to see Lulu, who was without doubt one of the loveliest babies ever born. It was a pity the poor child had been blessed with such a dead silly name.

Alice had only a vague idea where the yard was situated: somewhere in Seaforth not far from the playing fields. Benton Street rang a bell. For some reason John had always discouraged them from going there. She caught the tram to the terminus in Rimrose Road, walked under the railway bridge and emerged in Seaforth.

The first three people she asked had never heard of Benton Street, nor a firm called B.E.D.S. The fourth, a woman, had an idea the street was near the playing fields.

'That's right,' Alice said eagerly.

The directions were complicated. Turn right, then left, then right again at a big pub the woman couldn't remember the name of. Go half a mile down Sandy Road, turn left at a greengrocer's and Benton Street was the second turning on the right, or it might be the third.

Alice got wetter and wetter as she negotiated the complicated maze of streets. She thought about giving up, but decided she couldn't, not after having made it this far.

She was soaked to the skin by the time she turned into Benton Street and hoped John had a towel so she could dry herself. A wooden sign with B.E.D.S. painted on it was attached to a pair of tall iron gates, just round the corner in a place called Crozier Terrace, a cul-de-sac with no more than ten tiny houses either side.

Her heart sank when she tried the gates and found them locked. Surely John didn't lock himself in! Behind the gates a two-storey building had a light on upstairs. It was probably the office. Alice rattled the gates in the hope of attracting her husband's attention, but to no avail.

Disappointed, she turned away. After coming so far! She wondered where he could be. Maybe he'd gone to the timber yard for wood. Alice frowned. If that was the case, what was that smart green van doing parked inside the gates? Did it belong to John? It looked new, but he'd never mentioned having a van. She noticed a wire strung across the street attached to the top half of the building, the office. He hadn't mentioned having a telephone either.

'You'll find him at home, luv.'

'I beg your pardon?'

A woman had emerged from one of the tiny houses in Crozier Terrace. She was sensibly shielded from the rain in a plastic mac and hood. 'Mr Lacey, he's gone home to see his missus. I saw him pass me winder less than ten minutes ago.'

'You can't possibly have!' John had never been known to come home during the day. Anyroad, he'd have to go the other way, down Benton Street, not past this woman's window. There was no way out of Crozier Terrace.

'Please yourself, luv.' The woman shrugged. 'But I don't doubt the evidence of me own eyes. You'll find Mr Lacey in the end house, number twenty.'

She must be mad. Alice watched the woman walk away, then gave the gates another shake. Still no one came. She was about to walk away herself but, feeling curious, went down Crozier Terrace to number twenty. She took a step back and looked it up and down. It was a perfectly ordinary house, identical to the others, with pretty, flowered cretonne curtains. There was a vase of dried leaves in the window. The front door and the sills were painted maroon.

The woman had been talking nonsense. She couldn't possibly be right. On the other hand, how could she possibly be wrong? She'd referred to 'Mr Lacey'. She lived within spitting distance of the yard, so she must know John well. And another thing, Alice's heart began to pound painfully in her chest, it was John who insisted on maroon every time he painted the outside of their house in Amber Street. She would have preferred bottle green herself.

'His missus,' the woman had said. 'He's gone to see his missus.'

'But that's *me*,' Alice said aloud. She wondered if she should go home, *run* home, forget the house, what the woman had said, just wait for John tonight and tell him about Orla. She would never mention having been to the yard. Perhaps it would be best not to know whatever secrets might lie behind this door.

But she *had* to know. She would never rest until she did. There was still a chance that the woman had got things wrong, that it was another man who looked like John who'd passed her house. Except she'd called him Mr Lacey.

Maybe there were two Mr Laceys and they were similar!

Alice took a deep breath and knocked on the door.

After a few seconds it was opened by a young woman, heavily pregnant, with lovely soft fair hair. Through the door Alice glimpsed a simply but comfortably furnished parlour with a plain brown fitted carpet – she'd always fancied fitted carpets in her own house. There was something wrong with the young woman's face – she had a hare lip. Without it, she would have been extraordinarily pretty. A tiny girl, little more than a baby, clung to her leg and Alice felt herself go cold. The little girl could have been Orla at the same age. The young woman smiled, but didn't speak.

'John Lacey,' Alice said in a cracked voice. 'I've come to see John Lacey.'

'He's upstairs.' A little boy appeared. He had his mother's fair hair.

'Would you mind giving him a call, luv.' Alice still retained a shred of hope it was another man entirely upstairs.

'Dad!' the boy obediently yelled.

'Who is it, son?' John's voice called.

'A lady.'

There were footsteps and John came to the door. Alice, sick to her soul, was presented with the perfect picture of domesticity: the little girl, so like Orla, the boy with the fair hair, her husband, John, his arm laid casually round the shoulders of the pregnant woman.

When he saw Alice his face hardened and she glimpsed hostility in the brown eyes. He bundled his family out of sight, came outside, closed the door.

But by this time, Alice had already reached the end of Crozier Terrace and was running, racing, flying home. She didn't stop until she reached Amber Street.

Alice lay curled up in the armchair, knees pressed against her chest. There was something terrifying about her blank, staring eyes in a face that had lost all trace of colour. She looked like a ghost. Every now and then her body convulsed, as if she was about to have a fit, and the sobs that emerged fom her pale lips were strangely subdued.

A frightened Cormac had begun to cry, something he had hardly ever done when he was little. Maeve was visibly shaking.

Only Fionnuala, who could always be relied on to act sensibly in a crisis, managed to remain calm. 'What's wrong, Mam?' She shook her mother again and again. 'Mam, what's wrong?' But Alice seemed incapable of understanding, let alone providing answers.

'Perhaps our Orla's baby has died?' Maeve suggested.

'Or Orla herself?' Cormac's lip trembled.

'No,' Fion said. 'She would have told us. No, it's something different from that. She's had a terrible shock.'

Cormac managed to crawl on to his mam's knee, which he still did occasionally, despite the fact he was eleven and at grammar school. 'Mam!' He tenderly stroked her face. 'Oh, Mam!'

'Maeve,' Fion commanded, 'make a pot of tea. That might bring her round.'

Maeve hurried into the kitchen to put on the kettle. 'Should we fetch someone?' she asked when she came back.

'Who?' Fion asked simply. 'Anyroad, there's no need to fetch someone, she's got us. You know what I think we should do?'

'What?'

'Throw cold water on her. She's having a fit of some sort. I saw it once in the pictures. It's either water, or slapping her face and I don't know about you, but I couldn't bring meself to slap our mam. I prefer the water idea. She's already soaking from the rain, so it won't exactly hurt her.'

'Shall I fetch a bucketful?'

'A cup will do. *You're* the one who wants to be a nurse, Maeve Lacey. You should know about these things. Cormac, mind out the road, there's a good lad, we're going to throw a cup of water on our mam.' Fion dragged her brother off Alice's knee when he appeared not to hear.

'You do it.' Maeve handed Fion the water.

'You're going to make a hopeless nurse.' Fion took a deep breath and threw the water in her mother's face.

Alice screamed and violently shook her head for several seconds. 'Oh, my God!' she screamed again when she saw three of her children standing anxiously over her. 'What have I been saying?'

'Nothing, Mam. All you did was sort of cry.' Although relieved to see her mother all right again, Fion felt suspicious that things were being kept from her. Why should Mam be worried about what she might have said? 'Has Aunt Cora been at you over something?' she asked.

'No, luv.' Alice held out her arms and the children fell upon her. They might find out one day what their father had been up to, but they'd never hear it from her. She hugged them fiercely. 'I love you. I love you so much it hurts. Now, if someone doesn't make me a cup of tea soon, I think I'll bust.'

'The kettle's already on, Mam,' Fion and Maeve said together and disappeared into the kitchen. Cormac, with his mother all to himself, snuggled his face in her shoulder.

Alice felt dead ashamed. She had only a vague memory of being in the chair, having lost all grip on reality. There'd just been that awful feeling you had when you woke up from a horrific dream, unsure whether it was true or false. For the first time in her life the dream had turned out to be true. Perhaps her brain and her body had been fighting against the truth, praying for the dream to turn out to be just that, a dream.

John! Till the end of her days she would never forget the look on his face, as if she were a trespasser on his happiness. It would have been far preferable if he'd just walked out of Amber Street, left them. But to set up another home, with another woman, other children!

Fion and Maeve came in with tea on a tray and a plate of digestive biscuits. 'Is Orla all right?' Fion demanded.

'She's fine and the baby's lovely.' Alice realised she'd have to explain the hysteria. Now seemed the time to tell them their dad wouldn't be coming home. 'I went round the yard to tell your father about Orla and we had a big bust-up. He's not coming back.'

'But what about us?' Cormac wailed. Fion and Maeve didn't appear particularly upset.

'We never got round to discussing you, luv. I know' –

she had an idea – 'you can telephone him from the salon, arrange to meet somewhere.' She hoped John would be nice to the son he'd once loved so much, that he wouldn't regard him as a trespasser as he had done his wife. She remembered the other little boy and wondered what his name was. 'Son,' John had called him. 'Who is it, son?'

'A lady,' the child had replied.

It would be easy to cry again, but not now, not with the children there. She'd already frightened them enough. Cormac was still on her knee. She hugged him hard. He adored his dad and would miss him more than any other member of the family. Well, *this* family, she thought drily. From now on, John's other family would have him all to themselves.

'She looked so pretty, so nice,' Clare wrote quickly in her neat, precise hand. She started to weep again. 'I feel terrible. So should you,' she added, underlining the 'you'.

'I do,' John said in a heartfelt voice. He did indeed feel terrible, but he also felt very hard. He couldn't get Alice's shocked white face out of his mind, but there was no way he would let her spoil things between him and Clare.

Clare was writing again. 'We should have lived further away. It was always dangerous here.'

'We'll move as soon as possible.' He didn't want Danny Mitchell or one of the girls coming round to make a scene. They could yell at him all they liked, but he wasn't prepared to let Clare or his children be subjected to abuse, though he had a feeling Alice would keep things to herself. She'd be too ashamed and embarrassed to tell anyone, not even her dad or Bernadette.

He wondered aloud why she'd come to the yard in the first place and Clare wrote, 'Perhaps your daughter has had her baby?'

John smiled and stroked her swollen belly. If that was the case, it was possible he would become a grandfather and a father again within a single week.

'You should go to see the baby.' Clare supported the stumbling words with a movement of her hands, as if shooing him out of the house.

'I can't, not now.' He shook his head. 'Alice might be there. Anyroad, I'm not particularly interested.'

'Should be.' She nodded fiercely. 'Should be. Not right.'

'I'm the person to judge what's right or not.'

'I think we should wait a few days before we tell Orla about your dad,' Alice said when the children were ready to visit their sister. 'It's said every cloud has a silver lining, and your dad going means Orla and Micky can move into the parlour. That'll be nice, won't it, eh?'

Maeve and Cormac thought it a great idea, but Fionnuala wasn't so sure. 'Will the baby cry much?' she wanted to know.

'We'll just have to see, luv. Now, are you sure you don't mind me not coming with you? I don't feel as if me legs will carry me far tonight. Just tell Orla I'm a bit off colour, but I'll be at the front of the queue of visitors in the morning.'

'Are you sure you'll be all right on your own?' Fion asked.

Alice couldn't wait for them to go, to be on her own, to think. 'I'll be fine,' she said heartily. 'I'll be even better after a rest. Now, are you sure you've got your tram fare? Maeve, be careful how you hold them flowers, else you'll have the heads off. Cormac, put some stouter shoes on. It's still raining outside.'

She ushered them into the hall – her legs felt as heavy as lead – waved to them from the step, returned to the house, slammed the door, then let go.

'You bloody hypocrite, John Lacey!' she screamed. 'You made me life a misery, accusing me of having affairs, when all the time . . .' She aimed a kick at the skirting board and hurt her foot. 'You even called our Orla names.' What was it? A little whore. In that case, what was the women he lived with?

Unless she didn't know he was married! Perhaps he was a bigamist. If he was and if it hadn't meant she'd never be able to hold up her head in Bootle again she would have reported him to the police.

No wonder he handed over such a pitiful amount of housekeeping every week – he was buying fitted carpets for his other house, buying vans, having a telephone installed in the office. She would have loved a fitted carpet in the parlour. And it would have been nice for the whole family to have gone places at weekends in the van. When Cormac passed the scholarship, she could have rung him from the salon, not stayed up till midnight to let him know. In fact, if she'd known about the telephone she would never have discovered his double life – she would have merely rung to tell him about Orla.

Alice went into the parlour and kicked the bed that he'd slept on, then collapsed upon it, sobbing. Oh, God! It *smelt* of him. The whole house smelt of him: not just the bed, but the chairs, the very air. She had to get out of here and there was only one place she could go and think in peace, a place where there was nothing to remind her of John.

She sat in her favourite place under the middle dryer.

The nights were fast drawing in, it was almost dark. But it had been dull and miserable all day.

'It's been the worst day of me life,' Alice whispered.

Her anger had been replaced by, of all things, guilt. Guilt that he'd felt the need for another woman because his own wife hadn't been sufficiently understanding. She'd tried but, somehow, in some way, she'd let him down. Perhaps she'd been selfish, taking over the hairdresser's when he would have preferred her at home. Mind you, it had seemed dead unreasonable at the time and still felt unreasonable when she thought about it now.

The young woman at the door had had something wrong with her face, a hare lip. Perhaps he felt more comfortable with someone imperfect, like himself. But it was still no excuse for having betrayed his wife and children, for taking the coward's way out.

Alice jumped when there was the sound of a key being turned in the salon door. It turned several times before it was opened and Neil Greene said, 'It wasn't locked. Alice must have forgotten.'

He had someone with him, a woman, who was laughing helplessly. Alice wondered bleakly if she herself would ever laugh again. She prayed the light wouldn't be turned on – she'd look an idiot, sitting in the dark on her own.

'I can't see a thing,' the woman giggled.

'Just a minute,' Neil said, 'the switch is over here.'

The room was flooded with light. Neil took a startled step backwards and his companion uttered a little cry when they saw the red-faced, red-eyed, swollen-faced Alice, who remembered she hadn't combed her hair since morning and it had got soaking wet, as well as her clothes, which she hadn't changed. She must look like a tramp who'd broken in, in the hope of finding a night's shelter.

'Alice!' Neil's face was full of concern. 'Are you all right?'

'I'm fine. Our Orla had the baby and I didn't manage to get in earlier. I thought I'd come and tidy up a few bits and bobs.'

'In the dark?' Neil's companion looked considerably put out. She was smartly dressed in a grey flannel costume, yellow blouse and hat. Her hair was perfectly set in a series of stiff, artificial waves. Alice would never have allowed a customer to leave Lacey's with such unnatural-looking hair.

'I must have dozed off.' Alice stood up, too quickly. She swayed, nearly fell and had to sit down again.

Neil said, 'Jean, I think it would be best if you went home. I'll drop in at the bank at lunchtime tomorrow.'

Jean made a little moue with her mouth. 'But, darling . . .'

'Tomorrow, Jean.' Neil put his hands on her shoulders and propelled her towards the door. 'Goodnight.' The door closed and he turned to Alice. 'What on earth is wrong? You look like shit.'

'Don't swear,' Alice said automatically, then remembered he wasn't one of her children. 'I'm sorry.'

'You're quite right. Teachers shouldn't swear.' He regarded her sternly. 'Alice, will you please tell me what's the matter?'

'Put the light out.'

He switched off the light. 'Is Orla's baby all right? Is Orla herself?'

'Orla's fine, the baby's beautiful.'

'Girl or boy?'

'A girl. She's calling her Lulu.'

'That's a pretty name. Lulu Lavin, sounds like a

164

flower.' He came and sat beside her. 'Are you going to tell me now that it's dark?' His voice sounded very close, only inches from her ear.

'I can't, Neil,' she said brokenly. 'You're being very kind, but I can't tell anyone, not even me dad or me best friend. It's something truly awful.'

'A trouble shared is a trouble halved, so people say.'

'I've said it meself more than once, but I'm not sure now if it's true.'

'If it's really so awful, Alice, you should tell someone. It doesn't have to be me. You shouldn't keep it all to yourself.'

Alice said wryly, 'You sound as if you know about such things, but I can't imagine anything awful's ever happened to you.'

He was always cheerful and extraordinarily good-humoured, as if he found the world a wonderful place to be. She understood he was an excellent teacher – everyone at St James's liked him, though it was considered a mystery what he was doing there when he could have been teaching at a public school, or in a different job altogether. He'd been to university and had a Classics degree, whatever that was. He came from somewhere in Surrey and wasn't short of a few bob – one of her customers who knew about such things said his suits and shoes were handmade. His car was an MG sports.

His mam and dad were referred to as 'moms' and 'pops', and he had an elder brother called Adrian and a sister, Miranda, whose twenty-first birthday it had been in August. Instead of a party, Miranda had had a dance at which some well-known orchestra had played: Ted Heath or Ambrose or Geraldo, Alice wasn't sure. It wasn't that Neil showed off, but he sometimes talked about his private life.

It could have been embarrassing, having someone so dead posh living in the upstairs flat, but Neil hadn't an ounce of side. Alice had always felt completely at ease with her tenant. And he was always gentle with Fionnuala, whose crush on him was plain for all to see.

'What are you doing tomorrow?' he asked.

'Why, coming into the salon, like normal,' she said, surprised at the question.

'Act as if nothing dreadful has happened, laugh, smile, be your usual sunny self?'

'Well, yes, of course.'

'We all do that, Alice,' he said with a dry laugh. 'We all put on a show, no matter how we feel inside. What makes you think I'm any different?'

'I'm sorry, luv.' Alice impulsively laid her hand on his. 'I was being insensitive. It's just that you act as if you don't have a care in the world.'

'It wasn't always so. Seven years ago I wanted to kill myself.' He put his other hand on top of hers. 'If I tell you about it, will you tell me in turn why you are looking so utterly wretched? I got the fright of my life when I turned on the light. I thought the hairdresser's must be haunted.'

'I'm sorry,' Alice said abjectly. 'And I made you get rid of poor Jean.'

'Poor Jean will already have got over it.' He pulled her to her feet. 'If we're going to exchange confidences, let's go upstairs where it's comfortable and we can do it over a cup of coffee or, better still, a glass of brandy. A drink will probably do you good.'

'Give us a minute first to comb me hair.'

There were still a few pieces of furniture in the flat that had belonged to Myrtle – a sideboard, a glass-fronted china cabinet, the bedroom suite, though Alice had bought a new mattress. The two armchairs, the small table with matching chairs and the kitchen dresser were good quality second-hand.

She'd been upstairs a couple of times since Neil moved in. He had added things of his own – some exotically patterned mats that had come all the way from Persia, lots of bright pictures, a pair of table lamps that cast a rosy glow over the rather gloomy room. The china cabinet was full of books and there was a statue of an elephant on top, which Neil said was made of jade. There were more jade statues on the mantelpiece.

'It's lovely and cosy up here,' she said when he switched on the lamps.

'That was my intention. Would you like coffee or brandy? I suggest the latter.'

'That would be nice, though not too much, else it'll go to me head.'

He grinned. 'That mightn't be such a bad thing. Now, sit down, I'll get the drinks, then I'll tell you the story of my life.'

Instead of an armchair, Neil sat on the floor with his back against it, his long legs stretched out across the mat. He turned on the electric fire, not the element, just the red bulb behind the imitation coals. The room looked cosier still.

'You know I was in the Army, don't you?' he began.

Alice nodded. 'You joined in nineteen forty-two when you were eighteen.' She also knew he didn't have to join. He'd been accepted by Cambridge University and could have stayed to finish the course, by which time the war would have been over.

'What you don't know, Alice, is that I got married when I was twenty.'

'Married!' she gasped, startled. He appeared to be one of the most *un*married men she'd ever known.

Neil wagged his finger. 'Don't interrupt. I'd like to get

this over with as quickly as possible. I married my childhood sweetheart, Barbara. Babs everyone called her. She was, still is, no doubt, quite gloriously pretty. Our parents had known each other for years before we were born. Even now,' he said thoughtfully, 'I'm not sure if we ever loved each other, or it was a case of doing what was expected of us. It *seemed* like love, it *felt* like it and we were happy to go along with our parents' expectations – superbly happy, I might add.'

He stared into the fire, as if he'd forgotten Alice was there. 'We married the year before the war ended. I was stationed in Kent at the time. I got special leave – we even snatched a weekend's honeymoon at Claridge's. That's a hotel in London,' he added in case Alice had never heard of it, which she hadn't. 'Babs worked for a government department, something to do with rationing. She had a little mews cottage in Knightsbridge. From then on, it's where I spent my leave, though she claimed to feel lonely when I wasn't there.' His lips twisted. 'Now that she was a married woman, she didn't lead the wild social life she'd done before. So I used to tell my fellow officers when they were going to London, "Drop in on my Babs. She'll make you feel at home for a few hours." And they did. Would you like more brandy, Alice?'

'Not yet. Perhaps later.'

'I think I'll replenish my glass.'

He got to his feet, a tall, extremely good-looking and suddenly rather tragic young man, Alice thought, even though she didn't yet know the end of the story.

'Nine months after the wedding,' he continued when he had returned to his place on the floor, 'we were posted to France. The Brits had taken it back by then. Soon we were in Germany, on our way to Berlin. We were in Berlin on the wonderful day the war was declared over. That night we had a party in the mess. Everyone drank too much, me included. Things got wild. Then a chap I hardly knew, I'd never spoken to before, mentioned this "little tart", as he called her, who he'd slept with in London. He intended calling on her the minute he got back. Her name was Barbara Greene and she'd been recommended to him as a "good lay" – that's an American term, so I understand. The chap said he felt sorry for her poor sod of a husband. Then another chap butted in who also knew Barbara Greene – she'd taught him a few tricks he didn't know, he said.' Neil laughed bitterly. 'Before long, it seemed as if the entire bloody regiment was claiming to have slept with Babs.'

'Oh, luv!' Alice breathed. 'That's terrible. What did you do?'

'I got blind drunk. I was probably the only Englishman on earth who wanted to kill himself on such a momentous night.'

'What did you do – *after* that night?'

Neil shrugged. 'Saw out the rest of my service, got demobbed, went to see my lovely wife and told her it was over. She wasn't particularly upset. We went our separate ways. A few years ago she asked for a divorce, but I refused. We're both Catholics, you see. I don't think a divorced teacher would be acceptable to a Catholic school board.'

'So, you're still married?'

'Yes. As I have no intention of ever marrying again, what does it matter?' He shrugged once more. 'Would you like another drink now? I definitely would.'

'I wouldn't mind a little bit. You're not going to get blind drunk tonight, are you?' Alice asked anxiously.

'No.' He stretched his arms, put them behind his neck and grinned. Suddenly he looked his old self again. Alice felt relieved. 'I'm over getting plastered. I'm over Babs, if the truth be known. But I shall never get over the sense of betrayal. How could she *do* such a thing? I still ask myself that from time to time.'

'What made you become a teacher?'

'I'm not sure.' He considered the question. 'After I finished Cambridge, I felt the urge to escape from the world I'd always known, do something entirely different. I took up teaching, much to my folks' horror. They thought it a terribly middle-class thing to do. They regard themselves as very much upper-class, you see.' He looked at Alice, his eyes sparkling with merriment. 'I've never told you this, but my father is Sir Archibald Nelson Middleton-Greene.'

Alice burst out laughing. 'That's a mouthful. Am I supposed to have heard of him?'

'No. I'm pleased you're amused rather than impressed.'

'Oh, I'm impressed all right.'

'Are you feeling better?'

'Loads better.'

'Me too. I've never told anyone all that before.' He refilled her glass for the third time. 'Now it's your turn to bare your soul.'

'It doesn't feel so bad now. I mean, it's still awful, it just doesn't feel as bad inside.' She told him the story right from the beginning, about how happy she and John had been with their four lovely children, then when John had burnt his face and everything had changed. She told him the awful things he'd called her. 'Then suddenly he changed again.' He'd started staying out a lot. They hardly saw him.

'Today I went round to the yard to tell him about Orla. He'd always discouraged us from going before. You'll never believe what I found.' She described knocking on the door and it being opened by the very pregnant young woman with fair hair and a toddler attached to her knee. 'She smiled at me ever so nicely.' Then the little boy came and shouted upstairs for his daddy. 'By then, I knew it must be John, but it still knocked me for six when he appeared. And his eyes! They were dead horrible. I felt about *this* big.' Alice held up her thumb and forefinger about quarter of an inch apart. 'But do you know what gets me more than anything?'

'What, Alice?'

'It sounds daft, but she had a fitted carpet. John knew I'd always wanted a fitted carpet for the parlour. It made me realise how much he put this other family before his real one. It's as if we don't matter any more.' She sniffed. 'Oh, Lord, Neil. I think I'm going to cry again and I haven't got a hankie.'

'I'll get you one.' Neil leapt to his feet and returned with a clean, but unironed, white handkerchief. To her total astonishment he knelt beside her and began to dry her eyes, which she thought a trifle unnecessary. There didn't seem any real need to kiss them either, so that she felt her lashes flutter against his lips. It was years since John had touched her and it made her feel uncomfortable, even though it was undeniably very pleasant.

'You don't have to do this, you know,' she mumbled.

'I'm doing it because I want to, not because I have to.' Neil slid his arms around her waist. 'I've been lusting after you, Mrs Lacey, since the day I first set foot in the salon.'

'But I'm thirty-eight,' Alice gasped.

'I don't care if you're eighty-eight, you're utterly adorable.' He pulled her towards him and hugged her very tight.

'Neil.' She tried to struggle out of his arms. 'You've had too much to drink.'

'No, it's you who hasn't had enough. Stay still, Alice. I promise I won't touch you anywhere that's out of bounds.'

Alice sat stock still, knowing she should leave, but curiously reluctant to move an inch, while Neil traced her eyebrows with his finger, then her ears, her cheeks, her nose. The world had gone very quiet and, apart from the ticking of a clock somewhere, there wasn't a sound to be heard. Neil's firm finger traced her jaw and she could smell soap on his hand. John had always been a tender lover, but he'd never done anything like this. The finger moved to her lips and Alice felt as if her bones had melted inside her body. Then Neil bent forward and kissed her gently, ever so gently, on her forehead and she couldn't resist another minute. She flung her arms round his neck, feeling like a wanton woman, but not caring a bit.

Chapter 7
1956

Maeve Lacey got engaged on her twenty-first birthday. Her fiancé, Martin Adams, was a colourless, fussy young man who was a radiographer at Bootle hospital. They had been courting two years, but weren't planning to get married until Maeve was a State Registered Nurse and they had saved up a deposit for a house.

Alice was pleased that it all sounded so very sensible when compared with Orla's shotgun wedding. She remarked as much to her friend, Bernadette, who was helping prepare the food for what would be the party to end all parties that night.

'Me and Bob were sensible, and look where it got us?' Bernadette said darkly. 'Absolutely bloody nowhere.'

'Yes, but you're all right now.' Alice giggled. 'Mam!'

'Oh, shurrup.' Bernadette nudged her friend's ribs. 'Stop being so cheeky, else you might get your bottom smacked.'

Three years ago, when Alice had held a similar party on the occasion of her father's, Danny's, sixtieth birthday, Bernie had taken her courage in both hands and proposed.

'Neither of us is getting any younger,' she said to the astonished birthday boy. 'I can't stand you, Danny Mitchell. If the truth be known, you drive me wild, but at the same time I think we'd be good together. I fancy you something rotten and I know you fancy me, so don't look so outraged.'

Danny had spluttered something incomprehensible in reply.

'If you're agreeable,' Bernadette went on, 'I think we should get wed as soon as possible while we've both got a bit of life left in us. And before you accept, I should tell you I'd very much like a baby. I'm thirty-nine, so if we go at it hammer and tongs, there's still time for you to put me in the club.'

Danny had spluttered something incomprehensible again.

'Think about it,' Bernadette said kindly, patting his arm. 'Take your time, but try and let me know before the party's over, so we can announce it, like, while everyone's here.'

Four weeks later Bernadette became Mrs Danny Mitchell and stepmother to her best friend. Within a year Alice was presented with a brother, Ian, and a sister, Ruth, the year after.

Danny was rarely seen in the pub these days, only on Sundays after Mass. He was content to stay indoors with his pretty wife and two young children, and watch the new telly at night, much to the chagrin of the numerous women who'd had their eye on him.

'You've made me dad very happy,' Alice said as she rolled sausage meat into a length of puff pastry. 'And he thinks the sun shines out Ian's and Ruth's little bottoms. I never thought I'd see the day when he'd take two kids in a pushchair for a walk in North Park.'

'Well, he didn't have much alternative, did he?' Bernadette sniffed. 'I'd promised to give you a hand.' She removed a baking tray from the oven. 'How many jam tarts do you want? There's a dozen here and another dozen just on finishing.'

'Well, there's thirty coming,' Alice said thoughtfully, 'but not everyone will want a tart. I reckon that's enough.'

'What shall I do now?'

'Pipe some cream on those little jellies, then sprinkle them with hundreds and thousands. Oh, by the way, could you bring some teaspoons when you come tonight? I haven't enough to go round. And some glasses too, if you've got any.'

'Of course we've got glasses. What do you think we drink the sherry out of at Christmas – mugs?'

The two women worked in contented silence for a while, each preoccupied with her own thoughts, while the smell from the kitchen became more and more mouthwatering. Two cats sat on the backyard wall, enjoying the crisp November sunshine and hoping they might be thrown the odd sausage roll.

'Who's looking after the salon today?' Bernadette enquired. 'Sat'days are your busiest day.'

'Our Fion. She's going to manage the new branch in Marsh Lane when it opens after Christmas, did I tell you?'

'Yes.' Bernadette rolled her eyes. 'New branch! Get you, Alice Lacey.'

'To think I used to look up to you when you had that good job with the Gas Board.' Alice wrinkled her nose and looked superior. 'Now you're just a housewife and I'm about to have me own chain of hairdressers.'

'I'd hardly call two a chain.'

'It's a *little* chain.' She laughed happily. 'It seemed a shame not to take on Gloria's when I discovered it was closing down – we were overstaffed once Fion got her certificate and I couldn't possibly have got rid of Doreen to make way for her. Doreen's going to Marsh Lane with

Fion and I'm taking on another qualified assistant for meself. Patsy'll stay with me, naturally.'

'Their Daisy never got on the stage, did she?'

'No, she's married now, with two kids. Her husband's a chimney sweep if you'd believe it.'

'Well, I suppose chimney sweeps need wives the same as other men.'

'I think', Neil said, 'that I could become quite a fan of Elvis Presley.'

'He's OK,' Alice conceded. 'Our Fion's mad about him. She's got all his records. I prefer Frankie Laine meself.'

'This is a great party.' Neil put his hands on her hips and squeezed.

'Don't!' Alice said in a scandalised voice. 'Someone might come in.' They were in the kitchen in Amber Street and the party was going full swing. Elvis Presley was singing something about his blue suede shoes. 'Get out the way, Neil, while I make a pot of tea.'

'Don't you think people will have guessed by now how things are? It's been five years.'

'There's no reason for people to have guessed anything,' Alice said primly, 'and I've no intention of providing them with proof. I've got me reputation to consider and you've got your job. You'd be out on your ear if you were found having an affair with a married woman.' Like her, Neil was usually very discreet about their relationship and she wondered if he'd had too much to drink. 'Anyroad, me daughter's twenty-one today and I've got things to do,' she said brusquely. '*And* she's got engaged. Oh, hello, Cormac, luv. What can I do for you?'

'Are there any more jam tarts, Mam?'

'Sorry, luv. I thought two dozen'd be enough. There's

plenty of jellies, though, some iced fairy cakes and loads of chocolate biccies. You'll find them on the sideboard in the parlour.'

'Ta, Mam.' Cormac vanished.

'He's not going to grow very tall,' Alice said. 'Not like his dad.'

'He's only sixteen, time to grow taller,' Neil said comfortably.

Maeve came in, her face flushed with happiness. 'Are there any clean glasses, Mam?'

'There will be if you fetch some dirty ones for me to wash.'

'I'll get some. Oh, by the way, Neil. Thanks for the scent. It's lovely.'

'I didn't know whether to buy a present for your birthday, or the engagement. Perhaps I should have bought one for each.'

'The scent's perfect. I haven't begun a bottom drawer yet.'

'She seems so certain of everything,' Alice said when her daughter had gone. 'It hasn't crossed her mind that things might change, not always for the better. Mind you, I was just as certain at her age.'

'So was I.' Neil sighed. 'But it's only natural that we expect our lives to pass smoothly along without a hiccup. If we were waiting for everything to fall around our ears, as it did with you and me, we'd all go bonkers.'

Alice opened her mouth to speak, but a girl she had never seen before came in and asked for the lavatory, Maeve brought the dirty glasses, someone asked if there were any more jam tarts and a lad rushed into the yard to be sick. Alice had the worrying feeling it had been Maurice Lacey, who wasn't old enough to be drinking.

Before he disappeared Neil blew her a kiss, which she affected to ignore in case anyone was watching. She poured a glass of sherry and decided to circulate, make sure the guests were enjoying themselves.

In the living room, Fion was conversing with Horace Flynn, whom she had insisted on inviting. Apparently it was all part of the war she had declared on Cora. Alice would have preferred her daughter in the parlour where everyone was dancing. She despaired of Fion ever finding a friend, let alone a man friend – other than their revolting landlord.

Cormac was doing card tricks for an admiring audience, Micky Lavin and Bernadette among them.

She found her dad sitting on the stairs with Orla. 'The ancient and the pregnant are having a bit of peace and quiet,' Danny quipped.

Orla was in the club again with her fourth child. The girl was sorely in need of advice on birth control, but had bitten her mother's head off when she had broached the subject. Still, the family now had a nice little house in Pearl Street since Micky had finished his apprenticeship and was earning a proper wage.

'How are you feeling, luv?' Alice asked sympathetically. It must be galling for someone only twenty-two and heavily pregnant to be surrounded by people mostly the same age who were all single, childless and obviously having a good time.

'How do you think I feel?' Orla snapped. She sometimes wondered if all she had to do was be in the same room as Micky to conceive. She'd heard it was unlikely to happen if you did it standing up. Well, *they'd* done it standing up and Lulu had arrived nine months later. The rhythm system had produced Maisie, the withdrawal system Gary. After Gary, Micky had worn a French letter, but here she was, once again looking like a bloody elephant. Micky must have bought the only French letter ever made that leaked. Every time a baby was born, they forced themselves to hold fire for at least six months, otherwise there'd be children popping out twice a year. When the six months was up, they'd leap upon each other the way people dying of thirst would leap upon a glass of water, draining the glass and wanting more. It wasn't a bit fair and she was fed up with Mr Lavin joking it was about time Micky tied a knot in it.

In future they'd just have to abstain, like priests. The trouble was, she loved Micky to death, though she wouldn't have dreamt of telling him. It was torture to lie in the same bed and not touch each other. And the children were too beautiful for words. Even so, it still wasn't fair.

Nothing seemed fair to Fionnuala either. Everyone was having a great time, but she'd been stuck with Horace Flynn the whole night because there wasn't another person in the house willing to speak to him. Of course, it was her own fault for asking him, but he'd seemed grateful and flattered – Fion suspected she was the only one in Bootle who treated him like a human being. She was definitely the only woman who allowed him to pinch her bum, something he did every time he came to the hairdresser's, which was often. Fion would grit her teeth and pretend to smile. 'Ooh, Mr Smith, don't be naughty!' she would say and move out of the way.

Mam didn't realise the sacrifices she was making to keep Horace Flynn on their side – he never went round to Garibaldi Road these days. The lease would be renewed again in a year's time and Fion hoped they might get it for nothing if she continued to let him pinch her bum. She just prayed he'd never stroke it.

It was galling to think that it was *her* records being played in the front room. 'Love me tender, love me do,' Elvis Presley crooned. Yet not one of those lads had thought to ask her to dance. Didn't they realise she was a fully qualified hairdresser who would be managing her own salon after Christmas?

Oh, if only she didn't feel so *old*! Old and fat, wretched and lonely. Her youth was passing her by, had already passed. She was twenty-three, but had never been kissed by a boy, yet one of her sisters was pregnant for the fourth time and the other had just got engaged. It was even more galling to think they were both younger than she was.

It was a relief when Mr Flynn decided to go home because it was getting too hot. He courteously shook her hand and rolled out of the house on his fat little legs. Seconds later, Neil Greene came and sat beside her, and Fion suddenly didn't know what to do with her hands. He was so handsome, yet not the least bit conceited and very kind. Talking to Neil always made her feel warm inside. She often wondered if he was in love with her, but too embarrassed to say. She fluttered her eyelashes at him encouragingly, but all he talked about was mundane things like the weather and what a great party it was, and he'd like to bet she was really looking forward to being in charge of the new Lacey's in Marsh Lane.

Alice, who happened to be passing, thought with a pang how pathetic Fion looked. The poor girl would feel betrayed if she ever discovered what was going on between her and Neil.

She'd never dreamt she was the sort of woman who'd have an affair, but Neil had caught her at a particularly vulnerable time and it had turned out to be quite wonderful. She had forgotten what it felt like to be loved, to feel feminine and wanted. And it was dead exciting, pretending to work late at the salon and going up to see Neil instead. Or remembering during the evening that there was something she'd forgotten to do.

'I'll just nip round to Lacey's,' she would say, giving a mythical reason, and Neil would be waiting for her, sometimes already in bed, because Alice wasn't prepared to stay long. He wasn't a masterful lover like John. Neil was always concerned that she was enjoying herself as much as he was.

So, what harm was she doing, apart from committing a sin? She wasn't sure if it was a mortal or a venial sin and there was no way she was going to ask a priest. Anyroad, it was only temporary, though it had already gone on longer than she'd expected. Somewhere in the world, she felt convinced, there was the perfect girl for Neil, someone bright and attractive who would give him children, the sort of girl he'd gone out with before but had been too scared to get serious with in case she turned out to be like Babs. *She* was nothing like Babs, *he* was completely different from John and she suspected that was where the attraction between them lay. But one of these days Neil would meet the perfect girl and have no use for Alice any more.

Alice wasn't sure how she would feel when that day came. Devastated, she suspected. She would miss him for as long as she lived. Perhaps that's why she was always so brusque with him, always in a hurry to get back home, because she didn't want him to feel guilty when the time came for him to let her go.

John Lacey had forgotten that today his daughter, Maeve, was twenty-one. He didn't know she had got engaged, or that Orla was expecting her fourth child, that Fion was now a qualified hairdresser and that Cormac had achieved six top-grade O levels before going into the sixth form at St Mary's in September. He wouldn't have known his mother, Meg, had died, had he not read it in the paper. He had decided not to attend the funeral.

It was years since Cormac had rung the yard, asking to see his dad. John had refused, though it had hurt. Cormac had been the favourite of his children, but he felt the need to shed his first family, leave them behind, concentrate on the new.

'Would you like more tea?' Clare said stiffly.

'I wouldn't mind.' He pushed the empty cup across the table. The atmosphere was thick with bitterness and suspicion.

'Is this how you treated Alice?' Clare curled her pretty pink mouth. 'Did you accuse her of going with other men, call her a prostitute, ask how much she'd earned?'

John ignored the question. 'I'd still like to know why the hell you were so late getting home,' he growled.

'I've already told you half a dozen times. It was such a lovely evening. Instead of catching the train from Exchange Station, I walked along the Docky as far as Seaforth and caught the train to Crosby from there. I watched the sunset. Is that a crime?'

'Did you call in the Arcadia, look up some of your old customers?' he sneered.

'No, I did not. I merely enjoyed a pleasant shopping trip to town. I bought a few early Christmas presents. I had a nice time. It's a pity you had to spoil it.' Her voice was as clear and tinkling as a bell.

It was happening all over again, the same thing that had happened with Alice. It was too late now, but he desperately wished he hadn't persuaded Clare to have surgery. He had read about it in a magazine. 'What do you think?' he asked, showing her the article. At first she had been reluctant. 'I have you, I have the children, I'm quite happy as I am,' she had written on her pad. How many pads had she completed in her short life? he had wondered.

'Yes, but you hardly ever go out,' he said. 'Have it

done for the children's sake, if not for mine. They've never heard you speak, not properly. It doesn't affect them now, but it will when they grow older. Let at least one of us be perfect.' He remembered smiling.

Clare had reached out and touched his scarred face. 'What about you?'

'Nothing can be done about me, I'm afraid. The surgeon actually insisted it didn't look too bad.'

She shook her head. 'Surgeon right.' Then she wrote, 'Hardly noticeable, becoming weathered, like a tree or a house.'

The treatment had taken two years, it was more difficult for an adult. She was in and out of different hospitals as bit by bit her mouth and face were repaired with dental surgery, plastic surgery, reconstructive surgery to her palate. At first her voice had been hesitant, whispery, gradually becoming louder, clearer, more confident. She was left with a slight, attractive lisp.

Throughout the two years, during the times she was away, John had been totally supportive. He had arranged for a woman to look after Lisa and David who had yet to start school when the treatment started. He left the yard early to collect Robbie from school, make the tea. They'd been living in Crosby for years, in a large, semi-detached house not far from the shore – he could afford it; B.E.D.S. was doing extremely well.

She hadn't complained, not once, when she returned from various hospitals with her face swollen or badly bruised or in obvious pain or unable to make the slightest sound, though sometimes she looked frightened.

The time came when there was no more bruising, no more pain, no more operations. She began to say the words she'd always known, but could never say before. He'd always understood she was clever, but hadn't realised how clever until she began to talk – about politics, literature, religion, of things he didn't know about himself. She seemed to have opinions on anything and everything, as if she'd been storing them in her head, unable to express them before.

John suddenly realised she was an attractive, clever woman, with steady grey eyes, a small straight nose and a perfect, absolutely perfect, mouth. Even her hair looked different – fuller, shinier, more flattering around her face.

He must have been mad! If *he* thought her so attractive, so would other men. How stupid to have allowed, actually encouraged, her to become an object of admiration! Would he be able to trust her now that people didn't avert their eyes or regard her with an unhealthy fascination? How long would it be before she realised how lovely she was?

His brain was being split in two again, as it had been after that damned fire. He knew in his heart that Clare would never be unfaithful, just as he had known the same about Alice, but there was a different message in his head. He'd already started coming home from the yard at unexpected times to check on her. If she was out shopping, he'd wait until she came back, examining her face to make sure it didn't contain an expression that shouldn't be there. Once she'd been upstairs when he let himself in and he'd later searched the bedrooms, looking under beds and in wardrobes in case there was a man hidden there.

Clare wasn't as patient with him as Alice had been. She quickly lost her temper if he became suspicious. He wondered if her true personality was beginning to emerge, if the real Clare had been hidden until now.

'What did you buy in town?' he asked, doing his best to make his voice pleasant.

'Jumpers for Robbie and David, a woollen frock with smocking on the shoulders for Lisa. I thought I'd keep them for Christmas. I also bought a few small things for their stockings. Oh, and some more decorations. We hadn't enough last year.'

'Didn't you buy anything for yourself?'

Her eyes sparkled. She must have forgiven him for the things he'd said before. She leapt to her feet – even her movements seemed to have altered, she was more lively, more alert – and delved among the carrier bags on the floor. 'I bought myself a frock, almost a party frock. I've never had one before. I thought we could go somewhere on New Year's Eve, a dinner dance, maybe. The woman next door's always offering to babysit. I got it from Lewis's. What do you think?'

She held the frock up against her. It was black velvet, with a ruched bodice, a gently flared skirt and a scooped neck. The sleeves were long and tight, ending in a point. It was an entirely modest frock, but John felt a tightness in his chest when he visualised her wearing it. She would look a knock-out, turn every man's head.

'Oh, and I bought some high heels,' she said excitedly. 'Not very high, I'm not used to wearing them. They're black suede. See!' She slipped out of her old flat court shoes into the new ones and held out a foot for him to admire.

John could stand it no longer. 'Get them off!' he snarled. 'You're not going outside wearing them damn things, nor that frock. And we're not going to no dinner dance either. We'll stay at home on New Year's Eve like we always do.'

She looked at him with curiosity rather than anger. 'What's the matter with you? Did I have my face done for your eyes only? Am I supposed to stay indoors for the rest of my life just to please you?'

'You were quite happy to stay in before.'

'I was.' She nodded gravely. 'I was happy about

everything before, but one of the reasons you persuaded me to have the operations done was so I could go out more. Today was the first time I've gone shopping on my own and been able to ask for things without feeling a freak. Why are you so intent on spoiling everything? Would you prefer I had the treatement reversed, be made the way I was before?'

There was much truth in the last remark. It had all been his idea and now he resented the result. As ever, pride prevented him from explaining how he felt. 'I'm going to bed,' he muttered.

He had reached the door when Clare said softly, 'John.'

'What?' He turned.

She was looking at him pityingly. 'I'm grateful for everything you've done for me,' she said in the same soft voice, 'although I realise it was done solely for selfish reasons. There was a time when you wouldn't have given me a second glance, when you wouldn't have set foot inside the Arcadia. But you did and we met, and the years since have been the happiest of my life.'

She gestured towards a chair, and he returned to the room and sat down. There was a feeling in his bones that what she was about to say was of tremendous importance. His legs were unsteady.

'I've grown to love you,' she continued, 'though I suspect you've never loved me. Please don't interrupt, John,' she said imperiously when he opened his mouth to argue. 'Let me have my say. If you truly loved me you wouldn't act the way you do. You would want me to be happy, not resent me. John.' She leant on the table and stared at him intently. 'I would like us to grow old together, but I am not prepared to be bullied and made a prisoner in my own house.'

'But . . .' he began, but Clare seemed determined not to let him get a word in edgeways.

'If you continue being so suspicious, cross-questioning my every move, then I shall take the children and leave, because you are making our lives unbearable. And that's not the only reason,' she went on. 'I shall leave before you go somewhere like the Arcadia, find a woman you don't feel inferior to and end up betraying me in the same way that you betrayed Alice.'

Where was he? Cora fretted. It was two o'clock in the morning and she'd never known Maurice stay out so late before. Billy's snores rumbled through the house. The snoring had been the reason she'd given for sleeping in the spare room over the last few years. Billy hadn't seemed to mind. Sometimes she wondered why he bothered coming home. It could only be for the warm bed and hot dinners — it certainly wasn't for his wife.

And now Maurice was going the same way. He'd become a labourer, just like Billy, though she hoped, unlike Billy, he'd learn a trade: bricklaying, plastering, something. Now he was earning money of his own and she hardly saw him. Even at weekends he went to the football with his mates and didn't reappear till all hours. Sundays he did the same disappearing act after a late Mass. She suspected he haunted pubs — well, he'd been shown a good example by Billy. Only sixteen, he could have passed for twenty.

There were times when she could have cried at the way things had turned out, but she'd never been given to crying and wasn't sure if she knew how.

Feeling restless, Cora edgily circled the room, picking up the occasional ornament that had given her so much pleasure to buy, but gave no pleasure now. What point was there in the place looking nice when she was the only one who saw it? Whom was she impressing with the house in Garibaldi Road, so much superior to the one in O'Connell Street? No one except herself.

There should be people to show it off to – friends, relatives, but Cora had never had a friend and she'd seen off her only relatives, the Laceys, years ago. Maeve Lacey was twenty-one today and getting engaged at the same time. Perhaps that was where Maurice was, at the party. He continued to be friendly with Alice and her kids, despite his mam's coldly expressed disapproval.

She'd heard about the party on the grapevine. Cora shopped in Marsh Lane and found it a simple matter to keep up to date with the Laceys' affairs. She knew Alice was taking over Gloria's and that Cormac had done so well in his exams that he was likely to go to university.

The key turned in the front door and Maurice came stumbling into the hall. 'Where have you been?' Cora demanded. He looked drunk, she thought.

'A party, Mam. Had a smashing time.'

'Was it Maeve Lacey's?'

'Yeh. I'm going to save up for a gramophone, buy some records. Fion had records and they were really the gear. Elvis Presley.'

'*I'll* buy you a gramophone,' she said. It would be painful, drawing the money out of the bank, but she was often driven to buying him things in the hope of winning him back, though nothing so far as expensive as a gramophone.

She was pleased when his face brightened in gratitude, but would have appreciated a kiss. 'Ta, Mam,' he said. 'I'm off to bed. I'll sleep in tomorrer, go to midday Mass.'

'I'll bring you up a cup of tea around half-eleven,' Cora promised. She watched him go up the stairs two at a time. He was every bit as good-looking as his dad, but was turning out to be a bitter disappointment. But how was she to have known that?

It was time she went to bed herself, except she hardly slept. Her mind never felt rested, never at ease. It used to be full of plots and plans for the future, but now it was more concentrated on the resentments of the present and the past.

It would have been nice to have gone to the Laceys' party. Much better than being at home by herself, with no one to talk to and the house like a tomb. Orla was likely to drop her baby soon and there'd be another big do for the christening. Cora wouldn't have minded going, buying a new frock, even getting her hair set.

Well, she knew what had to be done if she was to get back in with the Laceys. She'd have to tear up that agreement, rip it in two in front of Alice's eyes and give her the bits. After all, the investment, if you could call it that, had been returned a thousand times. It might even result in a resumption of relations with Horace Flynn – these days he only came round to Garibaldi Road to collect the rent.

She'd do it Monday, call in the hairdresser's when she went to Marsh Lane shops. She might even buy a present for Orla's baby so they'd feel obliged to ask her to the christening.

Her mind wasn't at its normal feverish pitch when she went to bed and she fell asleep with unusual speed. During the night she was woken by the familiar creak of the third-to-top stair. Either Billy or Maurice was going to the lavvy. But the lavvy was on this floor and there was no need to go downstairs. The creaking sound must have come from the landing, though she could have sworn it was the stairs.

★

'I think,' Alice announced, 'I'll nip round the salon and practise a bit with them new mesh rollers.'

'Why don't you practise at home?' enquired Fion.

'Because the rollers are at the salon. They only arrived yesterday.' Alice wished she'd thought of another excuse. On reflection, this one seemed rather weak.

'Can I come with you?' Fion said eagerly. 'I quite fancy a bouffant hairdo. They're all the rage in London.'

Alice tried to think of a reason for saying no, but couldn't. It was Sunday afternoon and, as usual, Fion was the only one in the house besides herself. Apart from two cigarette burns on the parlour carpet, the house was pristine after Maeve's party the night before.

She was about to say, 'All right, luv,' because it would have been cruel to say anything else, when Maurice Lacey came in the back way, apparently to see Fion for some odd reason, and she was able to escape.

Alice always felt as if she was entering a different world from the one she knew when she went into Neil's flat. Wedding lines had given her and John permission from the Lord to make love, but lying in Myrtle Rimmer's old bed with Neil made Alice feel another person altogether, as if she'd removed her cloak of conventionality and left it outside Neil's door.

There was something faintly indecent, yet at the same time totally delicious, about letting Neil's tongue flutter against her nipples, his hands caress her body, every single part of it. Sometimes the sensations were so intense, so amazing, that she cried out, which Neil said later when she expressed embarrassment was perfectly all right and women did it all the time.

On the Sunday after Maeve's party Alice unlocked the salon door and went inside.

'Is that you?' Neil called.

'No, it's me.' Alice laughed and ran upstairs.

She couldn't find it anywhere. In the end, Cora removed every single piece of paper from the bureau and went through them one by one, but there was no sign of the agreement Alice Lacey had signed ten years before.

Could she have put it somewhere else? No, Cora decided. The bureau in the parlour was where she kept all the paperwork – the electricity and gas bills, receipts for this and that, Maurice's vaccination card, birth certificates. Everything.

It *had* to be here somewhere. She went through the papers again, emptying envelopes in case it had been mistakenly put inside. She was frantic by the time she'd finished and it still hadn't come to light. Perhaps it had been thrown away. Every now and then she sorted out the papers, threw away the old bills, but she surely wouldn't have been so daft as to throw away that agreement, even accidentally.

Mind you, finding the paper wasn't important. All she had to do was *tell* Alice she'd torn it up, that she wouldn't be asking for her share no more – and she'd be accepted back into the Lacey clan. Today was the day she called for her cut, but today she'd tell them they could keep it, though in a nicer way than that.

Cora fetched her shopping bag from the kitchen, put on her camel coat and zip-up boots, tied a headscarf round her pale, greying hair and set off for Marsh Lane.

She did her shopping first. Outside a shop that sold baby clothes she paused and examined the window display. A matinée coat would be nice for Orla's baby, white or lemon so it would do for a boy or a girl, booties to match. She'd get them tomorrow and ask for them to be wrapped in tissue paper before they were put in the bag.

There was a funny sensation in her belly when she turned into Opal Street. She'd made a mint out of that agreement, but it had caused a lot of bad blood and she wasn't sure if it had been worth it. Alice Lacey might be out of pocket, but *she* was the one who'd suffered most.

The bell tinkled when she opened the door. The salon was getting smarter with the years. There were tiles on the floor that looked like polished wood and three gleaming black dryers with leather chairs underneath. The colour scheme had been changed from mauve to orange, though Alice referred to it as 'apricot'. Just inside the door an elegant white desk housed a telephone and the appointment book. The old sinks had been replaced with shallow cream basins on which fat, stubby taps sparkled beneath the neon strip lights.

Although it was Monday morning, the place was already busy. The dryers were all occupied and two of the sinks. That Patsy woman, whom Cora had never been able to take to, was collecting dirty cups.

Alice looked up at the sound of the bell. Her eyes went cold when she saw Cora. 'The envelope's in the left-hand desk drawer as usual,' she said shortly.

'I'd like to talk to you,' Cora said eagerly.

'I'm busy right now, as you can see.'

'*I'll* talk to her.' Fion abandoned the tint she was applying and made for the kitchen.

Cora followed. It wasn't quite what she'd planned, but she couldn't very well say what she'd come to say in front of a crowded salon. And Fion would do just as well as Alice to be told the agreement no longer stood, perhaps better. She quite looked forward to seeing the girl's face collapse when she heard the news.

A kettle simmered in the kitchen. Cora coughed importantly, 'I've come . . .' she began, but Fion interrupted.

'I know quite well why you've come. Aunt Cora, to collect the money you've been doing me mam out of for years.' Fion glared at her aunt. 'You're not getting another penny off Lacey's and I'll tell you why.' She smiled unpleasantly. 'No, I won't tell you, I'll *show* you.' She produced a yellowing sheet of paper from the pocket of her overall and waved it in front of Cora's eyes. 'Recognise it? It's the agreement me mam was daft enough to sign. Now just watch, Aunt Cora.' The girl was clearly enjoying herself. She thrust the paper in the flames spurting from beneath the kettle and it immediately caught alight.

Cora watched numbly as the burning paper was thrown into the sink where it quickly became a few charred scraps. Fion turned on the tap and the scraps disappeared down the drain.

'There!' she said with a loud, satisfied sigh.

'Where did you get it from?' Cora whispered.

'I'll leave you to work that out for yourself.'

'Maurice! Maurice gave it you.' She remembered the footsteps on the stairs on Saturday night. Fion must have asked him to get it at the party, to steal it, actually to steal it from his own mam. Cora felt sick to her stomach. 'Can I use the lavvy?'

'You know where it is.'

'Fion,' Alice called. 'What are you doing? Mrs Finnegan's only had half her tint.'

'Coming, Mam.' Fion smiled slyly at Cora. 'Mam's going to be dead pleased, I'll bet.'

'Yes.' Cora scarcely heard. Everything had been turned upside down. Maurice had betrayed her. Her son's loyalty lay, not with her, but with Alice and her family. No one wanted her: not her husband, not her son. No one.

He was beautiful, but then all her babies had been

beautiful. Orla looked proudly down at Paul, her new son.

'He's a fine little chap,' Micky said, equally proud. 'Can I hold him for a bit?'

Orla carefully put the baby in his arms. 'I suppose your mam's spoiling the other three something rotten.'

'Well . . .' Micky grinned. 'Not quite as much as me dad. They're being stuffed with sweets that came from you know where.'

'I know exactly where. The lorry some Lavin or other always seems to be at the back of.'

'Your mam's having them all day tomorrow. She said the salon's overstaffed at the moment, so she can take time off. We're very lucky with our families, Orl.'

'I know,' Orla said soberly. 'We're dead lucky with the kids, too. Some woman had a baby just before me and it died within an hour.'

'Are we dead lucky with each other, though?' Micky glanced at her from beneath his long black lashes.

Orla hadn't thought it possible to blush in front of a man by whom you'd borne four children, but blush she did. 'I reckon so, Micky,' she said in a subdued voice. 'I reckon we're lucky all round in every possible way.'

Their lips met over the new baby and Orla felt the inevitable swirl of desire. She realised that, even if she wore an iron chastity belt, Micky would only have to sneeze and she'd get pregnant.

After he'd gone, the midwife came in. It was the same one who'd delivered Lulu five years ago. 'You're becoming quite a familiar figure in these parts,' she said with a grin. 'I see from your notes this is your fourth.'

'If you work here long enough you'll be present at me twenty-fourth,' Orla said gloomily − it was actually possible to feel happy and gloomy at the same time.

'Have you considered birth control?' the midwife said

helpfully. 'I know it says on your chart that you're a Catholic, but I hope you don't mind my saying this, the Pope's not likely to lend a hand if you have a child a year for the rest of your life.'

'We've tried birth control, but nothing works.'

'Have you heard of the Dutch cap?'

'No.'

'And there's something new, a birth control pill. It only came out last year, so I don't know much about it.'

'We'll try *anything*,' Orla said eagerly. 'Just tell me where to go.'

Chapter 8

It was surprising, but the Lacey's in Marsh Lane was attracting only a very small clientele. Business had been good at first, but had gradually petered off until the salon was doing only half the business of the one in Opal Street.

Whenever she had a spare minute, Alice went round to see if she could recognise what the problem was. She'd had the salon painted in the same warm apricot shade as the other, the same wood effect tiles laid on the floor. There were new lace curtains on the windows and strip lights fitted to the freshly painted ceiling. It looked very different, but the new decoration was a definite improvement on the old. No one could possibly have taken offence.

Yet, as the weeks passed, fewer and fewer women came. Why? Alice wondered.

She got her answer in April when the Marsh Lane Lacey's had been open for four months and Doreen Morrison handed in her notice. Doreen was in her fifties, unmarried, with platinum-blonde hair, always perfectly made up. She was never without a man friend and, years ago, had gone out with Danny Mitchell more than once. She still worked part-time, afternoons and all day Saturday.

'It's not your heart, is it, luv?' Alice said anxiously.

Doreen was a top-class hairdresser and she'd be more than sad to lose her.

'My heart's fine, Alice, it's . . .' Doreen paused.

'It's what, luv?'

The woman looked embarrassed. 'I don't like to tell you.'

'If something's wrong, Doreen, I've a right to know.'

'Well . . .' She still looked reluctant. 'Well, to tell the truth, Alice, it's your Fion. She's impossible to work with. Chrissie's also talking about handing in her notice.' Chrissie O'Connell was the junior, a helpful, friendly girl.

'What does our Fion do that makes her so impossible to work with?' Alice enquired coolly, torn between wanting to side with her child, yet knowing Doreen wouldn't leave without good reason.

'See, I knew you'd be upset. I can tell by the tone of your voice.' Doreen sounded upset herself. 'I wish I hadn't told you.'

'I'm glad you did.' Alice nodded encouragingly. 'Go on.'

'It's just that she's so rude, Alice: to me, to Chrissie, to the customers, except if they're old and then she gushes over them so much the poor dears can't stand it. It was all right when she was working alongside you. You probably didn't notice, but you kept her in line, kept laughing and apologising for her. I tried that a couple of times, but she put me firmly in me place. Told me *she* was the one in charge.' Doreen warmed to her theme, clearly having been smarting over the situation for a long time. 'There's one customer couldn't stand the dryer too hot, kept switching it down every now'n again. Fion was very short with her, told her off in no uncertain terms, and the woman's never come back again, yet she'd been coming to Gloria's for ages. If a customer asks for a one-inch trim, Fion will take off two or three because she thinks it would look better. Or she'll argue over the colour of a tint, or insist someone doesn't suit a fringe when they've had a fringe for years. I often feel – you must, too – that I know better than the customer, but you've got to be dead tactful if you suggest they try something else.'

'I see.' Alice sighed. On her visits to the salon she had noticed Fionnuala was a little brusque, but perhaps she was so used to her daughter's ways that she hadn't realised how much it would grate on other people. She had hoped making her manageress would give the girl the confidence she so obviously lacked, but clearly Fion couldn't be left to run the business into the ground. 'I'll have a word with Fion tonight,' she told Doreen. 'In the meantime, will you think twice about giving in your notice?'

'Of course I will, Alice. I never wanted to leave, it was just that Fion . . .' The woman paused and didn't continue.

'I don't suppose you feel fit enough to work full-time?' Alice said hopefully. 'I'll need someone straight away to manage the place and Katy's only twenty-one and not long qualified.' Katy Kelly was Alice's assistant.

Doreen's beautifully made-up face flushed with pleasure. 'Well, actually, Alice, I wouldn't mind. I was rather hoping you'd ask when the new branch opened. It's only across the road from where I live and it never gets hectic like it did in town. The customers are nicer too, not so demanding. They don't mind waiting a few minutes if there's the occasional rush on. There's just one thing, though, you won't be leaving Fion with me, will you? That would be dead unfair on the girl, us swopping places, like. Despite what I said, I'm quite fond of her.

Her heart's in the right place and she means well. She just doesn't know how to cope with people.'

'I'll let you have Katy. Fion can work with me so I can keep an eye on her.'

'But it's not fair!' Fion raged. 'Oh, Mam, it's not fair a bit. Doreen Morrison has never liked me. She's just making it up.'

Alice's heart went out to her gauche, bungling daughter, who was on the verge of tears. 'Fion, luv, Doreen wouldn't have gone to the extent of handing in her notice if she was just making it up. That would be cutting off her nose to spite her face. And is Chrissie making it up? Because she's thinking of leaving too. And what about the customers? Every week there's fewer and fewer. They're not staying away just to get at you, luv. You're not old enough for the responsibility yet, that's all. You make them feel uncomfortable for some reason.'

'I'm twenty-four.' Fion sniffed.

'It's all my fault.' Alice decided to put the blame on herself. 'Managing a hairdresser's was too much to ask of someone quite so young.'

But this only made things worse, because Fion said tragically, 'Our Orla's got four children and Maeve's a nurse. Running a crappy hairdresser's isn't much when compared to them and I can't even do that properly.'

'Do you really think it crappy?'

Fion laid her head on her mother's shoulder and began to cry. 'No, I loved it. It made me feel grown up and important. Oh, Mam!' she cried, 'what's wrong with me? No one likes me. Everything I say comes out wrong, unnatural, like. I can even hear it meself, this dead false voice.'

'You don't sound false to me, luv.' Alice stroked her daughter's brown hair. 'And don't forget how brilliant you were with Cora. You really knew how to put her in her place. Me, I was willing to lie down and let her tread all over me.'

'You were dead annoyed when I got Maurice to steal that agreement.'

'Well, I must admit I was upset at first, but it wasn't nearly as bad as what Cora did to me in the first place. I realised that after a while. It's nice to have all the money to ourselves.' She'd been so shocked when she heard what Fion had done that she'd actually considered letting Cora continue to have her share, but everyone – her dad and Bernadette, the children – said she was stark, raving mad even to think of such a thing. 'Anyroad, luv, as from tomorrow you'll be back in the old Lacey's with me. It'll be just like old times, won't it?'

Fion nodded forlornly. 'I suppose so.'

Alice told Neil what had happened when he commented on Fion's return to the salon. It was Thursday night and they were in bed together, having just made very satisfactory love.

'Poor kid,' Neil said sadly as he smoothed his hand over the curve of her hip. 'It must be awful to be so self-conscious.'

'The thing is, Orla, Maeve and Cormac have always been so sure of themselves, which can't have helped Fion much. It doesn't help that she eats like a horse, either. She's the same height as Orla, but her waist's at least six inches bigger.'

'When I heard about Babs, I drank like a fish for months,' Neil said thoughtfully. 'I suppose some people do the same thing with food. Fion only eats so much because she's unhappy.'

'Then what on earth can I do to make her happy?' Alice wailed.

'I've no idea.' Suddenly, Neil pinched her waist and she gave a little scream. 'The other day I was offered tickets for a dance at Bootle Town Hall. I turned them down,' he said with an exaggerated sigh, 'because the only person I wanted to take refuses to be seen in public with me. Why don't I take Fion? It might cheer her up a bit.'

Alice looked doubtful. 'Oh, I don't know, Neil. She might get ideas.'

'What sort of ideas?'

'That you're keen on her. She's definitely keen on you, I've told you so before.'

'I could say she was just doing me a favour, getting me out of a hole, because the girl I planned to take had let me down and I didn't want the tickets to go to waste. Actually, I wouldn't mind going,' he said in injured tones. 'I have no social life because of you.'

'Don't tell lies, Neil. You're always off to this and that.'

'Anyroad, about this dance – did you notice I just said "anyroad", which means I've become a genuine Liverpudlian – shall I ask Fion or not?'

'It might cheer her up, as you say – I can take her into town and buy her a new frock – but don't build up her hopes, Neil. She's miserable enough as it is. I don't want her heart broken as well.'

Fion had virtually stopped eating altogether. She had a slice of dry toast for breakfast, nothing for dinner and more dry toast for tea, because she was determined to squeeze into a size 40 frock for the dance at Bootle Town Hall instead of the usual 42. Alice had agreed to leave it till the very last minute before buying the dress and was actually closing the salon early on the day of the dance, at two instead of four.

'I want something black and slinky,' Fion said excitedly. 'Or really, really bright red, with straps as thin as shoelaces.'

'We'll just have to see,' Alice said, looking at her sharply. 'Why are you getting so excited? It's only a dance.'

'Yes, but I'm going with Neil,' Fion replied dreamily.

'Only as a replacement for the girl he really wanted to take.' Alice hoped she didn't sound too cruel, but it seemed her worst suspicions had been confirmed – Fionnuala was behaving as if Neil had proposed marriage.

Fion said, 'I think that was only a ruse, Mam. I think Neil's always wanted to ask me out, but didn't have the nerve.'

'Neil's never struck me as being short of nerve. Anyroad, he's much too old for you.'

'Oh, Mam, don't be daft. He's only ten years older. Grandad's twenty-one years older than Bernadette and you didn't turn a hair when they got married.'

Alice wondered if she should ask Neil to withdraw the invitation, but Fion would be bitterly disappointed. But she'd be just as disappointed when she realised Neil had no intention of asking her out again. She supposed that as, either way, Fion was bound to feel let down, she might as well enjoy the dance and feel let down afterwards rather than before.

She pleaded with Neil to be gentle with her daughter and he looked at her, hurt. 'As if I'd be anything else.'

Fion felt as if she was, quite literally, walking on air. The dance was all she talked about – the clothes she would wear, what sort of shoes and that if she kept on starving herself she might manage to squeeze into a size 38. She persuaded Orla's Micky to teach her how to foxtrot and they practised in the parlour of the little house in Pearl Street. She endlessly discussed with her mother exactly how she should do her hair: in one of the new bouffant styles, or the smooth look favoured by Lauren Bacall, or piled on top of her head in little curls. Or dare she risk one of them shaggy Italian cuts like Claudia Cardinale?

'For goodness sake, Fion,' her mother said impatiently, 'it's only a dance, not a reception at Buckingham Palace.'

Mam just didn't seem to comprehend the awesome significance of Neil asking her out. Fion had long been convinced that he was attracted to her. He was always so incredibly nice, so warmly understanding. Whenever they spoke, he gave her his undivided attention and asked all sorts of questions. Of course, Neil was nice to everyone, but she could tell she held a special place in his heart. He probably hadn't asked her before because he thought Mam might disapprove or Fion might turn him down. She didn't delve too deeply into exactly why he'd asked now, but he'd asked and that was all that mattered.

It was easy to imagine a bright, starry future – marrying Neil in about a year's time – she'd be down to size 36 by then and would wear one of those wedding dresses with a three-tiered skirt and have a bouquet of white roses with trailing ribbons. Orla could be a matron of honour and Maeve a bridesmaid – gosh, she'd, actually be getting married *before* Maeve! They would live somewhere dead posh like Crosby or Blundellsands, because teachers didn't normally live in places like Amber Street, except if they were unmarried, like Neil – like Neil was *now*.

The dance was three weeks away, two weeks, then only seven days. Fion continued to starve herself. Mam made her drink a glass of milk night and morning, and said it wouldn't do her any harm to lose a few pounds, dance or no dance. Mam positively refused to get into the spirit of things.

Only twenty-four hours to go. Fion lay on the bed in her room, her face covered in a mud pack and her feet on the headboard, which made the blood rush to the head and was good for the hair or the skin or the brain. Something.

Mam shouted up the stairs, 'I'm just nipping round to the salon for a few minutes. One of the dryers is playing up. I think it needs adjusting.'

'OK, Mam,' Cormac shouted from his bedroom in the new, deep voice he'd recently acquired. He was studying for yet more exams, but never seemed to mind.

'Tara, Mam,' Fion said tightly for fear she'd crack the mud pack, which felt like concrete and still had another five minutes to go.

The five minutes seemed to take for ever. Fion went downstairs and splashed the mud off in the kitchen. She went into the living room and examined her face in the mirror over the mantelpiece, and tried to decide if her skin looked softer, clearer, healthier, firmer, all the things it had promised on the packet. She wasn't quite sure. Mam had said the mud pack was a waste of time and money because Fion already had beautiful skin.

She had nice hair, too, thick and brown. But it was a very *ordinary* brown. Perhaps if Mam used one of them Tonrinzes when she set it tomorrow morning, auburn, say, it would bring out the highlights. She wondered if Mam had auburn in stock. She'd ask the minute she came home. No, she wouldn't. She'd go round now and check and, if necessary, call in the chemist's first thing tomorrow and buy one.

There was no need for a coat, not even a cardy, on such a lovely May evening. The sun was sliding behind the roofs of the houses, a great, flaming ball, briefly turning the grey slates into sheets of gleaming gold. Fion hummed to herself as she hurried along the street and through the entry into Opal Street. She opened the door of the salon, expecting to find her mother fiddling with a dryer – she hadn't noticed one was giving trouble. She was surprised to find no sign of Mam, either in the salon or the kitchen. The back door was locked, so she wasn't in the lavvy.

Perhaps she'd decided to call on Bernadette and Grandad, or she might have gone round to Orla's. Fion checked the box of Tonrinzes, found an auburn and was about to leave, when she realised she hadn't brought a key to lock the door – and why had it been unlocked in the first place? Mam must have forgotten to lock it when she left. Never mind, Neil would do it when he came home. She assumed he was out as there wasn't the faintest sound from the flat, no gramophone, no wireless.

She was about to leave a second time when she heard a woman laugh. The woman laughed again and Fion recognised Mam's warm, rusty chuckle.

From upstairs? Fion frowned. There was nothing wrong with Mam being upstairs, but why had it been so quiet until she laughed? And there was something odd about the laugh, something *intimate*.

Fion went to the bottom of the stairs. For some reason she felt reluctant to call out, announce her presence. She crept up a few steps until her eyes were level with the landing floor and glanced through the banisters. Neil's parlour, once a bedroom, was at the front. The boxroom was now the kitchen and the bedroom overlooked the backyard.

The doors to the parlour and kitchen were wide open, the one to the bedroom firmly closed and it was from behind this door that Fion heard her mother laugh again. Then Neil said something in a tone of voice she'd never heard him use before, soft and tender, throbbing with passion.

Mam was in bed with Neil Greene!

She could never remember leaving the salon, going home, but she must have done, because she was lying on the bed again – not crying, because she would never cry again, just staring at the ceiling, cold and shivering, numb with shock. Neil was in love with Mam, not her. He'd probably invited her to the dance because he felt sorry for her. It might even have been Mam's idea, to sort of make up for being demoted, for no longer being manageress of Lacey's in Marsh Lane.

'My life is a failure,' Fion said aloud.

'Did you just say something, sis?' Cormac shouted.

'No,' she shouted back.

'A complete failure.' She was whispering now, though there was no need to whisper, because everyone knew. Doreen Morrison and Chrissie O'Connell had refused to work with her, the customers hated her, her family felt sorry for her. 'I'm useless. There's something wrong with me.'

Fion felt overwhelmed by a black cloud of hopelessness and despair. When Mam came home, she shouted that she had a headache and had gone to bed early, and no, she didn't want an aspirin, thanks.

'I think you should start eating properly again as from tomorrer,' her mother called. 'I reckon you're overdoing it.'

'Yes, Mam.'

Maeve came home from her night out with Martin and Fion pretended to be asleep. She remembered she'd planned on having Maeve as a bridesmaid and wanted to curl up in embarrassment at even thinking such a thing. What a fool she'd been! And what was going to happen tomorrow? There was no way in the world she would go to that dance with Neil, and what reason could she give for refusing? If only she hadn't gone on about it so much to everyone she knew.

There was only one thing for it, Fion decided after a while, she'd just have to leave home.

When Fion woke up it was daylight, bright and sunny, though when she looked at her watch it was only six. The house was silent. She lay watching the sun filter through the curtains and asked herself if she still wanted to leave home.

She decided she did and that she would leave now, without telling anyone, before they got up, though she'd write a note. If she told Mam first, she'd only try to talk her out of it. Anyroad, she liked the idea of giving everyone a shock. Once she'd gone, they might appreciate her a bit more. She would come back in a year's time having made her fortune. Fion visualised herself with 36-inch hips and wearing a dead smart costume – black and white check with a velvet collar. She would be nice to everyone, not a bit toffee-nosed.

Unfortunately, the family didn't possess a suitcase. She managed to squeeze her underwear and a nightdress into the leatherette shopping bag that hung behind the kitchen door, and two frocks, a cardigan and some stockings into an Owen Owen's carrier bag with a string handle. She'd just have to wear her coat, which was a pity, because the day looked as if it was going to be a scorcher. It took some time deciding which shoes to wear, because sandals would look silly with the coat and heavy shoes equally silly in hot weather. In the end she decided on the shoes and managed to squeeze a sandal into each of the bags.

What to say in the note? One of Cormac's exercise books lay on the table. Only a few pages had been used.

She tore a page out of the middle, picked up Cormac's fountain pen and sat staring at the blank paper. She wanted to write, 'I'm going because I'm dead miserable and no one loves me,' so they'd all feel guilty and sorry for the way she'd been treated. But it might be better to leave them full of admiration for her bravery and spirit of adventure. 'I'm off to see the world,' she could put. 'Don't know when I'll be back.'

Upstairs, the springs creaked on the double bed and Fion wasn't sure what got into her, because all she wrote on the paper was, 'I know about you and Neil. Tara for ever, Fion.' She folded it up and tucked it behind a statue on the mantelpiece, because if Mam found it straight away she'd only come chasing after her. Flinging her handbag over her shoulder, she picked up the bags and left by the back way, which was quieter.

A few minutes later Fion had reached Marsh Lane, already having doubts and wishing she'd left the note in a more conspicuous place. She kept looking back, praying Mam would appear and persuade her to come home. If only she had a friend in whom she could confide, who would give her some encouragement, say she was doing the right thing. Or even talk her out of it, which would be even better. But there was no one.

Except Horace Flynn! He was the only person who didn't make her feel stupid, who was always pleased to see her. It was very much out of her way, but she'd call on him and say tara.

Horace Flynn didn't welcome the knock on his door at such an unholy hour. It was barely seven. If he hadn't thought it might be the postman with a registered letter containing someone's unpaid rent – it happened occasionally – he would have ignored the knock and stayed in bed.

Wrapping his roly-poly body in a plaid dressing gown, he went downstairs and found Fionnuala Lacey outside. Had it been anyone else in the world, he would have given them the sharp edge of his tongue, slammed the door in their face, but he'd always had a soft spot for Fionnuala, though even she wasn't exactly welcome at such an early hour.

'I'm running away from home,' the girl said breathlessly. 'I've come to say tara.'

The landlord was a lonely man, entirely friendless until he'd struck up a sort of relationship with this unsophisticated and rather naïve young woman. He felt hugely flattered that she'd come out of her way to say goodbye and stood aside to let her in. 'I'm very sorry to hear it,' he said, which was true. 'Would you like a cup of tea?'

'I'd love one. There wasn't time at home. I had to leave before anyone got up, see.'

'Is there any particular reason why you're running away from home?'

Fion followed him down the hall into the nicely furnished living room. She couldn't very well tell him about Mam and Neil. 'I'm twenty-four,' she said. 'I thought it was about time. I'm going to have lots of adventures.'

'I hope you do,' said Horace Flynn, who'd left Ireland forty years before in search of adventure and ended up a landlord whom no one liked. He noticed Fion's two inadequate bags. 'Would you like a suitcase?'

'If you've got one to spare. Call it borrowing. I'll bring it back one day.'

'Keep it. I doubt if I'll ever need it.' Horace put the kettle on and went upstairs. He returned with a leather case with straps, which someone had once given him in lieu of rent.

Fion looked pleased. 'That's big enough to take me

coat. I'll change me shoes, if you don't mind, put me sandals on.'

'Go ahead.' The kettle boiled. Horace made the tea and returned with two dainty cups and saucers on a tray. 'Do you take sugar?'

'I did till a few weeks ago. I don't now.'

'I thought there was a big dance tonight? You were buying a frock this afternoon, getting your hair done. You seemed to be looking forward to it, if I remember right.'

'I was, but I'm not now.' Fion shrugged nonchalantly. She was kneeling on the floor, folding her clothes inside the case, trying not to let him see her underwear in case it inspired him to pinch her bottom.

Horace sighed. 'I'll miss you.'

'I'll miss you too.'

It was worth being dragged so early out of bed for that. 'Have you got enough money?' Horace was astonished to hear the words come from his lips.

'Yes, thanks. I've got twelve pounds. It's me birthday money. I mean, it's what I've been saving up to buy presents.'

'That won't go far – where are you going, London?'

'I hadn't thought about it. I suppose London seems the obvious place.' People didn't run away to Birmingham or Manchester or Leeds.

'Just a minute.' Horace went into the parlour and opened the strong box which he kept hidden inside an antique commode. He removed twenty pounds, returned to the other room and handed the money to Fion.

She blushed scarlet. 'I can't take all that! It wouldn't be right.'

'It wouldn't be wrong either. If you like, look upon it as a loan. Once you're on your feet, you can pay me back. You don't want to come running home with your tail between your legs because you're out of money, do you?'

'No.'

Horace had the feeling that she didn't want to run away, that she wouldn't have minded being talked out of it. He felt tempted to dissuade her, because he would have preferred her to stay, but was prevented by a feeling of unselfishness that surprised him. He glanced at her fresh, innocent, unhappy face. It would do her good. She'd make proper friends, learn to be independent, find herself.

'Good luck,' he said.

Fion gulped down the remainder of her tea and got to her feet. 'I'd better get going.'

'You'll find plenty of cheap bed and breakfast hotels around Euston Station. They usually have the prices in the window. It would be best to stay there until you find somewhere permanent to live. Don't speak to any strange men,' he added warningly, suddenly concerned that the station would be teeming with men waiting for young girls like her to prey on, offering somewhere 'safe' to live.

'I won't. Thank you, Mr Flynn.'

He picked up the suitcase and took it to the door. 'Good luck again.'

'I'll send you a card as soon as I'm settled.'

'I'd appreciate that. I shall worry about you.'

'I know about you and Neil. Tara for ever, Fion.'

Alice's heart thumped painfully when she read the note that had been left on the mantelpiece. It was the first thing she'd noticed when she came downstairs.

How did Fion know? It could only be that she'd come

to the salon last night and heard Neil and her upstairs. She remembered thinking she'd heard a noise.

'I'm sure the salon door just closed,' she'd said.

'As long as it didn't open,' Neil had replied lazily. 'Come here! It's been a good five minutes since I've kissed you.'

She'd let him kiss her, forgotten about the noise. Until now. Poor, poor Fion! She'd be heartbroken. Alice, overwhelmed with guilt, was desperately trying to think of the best way of dealing with the situation when it dawned on her that Fion had written 'Tara for ever'.

She went to the bottom of the stairs. 'Fion!' she called, hardly able to breathe as she waited for an answer.

It was Maeve who shouted back. 'She's not here. She woke me up at the crack of dawn creeping about. That wardrobe door creaks like mad, Mam. It needs oiling.'

'Oh, my God!'

'What's up, Mam?' Cormac had woken.

'It's our Fion. I think she's run away.'

But she wouldn't run away for long, Alice told herself, not Fion. Fion was too clinging. She needed her family far more than the others. She wouldn't know how to manage on her own. Alice would like to bet she'd be back before the day was out – it might even be within a few hours, because she hadn't the nerve to go too far. Why, she might even be wandering around North Park at this very moment, already thinking about coming home.

When she did, she would have to be told what had happened between Neil and her mother as tactfully and as gently as humanly possible and then hope they would be able to keep the secret between the three of them.

Alice tried not to worry too much as the hours passed and still Fion didn't come home.

★

The hotel was called St Jude's, merely a large terraced house amid a long row of identical properties. It was spotless, but cleanliness was its only good point, unless you counted the strong smell of disinfectant that pervaded every nook and corner. Fion had never seen such a miserable room as the one in which she had just unpacked her case, transferring the clothes on to wire hangers in the wardrobe. A bottle-green candlewick quilt with bare patches covered the double bed and the heavy curtains were the same gloomy colour. The walls were possibly gloomier, a pale, muddy brown. There wasn't a single picture or ornament, just a dressing table and tallboy, that didn't match each other or the wardrobe. The floor covering was cheap and shiny, and boasted a faded rug beside the bed. She hadn't exactly been expecting luxury for 12/6d a night, but this was soulless, infintely depressing and suprisingly cold, considering it was such a lovely warm day outside.

'I'll go home tomorrer,' she said to herself. 'I've made me point, staying away a whole night.' She would give Mr Flynn his twenty pounds and his suitcase back.

When she arrived at Euston, she had contemplated catching the same train back, but something had prevented her, she wasn't sure what. Shame, perhaps, at the idea of running away and returning home the same day. Orla would laugh her head off, Maeve would disapprove, even Cormac would be cross with her for upsetting Mam. And poor Mam was probably doing her nut. She shouldn't have mentioned Neil in that note. After all, your mother having an affair wasn't a justifiable reason for leaving home. Neil was only being kind, asking her to the dance. And Mam had offered to do her hair and buy her a new dress. She was even closing the salon two hours early so they'd have time to shop.

Fion looked at her watch: seven o'clock. She'd taken

ages wandering around, trying to pluck up courage to enter a hotel, and had chosen this one because it was called after a saint, though she'd never heard of Jude and he mightn't even be a Catholic saint. Then she'd taken just as long sitting on the bed and trying to pluck up more courage to go out. It was twelve hours, almost to the dot, since she'd walked out of Amber Street. She shivered, feeling very odd and out of place in this miserable, anonymous room.

It was too early to go to bed because she wouldn't fall asleep for hours. She glanced from the bed to the door and decided she couldn't possibly stay in, not on such a beautiful evening. She'd have a wash first, but remembered she'd forgotten to bring soap and a towel, a hairbrush, lipstick, her toothbrush.

Fortunately there was a linen towel as stiff as cardboard folded over the sink and a tiny slab of yellow soap. Fion splashed her face, and rubbed her finger on the soap and cleaned her teeth. It tasted dreadful. After changing into one of her frocks, she ran her fingers through her hair, collected her bag and left to explore London.

There was a notice behind the front door announcing, THIS DOOR WILL BE LOCKED AT 10.30 p.m. Fion was about to leave, when the door marked RECEPTION opened and the woman who'd taken her money poked out her head.

'Have you read the notice?' she demanded.

'Yes, thank you.' She was a horrible woman, all sharp corners, even on her face.

'Well, just make sure you remember. I don't open the door to no one after half past ten.'

'I'll remember,' Fion said politely, wondering what on earth she was doing in this strange city, being spoken to by a strange woman as if she were a piece of dirt, when she could have been at home. She must be mad.

Outside, a huge, glittering sun hung low in the sky.

This was the same sun that was setting on Amber Street the day before when she'd been on her way to the salon. Things had changed so much since then.

Fion made her way back to Euston Station, then wandered along Euston Road, which was busy with traffic, though there were few pedestrians. She came to a road full of shops, all closed, naturally, though there were more people around. It was called Tottenham Court Road, she noticed as she crossed towards it, and it was very long.

At the end she reached a busy junction where a man was selling newspapers, shouting in what could have been a foreign language for all the sense it made. There was a cinema with a large queue outside, several cafés and a stall offering souvenirs of London: mugs and tea towels and replicas of London buses. People were pouring up steps from the bowels of the earth. Fion rounded a corner and found herself in Oxford Street.

She'd heard of Oxford Street. She must be in the very epicentre of London. Regent Street was probably not far away and Piccadilly Circus. Returning to the kiosk, she bought a map of London, despite it being a waste of money. After all, she was going home tomorrow. She noticed the film on at the cinema was *War and Peace* with Henry Fonda and Audrey Hepburn, which she'd planned on going to see with Mam when it came to Liverpool.

There was a self-service café at the top of Oxford Street. Fion went in for something to eat and to study the map – she must have lost pounds today, all she'd had was Horace Flynn's tea.

After she'd devoured two ham sandwiches and drunk a pot of tea, she found Piccadilly Circus on the map and began to wander towards it, pausing frequently to stare at the beautiful clothes in the very expensive shops. Regent Street was particularly grand and even more expensive.

The sun was setting lower now, casting sharp black shadows across the street, and the pavements were crowded with pedestrians, some wearing evening dress, obviously off to nightclubs or cocktail parties or theatres, or wherever people went in London on Saturday nights. As she passed a place called the Café Royal, a big, black car drew up and two women alighted, both wearing long satin frocks and smelling richly of perfume. One woman had a white fur cloak draped round her shoulders, which Fion thought was showing off a bit, as it was far too warm a night for furs.

She found she had arrived at Piccadilly Circus, which was drenched in golden sunshine and throbbing with life. The steps around the statue of Eros were crowded and neon lights flashed palely in the evening sunshine. Fion glimpsed a Boots chemists, still surprisingly open. She went in and bought the toiletries she'd forgotten to bring, which made a big hole in her money. Then she dodged through the traffic towards Eros, climbed a few steps, and sat down between an elderly couple with a small dog and a young man with a haversack at his feet. The dog, on a lead, came waddling towards her. She stroked it and the couple smiled. 'He won't bite,' the woman said. 'Lovely evening, isn't it?'

'Lovely,' Fion agreed and found herself smiling broadly for no reason, conscious of a strange mechanism behind her eyes making them sparkle brilliantly. She gasped and excitement coursed through her body like an electric shock, accompanied by a feeling of enormous triumph. Maeve might well be a nurse and Orla have four children, but neither had ever made it to London on their own. No one she knew had sat on the steps of Eros on Saturday night, breathing in the heady atmosphere, the *foreignness* of it all.

The young man beside her thrust a bar of chocolate in her direction. Fion took a square and muttered her thanks. It was dark and tasted bitter. It turned out the young man, like the chocolate, came from Belgium. He spoke only a few words of English and Fion didn't know a word of French, so communication was limited, though very pleasant. He left after a while, saying something about a youth hostel. Fion remembered she had to be back at the hotel by half-ten. Somewhat reluctantly, she started back. She'd probably walked further than she'd thought and had better give herself at least an hour. According to the map, the steps leading down to the bowels of the earth that she'd passed several times were stations on the London Underground. The system looked very complicated and this wasn't the time to try it out for the first time.

She would disentangle the workings of the Underground tomorrow and hoped it would be a nice day to explore the further wonders of London.

Fion entirely forgot that tomorrow she had made up her mind to go home.

While Fion was on her way back to the hotel, in Liverpool in the flat above Lacey's hairdressing salon Alice and Neil Greene were having an argument, something that didn't happen often. They usually got on exceptionally well. Had things gone as planned, Neil and Fion would have been at the dance by now.

They were in the parlour, fully dressed, sitting separately on each side of the empty fireplace. Alice had flatly refused to go to bed. She'd come for one reason only, to tell Neil their relationship must end.

'Just because Fion found out?' His jaw sagged.

'No, of course, not,' Alice snapped. 'Well, yes, in a way, I suppose it is. If Fion found out, then so can other people. I'm surprised we've gone a whole five years without anyone finding out before.' The trouble was, time had flashed by. It was half a decade since she'd confronted her husband in Crozier Terrace and discovered he was leading two lives, yet it felt like only yesterday. 'She must have heard us, Fion, last night when we were upstairs. Remember I said I thought I heard the door close?'

'Hmm.' Neil stared at the ceiling, then said casually, 'Why don't we get married?'

'Oh, don't be stupid, Neil,' Alice said more brutally than she intended. 'In case you haven't noticed, you've already got a wife and I've got a husband.'

'Babs regularly asks me to divorce her. You could divorce your husband; you've got enough grounds.'

'Oh, yes, and have me dirty linen washed all over Bootle. I'd look a right fool, wouldn't I? Me husband sets up house with another woman, has another family. What would people think?'

Neil said gently, 'Is that all that matters to you, Alice? Your reputation, what people think? Surely happiness, yours and mine, comes first?'

'I wouldn't be happy, knowing people were laughing at me behind me back,' Alice replied. 'And what about me kids? I've never told them what their dad got up to. They think he just left home, full stop. I'd sooner they never knew. They've already been hurt enough, particularly Cormac.'

'In other words there's no hope for us.' His face looked very drawn all of a sudden. 'I suppose it's no use asking you to come away with me so we can live together somewhere else?'

'No use at all, Neil. I belong here, with me family.'

'Have you ever loved me? You've said it enough times.'

'I *do* love you, Neil.' But not enough to get divorced. Even if the divorce went through without a public scandal, she wasn't the type of woman who got rid of her husband. She'd married John for better or for worse. They were joined together in the eyes of God for ever and a day. 'Oh, luv,' she said, more gently now, 'I shouldn't have let it go on for so long. I've been wasting your time, preventing you from meeting someone else. Even if there was nothing to stop us, I would never marry you, Neil. You're too young, I'm too old and I could never bring meself to meet your family, not with me speaking the way I do. I'd like you to marry someone young enough to give you children. Mind you, if word got round you were getting divorced, you'd lose your job. You work in a Catholic school, remember.'

Neil almost laughed. 'I suppose that means I'm stuck with Babs for the rest of my life.'

'Unless you get another, different kind of job, I suppose it does.'

'So, this is the end?'

'No, luv, it's just the beginning. It's been very nice, but we've been wasting each other's time all this while.'

'I certainly haven't been wasting *my* time and I would have described it as more than just nice,' he said drily.

'Oh, Neil, so would I!' Alice ran across the room and threw herself on to his knee. 'It's been truly wonderful, I'll never forget you, but all good things have to come to an end.'

He kissed her softly. 'Not necessarily, my darling.'

'This good thing has, Neil.'

'Do you have to sound so sensible?'

'It's about time one of us did. I'm almost glad our

Fionnuala found out. It's made me see things clearly at last.'

He began to kiss her more passionately and she couldn't find the strength to push him away – perhaps the truth was she didn't want to find it. She wished she weren't so sensible, so religious, so cautious, that she could find the courage to live with him openly and not give a damn about being respectable and what anyone thought. Or that she were harder, like John, able to leave the people she loved behind without a second thought.

But she was none of these things. She was Alice Lacey, who had four children, who lived in Amber Street, Bootle and owned her own hairdressers'. Somehow Alice knew she would never escape these simple facts, because deep down in her heart she didn't want to. She was her own jailer, bound by conventions she would never break. Even her love for Neil, which was far greater than she had ever admitted either to him or to herself, wasn't enough to change her.

He was carrying her into the bedroom and she didn't protest.

'We didn't know last night we would never make love again,' he whispered, 'and I'd like the last time to be special. Promise you'll never forget me, Alice.'

'I promise,' she cried.

It was an hour later when Alice crept out of the flat, leaving behind a shattered lover and some part of herself.

She prayed he'd soon see sense, realise he was wasting his time with a woman who wasn't willing to be seen with him in public, a woman who could never marry him, bear his children.

Oh, but she would never forget him, Alice thought as she hurried home, fighting back the tears.

She increased her pace. Neil wasn't the only person

who made her want to cry. There'd been no sign of Fion all day. Perhaps she was home by now . . .

But when Alice got back to Amber Street, Fion wasn't there. A worried Orla was, as well as Maeve and Martin, who'd been to the pictures and come back early just in case Fion had shown up.

The only person seemingly unconcerned was Cormac. 'She'll be all right,' he'd said earlier. 'Our Fion will manage better on her own than any one of us.'

'What makes you say that, son?' Alice asked curiously.

'Because she's unhappy, not like us. She's searching for something we've already found. Of course, she might come back today or tomorrow, but if she manages to stick it out for longer, then I doubt if we'll see her in a long time.'

Which didn't exactly cheer Alice up on top of everything else.

Chapter 9

The girl who served Fion's breakfast next morning was a distinct improvement on the woman she'd met the previous night. 'How would you like your bacon, darlin'?' she enquired, smiling sweetly, when she removed the cornflake bowl. She was about eighteen, not exactly pretty, but with big, velvety brown eyes. Her brown hair was badly cut, as if she'd hacked it off herself.

'Well, I don't like it crisp.'

'Neither do I. I'll do it medium, shall I? I won't be a jiffy.'

The dining room was every bit as miserable as the bedroom, possibly worse, with a depressing painting of a frantic-looking stag in the middle of a forest hanging above the blocked-up grate. There were only five other people there: a middle-aged couple, two Chinese girls and an elderly man who wished her good morning when she entered.

Fion sat in the window and ordered cornflakes, bacon and egg, and a pot of tea. Having this admittedly small control over her life gave her a heady feeling of adult responsibility.

The girl arrived with a slice of pink bacon, a neatly fried egg and half a tomato on a plate, as well as a rack with four triangular slices of toast. There was a saucer containing pats of butter and a small bowl of marmalade already on the table.

'Thank you, that looks lovely.'

'Let's hope it tastes as nice as it looks.'

'It did,' Fion said when the girl came to collect her plate. By now, only the elderly man remained, having finished eating and smoking a cigarette. 'Taste as nice as it looked, that is. Do you make the meals as well as wait on tables?' It seemed a lot for one person to do, especially one so young.

'Only on Sundays, when there's not usually many guests. Are you on holiday?'

Fion wasn't sure why she was there. 'I'm going sightseeing today,' she said, which didn't really answer the question. 'I thought I'd start off at Marble Arch and walk through Hyde Park.'

'Well, you've picked a smashing day for it. I hope you see all you want to see. Oh, by the way, Mrs Flowers wants to know if you're staying another night. She said you only paid for the one.'

Mrs Flowers seemed a most unsuitable name for the sharp cornered woman. 'That's right, I wasn't sure. I'll definitely be staying another night. I'll knock on Reception and pay on me way out, if that's all right.'

'That'll be just fine.'

It genuinely was a smashing day, Fion thought outside, just as the girl had said. For some reason she could smell blossom, though there was no sign of any trees. At Euston Station she bought a guidebook – more waste of money if she didn't intend to stay – then located the entrance to the tube.

She felt quite proud, after buying a ticket, of being able to negotiate her way to Marble Arch, emerging in sunshine that seemed to have got brighter during the short journey underground.

Large crowds were gathered just inside the park and

she noticed several men perched on boxes loudly sounding off about all sorts of things – according to the guidebook, this was Speakers' Corner. One man appeared to be arguing that the world was flat. Fion listened for a few minutes and decided he was daft. She was about to explore the vast greenness of Hyde Park, when at the edge of the crowd she noticed a woman speaker surrounded by about a dozen men, all heckling so ferociously that the poor woman could scarcely be heard above the chorus of insults being thrown in her direction.

'And why shouldn't women be paid at the same rate as men?' the woman wanted to know in a dead posh voice. 'Equal pay for equal work. It's already happening in the public sector, the NHS, the Gas and Electricity Boards, the Civil Service, so why not in the private sector too? It makes sense if you think about it.'

'Rubbish!' yelled a man. '*I've* just thought about it and it makes no sense to me.'

'Women are the weaker sex. They can only manage half the output of a man,' another man yelled.

'Now it's *you* who's talking rubbish,' the woman countered. She didn't seem the least bothered by her voluble and antagonistic audience. She was very tall, with intense black eyes and greying hair. 'During the war, women did the work of men. They worked on lathes and milling machines, they riveted, they welded . . .'

'They screwed,' one man interjected to gales of male laughter.

'They drove lorries and tractors,' the woman continued as if she hadn't heard, 'dug fields, planted corn, joined the Army, the Navy and the Air Force, worked in field hospitals, delivered post . . .'

'Took off their knickers,' the same man shouted and was greeted with more hearty laughter.

'Why don't you take *yours* off, luv? Give us an eyeful.'

'She's nothing but a bloody lesbian. I bet she only shows herself to other women.'

Fionnuala, at the back of the crowd, was aware of the same hot feeling inside her head that she'd had when Cora Lacey tried to bully Mam. 'You're worse than animals, youse lot,' she screamed. 'If it weren't for women, not one of you would be here. Men like you ought to be strangled at birth. You're not fit to live, not one of you. Haven't you heard of free speech? It's what we fought for during the war, but you're not willing to listen to a word you don't agree with.'

The men had turned from the speaker and were regarding Fion with glazed eyes. 'Now, you look here . . .' One took a threatening step towards her, but Fion took an even more threatening step towards *him*.

'Don't like it, do you?' she sneered. 'Don't like it when someone insults *you*. You're lily-livered cowards, that's why.'

'If you were a bloke, I'd give you a punch on the nose.'

'Oh, yeah! Just because me opinion's different from yours?'

The men began to drift away, having lost interest, or perhaps they preferred their own rude heckling to being verbally assailed by a woman, particularly one so young with a Liverpool accent.

'Well, you were a great help, I must say,' the speaker remarked when the men had gone and she was surrounded by just Fion and fresh air. 'It's best to have an audience, even if they're an unpleasant lot, than to have no audience at all. I might have got through to at least one of them.'

'I'm sorry.' Until then, Fion had been feeling very

225

proud of herself, expecting the woman to welcome support from a member of the same sex.

'That's all right.' The woman grinned cheerfully. 'I know you meant well but, in future, try to structure your thoughts, make pertinent points, don't just come out with mouthfuls of invective. It doesn't get us anywhere. By "us", I mean women.'

'I'm sorry,' Fion repeated.

'That's all right. I'll just have to start again. Here, take a leaflet, so next time you let off steam you'll have the facts at your disposal.'

Fion wandered away. When she looked back, the woman was once again surrounded by a small group of men, several of whom were already shaking their fists.

She tried not to let the incident spoil her day, though every now and then she would find herself thinking up more insulting things she wished she'd said and tried to structure the insults into pertinent points. She read the leaflet, which had been issued by the Equal Pay Campaign.

The park was gradually becoming fuller. People had come to sunbathe, to fish, talk, watch their children play, to sit and lean against a tree and read the Sunday paper, or just stroll across the emerald-green grass on what was undoubtedly a glorious morning.

After studying the map, Fion realised she was now in Kensington Gardens and there should be a café around somewhere. She was longing for a cup of tea, after which she'd go to the Natural History Museum, then catch the tube to the Tower of London. Tonight she'd have a meal in Lyons Corner House, which she'd noticed by Marble Arch, then go to see *War and Peace* in the cinema at the top of Tottenham Court Road.

Late in the afternoon she remembered it was Sunday and, for the first time in her life, she hadn't been to Mass.

She caught the tube to Westminster Cathedral and went to Benediction instead. It didn't make up for Mass, but would do just for today.

The room in St Jude's was beginning to look a bit like home. On the dressing table there were a hairbrush, a lipstick and a *Woman's Own* with a picture of Princess Margaret on the front: toothbrush, paste and a pink flannel on the sink, and that day's pants hanging underneath to dry. On the bedside table the guidebook and map were waiting for her to study when she got into bed, so she could decide where to go tomorrow.

It was strange, but she had felt much lonelier in Liverpool, living within the bosom of her closely knit family, than she did in this anonymous city where she didn't know a soul. It was as if she was no longer her mother's daughter, no longer sister to Orla and Maeve. She badly missed Cormac because he was the only person who'd never done or said anything that made her feel bad about herself.

Before opening the guidebook Fion counted her money. She hadn't touched Mr Flynn's twenty pounds, but the twelve pounds she'd saved for presents had almost gone. Twelve pounds! In only two days! At this rate there'd be no money left by the end of the week. And what was she supposed to do then?

There were two obvious answers: return to Liverpool, or obtain more money, and the only way to do that was to get a job. Fion found it a tiny bit disturbing that she much preferred the second answer to the first.

'I'm sorry, Missus,' the police sergeant said portentously, 'but your daughter's an adult. She can leave home if she wants. You can't expect us to go chasing after a woman of twenty-four. Under eighteen, yes. Over eighteen, folks can do as they please and it's no one's business but their own.'

'But she's only a very *young* twenty-four. She's never even been to the pictures by herself.'

'She's still twenty-four. And she didn't just disappear into thin air, did she? You say she left a note. Have you got it with you?'

'No.' Alice had only shown the note to Neil.

'Did it say where she was going?'

Alice sighed. 'No.'

'Well, it would seem she doesn't want you to know.' The policeman suddenly softened. 'Try not to worry, Missus. She'll soon realise which side her bread is buttered and come back.'

'Let's hope so,' Alice muttered as she left the station.

Fion had been gone almost a week. Alice would have worried more had not Cormac been so convinced she was all right. As it was, she felt guilt-stricken that she'd allowed Neil to ask the poor girl out, build up her hopes, then have them dashed so cruelly. Fion was such an impressionable girl. How must she have felt when she heard her mother and Neil together? She must have come round to the salon for some reason and it could only be to do with the dance the following night. She'd been so excited, *too* excited.

Her other daughters shared their mother's guilt, particularly Orla. 'I should have been nicer to her,' she wailed. 'I was horrible most of the time, yet I felt dead sorry for her.'

'Perhaps she left because she didn't want people feeling sorry for her,' Cormac suggested.

'*I* dropped her like a hot brick when I met Martin,' Maeve moaned. 'We always went to the pictures together on Sunday nights, but we haven't gone for months.'

'It was wrong of me to have made her manageress of the new salon, then just snatch the job away. I should have thought before I acted. She was far too young.' Then there was the business with Neil, which she couldn't reveal. Alice wondered what Fion was doing right now, on Friday night, six days after she had so abruptly left. Whatever it was, wherever *she* was, the poor girl was bound to be alone and as miserable as sin.

Fion was in a pub, the Golden Lamb on Pentonville Road, with Elsa, Elsa's dad, Colin, and Elsa's grandma, Ruby. The pub was bursting at the seams, there was sawdust on the floor, a spittoon in the corner and most of the customers were already sociably drunk. Hidden from view, a pianist was thumping out 'Somewhere Over the Rainbow', his or her foot stuck firmly on the loud pedal.

Elsa was the girl who served the breakfasts in St Jude's – and cleaned the rooms and made the beds, Fion discovered after she'd been there a few days.

'I need to find somewhere to live,' she had confessed to Elsa a few days ago when the money from Horace Flynn was reduced to half. 'Do you know of anywhere?'

They had already started to chat while the breakfast tables were being cleared. She had told Elsa that she'd left home, not run away, which sounded a bit silly at her age.

The hotel was almost full, mainly with commercial travellers – one had given Fion a folding clothes brush and a window leather.

'I'll ask around, darlin',' Elsa promised. 'Do you want lodgings or a place where you look after yourself?'

'Which is cheapest?'

'Lodgings. You get breakfast and an evening meal for an all-in price.'

'Lodgings, then. I prefer the other, but I'll wait till I'm settled in a job.'

'What sort of job?'

'I'm not sure.' Fion made a face. 'Any sort of job as long as it's not hairdressing.'

'Elsa, dear!' Mrs Flowers called from the kitchen. She was always very nice to Elsa. At first, Fion had been surprised, until she realised Elsa was an exceptionally hard worker and very reliable.

'See you tomorrow,' the girl said.

Fion drained the teapot, put the two remaining triangles of toast in her bag to eat later and set off for another day of sightseeing. She wouldn't spend a single penny she didn't have to, so the remaining money would last as long as possible. It meant no more pictures, which was a pity, as she'd be stuck for something to do at night. Yesterday, she'd seen *Seven Brides for Seven Brothers* and fallen in love with Howard Keel, the day before . . . *And God Created Woman* with Brigitte Bardot.

The weather was still fine and the busy London streets were flooded with sunshine. Fion mingled with tourists and shoppers, with office and shop workers, and felt extraordinarily happy. At one o'clock she went to Piccadilly Circus, bought coffee in a cardboard cup and sat on the steps of Eros, eating the toast and feeling on top of the world.

In the Golden Lamb Ruby Littlemore enquired, 'How's the digs, darlin'?' Ruby was mildly drunk on Guinness. She had jet-black, tightly permed hair, purple-painted lips and too much mascara. She was young to be Elsa's grandma, fifty-seven, but then Colin, Elsa's dad, was only thirty-eight and looked young enough to be her brother.

'Not so bad,' said Fion. 'The room's a bit small and nowhere's very clean, and I got tripe and onions for me tea, which I can't stand. Mrs Napier looked a bit put out when I asked her not to give it me again, as if she doesn't know how to cook anything else.'

'She'll think of something,' Ruby said. 'Blimey, you don't need more than one set of brains to come up with sausage and mash. Are you hungry, darlin'?' she asked in a concerned voice. 'Come back to ours later and I'll knock you up a plate of something.'

'Thanks, but I bought a meat and potato pie on the way.' It had been absolutely delicious.

'Come round tomorrer for your dinner, anyway. Sat'days, I usually make a stew with all the leftovers. Elsa doesn't work Sat'days. I don't know if she told you.'

'Yes, she's taking me to Camden Market to buy some dead cheap clothes. I didn't bring enough with me. We're going dancing at the Hammersmith Palais tomorrer night. I'm cutting her hair before. And I'd like to come to dinner, ta.' A midday meal wasn't included in the thirty-five shillings a week Mrs Napier charged.

'Elsa ses you're starting work Monday.' Colin Littlemore, sitting on Fion's other side, couldn't possibly be described as handsome. He was desperately thin, with brown, haunted eyes, hollow cheeks and a soft, curvy mouth. Nevertheless, Fion thought him enormously attractive, far more so than Neil Greene, who hadn't an ounce of character in his face. She thought it odd that she hadn't noticed that before. During the war, Colin had been taken prisoner by the Japanese and put to work building a railway. He had managed to stay alive, but returned home an invalid, unable to work, his health in ruins. There was something wrong with his lungs, he couldn't breathe properly and could only eat the tiniest of meals. He was sitting with an untouched glass of orange juice in front of him. His wife, Elsa's mother, had been killed during the war when the factory in which she worked was bombed.

Fion said, 'I saw a notice outside a factory just along the road. It said "Packers Wanted". It's called Pentonville Medical Supplies. I just walked in and they took me on straight away. I start Monday,' she finished proudly. She had a job and somewhere to live in London, and it was as if Liverpool and her family had never existed.

Colin wrinkled his thin nose. 'That company pays terrible rates.'

'Four and six an hour, but I don't care as long as it keeps me going.'

'You *should* care. The labourer's worthy of his hire. I knew a bloke who worked there once. He said they refused to recognise a union.'

Fion wasn't interested in unions. No one had ever talked about unions or politics at home, mainly about hairdressing. She was reminded of the leaflet she'd been given in Hyde Park, which was still in her bag. She took it out and showed it to Colin.

'Quite right, too,' he said after he'd read it. 'Equal pay for equal work; it makes sense.'

'That's what the woman said who gave it me. I suppose it does when you think about it; make sense, that is. Anyroad, I got really mad with the men who were trying to shout her down. I shouted them down instead.'

Colin smiled his gentle, boyish smile. 'Good for you, darlin'. If more people lost their tempers when they thought something was unfair, then the world would be a much better place.' He raised an eyebrow. 'What if Pentonville Medical Supplies are paying men more for doing the same job as women?'

'Oh, gosh! I hadn't thought of that. I suppose I'll get mad, like I did in Hyde Park.'

'Let's hope so.' He suddenly got to his feet. 'I'll have to go.' His voice was suddenly hoarse. 'This smoke don't

232

do me lungs no favours.' The smoke was rising towards the ceiling in white, wavy layers.

'I wouldn't mind an early night. I've had a busy week and I'm dead tired. I'll come with you – that's if you don't mind.'

'It'll be a pleasure, darlin'.'

'I'll just say goodnight to Elsa.'

The pianist was playing 'We'll Meet Again', when Fion and Colin Littlemore left the Golden Lamb and began to stroll down Pentonville Road. He was hardly as tall as her and as slight as a shadow. The tiny terraced house where he lived with his mother and his daughter was two streets along. Fion's digs were down a street almost opposite.

It seemed entirely natural for Fion to link her arm in his thin one. She thought how nice and uncomplaining he was, compared with her own father who'd made the whole family suffer for the injury he'd received during the war, finally doing a bunk and completely disappearing out of their lives.

They walked in companionable silence until arriving at the street where Colin lived. 'Would you like me to come in and make you a cup of tea?' Fion asked.

'I'd appreciate that, darlin'.' Colin patted her hand. He didn't think he'd ever met anyone so vulnerably innocent as Fionnuala Lacey. He remembered reading once that newly born chicks attached themselves to the first human being they clapped eyes on because they didn't have a mother. Fion had left home and attached herself in the same way to Elsa, then to Elsa's family, because she felt friendless and unbearably lonely. At the same time, he reckoned that if circumstances called for it, she could be quite tough.

'I'll send me mam a card tomorrer,' Fion said as they turned the corner. 'She's probably dead worried.'

'She's more likely climbing the walls.'

'I won't give her me address, though. I'll just say I'm all right.'

'That'll put her mind at rest. Actually, darlin',' he panted, 'I think I'll have to sit on the step a minute, get me breath back, before I go in the house.'

Fion sat on the step beside him. 'Is there anything I can do? Rub your back, or something?'

'No, but you can go in and put the kettle on. Here's the key.'

'Ta.'

He heard her run down the hall, anxious to help, then the rush of water in the kitchen, and thought she would make a good, caring mother – and a wonderful wife. With someone like Fion Lacey at his side, a man could conquer the world.

Colin smiled, then gave a little sigh. If only he were younger and in better health . . .

The young woman emerged from the art college into the grey drizzle of the late October day. She carried a large folder, the sides tied together with tape, underneath her arm. In her black and white striped slacks and baggy red jumper, and with her fair hair loose about her face, she looked like a teenager, but the man concealed in the doorway further down Hope Street knew that she was thirty and had three children, all old enough to be at school.

It was for this reason, to collect the children on time, that she was walking so swiftly and purposefully. He knew, because he had watched before, that she would walk all the way to Exchange Station rather than catch a bus somewhere more convenient like Skelhorne Street. A bus could get caught up in traffic and she might be late. She was a conscientious mother to her children.

More students came out of the college. One, a young man in his twenties, saw the young woman hurrying away. His face broke into a smile as he ran to catch her up. The woman smiled back, but didn't pause in her stride. The watching man shrank into the doorway when they passed on the other side.

What were they talking about? Would the chap accompany her all the way to the station? They might even catch the train together. The man in the doorway took a deep, shuddering breath. He smelt danger.

Clare and the young man parted on the corner of Lime Street and he went to catch the train to Rock Ferry. She wondered if John was still watching. Had he followed her this far? Or was he racing back to the factory in the van preparing for tonight's interrogation, starting with, 'Did you talk to anyone today?'

'Of course,' she would say. 'I couldn't very well spend the entire day at art school without speaking to a soul.'

'What about on the way home?'

As he'd seen her with Peter White, she'd have to concede that she had indeed spoken to someone on the way home. It was no good trying to laugh the questions away, because he would just persist and persist until he got an answer, even if it was an answer he didn't want.

'Yes, I spoke to someone on the way home. His name is Peter White, he lives in Rock Ferry and he's twenty-one. His mam and dad are Quakers. Anything else? Would you like his chest measurements? What he has for breakfast? How often he has his hair cut?'

But she wouldn't say all those things, because she'd done it before and John had called her 'insolent' and hit her. She would answer the question simply and leave it at that.

Passing St George's Hall, two men whistled at her

approach. She felt, rather than saw, them both turn and watch her walk away, and was aware of letting her hips swing more widely. It was more than a year since she'd had the operation and her perfectly mended face still gave her a thrill of delight when she caught sight of her reflection in a shop window or an unexpected mirror.

She would always be grateful to John, but he seemed to want more than gratitude and she didn't know what it was – to cocoon her from life, to hide her away out of sight of other human beings. It had been like a red rag to a bull when she said she wanted to go to art school because she'd longed to learn to draw – properly, not the scrawly, amateur things she'd done before.

John had done his utmost to stop her: threatened, bullied, refused to give her the money for the fees. Hit her!

'It's either art school or I'll get a job,' Clare said coldly. 'I'm not staying in the house by myself for the rest of my life.' She was bored out of her mind, full of unusual energy, the urge to explore, get to know people. But it was as if she'd escaped from the prison of her deformity and found herself in another, private, prison with John the warder.

'Meet anyone today?' John asked casually that night when she came downstairs after reading the children their story.

'I meet all sorts of people all day long.'

'I meant anyone special, that is.'

'I don't know what you mean by "special".' She knew she was being awkward, but 'special' seemed a strange word to use. Perhaps it was the only one he could think of to describe the short walk she'd taken with Peter White.

She could tell he was struggling to think of another way to pose the question and felt sick to her soul at the idea of having to relate in detail the entirely innocuous things she'd said to Peter. She wondered what his reaction would be if he knew Peter had asked her out! Imagine telling him *that*!

'I'm going to bed.' She got up abruptly. 'I feel very tired.' It was only half past eight and she resented having to go so early, but it was the only way to escape further interrogation. She would have liked to practise her drawing.

'I'll be up in a minute. I'm fair worn out too.'

Don't hurry, she wanted to say. Please don't hurry. These days, she couldn't stand him touching her. His eager, exploring fingers made her stomach turn. There was something so *possessive* about the way he made love. He made her feel like a thing, not a person.

This can't go on, Clare thought as she pulled the bedclothes around her shoulders. I can't put up with this much longer. I *won't* put up with it. She'd cast out on her own before and would do it again, though this time she wouldn't be on her own but would have three children. She thought of disappearing to another country, Canada or Australia, but the children had Lacey on their birth certificates and she didn't have wedding lines to prove she was their mother. John's authority would be required before they would be given passports and he mustn't know they were leaving. She had the uneasy feeling he might kill her if he found out.

She would finish the art course first so it would be easier to get a job. And she would need money. Fortunately, John was generous with the housekeeping. She'd start putting a few pounds aside each week. It would take a while, but she already felt better, knowing there was a future in which John Lacey no longer figured. She would be free.

'Our Fion? Oh, she's living in London,' Alice announced gaily. 'She went weeks ago. She's having the time of her life.'

'Is she working in a hairdresser's?' the customer enquired.

Patsy O'Leary answered: 'Yes, in this dead posh place in Knightsbridge, not far from Harrods, as it happens.' Patsy was innocently relaying the lie Alice had told her to explain Fion's sudden disappearence.

Alice went into the kitchen and the customer winked at Patsy. 'I suppose she'll be back in six or seven months and the population of the world will have increased by one.'

'Oh, no,' Patsy said, annoyed. 'Not Fionnuala. She's not a bit like that.'

The woman looked suitably chastened and changed the subject to one close to Patsy's heart. 'How's your Daisy's Marilyn?

'Oh, she's fine. You'll never believe this, but she's only nine months old and already walking . . .'

As Patsy had predicted, the customer didn't believe a single word.

Orla only had to mention once to her father-in-law that she would very much like a typewriter for him to arrive at the house in Pearl Street within a week, bearing an old, battered Royal. He winked. 'You'll never guess where this came from!'

'Oh, yes I do.' Orla had known where it would come from when she'd asked him to get it. The backs of lorries proved a useful source of supply whenever they needed something they couldn't afford. Lulu's new bike had come the same way and several other of the children's toys.

'It works OK,' Bert said. 'I've tried it. Managed to

type me own name, though it took a good ten minutes. Where would you like it, luv?'

'In the parlour. Thanks, Bert.'

'Any time, luv. All you have to do is ask.'

Orla was about to joke she wouldn't have minded a mink coat, but held her tongue in case one appeared.

'Now, you look here,' she said sternly to the children that night. 'This is not a toy to be played with. This is *mine*. Do you understand that?' She spelt the word out carefully. 'M – I – N – E. It belongs to your mum.'

'Can you get toy ones?' Lulu wanted to know.

'I'm not sure. I'll ask Grandad.'

'What's it for, luv?' Micky asked when he came home. Maisie and Gary were attached to his legs, and he was holding baby Paul in his arms. Lulu, her arms resting on the table, was taking far too much thoughtful interest in the typewriter.

'To make pastry with.' Orla rolled her eyes. 'What the hell d'you think it's for, Micky Lavin? It's to type on, you great oaf. People used to send little items of local news to the *Crosby Star* and I thought I'd do the same, as well as to the *Bootle Times*. I could even try and write articles. I wouldn't make much from it, but every little helps.'

'We're not short of money, are we?' Micky looked alarmed. Every week he handed over every penny of his wages and Orla gave him five bob back for himself. Otherwise, the housekeeping was a mystery to him.

'We're all right. Not exactly flush, so a bit extra's useful. It means we might be able to afford a holiday. In a caravan, say, somewhere like Southport.'

Micky's dark eyes brightened. 'That would be the gear.'

'Wouldn't it!' Their glances met and Orla's insides did

a somersault, though there was nothing remotely romantic about a caravan holiday in Southport. By now, Orla had expected to be living in Mayfair, interviewing famous people for a top newspaper or magazine. Instead, she was stuck in a little house in Bootle with a husband and four children. She didn't know if she was happy or not.

The children, Micky and Orla collapsed together on to the settee and hugged each other lavishly. Orla wasn't sure if this was happiness, but it would do for now.

Alice was in the throes of buying the lease on a hairdresser's in Strand Road that was closing down.

'Why do you do it, Mam?' Orla asked curiously. She had come round to see her mother one Sunday afternoon. Micky had taken the children to North Park and she felt bored on her own.

'Do what, luv?'

'Keep buying new hairdressers?'

'For goodness sake, Orla. I took over Myrtle's fourteen years ago. There's only been Marsh Lane since then.'

'You might soon have one in Strand Road. That'll be three.'

Alice shrugged. 'I'm not sure why. It's not the money. I suppose I find it exciting. Anyroad, our Fion's gone, and by this time next year Maeve will be married and Cormac at university. I need something to keep me busy, fill up me life, as it were.'

'Oh, Mam!' Orla cried. 'That sounds really sad.'

'Sometimes I feel really sad.' Alice glanced around the room which still had the same furniture that Orla remembered from her childhood. 'I sometimes wonder how things would have gone if your dad were still at home. If only he hadn't had that accident.'

'I'm fed up hearing about the stupid accident,' Orla said hotly. 'Anyroad, it wasn't that that mucked everything up. It was the way he behaved afterwards. There was a girl at school whose dad lost both legs in the war, but he didn't take it out on his family. People are funny . . .' Orla paused.

'Funny in what way, Orla?'

'Things happen and it brings out the worst in people, or it brings out the best. If Dad hadn't burnt his face, we would never have known he was capable of behaving the way he did, or that you were capable of running three hairdressers.'

Alice sighed wistfully. 'We were so happy until that ship went up in flames. From then on, the world just fell apart.'

Orla hurled herself across the room and knelt beside her mother. She slid her arms around her waist and laid her head upon her knee. 'No, it didn't, Mam. You kept the world together for us. We were still happy, despite Dad and even more happy after he'd gone.'

'You never know people, do you? I thought I knew everything there was to know about your dad.'

'Sometimes people turn out nicer than you'd expect,' Orla said encouragingly. She felt worried; it was most unlike her mother to be so despondent. 'Look at Horace Flynn. He brought you flowers the other day.'

'I know, he still comes round the salon. He misses Fion. They were friends, though I can't think why.'

Because they were two misfits together, Orla thought, but didn't say. 'Our Fion was always very kind,' she lied. Fion could be a bitch when she was in the mood.

'I wish she'd write,' Alice said fretfully. 'Oh, I know she sends cards from London, but they never say anything much. I want to know if she's happy, where she's living so I can write back. I want to know how she *is!'*

Two more years were to pass before Alice received news of her daughter. It arrived in a letter from Neil Greene and was dated November 1960.

Dear Alice,

I know we agreed not to write to each other, but something has happened I thought you'd like to know. Firstly – this is not the 'something' – my divorce from Babs came through the other day. You may not think this relevant but it is, because to celebrate my brother, Adrian, who incidentally became a fully fledged MP following last year's election, invited me to tea at the House of Commons.

I arrived at the House at about five thirty and wondered why there was such a commotion going on. It seemed as if hundreds of women, though it was probably only a few dozen, were gathered outside carrying placards, all shouting and screaming abuse at everyone in sight apart from themselves.

'A Woman's Right to Choose', the placards said, or 'Whose Body Is It Anyway?'. I remembered Adrian saying a Private Member's Bill to legalise abortion was being discussed that day. Although fully in sympathy with the Bill – unlike Adrian, who opposed it – my heart sank a little at the thought of fighting my way through a crowd of such vociferous females. It sank even further when one of the women grabbed me and I thought I was about to be attacked, or at least debagged and subjected to something shameful and possibly degrading.

But no! 'Hello, Neil,' the woman said. It took some time before I recognised it was Fionnuala. She looks wonderful, Alice. Very slim, taller somehow, long wild hair, rosy cheeks and lovely bright, bright eyes.

It was impossible to say much in such circumstances and I shall always regret not suggesting we meet some other time, but then I have always been a bit slow-witted. I managed to ask what she was doing. 'I'm a union organiser,' she said, which I found quite stagger-ing as I can't recall her being interested in politics. I was about to ask where she was living when we were both swept away by the crowds and lost sight of each other.

Fion may have made contact with you by now and you know all this but, in case not, I thought I'd write and let you know she looks fine and you have nothing to worry about.

As for me, I miss Bootle terribly. It was where I felt at home. One day I shall return, I swear it. I miss teaching, too, but it was unfair of me to continue to deny Babs a divorce, and divorce and teaching in a Catholic school were incompatible. I'm working in the City, doing something frightfully dull and frightfully unimportant in Insurance – having a father with a title and a brother in Parliament can work wonders when you're seeking a job. I'm seeing a woman called Heather, divorced like me. We sort of like each other.

An old colleague from St James's continues to send me the *Bootle Times* each week, so I keep myself abreast of what goes on. Congratulations on the new salon – I saw the advert announcing the opening and tried to imagine exactly where in Strand Road it is. How does it feel to have three?

I also saw the news about Maurice Lacey. He seemed a nice boy, though not exactly bright. It came as a shock to read he'd been sent to prison. What was it? Breaking and entering – a newsagent's, if I remember rightly.

I closely study the Birth, Marriages and Deaths

columns. I have been holding my breath, but there has been no mention of Orla under the first, though I noticed the announcement of Maeve's wedding under the second and saw the picture the following week. Was Martin as nervous as he looked? I see Horace Flynn has died. Such a strange man! I trust his properties haven't fallen into the hands of someone who will cause problems for you with leases.

My colleague told me Cormac was accepted at Cambridge. You must feel inordinately proud.

Well, I think that's all, so goodbye, my dearest Alice. You are rarely far from my thoughts.

Your glum and rather lonely friend,

Neil.

She found Neil's letter upsetting and wished they had never become lovers, just remained good friends. Then they could have remained friends when Neil moved away. Alice missed having someone to confide in, even if it were only by letter. These days, Bernadette was completely wrapped up in Danny and the children. Although she and Alice were the same age, Bernadette had had babies when Alice already had grandchildren and seemed to be growing younger as Alice grew older.

Even worse, although she was relieved to hear that Fion was safe and well, it shocked her to the core to learn she had actually been outside the House of Commons waving a placard in support of abortion. Alice was possibly more opposed to abortion than to divorce and the idea of one of her daughters promoting legalised murder filled her with revulsion. Still, no matter what Fion had been up to, she longed for her to come home.

December came, Cormac arrived from Cambridge and she put the contents of the letter out of her mind to concentrate on her son.

Cormac was twenty. He had never grown tall like his father, but had filled out a little. His shoulders were neither broad nor narrow, but they looked strong and the tops of his arms were surprisingly muscled – he'd played tennis all summer, both at Cambridge and, during the holidays, on the courts in North Park, and the long hours spent outdoors had turned his pale skin a lovely golden brown. His hair, a mite too long in Alice's opinion, hung over his forehead in a casual quiff, streaked with white by the sun. He kept pushing it out of his eyes with a brown hand. He looked sophisticated, but at the same time his face still retained the guileless, trusting expression he'd had when he was a little boy. Even then, no one had tried to take advantage of Cormac. He was genuinely liked by everyone and everyone seemed to want him to like them in return.

Alice had been worried university would change her son, that he would grow ashamed of Amber Street and his family. But university had done nothing of the kind. Cormac was proud of his roots. He'd spent weekends in other chaps' houses and they were big, cold morgues of places, where he said he'd hate to live all the time. Most of the chaps had spent their childhoods in boarding schools, which sounded dead horrible and which he would have hated even more. He still talked with a Liverpool accent, possibly not quite so pronounced as before.

Of course, other graduates made fun of the way he spoke, but he didn't give a damn. 'I tell them I'm working class and proud of it, and make fun of the way *they* speak – they call their folks Mater and Pater.' He said he was pleased to be home among normal people.

Working class or not, Cormac must have been popular in view of the number of Christmas cards that arrived for him from all over the country, even more than last year.

On Boxing Day he'd been invited to a drinks party in a chap's house in Chester. He might go, or he might not, he wasn't sure.

The young woman came into the salon a few days before Christmas. Alice and her assistants were at their busiest and the windows were blurred with steam. Alice looked up briefly, then turned away. Patsy was seeing to her. Then Alice looked again and wondered where she had seen the young woman before. It was the hair, more than anything, that looked familiar: very fair, very smooth, silky. Perhaps the woman had been to the salon before, though she didn't often forget a customer and this one was quite outstandingly pretty.

'Alice,' Patsy called. 'Someone would like a word with you.'

'Half a mo.' Alice was combing out Florrie Piper, still a regular customer and still insistent that her hair be dyed the colour of soot, even though she was gone seventy.

'Leave me be, luv,' said Florrie. 'I don't mind waiting a few minutes and admiring the decorations. And it's lovely and warm in here.'

'Ta, Florrie.' Alice went over to the newcomer who wore a smart double-breasted navy coat with a half-belt at the back and navy boots. 'How can I help you, luv?'

'Mrs Lacey? I'd like to speak to you in private.' The request was made so brusquely, without a 'please', that Alice blinked.

'Well, there's only the kitchen.'

'That'll do.'

Alice was aware of Patsy's curious eyes following as they walked through the salon. She felt just as curious herself. 'What's this all about?' she enquired when they were in the privacy of the kitchen.

'I'm leaving John.'

'I beg your pardon?'

'I'm leaving John, your husband. I'm going today. I shall pick the children up from school in an hour's time, then catch a train somewhere far away. I shan't tell you where because I don't want John to know.'

Alice's head reeled. She swayed, reached for a chair and sat down before her legs gave way. She felt confused and very old. 'What's all this got to do with me?' She could hear the tremor in her voice.

'I thought someone should know because he's bound to be very upset and I shall worry about him.'

'I don't understand. Who *are* you?' The woman looked much older close up, at least thirty. Alice remembered where she'd seen her before. '*You're* the girl from Crozier Terrace! You've got a nerve, coming here. There's some women who'd tear your eyes out.' She stared at the face, which had gone very pink. 'I thought you had . . .'

The girl tossed her head. 'I had a hare lip, but it's been fixed and ever since John has made my life unbearable. I wasn't prepared to put up with it any longer. It's taken ages to get the money together, find a place for us to live, get a job. But now I've done it and I'm leaving today. I knew, somehow, you wouldn't tear my eyes out from things John's said. I got the impression your marriage was over long before he met me.'

'Perhaps it was.' Alice was beginning to get her wits back. 'Just let me get this straight,' she said carefully. 'You're walking out, but it makes you feel guilty, so you've decided to plonk the responsibility for what you're doing in *my* lap?'

The woman's face went pinker. 'I suppose I have.'

'That's very nice of you, I must say. What makes you think I give a damn what happens to John?'

'Is there another chair?'

'No.'

'The thing is' – she leaned against the sink – 'in a way, I still love him. I feel terrible for what I'm about to do. I imagine him coming home tonight, finding us gone.' She twisted uneasily. 'He'll be devastated.'

'And you think me turning up with buckets of sympathy will make him feel less devastated?' Alice laughed in disbelief. 'I never want anything to do with him again.'

'I thought you might possibly care.'

'Well, I don't. And if you love him all that much, then why are you walking out?'

'Because I think one day I might hate him.' She stared at the older woman almost angrily. 'Surely you understand? I love him because I know how kind and gentle he can be. He's wonderful with the children.' She pointed to her lovely face. 'John was responsible for this. It's changed my life, but the trouble is it changed him too. He became a different person. He couldn't bear me out of his sight. Did he ever hit you?'

'Just the once.' It all sounded very familiar. Alice frowned. 'Has he hit you?'

'Rather more than just the once.'

Patsy stuck her head round the door, her ears almost visibly flapping. 'Your next customer's here, Alice, and Florrie's still waiting to be finished off.'

'I'll have to go.' Alice got to her feet. Her legs still felt as if they were filled with jelly.

'I hope I haven't upset you.'

'Of course you've upset me. Who wouldn't be upset under the circumstances? All *right*, Patsy, I'll be out in a minute.' Patsy disappeared with obvious reluctance. 'I tell you what, I'll ask me dad to go round and see John, make sure he's all right. I'm not prepared to go near him.' It meant she'd have to tell Dad what had happened, that John had got himself another family, that he hadn't just walked out. Neil was the only person who knew the real truth. 'Are you still living in Crozier Terrace?'

'No, we moved ages ago. We're in Crosby now, 8 Rainford Road. Thank you. I appreciate you being so nice about this.'

'I don't feel a bit nice,' Alice said drily. 'Out of interest, what's your name?'

'Clare Coulson.' She paused at the kitchen door. 'Goodbye, Alice.'

'Good luck, Clare.'

Danny Mitchell didn't think he'd ever been asked to carry out a task that filled him with such revulsion. If he arrived at Rainford Road and found John Lacey with a rope and about to hang himself, his first instinct would have been to help him tie the knot. But it was a long time since Alice had asked for his help, possibly too long. Danny was uncomfortably aware that he had neglected his daughter, so wrapped up had he been in his young wife and their children. Alice hadn't exactly lost her dad and her best friend when Danny married Bernadette, but as good as. Neither was available for her in the way they'd been before.

His heart was full of loathing for his son-in-law. Alice had explained to him and Bernadette the real reason why the marriage had broken down.

'Oh, luv! You should have told us all this a long while ago,' Bernadette cried. She looked anguishedly at Danny and he could see his own guilt reflected in her eyes.

'I felt ashamed,' Alice said simply. 'I didn't want anyone to know.'

'It's nothing to be ashamed of.' Danny's voice was gruff. 'John's the one who should be ashamed. He brings misery on everyone he touches.'

'Anyroad, Dad. This girl, this Clare Coulson, she's worried about him.'

'She's got a nerve!' Danny and Bernadette said together.

'Actually, I quite liked her. She's got spunk, which is more than I ever had. I just sat back and let things happen.'

'You say he actually hit her?'

'Yes, Dad.'

'I'll sort him out,' Danny said grimly.

'No one wants you to sort him out, luv,' Bernadette put in. 'You're just going to make sure he's all right, that's all, like Alice promised.'

'I'd like to sort him out with me fists.'

'John's years younger than you, Danny Mitchell. I don't want you coming back here with a black eye and a broken nose. Forget your fists and use your mouth instead.'

'Yes, luv,' Danny said meekly.

Danny had barely taken his finger off the bell when the door opened and he didn't think he'd ever seen a look of such naked misery on a face when John saw who it was. He'd clearly been expecting someone else.

'Can I come in a minute?'

John seemed to collect himself. He shrugged and stood to one side. 'If you must. I can only spare you a minute. I've got things to do.'

The business must be doing all right, Danny thought as he walked down the spacious carpeted hall into a large, charming room, which had clearly benefited from a woman's touch. There were vases of rushes, bowls of dried flowers, a cosy blue moquette three-piece, rugs and numerous pictures on the walls. Danny tried to take everything in without making it too obvious, knowing

Bernadette would subject him to the third degree when he got home. Perhaps it was because he knew the circumstances, but the room had a sad, deserted air, as if all the life had gone out of it. The fire was a mountain of grey ash with only the occasional glowing coal. It felt very cold.

'What can I do for you, Danny?' John stood, legs apart, in front of the fireplace. He didn't ask the visitor to sit down. Danny sensed he was coiled as tightly as a spring. It wouldn't take much to make this man explode. He longed to be at home in his own comfortable little house with his comfortable little wife.

'I'll come straight to the point,' Danny said bluntly. 'I'm only here for one reason, to make sure you're all right. Once you've assured me that you are, then I'll be off.'

John frowned slightly. 'Is there any reason why I shouldn't be all right?'

'I understand someone walked out on you today, someone called Clare. She came round and asked Alice to see to you, as it were.' Danny glowered. 'I don't appreciate our Alice being dragged into your affairs after all this time. I thought we'd done with you once and for all.'

The man's face had gone a dark, ugly red. 'Clare came to see you?'

'She came to see Alice.'

'She left a note. She didn't mention Alice. When the doorbell went I thought she'd . . .'

'Come back for another beating? I doubt it, John. I doubt if you'll see that girl again.'

'She actually told . . .' He turned away, put his hands on the mantelpiece, stared into the fire. Danny wondered if he was ashamed, embarrassed, or just angry. 'Did she say where she was going? She took the children. I'm worried . . .'

'No, she didn't. If she had, I wouldn't tell you. I don't have much time for men who hit their women.'

'I didn't mean to hit her.'

Danny gestured impatiently. He wasn't interested in anything John Lacey might have to say. All he wanted to know was how the man was bearing up before he made his departure.

Perhaps John had read his thoughts, because he turned round and said coldly, 'I can't think why Clare went to see Alice. I was a bit surprised, that's all, when I came home tonight and found she and the kids had gone. We haven't exactly been getting on in a long time. It'll feel strange for a while without the children, but even that has its compensations. They were dead noisy and I've always liked a quiet life.'

He was lying, it was obvious, but Danny didn't care. He'd asked and the man claimed to be all right. His task was done. 'I'll be off, then.'

'I'll see you out.'

'Don't bother. I'll make me own way. Tara, John.'

The front door closed. John Lacey fell to his knees on the rug in front of the fire. His mouth opened in a silent scream and he beat the floor with his fists. He wanted to roll up in a ball of pain.

Clare had gone, the children. He knew in his heart he would never see them again. He had driven them away, just as he drove everyone away. He prayed to God to make him die.

Minutes later, or it might have been hours, when God seemed unprepared to answer his prayer and John hadn't the courage to take matters into his own hands, he got to his feet and went round the house gathering together a few possessions, which he threw in the back of the van parked outside.

The landlord could have his house back, as well as everything in it. From now on he'd live in the office at the yard. From now on nothing mattered any more.

Chapter 10

Cora bought the *Liverpool Echo* especially. She opened it as soon as she got home and searched for Twenty-Firsts.

'LACEY, Cormac John. Many Happy Returns, son, on your twenty-first. With all my love, Mum,' she read.

There were three more entries for Cormac: from Maeve and Martin, from Orla and Micky and the children, and the last from Grandad, Bernadette, Ian and Ruth: 'Congratulations to a fine young man on reaching his majority.'

There would be no entries tomorrow for Maurice Lacey. Anyone who knew him would have laughed, because Maurice was in Walton jail.

Oh, the shame of it! Since the court case Cora had hardly left the house. She did the shopping Strand Road way where she wasn't known, rather than in Marsh Lane.

She still didn't know what had got into Maurice. He'd lost his job – he was 'unpunctual', according to his boss. Cora had considered it fortunate that he'd been called up to do his National Service almost straight away. It would do him good, teach him the discipline that Cora had failed to do. But the minute he came out he'd started hanging around with a girl, Pamela Conway, who had a reputation for being no better than she ought to be. It was Pamela's brothers who'd led Maurice astray, of that Cora was convinced. They were much older than him, with convictions for breaking and entering behind them. One had threatened a shopkeeper with a knife and wasn't long out of jail himself.

They'd *used* Maurice. He was a soft lad, easily led. He'd broken a window to get into the shop and it hadn't entered his daft head that someone might hear and call the bobbies. They were waiting for him when he came out, laden with boxes of cigarettes and baccy, almost certainly for the Conways to sell in the pubs at half price. He refused to clat on them. Cora suspected he was frightened.

For once, Billy had been in when the bobbies arrived and requested they come to the station, where he'd leapt at Maurice and had almost throttled him by the time he was pulled off. He wanted nothing more to do with him, he said. But when had Billy had anything much to do with his wife and son?

She recalled her own criminal past, though she'd been too clever to get caught. Perhaps thieving was inherited, like the same coloured eyes and hair. But if that was the case, Cormac . . .

Sometimes she forgot what the truth was.

By now, Cormac would be home from university for Christmas and there was bound to be a birthday do somewhere tonight – Alice threw parties at the drop of a hat.

Restless, Cora wandered round the house, touching things. It wasn't fair. Nothing was fair. Nothing had gone the way she'd expected. Horace Flynn had popped his clogs last year, but hadn't left her a thing. The chap who came to collect the rent said a nephew back in Ireland, a priest, had inherited the lot and wanted everything left the same. All the chap did was collect the leases and the rents, and send cheques to some church in County Antrim. When Cora asked why Horace's big house in Stanley Road remained empty, he knew nothing about it.

She wondered if Cormac's do would be held at home or whether Alice had booked somewhere bigger, seeing as how it was a twenty-first. Wherever it was, she wouldn't mind going and waiting outside so she could take a peek, see who was there – if she could do it without being noticed, that is.

They'd probably know in the Strand Road salon – she looked inside whenever she passed. It was always busy, but she'd never once seen Alice there. It looked a posh place, much bigger than the Laceys' in Opal Street and Marsh Lane. But she couldn't just barge in asking questions, she'd have to have something done to her hair. She'd get a trim, though she usually cut it herself, and give a false name. It wouldn't do to say she was a Lacey.

The thought cheered her up somewhat. It gave her a reason for getting out of the house. She'd go now.

Cora went into the hall and lifted her camel coat off a hook. It was twelve years old, but good quality and she wouldn't have dreamt of buying another until it wore out. She pushed her small feet into a pair of stout suede boots that were even older than the coat, then tied a scarf round her head. For some women, appearance was everything, but Cora didn't give a damn. She fastened the buttons in front of the full-length mirror. She was fifty-one and looked neither younger nor older. Not a soul in the world would have given her a second glance.

The woman in Lacey's who was doing her hair was called Enid. Cora would suit it shorter, she said. It would give it more texture and she'd look like June Allyson. 'She's a film star,' she went on in response to Cora's puzzled look. 'She was in *Little Women* and *Executive Suite.*'

'I don't get to the pictures much.'

'Don't you, luv? Me, I go at least three times a week.'

Cora said she'd prefer to stick to just an inch off, thanks all the same. She was about to add sourly that she had more important things to do with her time than go to the pictures three times a week, but remembered she wanted to pump the woman for information. This proved easy when she mentioned she was an old friend of Alice whom she hadn't seen in years. 'How's her kids getting on? Four she had, didn't she? Three girls and a boy – he was almost exactly the same age as me own lad.'

'In that case your lad must be round twenty-one, like Cormac. It's his birthday today. He's a smashing lad – I sent him a silver key meself. We're all going to his party tonight.'

'And where would that be?'

'You know Hilton's Restaurant on Stanley Road? Well, it's in the room above. There's at least fifty of us going. Alice has invited all the staff and Cormac has asked some friends from school and university. Did you know he's at Cambridge, luv? He's taking Chemistry, if you'll believe.' The woman couldn't have sounded prouder had Cormac been her own son. 'After he's got his degree, he's going to stay and get more letters after his name. When he leaves he'll be called doctor.'

Cora waited until eight o'clock before stationing herself across the road from Hilton's, a large restaurant well known as a venue for wedding receptions and parties. It was situated on the corner of busy Stanley Road and Greening Street. The double-fronted downstairs was in darkness. She could hear the noise of the party upstairs, the music and the chatter, the laughing and the singing, from all this way away, despite the passing trams and other traffic.

Why was she doing this, cowering in a doorway on a freezing cold night in December, listening to other people enjoying themselves? Because this night had been stolen from her, she told herself. This night should be *hers*. It should be *her* throwing the party for Cormac.

She waited a good hour, huddled inside her coat, stamping her feet, her gaze fixed hypnotically on the lighted upstairs windows opposite. There was no way she'd see a thing from here and she wanted to know what was going on. Spots of ice blew against her face as she crossed over and went down Greening Street to the side door of the restaurant where people had been going in. Hopping from one foot to the other, she stood hesitantly outside before pushing the door open, though she didn't go in. Narrow stairs led upwards and the noise here was deafening, a whooping and stamping of feet, as if people were doing some strange sort of dance. Cora had never been to a dance.

Dare she go in? Sneak upstairs, just peer through the door, so she didn't feel totally excluded from Cormac's twenty-first?

Well, even if she was discovered, she was unlikely to be chucked out on her ear. Alice would never be rude. Fion would have been, except she wasn't there. The woman in the salon said she was still living in London.

Cora crept upstairs, making not a sound in her crèpe-soled boots. To her left at the top there was a Ladies and a Gents, a kitchen and a door marked 'Office'. The whoops and stamping came from behind the door to her right.

Someone – it was Bernadette Mitchell – was coming out of the kitchen carrying a birthday cake with the candles already lit, too concerned with watching her feet in case she tripped over to notice Cora, who shot into the Ladies, heart thumping.

The music and the stamping suddenly stopped. There was utter silence for a minute, then 'Happy birthday to you, Happy birthday to you, Happy birthday, dear Cormac . . .'

They loved him. Everyone loved Cormac.

Cormac, Maurice. Maurice, Cormac. The names chased each other around Cora's brain. She'd thought she was doing a good thing all them years ago, but she'd done a bad one. If only she'd left things as they were, it would be Alice with a lad in Walton jail, not her. If only she could go back twenty-one years and put everything right.

The Ladies was a large room that doubled as a cloakroom. Two sides of the walls were full of coats, and there were two lavatories. Cora went inside one and closed the door. She pulled down the seat to sit on. They were singing 'For he's a jolly good fellow' now. Alice was probably hanging on to his arm, looking gormless. She didn't deserve Cormac for a son.

Oh, it wasn't *fair*!

There was a sudden rush of women into the Ladies. They kept trying Cora's door. 'Who's in there?' someone said. 'They've been ages.'

A few minutes later there was a knock. 'Are you all right?' It was that bloody Patsy woman who worked for Alice.

'Yes,' Cora replied gruffly.

The Ladies emptied. The music started again, quieter now, romantic music. She imagined the lights turned low and everyone dancing, and wondered if Cormac had a girlfriend with him.

Not long afterwards the women returned to collect their coats. The party must be over. From their conversation, they'd had a dead good time. After about fifteen minutes of bustle there was silence. Alice hadn't been in for her coat, Cora would have recognised her voice. Unlatching the door, she came out to find only a handful of coats left on the hooks and wondered if she could make it from the lavatory to the stairs without being seen, otherwise she might end up being locked in the building all night.

There was no one in the kitchen. Cora had reached the top of the stairs and was about to creep down as quietly as she'd come, when she noticed the door to the big room was open and there was still music, very faint, so faint that it was almost drowned out by the noise of the traffic outside.

She paused. At the far end, Orla and Maeve were dancing with their husbands: that no-mark Micky Lavin and the one who had a good job at the hospital, Martin. Danny and Bernadette were standing by a radiogram, sifting through records. Cora edged closer until Alice came into view. She wore a lovely bottle-green dress with a fluted hem and was sprawled on a chair, legs stretched out in front, clearly worn out. But Cora didn't think she'd ever seen such a look of perfect contentment on a face before. Alice quite literally glowed. Her face seemed to be exuding darts of electricity and Cora felt her own face prickle, as if from tiny electric shocks. Her sister-in-law was experiencing the happiness that was *her* due, the happiness that had been denied her all these years.

She edged closer, her eyes searching for Cormac. He appeared, inch by inch, bending over Alice. He wore black trousers and a white shirt that looked too big for him, she thought. It was all bunched up round the waist where it was tucked inside a narrow belt. He might have started off the evening with a tie, but wasn't wearing one now. The collar of the shirt was open, emphasising his slender neck. Cora's heart missed a beat. He looked dead handsome. He and Alice were laughing together about something. The whole scene looked like a painting of Happy Families. Then Cormac suddenly reached out and stroked Alice's hair.

Something snapped in the watching woman. Her head felt as if it was full of smoke: thick, black smoke, that swirled around and got hotter and hotter.

By now, Maurice would have kipped down in his cell. 'Lights Out' would have been called. Everywhere smelt of pee, he claimed. The food was awful. After a few months, Cora had stopped going to see him. She didn't know what to say and the other visitors were scum. She felt ashamed, mixing with them. She wasn't sure if she wanted Maurice back home. She wasn't sure if she loved him any more.

This was her son, her lad, the fruit of her womb, this fair-haired, clever, extremely dashing young man.

'Drat!' Alice had kicked something over. A glass of wine. The liquid spilled like blood on to the polished floor.

'I'll get a cloth from the kitchen.' Cormac began to hurry towards the door, towards Cora, the son towards his mother. God must have arranged for that glass to be knocked over.

Cora backed up so that she was in the kitchen when Cormac came in. He jumped, startled. 'Aunt Cora! I didn't know you were here. Why don't you go in the big room with me mam?'

She fixed her eyes squarely on his neat, good-looking face. 'You're mine,' she said in a deep, passionate voice that she didn't know she possessed.

'I beg your pardon?' Cormac said courteously.

'I said, you're *mine*,' she continued in the same

261

unnatural voice. 'The night you were born, I swapped you round for Maurice. I went for a walk in the hospital. Everyone was asleep, 'cept me. When I came to the nursery, Maurice was in the cot marked Lacey 1, and you were in Lacey 2. I changed you round.'

Cormac was actually smiling. 'Don't talk rubbish, Aunt Cora. I don't like to be rude, but I've never heard such ridiculous nonsense.'

'It's not nonsense, luv. It's true,' Cora insisted hoarsely.

He laughed. 'Things like that aren't allowed to happen in hospitals.'

'They happened that night. There was a raid. It was like hell on earth, women and babies all over the place: in the cellar one minute, in the wards the next.' Cora clutched his arm, but he shrugged her away.

'This is going beyond a joke.' His voice had become icy cold. 'I'm sorry about Maurice being in prison, Aunt Cora, but it doesn't mean you have to spoil *my* twenty-first for me.'

He thought she was saying things out of spite! 'Oh, luv,' she cried. She reached for him, but he moved away with an expression of distaste. 'I don't want to spoil anything, I just thought it was time you knew the truth. I told you, it was bedlam in the hospital, nurses rushing around like lunatics. There was this emergency. Alice wasn't shown her baby till next morning, when they gave her you 'stead of Maurice. It's not your twenty-first till tomorrer. It's Maurice who's twenty-one today.'

It seemed as if the reference to the birthdays, trivial in comparison with the other things she'd said, had sewn a seed of doubt in Cormac's mind. He went as white as a sheet. 'Just supposing,' he said carefully, 'just supposing there's a grain of truth in what you've said, what on earth would possess you to do such a wicked thing?'

Cora smiled slyly. 'Because I thought Maurice looked the better bet, but it turned out I was wrong.'

'Jaysus!'

She felt slightly uneasy at the sight of his gentle face contorted with horror and disgust. Perhaps she should have approached it differently, or at least thought things through before she opened her big mouth. Perhaps it would have been best if she'd told Alice first. Alice knew the way things had been that night and would have been easier to convince.

'Cormac!' Alice shouted. 'Where's that cloth?'

'Won't be a minute, Mam.' His face had cleared, become devoid of expression. 'I don't believe you. You're just making trouble, something you're very good at, going by past experience.'

'Just take a look at yourself in the mirror, son,' Cora said softly. She'd upset him badly, which was only to be expected. She felt a surge of sympathy that made her body ache, but no way was she going to deny that what she'd said was true. She'd already suffered enough for that one silly mistake. 'It's never crossed anyone's mind to notice, but you're the spitting image of me, your mam – the same shaped face, the same little hands.' Alice had long, thin hands, John's were broad. She held out her own hands, spreading the small fingers, regarding them impassively. 'See, son.'

For the first time in Cormac's life his legendary calm deserted him. 'Don't you dare call me "son". I'm not your son. I'd sooner die than be your son. I want nothing to do with you.' He could hardly speak. The words came out thickly, as if his tongue had got too big for his mouth.

Cora chewed her bottom lip. She didn't like seeing her boy in such a state, but what had she expected? For him to throw himself into her arms? All this must have come as a terrible shock. 'Why don't we get Alice out here?' she suggested.

'Does Mam *know*?'

'No, but it's about time she did.' She thought Cormac was about to hit her. He reared over her, pushed his face in hers. 'Don't you *dare* breathe a word about this to me mam, d'you hear? It would kill her. I don't want anyone else to know. Do you hear me, Aunt Cora. *I don't want anyone else to know.*'

'But,' Cora began, disappointed, because she wanted the whole world to know that *this* was her son: Maurice, the jail bird, belonged to someone else.

Then Cormac put his small white hands round Cora's scraggy neck and began to squeeze. 'If you tell another soul, Aunt Cora, so help me, I'll kill you. I swear it. No matter where I am, I'll come back and kill you stone dead.'

She was gagging. 'Leave go, son. I won't tell a soul.'

He removed his hands. 'You'd better not,' he said threateningly. 'And don't, don't ever call me son again.'

With a sense of perverse pride, Cora realised that soft, gentle Cormac, who everyone thought wouldn't have hurt a fly, who had never been heard to raise his voice in anger, meant every word. She herself had killed, a long time ago, two people. A chip off the old block, she thought. He's his mammy's son, that's for sure. She sighed happily. Cormac knew the truth and that was all that mattered. One of these days he'd come round and learn to love his mam.

Cormac went into the Gents and stared at himself in the mirror. Within the space of a few minutes the bottom had dropped out of his world. He hadn't realised how swiftly life could change, that you could be completely happy one minute, in the depths of despair the next.

He had never liked Aunt Cora. She gave him the jitters. There was something unhinged about her. As he grew older, he'd become convinced that she was mad and, if she truly was his mother, then he, Cormac, could easily become mad himself. He hadn't, for instance, considered himself remotely capable of murder, yet minutes ago he'd grabbed a woman by the throat with the intention of strangling her. He wondered if he would have done it if there hadn't been other people around.

By some obscene coincidence her name could actually be made from the letters of his: Cormac, Cora, as if, inadvertently, there'd been a connection between them all along.

The idea that everything that had happened so far in his life was due entirely to the quirk of a crazy woman wandering around a hospital in the dead of night made his stomach curl with horror. It was enough to make anyone lose his mind.

On the other hand he supposed he was lucky. It could have been *him*, not Maurice, brought up in the house in Garibaldi Road with a cane hanging on the wall.

Poor Maurice! Cormac shuddered.

He no longer felt sure who he was, whom he belonged to, which family was his. He told himself that Aunt Cora was talking rubbish, as he'd first thought, except that the person staring back at him from the mirror had the cold eyes and the nothing face of his detested aunt. The eyes were a different colour, that was all.

Oh, God! Why hadn't he noticed before? Why hadn't anyone? Until now, he'd always considered himself at least averagely good-looking, but the face in the mirror looked like that of a corpse.

'We don't know who on earth he takes after,' Mam said when people remarked Cormac was nothing like the rest of the family. No one had noticed the remarkable resemblance between the woman who now claimed to be his mother and himself. He would never, never be able to get his head round the fact that Alice wasn't his mam.

There was a knock on the door. 'Cormac, are you all right, son? I hope you haven't made yourself sick with all that beer. Oh, by the way, I've got a cloth meself.'

'I'm all right.' He couldn't bring himself to say 'Mam', he just couldn't. 'I'll be out in a minute,' he called.

Chapter 11
1965

Cormac lay flat on his back within a circle of brittle corn. He stared at the sky through the corn tunnel that grew narrower and narrower until the top seemed no bigger than his eye. The flattened plants beneath him stuck sharply into his body through his thin Indian top and flared cotton pants, though they didn't hurt. His arms were spread as wide as they would go and his hands were hidden within the yellow stalks. The tips of his fingers touched those of Wally on one side and Frank the Yank, snoring his head off, on the other.

He imagined himself a bird passing overhead and seeing himself and his friends spread out like a row of little paper men.

'Why is the sun red?' Wally murmured.

'I don't know,' Cormac answered. 'Why is every-where so hot?'

'Because the sun is so red, man. It's on fire.'

'I need a drink.' Cormac sat up and experimentally touched his bare toes. The fact that he was physically capable of such an act meant he was badly in need of a joint as well as a drink so that his senses would become sufficiently blurred.

He got to his feet and staggered towards a luridly painted coach that was parked in the corner of a field in Suffolk, Sussex or Surrey, he couldn't remember which. He knew they were on their way to play at a pop festival in Norwich, which would start the day after tomorrow. The farmer whose field they were on was so far unaware he had trespassers. If he noticed before they left that night, they would be turfed off sharpish with the aid of a couple of savage dogs, a shotgun, or possibly both.

Inside, the coach buzzed with flies. When bought, it had already been converted into a mobile home with six bunks, three each side, as close as shelves, a tiny sink and a table at the rear with fitted, plastic-covered benches. Behind a screen a chemical lavatory remained unused because no one was prepared to empty it and there was a tiny fridge that no longer worked. The windows had been painted over to provide privacy, apart from the one in the roof, which wouldn't open. The sun scorched through the glass like a blowtorch, turning the cramped space into an oven.

Cormac could hardly breathe in the suffocating heat. He opened the fridge and remembered it was broken when he came face to face with half a mouldy tomato. Nothing came out when he turned on the tap over the sink – the water tank must be empty. He searched everywhere, in the cupboard under the sink, under bunks, under the clothes that littered the bunks, but could find nothing except a few empty beer bottles that yielded not a drop when he attempted to drain them. In the process he knocked over a guitar, which fell to the floor with a hollow boom and he noticed one of the strings was broken.

Then he recalled that the girls had gone into the village to buy supplies: Tanya and Pol, but his memory was hazy as to the time they'd gone. It could have been five minutes ago or five hours.

Jaysus, the smell in here was foul. Someone had been sick the night before and everywhere reeked of vomit. Perhaps that was what attracted the flies. There was another smell, quite strong, and Cormac realised it was paint. The fiery sun was burning the paint off the outside of the coach.

He'd die if he didn't have a drink soon. Perhaps a joint would lessen his thirst. He remembered a joint was one of the reasons he was there and reached under the pillow on his bunk for the battered Golden Virginia tin in which he kept his stuff.

'Hello, friends,' he said affectionately to the contents of the tin: a packet of red Rizla papers and a book of matches nestling within a bed of tobacco and, most important, a lump of hash that felt warm. He spread the tobacco on a paper and shredded a portion of the hash with his fingernail so that it was evenly spread, then put back the remainder carefully. He lit the spliff, took a long, deep puff, then went out and sat in the shade of the coach, his back against it. It didn't feel even vaguely cool, but at least he was out of the sun.

'Hi, man.' Wally appeared. 'Is there anything to drink in there?'

Cormac shook his head. 'Not a drop, man.'

'Where's Tanya and Pol?'

'Gone somewhere. Where's Frank?'

'Asleep.'

'Shouldn't someone wake him? He'll get sunburn.' Did you get sunburn or catch it?

'I suppose someone should.' Wally must have decided it wasn't going to be him. He sat beside Cormac and gestured towards the joint. Cormac handed it to him. They shared everything, including the girls. Cormac and Wally had shared each other, only the once, but had decided it wasn't for them.

Frank the Yank provided most of the money. His pa had sent him abroad to escape the Vietnam draft and wherever they went, Frank only had to find a Lloyds bank and produce his passport, and massive amounts of cash would be handed over. It was Frank who'd bought the coach and they'd painted it together. The others signed on the dole if they stayed somewhere long enough, but that didn't happen often.

A pleasant fog had formed inside Cormac's head. He was no longer thirsty. This hazy sensation of wanting nothing, needing nothing, was something Cormac wished to retain for the rest of his life. His ambition was to get from one day to the next in the deepest possible daze without actually becoming unconscious – unconsciousness appealed, but was impractical.

The girls returned, loaded with shopping. Cormac feebly raised a hand in greeting. Pol smiled, but Tanya eyed them balefully.

'You're stoned,' she said accusingly. 'I bet you haven't cleaned up inside.' Tanya was tall, breathtakingly beautiful and extremely bad-tempered for most of the time. She wore a full-length flowered skirt and a skimpy T-shirt. Her mother was a famous model.

'Cleaned up inside?' Cormac and Wally said more or less together. They looked at each other. It was the first they'd heard of it.

'It stinks in there. It wasn't Pol or me who was sick. You promised you'd clean it.'

'Did we?'

'I'll do it.' Pol was short and slight, and merely pretty. She had crisp brown curly hair and a heart-shaped face. In her limp, shapeless cotton frock, she looked no more than sixteen, though she was twenty-one, three years younger than Cormac. 'As my horrible mother used to say, "If you want something done properly, then do it yourself".'

'Alice used to say something like that.' Cormac grinned.

'Where's Frank?' Tanya demanded.

'Asleep,' Wally said.

'In there?' She pointed to the coach.

'No, over yonder,' Wally said poetically and gave a vague wave in the direction of the field.

'Tsk, tsk. He'll get sunburnt.' Tanya marched away, her back rigid, like a schoolmistress. Cormac supposed that someone had to keep them in order. He was glad Tanya was around. And Pol. Particularly Pol.

'I'll put these away.' Pol staggered as she picked up one of the bags laden with shopping.

Cormac's innate courtesy came to the fore and he stumbled to his feet. 'I'll give you a hand with those.'

'Ta, Cormac. Phew, what a smell!' Pol gasped when they were inside the coach. She tripped over the guitar and it slid along the floor until it stopped under the table with a thump. 'We need to find a launderette and wash the sleeping bags. There's bound to be one in Ipswich, and they're usually open till late. I'll chuck everything outside for now.' With that, she began to grab the sleeping bags and the scattered clothes, and to throw them out of the door. The worst of the smell went with them.

Where on earth did she get the energy from? Cormac wondered. He himself would have found it a simple matter to wallow in filth for the rest of his life rather than wash a sheet. 'Is that where we are, Ipswich?' He'd only vaguely heard of the place before.

'About five miles away. Are you thirsty?' She was putting the food away under the sink.

'I think I might well be.'

'Would you like some lemonade?'

'That would be most acceptable.'

'Sit down, then, and I'll pour you some.'

'Thank you, Pol,' Cormac said gravely.

'When we stop in Ipswich to do the washing, it wouldn't hurt if you washed your hair, Cormac. It's getting quite matted. You could do it in a Gents toilet.'

'I like it matted.' Cormac touched the hair that went halfway down his back. It felt greasy and unusually thick.

Pol shrugged, easygoing. 'Please yourself.'

'I'll wash me hair for *you*.' He liked Pol very much, perhaps a bit too much. He was beginning to resent having to share her with Wally and Frank. Perhaps they should find another girl and split into three separate couples. 'I think I love you, Pol,' he said seriously.

'Oh, Cormac! You're too stoned to think most of the time.' She looked at him curiously. 'Why do you do it? I mean, I like a spliff myself, but you seem to be on a permanent high.'

'It's a long story, Pol. Something happened.' Cormac spoke slowly, carefully enunciating the words, hoping they made sense. 'One day, no, one minute, everything was perfect, next minute it was shit.'

'What was it that happened?'

'I discovered I wasn't the person I'd always thought meself to be.'

Pol looked impressed. 'That sounds deeply disturbing, Cormac.'

'Intensely deeply.' Cormac was about to reach for her, pull her on to a bunk, when Wally fell into the coach, following by Frank, who was being led by an irritable Tanya. Frank's face and arms were as bright red as his hair and slightly puffy.

'I'm all right, man,' he protested. 'Stop making a fuss.'

'You won't feel all right tomorrow. You'll be as sick as a dog. Is there calamine lotion in the first aid box, Pol?' It was Tanya's idea to have a first aid box, and Cormac had to concede it came in useful from time to time.

'I don't think so, no.'

'Then I suggest we leave now, straight away,' Tanya said briskly. 'We'll call in Ipswich, do the washing, fill the water tank, buy some calamine lotion. Are any of you three fit to drive?'

Cormac occasionally drove, even though he'd never had a lesson. 'I'm ferfectly pit,' he announced.

'Oh, yeh!' Tanya glared at Wally who had collapsed on the floor. Frank had started to shiver violently for some reason. 'It looks as if I'll have to drive myself. One of these days we'll be stopped by the police and I haven't got a proper licence.'

The surface of the large field had baked as hard as clay. It was impossible to imagine the soil having been soft enough for the huge tyres of tractors to have made such perfect moulds – they made comfortable seats, Cormac discovered, just wide and deep enough for his bottom to fit.

Pol sat between his legs, leaning against him. His hands lay limply on her lap. They sprawled at the very edge of the field, where they could hardly see the group playing beneath an awning that fluttered not an inch on such a windless day. The music stopped and there was a smattering of applause from the crowds that dotted the field like confetti. The audience included many children, most of them naked. A few of the women were bare to the waist. The numerous dogs seemed to have been trained to defecate and piss as frequently as possible.

Today, Pol wore a different frock, just as shapeless. He nuzzled her hair, which smelt of soap. His own hair, beautifully clean, was wondrous to behold: clouds of pale-blond locks held together at the back with an elastic band.

'Where do you come from, Pol?' he asked. She'd probably told him before, but he'd forgotten.

'Lancashire, same as you. Blackpool.'

'I went to Blackpool once. There was something called the Golden Mile.' He'd gone on the big wheel with Fion and Orla. Maeve had been too scared. Grandad had been there. It was before he'd married Bernadette.

'You should see the Blackpool Lights in a few weeks' time, they're terrific.'

'Shall we go together?'

'No chance, Cormac. I might meet my mother.'

'Would that be so awful?'

'Awfully awful. She's a bitch.'

'So's mine.' Cormac shuddered.

'I thought you said your mother was lovely.' She turned her face towards him and he kissed her nose. 'You're always on about Alice.'

'Alice isn't my mother, she just thinks she is.'

'Oh, Cormac, you don't half talk rubbish. Were you adopted or something?'

'No, I was given away at birth.'

'Who by, a bad fairy?'

'Well, yes, as it happens. Very bad.'

'You're something of a mystery, do you know that, Cormac?'

'I'm a mystery to meself,' Cormac said darkly.

'Are we playing here tomorrow?'

'I doubt it, not if Frank's still laid low with sunburn. And I think one of the guitars is broken.' The Nobodys were usually the first on the bill, hired to keep folks amused while they looked for somewhere to sit, or searched for their seats if the concert was indoors. Frank and Wally played guitar not very well. The only decent musician was Tanya who was brilliant with the fiddle.

Pol had a sweet, high voice and Cormac could rattle a tambourine as well as anyone. He was the group's manager-cum-roadie. At least, he was when he remembered. The Nobodys were unusual in that they recognised their limitations and weren't interested in either fame or money. It was just something to do, giving occasional point to their otherwise meaningless lives.

'I think I'll go back to the van, bathe poor Frank's head, or something,' Pol said.

'I'll come with you,' Cormac said with alacrity. He didn't want her alone with Frank, who might not be one hundred per cent incapacitated by the sunburn.

'There's no need, Cormac.'

'This group are shit and I need a rest.'

'What from? You've been sitting in that rut virtually all day.'

'I need a rest from sitting in this rut.'

Vehicles were parked nose to tail along the narrow country lane: buses, caravanettes, lorries, large vans, small vans, ambulances with the word 'Ambulance' painted out, the occasional car. According to the radio, it was the same for miles around. The police had decided to let the festival go ahead rather than turn hundreds of vehicles away. It would cause less hassle. On the radio, several local residents had huffed and puffed, and said it was disgraceful. Why weren't these people at work? How dare they descend on a peaceful, law-abiding community and create havoc? Pubs, restaurants, one or two garages, had signs outside, 'No Festival Goers'. The Nobodys were out of water again and it was impossible to get more.

'My skin won't let me move, man,' Frank complained bitterly when Pol and Cormac climbed into the coach. He was poised stiffly on a bench, elbows on the table, wearing only a pair of shorts with a pattern of butterflies.

The skin on his upper half was less livid, but still looked painful. His red hair looked crisp, as if it had been fried. 'My chest hurts when I breathe.'

'Shall I douse you in calamine?'

'Please, Pol.'

Cormac reached under the pillow for his stuff and began to roll a joint. The first puff brought on a sensation of enormous lethargy. He lay down and within seconds was asleep.

It was dusk when he awoke, slightly cooler. He could hear music thumping away in the distance. The spliff had burnt a perfect round hole in the nylon sleeping bag, but there was still half left. He was searching for the matches when he noticed Frank and Pol squeezed together on the bunk opposite, both asleep. Pol was naked, her small, perfect body glistening with perspiration, and Frank's shorts were around his knees. His red skin was splattered with pink calamine.

Cormac groaned. He'd come back with Pol to keep an eye on her, yet she and Frank had made love directly in front of his closed eyes. They badly needed another girl, someone for Frank. Wally could have Tanya, Cormac would have Pol.

Another girl! He made his unsteady way outside and began to walk in the direction of the music to look for another girl. Dusk was falling. There were lights on in some of the vehicles and he could hear the clink of dishes. The smell of food made him feel nauseous, though he'd had nothing to eat all day and possibly yesterday, for all he knew. A police car came zooming down the lane, blue light flashing. Cormac pushed a small child and an exceptionally hairy dog to safety. The child cried and the dog growled ungratefully.

Cormac had no idea why he should cry as he walked towards the music. He wasn't even conscious of crying until one of the great, bulbous tears pouring down his face landed on his bare foot and he thought it was raining. He looked up into the clear, dusky blue sky and realised he was crying and the rain was a tear. He was thinking about Pol and Alice and Grandad and his sisters, about Amber Street, about Bootle, Lacey's hairdressers, the schools he'd gone to, the friends he'd made. He thought about university and the fact that he hadn't gone back to finish his degree, about Alice's face when he told her. He thought about Cora Lacey.

'Here, look where you're going, luv.'

He'd collided with a woman coming from the opposite direction, leading two children by the hand.

'I'm sorry.' Cormac wept. 'So sorry.'

'It's not the end of the world, luv,' the woman said kindly.

Still crying, Cormac walked on, when a voice said incredulously, 'Is that you, Cormac?'

He turned. The woman with the children had stopped and was looking at him, her face as incredulous as her voice. She was tall, well built, but shapely and her long, wild hair was tied in a knot on top of her head. She wore a black T-shirt with a white CND sign on the front and narrow black pants. She was, unfortunately, too old for Frank, about thirty, and there was no room for the children in the coach.

'I'm Cormac, yes,' he conceded in a whisper.

'It's Fion, luv. Fionnuala, your sister.'

'Fion!' Cormac had never, in all his life, been so pleased to see anyone. He stopped crying, grabbed his sister and showered her face with kisses. She hugged him tightly in return and rubbed his back, as if he were a baby. One of the children, the boy, tried to pull her away.

'It's all right, Colin. This is Cormac, your uncle. Oh,

Cormac, you look bloody awful. Are you sick or something? C'mon, luv, we're only along here.'

The children ran ahead, stopping outside a smart white caravanette. Fion, holding Cormac firmly by the arm as if worried he'd run away, opened the door and pushed him through. Inside, the vehicle was cheerful and scrupulously tidy. Red gingham frills framed the tiny windows and there was a matching cloth on the table, as well as a small bowl of roses. The miniature stainless steel sink sparkled and a red carpet graced the floor. There wasn't a dish or an item of dirty washing in sight.

The grip of his sister's hand on Cormac's arm made him feel as if he had suddenly been plugged back into the normal world and the scene of domestic neatness reminded him of a time when he had known nothing else, when it had been a simple matter to get washed, wear clean clothes, brush his teeth, sit down to proper meals.

'Blimey, Cormac, you don't half pong,' Fion said bluntly. 'Have a wash, there's a good lad, while I make some tea. I'll find you a clean T-shirt in a minute. This is Colin and Bonnie, by the way. He's nearly five, she's nearly four. Say hello to your Uncle Cormac, kids, then get into your pyjamas. It's nearly time for bed.'

Bonnie pushed herself boldly forward. 'Hello, Uncle Cormac.' The boy hung back and sucked his finger.

'Hello, kids,' Cormac said, doing his best to sound like a proper grown-up uncle. 'Where's their dad?' he said to Fion.

'Dead. He died two years ago. His name was Colin too.'

'Oh, hell! I'm sorry.'

'So am I,' Fion said matter-of-factly. 'I loved him more than words can say, but he'd been in a Japanese prisoner of war camp and was dying when I met him.

When we got married we never thought he'd last six whole years, but he did and they were the best years of me life.' She gestured towards him with soap and a towel. 'Take your shirt off, luv, and chuck it away before you stink the place out. Are you hungry?'

'I wouldn't mind some bread and butter.'

'I think we can manage that.'

Cormac had never had a favourite sister, but had always felt more drawn to Fionnuala than he had to loud, aggressive Orla and quietly confident Maeve. There had been something very vulnerable about tactless, hopeless Fion, forever putting her foot in it, saying the wrong thing. To find his wretched self plucked off a country lane in Norfolk by the sister he hadn't seen in years and put down in this neat, cool place, where there was fresh water, healthily smelling soap, roses on the table and a kettle boiling for tea, was little short of a miracle.

'What are you doing here?' Fion asked while he was getting washed. The children watched with interest as they changed into their pyjamas.

'I belong to a group, the Nobodys. We're on tomorrow's programme, but Frank's too ill to play.'

'Never heard of you.'

'Nobody ever has, hence the name.'

'Mummy, he hasn't cleaned behind his ears.'

Fion grinned. 'Bonnie says to clean behind your ears, Cormac.'

'Sorry, Bonnie.'

'And under your arms.'

'Yes, Bonnie.' Cormac was beginning to feel vaguely happy.

In quick succession Fion opened a tin of beans, shoved toast under a grill, poured water on the pot. Within minutes the children were sitting down to beans on toast, and Cormac was drinking a mug of scalding tea and wearing a T-shirt with Amnesty 61 on the back. There seemed to be plenty of provisions. A loaf appeared, a plastic butter dish, a tin of cocoa, a bottle of milk, a packet of biscuits – custard creams. Cormac couldn't remember having seen such a rich assortment of food in years.

'Is the van yours?' he asked.

'No, it's hired. We're on holiday, on our way to Scotland. Some of my friends were coming here, so I thought I'd make a detour and let the children see what a rock concert's all about. Bonnie thought it great, but Colin hated it, didn't you, luv?' Colin had yet to open his mouth and merely nodded. Fion ruffled his hair and for some reason the gesture made Cormac want to cry again.

'Me and Colin,' Fion continued, 'big Colin, that is, though he wasn't all that big as it happens, went touring every year. It's the cheapest way of seeing the country. We didn't come last year, so it's our first holiday since he died.'

'Did you ever get near Liverpool on one of your tours, sis?' Cormac said mildly. 'Alice gets dead upset whenever your name's mentioned. She misses you. We all do.'

Fion glanced at the children who had eaten the beans on toast, drunk their cocoa and were now munching biscuits, listening avidly to the conversation between their mother and their newly discovered uncle. 'Come on, you two, bed.' She clapped her hands. 'I'll leave the light on and you can take the biscuits with you as a treat, seeing as how we're on holiday, like. Mind a minute, Cormac, there's a good lad.'

She folded down the leaves of the table, which was surrounded on three sides by thickly cushioned benches covered with red moquette, with storage spaces underneath. Several items of bedding were removed and laid on two of the benches. The children obediently lay down and Colin immediately began to suck his thumb. Then Fion produced two folding stools out of thin air and took them outside, round to the back of the van, out of the way of any traffic that might go speeding past. It was almost dark by now and the air was slightly cooler.

'They don't usually go so willingly to bed, but they're dead tired. Colin's quiet because the holiday reminds him of when his dad was alive. He still misses big Colin something rotten. It doesn't bother Bonnie, she can hardly remember him. Would you like some orange juice, Cormac? It's lovely and cold.'

'I'd love some.'

'Won't be a mo.'

Cormac glanced in the direction of the field where the concert was being held. By now, it was almost dark and searchlights criss-crossed the sky. Through the intervening hedges he glimpsed a blur of coloured lights and the thumping music could be clearly heard. It was a familiar number played by a familiar group whose name he couldn't remember.

Fion was back with two glasses and a carton of juice. 'Here you are, luv.'

'Ta.'

She sat on the stool, their arms touching. 'You asked why I've never been home, Cormac. The thing is, I don't rightly know. I've sent cards from time to time so Mam would know I was all right, like. I didn't give me address in case someone came and tried to persuade me to go back. A year later, when I married Colin, it seemed too late, too embarrassing, to let anyone know and the longer it went on the more embarrassing it got.'

'Alice wouldn't have felt embarrassed.'

'I know,' she said abjectly. 'I *should* write, break the ice, as it were, because I'll be coming home to Liverpool soon. Ruby, Colin's mother, died last month and Elsa – she's his daughter from his first marriage – married a soldier and went to live in Germany.' She sighed. 'So there's nothing to keep me in London any more. Me neighbours are lovely, but it's not the same as having your own flesh and blood around. I'd like the children to have a grandma, aunts and uncles, cousins. Colin's due to start school at Christmas and it'd be best for him to start in Liverpool, rather than have him change in a few months' time.'

'There's plenty of room for the three of you in Amber Street, sis.'

'Oh, I've already got a house,' Fion said suprisingly. 'Remember Horace Flynn? He left me his house in Stanley Road. He was the only one who knew I was leaving. I wrote and told him where I lived when I sent back this twenty quid he loaned me and he promised never to tell Mam. We wrote to each other often – he sent a present when me and Colin got married. The house has been rented out for years. It seemed like fate when I got a letter from the tenants giving a month's notice the same week Ruby died. Anyroad . . .' She refilled his glass with juice. 'How is everyone? Has our Maeve had any children yet? Has Orla had more? How are Grandad and Bernadette?' Her voice dropped, became husky. 'And how is our mam, Cormac? I've missed her, you know, every bit as much as she's missed me.'

Cormac didn't doubt it. He knew how easy it was to love someone to distraction, yet treat them with terrible cruelty. At this very moment he was breaking Alice's heart, but his own heart was cold and he didn't care. 'Maeve and Martin haven't had children so far,' he said.

'They're too wrapped up in their house in Waterloo. Orla still only has the four – they're growing up, Lulu's already a teenager. Grandad's retired. He's seventy-two, but as fit as a fiddle, and Bernadette and the kids are just fine.'

'And Mam?'

'How do you think, sis?' Cormac shooed away the dog whose life he'd saved and that had repaid him with a growl. 'You walked out seven years ago and haven't been seen since and her only son has more or less resigned from the human race.'

'Hmm.' Fion gripped her knees. 'I never visualised you becoming a hippy, Cormac. I've always imagined you working in a laboratory, mixing noxious liquids, or whatever it is you do in laboratories, having left university loaded with honours and distinctions. You did, didn't you?' she said anxiously when Cormac pulled a face.

'I didn't finish my degree, Fion. I didn't go back for the last two terms. Alice did her nut. I just missed having to do National Service, I'm pleased to say, otherwise I would have had to register as a conscientious objector.'

'Why do you keep calling her Alice, Cormac? She's our mam.'

He'd love to tell someone, share the knowledge that had been gnawing away at his soul for three and a half years.

'Why, Cormac?' Fion persisted.

'If I tell you, will you promise never to repeat it to a living soul?'

'Cross my heart.'

Cormac took a deep breath. His head felt lighter as he began to relate the story of his twenty-first birthday party, finding Aunt Cora in the kitchen, the terrible things she'd said. 'I can't describe how I felt afterwards.

My feet no longer felt as if they were on firm ground. I felt unreal, like a ghost. Living in Amber Street was a great big lie. I couldn't talk to Alice any more. I didn't know what to say, and what I did say sounded stiff and unnatural.' He shook himself, as if trying to rid himself of the memory of that dreadful period. 'I knew it was a waste of time going back to university; my brain seemed to have frozen solid and refused to work. The only place that I could stand was the Cavern, where I was able to drown in the music, it was so loud and I didn't have to think. It was there I met an old mate from St Mary's who was trying to get a pop group together to rival the Beatles. I joined as general dogsbody and chief tambourine player. I've been on the road with different groups ever since. I'm afraid none has come even remotely close to rivalling the Beatles.'

'No other group ever will.' Fion rocked back and forth on the stool. She didn't look as shocked as Cormac had expected. She said, slowly and thoughtfully, 'If I were you, Cormac, I wouldn't believe Cora. I reckon she's jealous, that's all, what with you doing so well and their Maurice being in prison – I met Neil Greene once in London and he told me. She was always trying to stir things up. Look at what she did to Mam with that agreement thing.'

'But, Fion,' Cormac wailed. 'I look so much like her. No one's ever noticed before. When you think about it, it's obvious she's my mother.'

Fion regarded him in the light falling through the window of the caravanette. 'I don't see a resemblance meself. You're probably just imagining it.'

Cormac shivered. 'I can't stand the thought of her being me mother. I have nightmares about it.' He often dreamed of how it might have happened, of Cora slithering through the sleeping hospital, arriving at the nursery, changing him over with Maurice. 'Maurice looked a better bet,' she'd said.

'If I were you,' Fion said again, 'I wouldn't take any notice of Cora. I'd try and pretend she never told you all that stuff.' She linked her arm in his. 'I'll never think of you as anything other than me brother, Cormac, and I know Orla and Maeve feel the same. Grandad thought the sun shone out of your arse. And Mam – you're not being very fair on Mam, luv.'

'Could you forget if it were you it had happened to?'

'No, but I'd want someone to talk to me the way I'm talking to you. It's almost quarter of a century since you were born and whatever happened that night isn't important any more. It's what's happened since that matters.' She gave him a little shake. 'You're Mam's son, our brother, Colin's and Bonnie's uncle.'

'But say if I'm not, Fion?'

'You *are*,' Fion said confidently. 'I remember the day Mam brought you home from hospital. You felt like me brother then, every bit as much as you do now. We all laid claim to you, Cormac. You're *ours*.'

Cormac was beginning to feel as if there was a way out of the morass in which he had been wallowing for so long. If he could just hold on to the fact that what Cora said didn't matter after all this time, that it was how things were *now* that was important. 'What about Uncle Billy,' he said, 'and Maurice?'

'I doubt if Uncle Billy gave a damn who Cora brought home from the hospital. As for Maurice . . .' She paused.

'I owe him a debt worth more than a kingdom,' Cormac said softly.

'*You* don't owe him a thing. If it's all true, not that for a moment I think it is, then I suppose it's hard luck on Maurice.' She wrinkled her nose. 'Well, worse than hard luck, having Cora for a mam.'

'Particularly instead of Alice. He would have grown up a different person altogether in Amber Street. He wouldn't have gone to prison for a start.'

'You can't say that for certain.'

'Yes, I can,' Cormac assured her.

'What's he doing now?'

'Living in the flat over the hairdresser's, where Neil used to live. Cora chucked him out.'

'She's mad,' Fion said flatly. 'She's not likely to say anything about this to Mam, is she? That would really put the cat among the pigeons.'

'I doubt it. I told her if she did I'd kill her. I meant it, Fion. It makes me wonder if one day I might go mad too.'

'Don't be silly. You're the sanest person I've ever known.'

'Once maybe, not now.'

'I'm going to tell *you* a secret, then I'll make us some tea and sandwiches.' Fion regarded him slyly. 'You'll never guess, but Mam was having an affair with Neil Greene. It was the reason I left home. I heard them in bed together and it made me feel such a fool.'

Cormac smiled. 'I already knew that, sis. You couldn't help but notice the way her eyes went all starry when she announced she was "popping round" to Opal Street for some reason. They were even starrier when she came back.'

'Jaysus, Cormac Lacey! Nothing escaped your gimlet eyes.'

Fion went to make the sandwiches. Cormac leant against the back of the van, suddenly conscious of the music in the distance. He'd forgotten where he was. The lane was busy. Children were being brought home from the concert and latecomers were on their way towards it. Two girls, conventionally dressed, rode by on bicycles –

he'd like to bet the young people of the area weren't as opposed to the festival as their elders.

The sky above was as clear as sapphire with a twinkling of stars and a perfectly round moon, but at the edges, just above the horizon, black clouds were banked, looking as impenetrable as mountains. This effect of nature, both impressive and oppressive, made Cormac feel very small, insignificant, in the great scheme of things. Looked at one way, the bombshell that had been dropped on the night of his twenty-first seemed trivial, not worth bothering about.

He wouldn't have minded a spliff, but his stuff was under his pillow in the coach and he didn't feel like going back, not yet. Anyroad, Fion might not approve of spliffs. He was grateful to his sister for bringing him down to earth, showing him there was a future.

As soon as he could, without letting down his friends, he would extricate himself and Pol from the life they were leading – from the life they were *wasting* – and . . .

Cormac paused in his reverie. Two young men were walking past, bare to the waist, supporting a girl between them. In their free hands the men wielded bottles of the local cider, a lethal concoction. The girl stumbled. The men roughly hoisted her upright. One squeezed her bottom through the thin cotton frock that looked ominously familiar.

Pol! She rarely drank. Half a bottle of that lethal brew and she'd be senseless. It was possible she was being taken back to the coach for her own safety, but somehow Cormac doubted it. He leapt to his feet. He had to rescue Pol.

It meant that when Fion emerged from the van with tea and sandwiches, her brother had gone.

★

It might have continued for ever and a day: the spliffs, the drink, missing gigs, driving nowhere, doing nothing, had it not been that Pol discovered she was pregnant.

'I can get the bread together for an abortion,' Frank said when they sat round the table for a conference. Everyone had been on tenterhooks waiting for Pol to start her period, but she'd missed two and was definitely pregnant. They wore a motley assortment of coats and jackets because it was November, and no one had any idea how to keep the coach warm, apart from using an oil heater, which brought on Wally's asthma. Being on the road had its disadvantages in winter. 'Abortion's legal in this country, isn't it?'

No one knew.

'I don't want an abortion whether it's legal or not,' Pol said defiantly. 'I want my baby.' She laid her hands on her stomach, as if she could already feel its shape inside.

'Don't be foolish,' Tanya snapped. 'This is no life for a baby.' A baby would clutter up their already cluttered lives. Tanya was very conventional. Cormac sometimes wondered if she was only there to annoy her family and had the firm intention of returning home when she felt she'd annoyed them long enough.

'I'll go away,' Pol said. 'I'll find a place to live, a bedsit, probably in London. The state will support me. I mean, us.'

'Who's the father?' Wally asked.

'I don't know, do I? It's either you, you, or you.' Pol nodded one by one at the three men.

'I'm afraid I can't offer monetary support, Pol.'

'No one's asked you to, Wally.'

'I'll buy the pram and the diapers and stuff, honey.'

'Thank you, Frank.'

'Come back to Liverpool and live with me, Pol,' Cormac said, wincing as he massaged the wrist that had been broken months ago when he'd rescued Pol from the two louts who turned out not to be taking her back to the coach, but to their own ex-Post Office van. The plaster had only been removed last week.

Everyone looked at him in surprise, including Pol. 'Hey, man. Isn't that a bit heavy?' Wally murmured.

'Live with you, Cormac?' Pol's grey eyes smiled into his. 'Why, I'd like that very much.'

'Oh, well, that's settled,' Tanya said, as if they'd just decided which pub to go to. 'Would anyone like a cup of tea?'

Chapter 12

Billy Lacey strolled along the Dock Road, a woman on his arm whose name he couldn't remember. It was August and still very hot, despite the lateness of the hour – at that moment Cormac Lacey was sitting in a remote Norfolk lane with his sister, Fionnuala.

The Docky wasn't nearly so busy as it had been when Billy was a lad and he'd come with his brother, John, to look at the ships. There was hardly any traffic, hardly any ships to look at. Even the smells had gone: the musky aroma of spices, coffee, perfumed teas and the strange, dusty smell that turned out to be carpets. He considered it a poor show that such a vital, throbbing part of Liverpool was being allowed to waste away and die. Only the moon, swinging freely – Billy was drunk – in the navy-blue sky and the soaring brick walls of the docks, the giant gates, remained the same.

Despite the jowlly cheeks and the monstrous beer gut that had long ago cancelled out his waist, leaving his trousers somewhat perilously supported by a narrow leather belt, at fifty-four, Billy was still a fine figure of a man, with his thick, dark hair and broad shoulders. A cheap suit adorned his burly body, the jacket hanging open because it wouldn't meet round his swollen belly. Yet he carried himself well. Not a few female eyes were cast in his direction as he swaggered along, linking the arm of his anonymous companion. She was taking him home for a nightcap. Billy wasn't sure which he was most looking forward to, the drink or what was to follow.

'Have you got a missus?' enquired the woman who was leading him towards the longed-for nightcap and her bed.

'She's left me,' Billy lied. For years now, possibly since the day after the wedding, he'd wished Cora would leave. He would have left himself, except he couldn't be bothered looking for somewhere else to live. Anyroad, he'd have to cook his own food, make his own bed, do his own washing. It was comfortable in Garibaldi Road, if nothing else. He and Cora hardly talked, but he wouldn't mind if she never opened her mouth again for the rest of her life. It was sad about Maurice: first jail, then leaving home, but Billy had never really felt that Maurice was his son. He belonged to Cora, who spoiled the poor lad rotten when she wasn't thrashing him with that bloody cane. He'd probably ended up dead confused. Billy knew he should have put a stop to it, but he'd never been much of a match for his wife.

He had no idea why he'd married her, Cora. He must have been pissed when they met, pissed when he proposed and pissed the day they got married – he could never actually remember saying 'I do', though his mam claimed he'd behaved impeccably at the wedding. Still, it had been done and it was a long time ago now. Billy had quite enjoyed his life, Cora or no Cora. He still did. Another woman mightn't have let him do as he pleased, be so glad to see the back of him. Mind you, it would have been nice to have had a few more bob in his pocket. As it was, Cora took scarcely a penny off him, but he still had to rely on finding some poor woman like the one on his arm, desperate for company, poor cow, to keep his belly primed nightly with ale. He had no idea where Cora got the cash from to keep things going and had never bothered to enquire.

'Are we nearly there, luv?' he asked.

'Yes, Billy. It's just round the next corner.'

The pubs had not long ago called time, otherwise there was no way Billy would have been out in the open, breathing in the fresh, warm air. They were approaching the Arcadia, a pub with such a wicked reputation that even Billy had never dared enter its doors, despite intimate knowledge of most of the ale houses in Bootle. A man and woman came out, arguing furiously. At least the woman was furious, the man appeared to be drunk, but not the boozy, mild sort of drunk that Billy knew. This geezer was paralytic. You could have cut off parts of his body and he wouldn't have known. The woman gave him a shove. 'You're bloody useless, you are,' she sneered. 'I'm giving you a wide berth in future.'

The man collapsed on to his knees, wobbled, then crumpled into the gutter. His eyes, staring upwards, were glazed, unseeing. His face looked as if it had been made of stone.

'Here, mate, let's give you a hand,' Billy said sympathetically. He leant down, put his hands under the man's armpits and hoisted him to his feet. 'Jaysus, you're as light as a feather.'

The man's head hung down, like a scarecrow's, as if he too needed a pole to keep it straight. It wasn't until they were face to face that Billy realised that the man he was supporting was his brother, John, whom he hadn't seen in years.

'Don't tell anyone I'm here,' John said to Cora next morning.

'Not if you don't want me to, luv.'

Cora was in her element. This was the man she had

desired all her adult life and now she had him under her roof, at her mercy, you might say.

She had never seen anyone so thin. No wonder Billy had been able to walk all the way from the Docky with his brother over his shoulder like a sack of coal. Last night they had conversed, she and Billy, for the first time in ages.

'Look who I found!' Billy said when she opened the door, him being unable to use his key, like. 'It's our John. I found him collapsed in the Docky.'

Billy looked upset. If things had been different he might have loved his wife and son, but his brother had been the only person he'd ever felt real affection for. 'I'm taking him upstairs, to Maurice's room,' he said gruffly. He stared defiantly at his wife, as if expecting her to object, but Cora flew ahead to put clean, aired linen on the bed and open the window of the stuffy, unused room.

'He hasn't a pick on him,' Billy said with unexpected tenderness when he laid John down. 'Is there a spare pair of pyjamas?'

'I'll get some.' When Cora came back, Billy was stripping John of his clothes. He looked as if he might object when Cora started to help, but must have decided two pairs of hands were better than one. John moaned once or twice as his clothes were removed and he was lifted into a pair of far too big pyjamas. Cora tucked the bedclothes around his waist.

'What shall we do now, Billy?'

'Leave him be. Let him sleep it off. He's as drunk as David's sow. He'll have a head on him in the morning.'

'He needs building up, Billy. He needs to stay in bed a week and be fed proper. He looks as if he's been neglecting himself something awful.'

'Do you mind if he stays?'

Cora shook her head vigorously. 'I always liked your John. Alice hadn't enough patience with him after the accident. I'm not surprised he left. Where's he been living?'

'I've no idea.'

'I wonder if he's still got that business of his?'

'I don't know, luv. I wrote to him twice at that place in Seaforth, didn't I? But he didn't answer. Mind you, that was years ago.'

They went to bed in their separate rooms. During the night Cora, even less able to sleep than usual, got up and went to look at their guest. The curtains had been left open to allow fresh air through the window and the room was brightly bathed in moonlight. She knelt beside the bed and gently stroked the damaged cheek, which by now was scarcely noticeable. The skin was no longer red and one side of the thin, sombre face was merely slightly more wrinkled than the other. Once he had more meat on him, it would be even less obvious.

Cora breathed a kiss on the thin lips of the man she had always wanted, then went through his pockets, the jacket first. He had three pounds, ten shillings in a wallet, along with a photograph of a fair-haired girl and a separate one of three young children, none of whom she recognised. There were some grubby business cards, including several for B.E.D.S. In another pocket she found a packet of ciggies, a lighter, a dirty hankie, a bunch of keys. His trouser pockets held nothing but change. She rubbed the material between her thumb and forefinger: good quality, but it smelt sour and was badly in need of dry-cleaning.

John was still asleep when his brother went to work next morning. Cora kept popping her head round the door, but it wasn't until midday that she found him staring vacantly at the ceiling. His head, his arms, lying loosely on the covers, were in exactly the same position as the night before, as if he hadn't the strength or will to move them. His eyes turned fractionally when Cora went in, but showed no surprise. He didn't appear particularly bothered where he found himself.

'I was wondering where I was,' he whispered. 'How did I get here?'

'Your Billy found you on the Docky and carried you all the way back. Would you like a cup of tea, luv?'

'I think I might, thank you, Cora.'

She put extra milk in the tea so it wasn't too hot, and had to support his head with one hand and hold the cup for him with the other. It gave her a feeling of intense satisfaction to have John Lacey so dependent on her.

When he'd finished he said, 'Don't tell anyone I'm here.'

'Not if you don't want me too, luv,' Cora assured him.

That afternoon she made him bread and milk, and fed it to him with a spoon. By the time Billy came home he was sitting up, propped against a heap of pillows, smoking a cigarette.

'I didn't know you smoked, mate,' Billy remarked.

John shrugged. 'I started years ago.'

'How are you feeling?'

'Exhausted,' John said thinly.

'What were you doing in the Arcadia, mate? It's a dump.' Billy regarded his older brother with concern. He'd missed John badly since he'd left Alice and had been hurt when his letters hadn't been answered. He found it upsetting to see this once strong, vital man lying like a shadow in the bed. Billy had been raised with the dictum 'Why can't you be more like your brother' constantly in his ear. Mam had made no bones about the fact she liked John best, that she was proud of him, whereas Billy was the family black sheep, the failure. Now it seemed their positions had been reversed and it made Billy feel uncomfortable.

'I can't remember going to the Arcadia,' John confessed. 'In fact, I can't remember anything much about yesterday.'

'Been on a bender, eh!'

'One bender too many, I'm afraid.'

Billy chuckled, though there was nothing to laugh about. He put his hand over his brother's thin one, slightly embarrassed. 'What's up, mate? How did you get yourself in such a state? You look like shit.'

'I feel like shit.' John took a long puff on the ciggie. 'Things happened, Billy. Things I'd sooner not talk about.'

'Whatever you say. Where are you living these days? What's happened to that company of yours?'

'I still do a bit of business − I've been living in the office for quite some time.'

'I'd've come and seen you if I'd known.'

John gave a curt nod of appreciation, but Billy had the odd feeling he wouldn't have been welcome and the even odder feeling that he wasn't particularly welcome now, that John would much prefer to be alone.

'You're looking well, though, Billy,' John said with an obvious effort. 'There's enough fat on you for both of us.'

Billy patted his monstrous stomach. 'It's the ale.'

'You always had a weakness for the ale.' John's mouth curved drily. 'I didn't have any weaknesses, did I? I was the perfect husband, the perfect father, a good provider for me family. Then this happened' − he pointed to his face − 'and I turned out to be weaker than most men. Another bloke would have taken it in his stride and got on with things. I let it ruin me life instead. Nothing's been the same since.'

'It was a brave thing you did that day, John.' Billy had had little experience with conversations of this sort. There was a break in his voice when he said, 'There's hardly another man in the world who would have tried to save that sailor. You should have got a medal.'

'They offered me a medal, but I turned it down, just like, in a way, I turned Alice down, as well as me children. I was determined to suffer and I wanted everyone to suffer with me.'

'Perhaps there's time to put things right yet. Alice is still on her own.'

John didn't answer. Cora came in with a bowl of home-made soup and announced Billy's tea was ready downstairs.

Cora was disappointed when John insisted on feeding himself. She sat on the bed, watching. 'There's jelly and custard for pudding,' she said when he'd finished.

'Maybe later. Thank you, Cora. You and Billy are being very kind. Where's Maurice, by the way? Isn't this his bed I'm in?'

He mustn't have known Maurice had been in jail. Cora wasn't about to tell him now. 'He wanted his independence. He's got his own place. It's in Opal Street, over Lacey's, as it happens.'

Later, Billy came back upstairs and Cora went down. For the first time in years, Billy didn't go to the pub. John softened slightly and the brothers reminisced, reminding each other of things that had happened when they were children. Billy had the most to say, his voice was the loudest. His laughter boomed through the normally silent house, awakening it.

Cora sat with the television on, but the sound turned down, listening, planning tomorrow's menu and the other things she'd do. She'd get John's suit cleaned – his shirt and underclothes were already washed and ironed, his tie sponged. She'd ask if he'd like some books from the library. Unlike his brother, John Lacey had always been a reading man.

John couldn't possibly have been looked after more tenderly and efficiently. 'You should have been a nurse, Cora,' he said when, after seven days of cosseting and being fed bland though nourishing meals, he felt up to coming downstairs for his tea.

It was possibly the first time in Cora's life that she had blushed. 'You just needed a bit of building up, like,' she mumbled. 'You'd let yourself go.'

'I've been letting meself go for years.'

'There's no need for it any more,' Cora assured him eagerly. 'You can stay with us for always. There's plenty of room.' It would be one in the eye for Alice when she discovered her husband was living in Garibaldi Road. Cora had promised not to breathe a word, but it was bound to get out some time.

'We'll just have to see,' John said, lighting a ciggie.

A few days later John announced he felt like a walk. Cora accompanied him round the block, proudly linking his arm. By now, August had turned into September and the air felt cooler. The flowers in the gardens smelt as sweetly as wine. She sniffed appreciatively. Normally, she never noticed such things.

'I enjoyed that,' he said when they got back to the house. 'I might go again tomorrow, further afield.'

'I'll come with you.'

'That would be nice.' His face was filling out, his suit already fitted better. He looked dead handsome, she thought. He had yet to smile, but John Lacey was a dignified, serious man, not much given to laughing and smiling. She wished there were a way of getting shot of Billy, so there'd be just the two of them left in the house.

She bought John a shirt because he only had the one and Billy's swam on him. It had a striped body and a white collar. 'The man in Burton's said it's the latest fashion.'

'Cora! You've made me feel dead embarrassed.' She could tell, though, that he was pleased. It was probably a long time since a woman had made a fuss of him, got him a prezzie.

'This is very smart. I'll wear it tonight.'

'Let me iron the creases out first.'

Billy said John looked like a stockbroker or a solicitor in the shirt and addressed him as 'Sir', while they ate their tea. When the meal was over John announced he was going out. There was someone he wanted to see.

Cora's blood turned to ice. She knew for certain he was going to see Alice and her heart seethed with jealousy. Something told her he intended asking Alice if she would have him back.

'Will you be long?' she asked when he was ready to leave, hair combed, freshly shaved, wearing the shirt *she'd* bought.

'I've no idea, Cora.'

Alice was sitting with her feet on a stool. She'd had a busy day, but then all her days were busy. It was something of an anticlimax to enter the unnaturally quiet house. The emptiness always reminded her of her two missing children. Where was Fion? she wondered fretfully. Why didn't she come home, if only to visit? And she worried constantly about Cormac. At least she saw him from time to time, but something had happened to him that she didn't understand. He appeared withdrawn, almost sullen, yet he was a lad who'd always looked upon the world with such obvious delight.

She hadn't been home long when, much to her relief, the back door opened and Bernadette yelled, 'It's me.'

'Put the kettle on while you're out there,' Alice yelled back. 'How's me dad and the kids?' she asked when her friend plonked herself in an armchair with a deep sigh.

'Everyone's fine. How's yourself?'

'A bit bored, if the truth be known. I quite fancy some excitement.'

'How about the pics? Danny's given me the night off. We could go into town. Henry Fonda's on at the Odeon. I could *eat* Henry Fonda.'

'Oh, we all know the things you'd like to do to Henry Fonda, but when I said excitement I meant something a bit more personal, not watching Henry Fonda having all the excitement.'

'Well, I'm afraid, Ally, that it's the pics or nothing.'

'I suppose the pics are better than nothing,' Alice grumbled. The kettle whistled in the kitchen. 'You can make that tea while I get changed. I won't be a mo.'

Alice had changed into a green linen costume with a fitted jacket and pleated skirt and was brushing her hair when the knock sounded on the door.

'I'll get it,' Bernadette shouted.

There was a long silence. Alice was about to ask 'Who is it?' when Bernadette came into the bedroom. Her face was white.

'It's John,' she said.

'John who?'

'John Lacey, daft girl. Your husband. I'll be getting along home.'

'Don't go, Bernie!' Alice cried, but Bernadette mutely shook her head and ran downstairs. Alice stared at her own white face in the mirror for several seconds before going downstairs herself, holding tightly to the rail to support her trembling legs.

John was standing in the living room. He looked fit enough, she thought, though showed every one of his fifty-six years. He'd also lost a bit too much weight. She would have had to look at him twice if she'd met him in the street before recognising him as the man who was still her husband.

He inclined his head. 'Hello, luv.'

'Hello, John.' She would have preferred it if he hadn't called her 'luv'. It didn't seem right after they hadn't seen each other for so long a time. 'Sit down,' she said politely. 'How are you?'

'Ta, luv.' He sat in his old place under the window. 'I've felt better, but I've felt worse, too. I've been living the last few weeks at our Billy's.'

'I didn't know.' Her voice was very cool – and perfectly steady, she noted with relief. She didn't want him to know how badly she was shaking inside. She prayed she looked as calm as he appeared to be.

'You've hardly changed a bit,' he said.

Alice squirmed uncomfortably when she saw the obvious admiration in his eyes. She didn't reply.

'How are the kids?' he asked.

'Fine. Fion's in London. I'm not quite sure where Cormac is right now. He travels a lot, like. Maeve's married and Orla has four kids, two boys and two girls.' She remembered it was the day Lulu was born that she'd discovered he'd got himself another woman and a brand-new family.

'I suppose our Cormac's in a dead good job. I take it he went to university?'

The 'our' Cormac was another mistake. 'He decided not to in the end,' Alice said coldly. If his father had been around he might have been able to talk his son into completing the last two terms. 'He went into the music business instead. He's in a group that plays all over the country.'

He didn't ask what the group was called, what Fion was doing in London, where did Orla and Maeve live. Alice sensed he'd come for a purpose and it wasn't to know how his family were.

'Would you like some tea? Bernadette made some just before you came.'

'Please, luv.'

She went into the kitchen, poured the tea and wished he'd stop calling her 'luv'. It was getting on her nerves.

'You've got the place looking nice, luv,' he said when she came back. 'All this furniture's new, isn't it? I remember you going on about how much you wanted a fitted carpet.' His eyes swept approvingly around the room. 'Hairdressing must pay well.'

'I've got three salons now.' She resented being reminded of the days when she'd been dependent on him. 'I'm able to buy me own carpets.'

John gnawed his bottom lip. He glanced at her covertly. The coolness of her tone must have got through to him. 'I suppose you're wondering why I'm here?'

'It had crossed me mind.'

'Well, luv, I won't beat about the bush. I'll be totally honest with you. Do you mind if I smoke?'

Wordlessly, Alice fetched an ashtray, though the request surprised her. In the past he'd always claimed smoking was a complete waste of money: 'You may as well set light to a ten-bob note every week or so.' She noticed he'd lost some of his composure. His hands were unsteady as he lit the cigarette.

'The truth is, luv,' he said in a rush, 'I've been going

further and further downhill over the last few years until a few weeks ago when I hit rock bottom. I don't want to stay at our Billy's for ever.' He paused. 'I was wondering if you'd mind if I came back home?'

Alice folded her arms over her chest, pressing them against herself so hard that it hurt. At least he'd been honest, as he'd promised. He didn't want to come back because he loved her or he'd missed her, or he wanted to be near his children. He wanted to return because he'd reached rock bottom and had nowhere else to go.

'It's bloody miserable on your own, luv,' he said forlornly.

'I already know that, John. I've been on me own for thirteen years.'

'Well, it'll be nice to have a man around the house for a change,' he said with an attempt at jocularity.

She looked at him directly. 'Not if the man is you. Am I so pathetic that you think *any* man will do for me? Including one who walked out on me for a younger woman and wouldn't be here if that woman hadn't walked out on *him*!'

'It was nothing like you think with Clare. I wouldn't have had anything to do with her if it hadn't been for me accident.'

'Your accident!' Alice laughed bitterly. 'Oh, we all know about your bloody accident. I'm surprised you didn't put a notice in the papers and announce it to the world. You'd think you were the only person who'd ever been hurt. In turn, you hurt everyone who loved you. I'll not forget when you moved in permanently with Clare. Cormac kept ringing the yard. He wanted his dad, but you'd have nothing to do with him. You were dead cruel, John. Cruel and selfish. People don't go that way because they've had an accident. It must have been there always. You just hadn't shown it before.'

'I'm sorry, Alice.' His body had gone limp. He lit another cigarette from the stub of the first and seemed to have trouble making contact.

'So you should be,' Alice said brutally, then immediately regretted it. 'Look,' she said more kindly. 'There's nothing to stop you coming round now and then for a cup of tea. I could arrange for Maeve and Orla to be here.'

'I doubt if they'd want to see me.'

On reflection, Alice doubted it too. 'You could still come round. I could make you a meal.'

'Do you really want me to?'

She couldn't meet his eyes because she could think of few things she wanted less. Until that night she hadn't realised he meant so little to her, that she actually disliked him. 'Of course,' she said.

It was John's turn to laugh. 'I think I get the picture. Perhaps I should have said I wanted to come back because I love you.'

'It wouldn't have made any difference. And it wouldn't have been true.'

'Oh, yes, it would, Alice. I *do* love you. I've never loved anyone else the way I love you.' His face collapsed. He was almost crying and it was horrible seeing a man like John Lacey so close to tears. He dropped the cigarette. The glowing end fell on his shirt, and she leapt to her feet and knocked it away before it burnt a hole, then picked up the ciggie off the carpet. She was still holding it when John grabbed her legs and laid his head against her stomach. 'I do love you, Alice.' He sobbed. 'I can't go on living the way I am.'

She pushed him away, wanting to cry herself. 'But I don't love you, John.' She only wished she did. Then she would have been happy to take him back.

He collapsed into the chair. 'What am I to do?' he asked pitifully. 'Where am I to go?'

'Home.'

'I haven't got a home.'

'Back to your Billy's, then.'

'I can't stay there for ever. You know how much I've always loathed Cora.'

Alice had reached the point where *she* had begun to feel cruel and selfish. 'I'll find you a home, a little house somewhere,' she said desperately. 'I'll give you the money for the furniture if you're short.'

It was a genuine offer, made because she felt genuinely sorry for him, but it immediately brought her husband to his senses. His face turned to stone. 'Do you really think I'd take money off a woman?'

'I'm offering to help, John, that's all.'

'I don't want your help, or your sympathy.'

'What else do you expect when you start crying?'

He got to his feet. 'I have the distinct feeling I've made a fool of meself. I think I'll go now.'

'John.' She put her hand on his arm, but he shrugged her away. Alice had a sense of déjà vu. In the past, he'd done the same thing when she'd been trying to reach him and had been rewarded with the same churlish rejection.

'Goodnight, Alice.'

Alice shut her eyes until the front door closed. She didn't open them until she heard someone coming in the back way.

Seconds later her dad barged in, livid with anger. 'Is he still here?' he demanded.

'No, Dad. He's gone.'

'What did he want?'

'To come back.'

'The nerve of the bugger. I hope you told him to go

. . . to go . . .' Danny paused, trying to think of a way of putting it without using an unacceptable expletive. 'To go and jump in the lake.'

'I just said no, Dad.'

'He's upset you, hasn't he? I can tell by your face.'

'Oh, Dad,' Alice cried. 'He seemed so *tragic*. I feel sorry for him. What's going to happen to him now?'

'That's no longer any of your concern, girl. You're too soft, you are. If John Lacey's tragic, then it's his own fault. He's already put you through enough. Come on, luv.' He put an arm round her shoulders. 'Come back to ours and have a cup of tea, then you can go to the pictures with Bernadette. Even better, go somewhere and have a nice meal and a jangle.'

Alice willingly allowed herself to be led away. Anything would be better than being left with her own thoughts. She just wished she didn't have the horrible feeling that she'd let John down.

If only you could relive certain scenes in your life and do them differently! He should have been more controlled with Alice, more practical. He shouldn't have broken down, made himself look pathetic. Perhaps he should have asked more questions about the children, then approached the subject of him coming home more casually, skirting round it, like, as if the idea had just come to him. As it was, he'd made a terrible show of himself. His flesh crawled, thinking about it.

She'd looked so lovely, too: fresh and young, elegant in that green costume. She'd changed, though, since they used to live together. She'd never have said the things then that she'd said tonight – 'Do you think *any* man will do me?' – as if he was just a piece of shit.

In Marsh Lane, John paused outside an off-licence and realised how much he needed a drink. A sup of liquor hadn't passed his lips since the night Billy had carried him home from the Docky. He'd sworn never to get in such a state again, but now he felt like getting smashed rotten. He went into the shop and bought a bottle of whisky, the cheapest there. Outside, he stopped in the first doorway, unscrewed the top, put the bottle to his lips and swallowed deeply. The alcohol seemed warmly familiar as it poured down his throat and he immediately felt better, more in charge of himself.

He walked towards Garibaldi Road, only slightly unsteady on his feet, anger mounting. Who did Alice think she was? Had she forgotten that they were still man and wife, that he had rights? It could be she had no lawful right to turn him away. It could be that the house in Amber Street was still legally his. It was *his* name that used to be on the rent book. He might go and see a solicitor tomorrow.

Cora opened the door as he was struggling with the key. 'I'll give you a key if you like, luv.' She nodded at the one in his hand. 'That must be for somewhere else.'

'Sorry.' He frowned at the key. It was for the padlock on the gates of the yard.

'You weren't gone long,' Cora said, slyly pleased. There'd obviously been no great reconciliation.

'Where's Billy?' John lurched into the hall.

'He went out not long after you. Why don't you come and watch telly till he comes home?'

'I'd sooner go to bed early, if you don't mind. I feel very tired.'

'Anything you like, luv.'

Cora could smell the drink on him. As he went unsteadily upstairs, she saw the whisky bottle protruding from the pocket of his jacket. Alice must have turned him down.

What John didn't realise was that the woman who was

perfect for him was directly under his nose – herself. They thought the same black thoughts, they looked darkly upon life, they didn't suffer fools gladly, they took great risks.

For the next two hours she sat in front of the empty grate, hands clasped on her lap, unmoving. Billy came in and wanted to know if John was home, and she told him he was in bed, but didn't mention the whisky.

'I think I'll turn in meself,' Billy announced, yawning.

Within minutes she could hear him snoring. And still Cora sat, shoulders tense, arms stiff, hands held together tightly, like a knot in a rope. Dare she show John, that very night, how exactly right they would be for each other? Billy wouldn't hear. The house could fall down around Billy's ears, but you'd still have to shake his arm to wake him.

Dare she?

She'd known he was for her the very second she'd set eyes on him. She felt certain something had passed between them. But he wasn't the sort of man who'd steal his brother's girl. He'd pretended to ignore her, but she could tell he wanted her as much as she wanted him. Alice, wishy-washy, gormless Alice Mitchell, was merely a substitute for the woman he really loved.

Cora went upstairs and changed into her best nightie. It was blue, that brushed-nylon stuff, and she'd got it in a sale in T. J. Hughes's. She undid her bun and combed her greying hair loose around her shoulders. There was scent somewhere, Californian Poppy, that Alice had given her for Christmas in the days when she'd been made welcome in Amber Street. She found the tiny bottle in a drawer under her stockings and dabbed some behind her ears.

Then she crept along the landing to the room where John Lacey slept.

He lay sprawled on the bed in his vest and underpants, his suit and the shirt she had bought him thrown carelessly on the floor. On the bedside table the whisky bottle was three-quarters empty and the clean ashtray she'd provided earlier overflowed with butts. The smell of smoke, of whisky fumes, only increased Cora's desire. She leant over the bed and started to touch him.

'Darling!' John reached for her and began to stroke her body through the scratchy nightdress. Cora pulled it over her head, leaving herself entirely exposed to him, giving herself, touching him as he touched her. Her body arched and shuddered with pleasure beneath his exploring hands. Then he thrust himself inside her and she had to hold back a shriek as a feeling, impossible to describe, began to grow and grow in her gut, like a firework, sizzling away, getting brighter and brighter, louder and louder, as it prepared to explode in a shower of stars and sparks.

Then the explosion came and her body, from head to toe, was encased in a silent scream of ecstacy. Cora had been waiting all her life for this day, for this hour, for this single minute.

She fell back on the bed, blissfully exhausted. John grunted, collapsed beside her and immediately fell asleep, but she didn't care. She snuggled against him and put her arm round his waist.

'That was nice, luv. It was never that way with your Billy,' she whispered. 'Later on, we'll do it again. We'll do it again and again for the rest of our lives. We're soulmates, you and me. I bet I could tell you things and you wouldn't be the least bit shocked.' She looked at his face, wondering if he could hear. 'I've never breathed a word about this to a soul, but I killed two people once. They were me aunties, Kate and Maud. You see, luv, me mam wasn't married when she had me and she died right after I was born. I never knew who me dad was. Kate and Maud, they took me in, but they didn't like me. Oh, no, they didn't like me a bit. I was a "badge of shame", they said. They treated me worse than an animal, fed me scraps, hit me and kicked me whenever they felt like it. I got hardly any learning. I never even learnt how to be happy, like. So, you know what I did?'

She paused, half expecting him to say, 'What, luv?' but there was no answer. 'I murdered them. I set fire to the house we lived in. I waited in the backyard till I heard them scream, then I waited till the screaming stopped, then I ran away. Sometimes, in the dead of night, I can still hear them screams. I can even smell the fire. It's the reason I can never sleep.' Cora sighed. 'Are you comfy, luv?' She adjusted the pillow beneath his head, pulled the sheet over them both. 'You have a nice rest, now, and when you wake up I'll make you feel dead happy again.'

Cora had never known what it was to relax, for her body to feel rested, her soul to be at peace, her brain to feel as light as air, and free for once of the thoughts and memories that plagued her. Before long, although it was the last thing she intended, she, too, was fast asleep.

The palest of grey light was creeping through the window when John Lacey woke. The birds in the garden had just begun to sing. For a few seconds he felt disorientated.

He recognised the lampshade hanging above him and remembered he was at Billy's. It took several more seconds before he realised there was someone in bed with him: a woman. For one mad moment he thought it might be Alice. He'd been to see her the night before. But the hair just visible in the still dusky shadows of the morning was the wrong colour. Anyroad, Alice had turned him down and he'd bought a bottle of whisky.

He'd obviously gone somewhere, met a woman and couldn't remember a thing about it — it had happened before. He must have been plastered out of his mind to have brought her back to his brother's house.

Jaysus! He was longing for a fag. As soon as he'd smoked it, he'd get rid of his companion of the night as quietly as possible. Gingerly he eased himself out of bed. The ciggies were on the bedside table. He lit one, breathed in deeply, then noticed the blue nightdress thrown over the foot of the bed.

His reflexes must be working dead slow this morning, because it took John quite a while to realise the significance of this. There was only one person the nightdress could belong to.

Cora! He stumbled backwards, horrified. Cora Lacey was lying in his bed, naked. They must have . . .

Christ! He wanted to be sick. Something stirred in his sluggish brain, a memory, of hands touching him, of him touching back. He could remember them making love — and that it had actually felt good. He gagged. He had to get out of here.

Frantically he picked up his clothes, the ciggies, the remainder of the whisky and carried them on to the landing, where he clumsily got dressed, thrusting his foot into the wrong trouser leg, buttoning up his shirt all crooked. As he did so other memories returned, of a voice in his ear talking about murder, about burning people alive in their beds, listening to their screams.

Outside, a fine grey mist hung in the air and he could feel the moisture on his face as he walked towards Seaforth, towards the place that had been his home since Clare had left with their children.

Every now and then he stopped and took a mouthful of whisky. If he drank enough for long enough it might drown out the memory of last night.

By the time he reached the yard the whisky had gone and he could hardly walk. He flung the empty bottle into the gutter, where it smashed into a thousand brilliant shards. It took some time to fit the key into the padlock on the gates, more time to unlock the door of the two-storey building that was a store room, an office and the place where he lived – there was little use for an office these days. B.E.D.S. was all washed up. He'd been neglecting the firm for years. He owed money for the materials going rotten in the yard.

Somehow he managed to climb the stairs, where he collapsed on the filthy bed and immediately lit a ciggie.

The place stank, but he couldn't be bothered getting up and opening a window. He couldn't remember when it had last been cleaned. For years, now, he had let himself wallow in his misery, in the dirt of his surroundings. He had let B.E.D.S. collapse around his ears.

It never ceased to amaze him that a man as sensible as he'd always considered himself had made such a total and completely unnecessary mess of his life, culminating in last night's misadventure with Cora. He squirmed at the memory and wondered if he'd just imagined the things she'd said. Was his brother's wife a murderer?

In a minute he'd look for something to drink. He'd drink himself completely senseless, so he wouldn't be able to think. There were times, like the night Billy had found him on the Docky, when his mind was nothing but a blank.

The fag had burnt so low he could feel the heat on his lips. He spat it out and reached for another. The effort of stretching made his head swirl crazily and John didn't mind a bit when he found himself sinking into welcome unconsciousness.

The stub of the cigarette had landed on the bed, rolled under the pillow. John Lacey was too far gone to notice when the pillow began to smoulder.

Chapter 13

The police were still trying to trace the relatives of John Lacey, the man whose charred body had been found after the fire in the timber yard had been extinguished, when Fionnuala Littlemore returned to Liverpool with her children.

It was Sunday afternoon, and Fion came in the back way just as Alice was preparing a salad for Maeve and Martin who were expected later for tea.

'Hello, Mam,' Fion said, as casually as if she'd been gone five minutes, not several years.

'Fion!' Alice dropped a slice of ham on the floor. 'Oh, Fion, luv. It's good to see you.' She flung her arms round her eldest daughter, stroked her face. 'How are you, luv? Where have you been? And who are these?' Only then did Alice become aware of the children.

'This is Colin and this is Bonnie, and we've been living in London. Say hello to your grandma, kids.'

'They're yours?' Alice dropped more ham.

'Very much mine, Mam. And before you ask, their dad, me husband that is, died two years ago.'

'Oh, luv!' Alice burst into tears for the son-in-law she'd never met and hadn't even known existed. 'Oh, they're lovely children,' she said tearfully. 'Let's take a look at you.' She knelt down and examined Colin's face. 'You must take after your dad, because you're nothing like our family. And you' – she turned to Bonnie – 'are the image of your mam.'

Both judgements seemed to please the children inordinately. Alice forgot the salad and took them into the living room.

Fion immediately made herself at home. 'I'll put the kettle on, Mam. I'm dying for a cuppa.'

'I wouldn't say no to a cuppa either.' Alice drew her new grandchildren on to her knee. They went willingly. 'You're prettier than Ruby,' Bonnie said.

'Who's Ruby?'

'Ruby was their other grandma,' Fion said as she came in. 'She was much older than you. She died a few months ago. That's why we're back home.'

She'd come home for good! Alice did her best not to feel glad that the unknown Ruby had died, otherwise Fion, who'd clearly not acquired an ounce of tact in her absence, would still be in London. Her daughter had acquired one thing, though – confidence. Alice watched as Fion unzipped a small travelling bag and began to root swiftly and efficiently through the contents. She seemed very sure of herself. She was slimmer and had grown her hair, which was gathered in an untidy knot on top of her head. Long wavy tendrils had escaped and trailed over her neck and ears. Her outfit was a bit peculiar: black slacks and a thin black jumper under a brightly coloured patchwork waistcoat. Neil Greene, who'd met her in London, said she worked for a union.

'Oh, it's good to see you, Fion,' Alice cried. 'You look wonderful.' Her mind went back to the day Fion, her first child, had been born. She'd arrived two weeks late, after a long, tiresome labour, very early in the morning. At almost nine pounds, she was the biggest of Alice's babies – and the biggest in the maternity home, she remembered. John had been so proud. She recalled him taking his daughter in his arms, looking down at her, his eyes filled with love. It had never crossed her mind that one day that love would disappear.

'It's good to see you, Mam,' Fion said practically. 'And you don't look so bad yourself.'

'Where's your luggage, luv? You won't last long out of that small bag.'

'I've got more than luggage, Mam. I've got furniture. It's coming in a van tomorrow.'

Alice felt alarmed. 'But there isn't the room here for furniture, Fion.'

'I know that.' Fion snorted. 'I'm not an idiot. The furniture's going to me house on Stanley Road.'

'You've got a house!'

'It's Horace Flynn's old house that he left me in his will.'

'Bloody hell!' exclaimed Alice, who usually managed not to swear if children were present. 'Who'd have thought it, eh? Wonders will never cease.'

'Is our Orla still living in Pearl Street?'

'Yes, luv,' Alice said weakly, still trying to come to terms with the incredible fact that Horace Flynn's house in Stanley Road now belonged to Fion. 'Maeve's in Waterloo. Her and Martin are coming to tea.'

'I'll go round and see Orla in a minute. I'll leave the kids with you, if you don't mind.'

'As if I'd mind being left with these two little darlings,' Alice cried, hugging the children to her. 'Ask Orla and everyone back to tea. I'll take Colin and Bonnie round me dad's and see if Bernadette can lend us some food. Oh, I can't remember when I last felt so happy.' Fion's return more than made up for John's recent visit, the memory of which still haunted her.

To make things even better Fion had news of Cormac. 'I think he might soon be back as well.'

'Did he say what was wrong?' Alice asked anxiously. 'I think something must have happened at university to make him not want to go back. He was doing so well, too.'

'He didn't say anything, Mam. Perhaps he'd been studying so much his brain got tired. I've heard it can happen.'

Alice sighed blissfully. 'I can't wait to have him home. It'll be just like old times, all four of you here. And these two little 'uns will make it absolutely perfect.'

'Oh, so you saw fit to show your face again, Fion Lacey.' Orla's face was cold when she opened the door to find her sister on the step. 'You know, Mam was dead upset when you walked out.'

'She was dead upset when Micky Lavin put you up the stick,' Fion said, grinning. 'So I reckon we're even when it comes to upsetting Mam. And it's Fion Littlemore, if you don't mind. I'm a mother now of two small children.'

Orla's cold expression vanished and she grinned back. 'It's great to have you home, sis. You look marvellous. Our Maeve's become a real pain since she got married. All she talks about is her bloody house.'

'It's good to *be* home, Orla. Now, are you going to let me in, or must I stand on this doorstep for ever?'

An impromptu party took place at the Laceys' that night. Danny Mitchell went to the off-licence and returned laden with wine, beer and crisps. Bernadette quickly made two dozen sausage rolls. Orla, never an expert in the kitchen, coaxed Lulu into making a tray of fairy cakes. Maeve was telephoned and asked to bring whatever was available.

'I bought a tin of iced biscuits for Christmas the other

day. I'll fetch them and anything else I can find,' Maeve promised. 'Tell our Fion I can't wait to see her.'

'Jaysus! She's become so *efficient*!' Orla groaned. 'Who in their right mind buys biscuits for Christmas in September?'

'Our Maeve does, obviously. It's no worse than someone with four children not being able to rustle up a fairy cake.'

'You've not changed, Fion. You were always one to call a spade a spade.'

'I could never understand why anyone would want to call a spade anything else. Are my Elvis records still around, Mam?'

'They're in the parlour, luv. You'll find Cormac's there too. He was fond of Gerry and the Pacemakers and Herman's Hermits – and the Beatles, of course.'

It's quite like old times, Alice thought as she prepared a mountain of sandwiches and listened to her daughters bicker. But there was no spite behind it now. Fion wasn't jealous of Orla any more. She felt her equal.

Eight o'clock. Most of the adults were slightly tipsy. Colin and Bonnie were upstairs, tired after the long journey from London, fast asleep in their mother's old room. The other children were in the parlour playing something that seemed to require a great deal of noise.

The weather had changed. The long Indian summer had ended late that afternoon when the sun abruptly disappeared and the sky became a solid mass of black, leaden clouds. Thunder rumbled in the distance, lightning flashed. Every now and then there would be a splattering of rain against the windows. A downpour was expected any minute.

In Amber Street the lights were on and the weather

did nothing to dampen spirits. The three men were contemplating going to the pub for a pint.

'But we've got beer here,' Alice pointed out.

'It tastes different in a pub,' Danny claimed.

'What happens if it rains?' Orla wanted to know. 'I'm not pressing your best suit if it gets soaked, Micky Lavin.'

Maeve looked reproachfully at Martin. 'Fancy deserting me for a pint of beer!' the look said. Martin affected to ignore it.

'Well, will we or won't we?' Danny demanded.

Micky slapped him on the shoulder. 'I say we will.'

'Me, too.' Martin was still avoiding Maeve's accusing stare.

Lulu appeared in the doorway, her blue eyes round and slightly scared. 'There's a police car stopped outside,' she said. 'The man's just got out.'

There was a knock on the door.

Alice still felt shattered next day. 'It's all my fault,' she said hoarsely. 'If only I'd taken him back!'

'Don't be daft, Mam. If I'd come home and found him here I'd have been out the house again like a shot.'

'Don't say things like that, Fion.'

'Well, don't you go saying stupid things like it's all your fault. It's nobody's fault but his own. The police said the fire was started by a cigarette. He could have done the same thing here and it wouldn't have been just him who'd gone up in smoke, but you as well.'

Alice sighed. 'You sound awfully hard, luv.'

'I'm just being sensible, Mam,' Fion said more gently. 'Why don't you go in to work, try and forget him.'

'As if I could forget your dad! He was everything to me once.' Alice looked imploringly at her daughter. 'You'll come to the funeral, won't you, luv? I wish we could get in touch with Cormac, tell him.'

'I'll come for your sake, Mam, not his. Orla and Maeve are coming for the same reason, and Grandad and Bernadette. As for Cormac, he's lucky to be out of it. I only wish I'd left coming back another week and I'd've been out of it too.'

Billy Lacey was the only person to cry at his brother's funeral. His sobs sounded harsh and bitter across the deathly wastes of Ford Cemetery. It was a strange morning, neither warm nor cold, not quite sunny, not quite dull.

Billy's wife made no attempt to comfort him. The other mourners would have been surprised if she had. Cora's face was as strange as the morning. She gave no sign to show that she cared her brother-in-law had gone.

It was left to Maurice who, at twenty-five, could have been the double of the young John Lacey, to step forward and put his arm around the broad, heaving shoulders.

'Never mind, Dad,' Maurice mumbled awkwardly, and father and son embraced, as they had never done before.

Alice wouldn't let herself cry, because the tears would have been for herself, not John. They would have been hypocritical tears. She was sorry John had died such a horrible death, but her prime emotion was guilt that she might have stopped it.

John's daughters were there purely for their mother's sake. Alice was a stickler for appearances. It mattered to Mam what people, particularly the neighbours, thought. However, so far, none of the neighbours had guessed that the John Lacey, whose death in a fire in Seaforth was reported in the local paper, was the John Lacey who had once lived in Amber Street.

Good riddance to bad rubbish, Danny Mitchell

thought as the coffin was lowered into the grave. Our Alice should be glad to see the back of him.

Bernadette Mitchell thought more or less the same.

Only one piece of paper remained that had belonged to John Lacey. All the rest had been destroyed in the fire, every scrap; the unpaid bills, the files, the audited accounts going back for years, every single letter John had ever received and the carbon copies of those he had sent, the photos of Clare and their children.

The paper that remained had been lodged in a bank. It was a deed, confirming that John had owned the freehold of the piece of land fronting the corner of Benton Street and Crozier Terrace. Alice, as the lawfully wedded wife of the deceased, was now the legal owner, so the bank informed her in a letter.

'I don't want it,' she said with a shudder when she showed the letter to her dad.

'Then get the place cleaned up. It's bound to be in a mess. And sell it,' Danny advised.

What would she do with the money? There was money piling up in the bank from the three salons, but none of her children was prepared to take a penny. Maeve and Martin had refused help with their mortgage, and Micky Lavin had been indignant when she'd offered to buy him and Orla a house. Cormac had lived happily on his grant at university and she had a feeling Fion wouldn't let her pay for Horace Flynn's old place to be done up – it was dead shabby and the plumbing made some very peculiar noises.

Why was she bothering to make all this money when there was nothing to spend it on? She was fed up with her customers wondering aloud why she was still in Amber Street, why she hadn't bought herself a nicer house in a nicer place.

'Because I'm perfectly happy where I am,' she would reply. She felt very dull and unimaginative.

Fion was looking for someone to care for the children so she could go to work. Alice could sell the salons and become a full-time grandma.

'No, I need more than that,' she told herself. 'I may well be dull and unimaginative, but I need to *be* someone, not just a mother or a grandmother, not just a wife. I need to be special in me own way.'

Since John's death, Billy Lacey had taken to calling on his sister-in-law on his way home from work. Alice was the closest link to the brother he had lost, found, and finally lost again.

He couldn't understand why John had left the house in Garibaldi Road, he said repeatedly. 'He was in bed when I came home the night before, but gone next morning, without a word of explanation. I thought he was happy there. He *seemed* happy. Cora liked having him. He could have stayed for ever as far as we were concerned.'

Alice didn't mention it was the night before that she'd turned John away. She already blamed herself enough and she didn't want the burden of Billy's blame as well.

'Have you ever been to that timber yard place?' Billy asked.

'Just the once.'

'I should have gone meself. It's not far. I shouldn't have let him sink into such a state, me own brother, like.'

'Don't reproach yourself, Billy. John knew where you lived. It was him who walked out, on all of us, including you. It was up to him to keep in touch, not for you to search him out.' Alice wished she could take her own sensible advice. She showed Billy the letter from the bank.

'Do you mind if I take a look at the place?' His face brightened. 'I'll tidy it up if you like.'

He would have been hurt if she'd turned him down. She accepted his offer with a show of gratitude, though she didn't give a damn what happened to the yard. Billy perked up considerably and decided to go round to Seaforth there and then.

'I'll call for our Maurice on the way. The two of us can do the job together.'

At least one good thing had come out of John's death: Billy and his wayward son were now reunited.

The iron-barred gate was secured with a padlock and chain. The men peered through the bars at the dismal remains of John's once thriving business. The building he had lived in had almost completely burnt away. There were no walls and only the skeleton of the roof remained, the beams silhouetted starkly against the livid evening sky – more rain looked inevitable later.

The yard itself was covered with ash and soot, mixed with other debris, including curls of black tar paper, like apple peelings, from the roof. Pools of black water reflected the angry yellow sky. The few lengths of timber stacked around the walls had been badly singed. There was a rusty van with a flat tyre.

'We'll have to get a key from somewhere to match the padlock,' Billy said.

'It'll be a job and a half, clearing this place up,' said Maurice.

'You don't mind though, do you, son? After all, it's not as if you've got anything else to do.'

'I don't mind and no, I haven't got anything else to do.' Maurice's voice was bitter. A prison record didn't help when you were looking for a job. Maurice hadn't worked since he'd come out of Walton jail, though he'd never stopped trying.

'I didn't mean it like that, son.'

'I know, Dad. I was a fool to break into that newsagent's. I only did it to impress some girl – I can't even remember her name. I know I shouldn't make excuses. I was an adult. I should've known better, but her brothers talked me into it.' Maurice laughed drily. 'They made it sound so easy.'

They began to walk back towards Bootle. 'You know,' Maurice said after a while, 'we could do something with that yard.'

'Such as?'

'I'm not sure. Remember that place I used to work, the builders' merchants? Something like that.'

'We'd need money to get started, son.' Billy jangled the coins in his pocket. They were all he had until he got paid on Friday.

'You can borrow money from the bank to start a business. Not that they'd lend it me,' Maurice said hastily. 'Not with my record. But they might lend it you. After all, we've already got the premises.'

'Who said we've got the premises. Alice wants the place sold.'

'She won't sell if we tell her our plans,' Maurice said with utter conviction. 'Not Auntie Alice. Anyroad, once we get going we'll pay rent. We might even buy the site off her one day.'

'What plans?' Billy asked, bewildered.

'The plans you and me have to start our own business. Dad.' For the second time in a week Maurice placed his arm round his father's shoulders. 'I wonder if that van goes?'

Cormac came into the salon wearing an Afghan coat that

looked as if it had been gnawed by a hungry animal, red cotton trousers and open-toed sandals, despite it being November and very cold. His long fair hair was tied back with a ribbon. He looked a sight.

Alice was torn between the joy of seeing him again and worry that her customers would recognise who he was. She rushed her once-perfect son into the kitchen. 'Fion said to expect you one day soon.' She longed to kiss and hug him, but Cormac seemed to have gone off that sort of thing. 'Are you hungry, luv? Shall we go home and I'll make you something to eat?'

'I've just eaten at Fion's, thanks.'

'You went to see Fion first?' Alice felt hurt.

'I wanted to put my stuff there.' For some reason he refused to meet her eyes. 'I'll be living at Fion's, on the top floor. I hope you don't mind.'

'Of course not.' Alice minded very much, but didn't show it. 'Your room's always there if you change your mind.'

'The thing is' – he shuffled his near-naked feet – 'I've brought a girl. We'll be living together.'

Alice swallowed and reminded herself that young people did this sort of thing nowadays. 'I hope she's nice. What's her name?'

'Pol. She's very nice. She's also pregnant.'

To Alice's surprise she burst out laughing and at the same time thanked God he hadn't expected to live in Amber Street with his pregnant girlfriend. 'What else are you going to tell me, that she's got two heads?'

Cormac smiled for the first time. 'No, just one head, Mam. Fion said to come round tonight so you can meet her.'

It might have been a mistake, but he'd called her Mam, something else he avoided these days, along with the hugs and kisses.

★

Horace Flynn would have turned in his grave if he could have seen the state of his house, which hadn't seen a lick of paint in years. The few pieces of expensive furniture still remaining were covered in cigarette burns and the scars of too hot cups. Cats — Fion already had two strays — had scratched curves in the legs of the mahogany table, the six chairs that went with it and the lovely sideboard that used to house Horace's pretty ornaments.

Fion's own furniture was cheap stuff, similarly marked with years of wear and tear. Alice suspected it had been bought second-hand.

She had insisted on paying for the curtains to be cleaned — they were too thick and heavily lined to wash — because they made the rooms smell musty. 'Regard it as a prezzie,' she said to Fion. 'People usually buy each other house-warming presents.'

The long velvet parlour curtains had emerged from the cleaners in tatters. 'They were rotten,' the woman assistant announced when Alice went to collect them. 'I'm afraid we can't pay compensation.'

Alice had bought replacements, but Fion didn't notice that the curtains that went up in the parlour were different from the ones that came down. Fion seemed oblivious to her surroundings. The shabby furniture didn't bother her. Neither did the clanky, grumbling plumbing, the ancient bathroom, the tatty carpet on the stairs, the grimy ceilings, the wallpaper peeling in the corners . . .

And it wasn't just stray animals Fion had started to collect, but human beings too. Alice had no idea where she found them. The three Littlemores lived on the vast ground floor. On the floor above, in the front bedroom, a Mrs Freda Murphy spent her days knitting unwearable garments for the children.

'Where did she come from, luv?' Alice asked curiously

when Freda first turned up. Fion had scarcely been living in the place a week.

'Her son was all set to throw her out. The thing is, Mam,' Fion said indignantly, 'the rent book used to be in her name, but he persuaded her to change it.'

How had Fion *known?* Alice didn't bother to pursue the matter.

Not long afterwards the Archibalds arrived, Peter and Geoffrey, twin brothers in their thirties, who occupied the bedroom at the back. 'They've been in a mental home, poor things,' said Fion.

'Are you sure they're safe, y'know, with the children, like?' Alice asked nervously.

'There's nothing wrong with them, Mam. They went in the mental home by mistake. Anyroad, it's only temporary. The corporation have promised to find them a proper house.'

Now Cormac was moving into the top floor with a pregnant girl called Pol and there were still two bedrooms empty. Alice dreaded who might turn up next.

Yet the strange thing was that she loved being at Fion's. The fire in the living room was always lit, the shabby chairs were comfortable, tea was permanently in the pot for anyone to help themselves. The telephone rang non-stop, because Fion, who never used to have a single friend, now seemed to have dozens. Alice discovered she was a member of numerous organisations and charities, and was always in the throes of arranging fund-raising events: jumble sales, coffee mornings, parties, lectures. She had persuaded her mother to help at a Christmas bazaar early in December. A few weeks ago she had taken the children down to London for a CND march.

'What's CND?' Alice asked.

'The Campain for Nuclear Disarmament. Honestly, Mam, you're dead ignorant. All you know about is hairdressing.'

Alice humbly agreed.

She felt very nervous the night that she went to meet Cormac's pregnant girlfriend. She prayed that they would like each other and that Pol would make a suitable wife – she assumed they would get married one day – for Cormac, who was a remarkable lad and would make a wonderful husband.

Freda Murphy opened the door to Alice's knock, the long needles of her untidy knitting tucked under her arms. Two strange children were playing in the hall with Colin and Bonnie.

In the living room a woman with a black eye was talking in a high-pitched, angry voice to Fion.

'Hello, Mam,' Fion said calmly. 'This is Jenny. She's staying with us a while until the police do something about her louse of a husband. Our Cormac's upstairs with Pol. Tell them to come down in a minute; I've made some scouse.'

'You gave birth to an angel when you had that girl,' Freda remarked when Alice reappeared.

'Did I really?' She went up two flights of stairs. The top floor was merely one large room with a sloping ceiling and windows at both ends.

'Come in,' Cormac shouted in answer to her knock.

Alice took a deep breath, opened the door, and found Cormac and a young girl sitting crossed-legged on the floor, facing each other and holding hands.

'We're doing breathing exercises,' Cormac said. 'We've bought a book on what to do when you're having a baby. This is Pol, by the way. Pol, say hello to . . . to my mother.'

'Hello, Mrs Lacey,' Pol said in a breathless, childish

voice. She scrambled to her feet, a rosy-cheeked girl, with guileless eyes and curly brown hair. She wore an ankle-length cotton skirt and a coarse woven top. Her feet, like Cormac's, were bare. She looked no more than sixteen.

'Call me Alice.' They shook hands. Pol's hand was very small and limp. 'How are you feeling, luv? When's the baby due?'

'I feel fine. I haven't been sick or anything. I'm not sure when it's due.' She looked vague.

'Well, the doctor should be able to tell,' Alice said comfortably. 'He'll send you to the clinic where they'll keep an eye on you.'

Pol gave a tinkling little laugh. 'Oh, there's no need for doctors and clinics, Alice. As long as I look after myself, eat properly and do the breathing exercises I shall be OK.'

'I see.' Alice was horrified. She glanced at her son, still sitting cross-legged on the floor, eyes closed, apparently in a trance. He must approve of Pol's plans for her pregnancy. Still, she had always made a point of not interfering in her children's affairs and wasn't going to start now. 'Oh, well, but you need to book into hospital, so they'll be expecting you.'

'There's no need for that either.' Pol regarded her pityingly. 'Cormac's going to deliver the baby here.'

'He'll sew you up, will he? If you need stitches, like.'

'She won't need stitches,' Cormac said without opening his eyes. 'She'll be too relaxed to tear.'

Jaysus! Alice announced the scouse would be ready soon and escaped downstairs. The pair were crazy, out of this world.

Fion was alone, stirring pans in the old-fashioned kitchen. A cat watched with interest from its unhygenic position on the draining board. She looked up when her mother came in. 'What did you think of her?'

'She seems very nice, but awfully young.'

'She's twenty-one, older than she looks.'

'Has she told you her plans for having the baby? They're not very sensible, Fion. I'm worried.'

'She'll change her mind nearer the time.'

'Lord, I hope so. Our Cormac's a clever lad, but I'm not sure if he's up to delivering a baby.'

The Christmas bazaar was to raise funds for an orphanage in Ethiopia. Fion put Alice in charge of the bottle stall. The main prize was a bottle of whisky. Every bottle had a raffle ticket attached, the numbers ending in a nought. People bought tickets for sixpence each and if they picked one that matched the number on a bottle it was theirs.

Naturally, everyone wanted to win the whisky. The trouble was the winning ticket wasn't in the box. Fion had taken it to put in later when most of the bottles had gone.

'You can't do that!' her scandalised mother gasped.

'Of course I can, Mam. If the whisky's won right at the start, no one will want a go any more. Don't forget, it's all in a good cause.'

Alice had been hoping to enjoy herself. Instead, she felt like a criminal as she tended her colourfully decorated stall. Carols issued from a loudspeaker and their innocent message made her feel even more sinful. She was very busy, always surrounded by a crowd, and the prizes – the bottles of chop sauce, vinegar, shampoo, lemonade, mayonnaise – rapidly diminished as the afternoon progressed. The more they diminished the more the eager participants saw their chance of winning the whisky, which had started to look very lonely, not quite by itself but almost.

Where the hell was Fion? She couldn't leave the stall and look for her. Alice began to panic. Any minute, now, someone would guess the ticket for the whisky wasn't there and she'd be driven from the hall by a justifiably angry crowd. She felt conscious of her burning face, her racing heart.

'Are you all right,' said a voice. 'It's Mrs Lacey, isn't it? Fion's mum.'

She'd noticed the slightly balding man who seemed to be in charge of things. He was about her own age, casually dressed in a black polo-necked jumper and baggy corduroy pants, his craggy face deeply tanned, as if he'd spent many years abroad. He had a slow, gentle, very patient smile.

'No, I'm not all right,' Alice said in a cracked voice. 'I need our Fion urgently.'

'I'll find her for you.'

Fion arrived seconds later. Alice stared at her accusingly over the heads of the crowd surrounding the stall.

'Can I have a go, Mam?'

'I think you better had.'

Only Alice noticed the ticket already in Fion's hand when she dipped it into the box. 'If she brings it out again and claims the whisky I'll bloody kill her,' she vowed. Luckily for Fion, she withdrew a losing ticket. Not long afterwards the whisky was won by a little boy and immediately appropriated by his delighted father. Alice breathed a sigh of relief.

'Would you like a cup of tea?' The man in the black jumper was back.

'I'd give my right arm for a cup of tea, ta.'

'There's no need for such extremes.' He smiled. 'You can have one for nothing.'

Now the whisky had gone, so had all interest in winning the motley collection of bottles that remained. Alice sank on to one of the chairs against the wall behind.

The helpful man returned with two cups of tea and sat beside her. 'My name's Charlie Glover. Do I call you, "Fion's Mum" or "Mrs Lacey"?'

'I'd prefer Alice and I don't know what I would have done without you earlier. You were a great help.'

'Pleased to be of service, Ma'am.' He smiled his lovely smile. His eyes were dark-grey with little shreds of silver.

Alice wondered why she was noticing a strange man's eyes, his smile. She was fifty-one, for heaven's sake. She'd lost all interest in men years ago. 'Have you been living abroad?' she asked conversationally.

'Yes, Ethiopia. I used to run the orphanage we're raising funds for.'

'Used to?'

'I thought it was time I had a rest and a change,' he explained. 'I'm staying with my brother and his wife in Ormskirk.' His voice was deep and pleasing, and Alice detected the faint trace of a Lancashire accent. He spoke slowly, with the air of a man unused to being interrupted. 'In another three months I'm off to the Transvaal, this time to take over a hospital on the borders of Swaziland.'

'You're a doctor?'

'Yes. I work for a charity called Overseas Rescue.'

'Gosh! It all sounds very exciting.'

'It's more worthwhile than exciting.' He half smiled. 'My wife used to love it when we moved somewhere new, but she sadly died ten years ago.'

Alice put her hand on his arm. 'I'm so sorry.'

'That's kind of you. Fion told me her father died recently. You're being very brave about it.'

She felt uncomfortable. 'Me and John hadn't lived together in a long while. I was upset he died, but not devastated. Mind you' – her lips twisted wistfully – 'I would have been devastated once.'

'You obviously have good memories to look back on.' He got to his feet. 'Duty calls. I'm due to draw the raffle any minute.' To her surprise he sat down again. 'Look, are you doing anything tonight?'

'Nothing particular. I'll probably watch television,' Alice replied, taking the question literally and wondering why he seemed so pleased by her answer, why his grey eyes lit up.

'Then why don't I take you out to dinner instead?' he said eagerly. 'Somewhere in Southport would be nice.'

'Dinner!' she exclaimed, immediately flustered. 'Oh, no. No, I couldn't possibly. Thanks for asking, but no . . . excuse me. I've just seen my other daughter. Orla!' she called and almost ran over to the door that Orla had just entered by. 'What are you doing here?' she asked breathlessly.

Orla waved the notebook in her hand. 'Covering the bazaar for the paper. Have you been trying to run a four-minute mile, Mam? You're all puffed out and as red as a beetroot.'

'I've been working hard on a stall, that's all.'

'Where's our Fion? I need to know how much she raised, then I've got to interview a chap called Charlie Glover. He wants to appeal for funds for some hospital abroad.' She made a face. 'I once envisaged meself interviewing film stars and politicians, not reporting on a grotty bazaar. You know how much I'll get for this?' She waved the notebook again. 'Tuppence a line!'

'Oh, stop moaning, luv.'

Orla was jealous of Fion, with her active social life, loads of friends and part-time job at Liverpool University

333

where she worked in the Students Union. Beside that of her sister, Orla considered her life hideously dull and uneventful, and the Lavins' house in Pearl Street poky in the extreme compared with the one in Stanley Road. 'Ta, Mam. You're all sympathy,' she said tartly.

'Tell Fion when you see her I've gone back to Stanley Road, and that I've taken Colin and Bonnie. They look dead bored. And by the way, that's Charlie Glover over there, about to draw the raffle.'

Alice was gently frying sausages when Fion arrived home, looking flushed and exhausted. 'We raised over two hundred pounds,' she said triumphantly. 'Where's the kids?'

'Watching telly. They said they were starving, so I've fed them. All I could find in the fridge was sausages, so I've done the same for us. You've got no spuds, either, only frozen chips.'

'I need to do some shopping,' Fion said vaguely. 'By the way, what did you do to poor Charlie?'

Alice nearly dropped a fork in the sausages. 'Nothing that I know of. We just chatted a bit, that's all. Why, what did he say I'd done?'

'Nothing, but he talked about you non-stop while we were packing up. He obviously fancies you dead rotten, but when I invited him back to tea and said you'd be here he claimed you wouldn't be too pleased.' She stared accusingly at her mother. 'Why on earth should he say that, Mam?'

'He asked me out and I refused.' Alice went red.

'Idiot!'

'I am not an idiot, Fion. I didn't want to get involved, that's all. I wouldn't have known what to say. I'm quite happy staying in and watching television.'

'Well, you shouldn't be.' Fion lit the gas under the

chip pan, already full of fat that hadn't been changed in weeks. 'You're not exactly old and Charlie's quite decent-looking for somone in his fifties. You should have grabbed the chance to enjoy yourself for a change. Our Orla agreed.' Her eyes narrowed calculatingly. 'If you'd played your cards right, you could have gone with him to the Transvaal in a few months' time.'

'What as, one of the cleaners in his bloody hospital?'

'No, as his wife. You're not half daft, Mam. He fell for you like a ton of bricks.'

Alice's heart gave a little lurch. 'Are you after getting rid of me, Fion?'

Fion laid her chin on Alice's shoulder. 'No, Mam. I just want you to be happy, do something interesting and exciting for a change. I don't like you living on your own in Amber Street. You're going nowhere fast. Why don't you tell Charlie you've changed your mind? Give him another chance; he'd leap at it.'

'He might be a Protestant.'

'For God's sake, Mam,' Fion said, exasperated. 'As if that matters at your age.'

'I'll think about it,' Alice promised, though she had no intention of doing any such thing.

That night the television was on but Alice wasn't watching. Instead, she was going over the events of the afternoon. She didn't want to leave Amber Street, let alone travel to the other side of the world. She didn't even want her humdrum life interrupted by having dinner with a man she hardly knew.

She wasn't particularly happy, but nor was she particularly sad. She just existed, went from day to day, living a life in which little happened that was exciting or remarkable. Babies were born; people died; there was an occasional juicy bit of gossip in the salon; she sometimes went to the pictures with Bernadette; her children and *their* children came to tea on Sundays. Every now and then she threw a party. She'd got used to being the proprietor of three hairdressing salons and they had long ceased to be a source of pride.

It wasn't much of a life, but it was the life she wanted.

No one thought to close the curtains when Alice Lacey held a party on Christmas Eve. From the parlour a sharp ray of yellow light fanned across the dimly lit street. There were other parties in Amber Street that night, other lights, making the unlit areas darker and more starkly defined, shadowy. It was a beautiful night, calm and tranquil, not particularly cold for the time of year. There was no moon, but the black sky was littered with stars.

The solitary figure of a woman lurked in the shadows outside the Laceys', peering through the window, dodging from one side of the glass to the other. The woman wore the same camel coat, the same clumsy fur-lined boots that she'd worn four years before when she'd spied on Cormac's twenty-first. She spied on him now, watched him lounging against the wall, looking a bit fed up, she thought.

She was disappointed in her son, who'd given up university for some reason and had actually been seen in the labour exchange, shamelessly queuing for his dole money. She didn't approve of his long hair and the way he dressed, like he'd just picked stuff out of a ragbag. The girl, Pol, was there, obviously in the club. No one knew if she and Cormac were married. By all accounts Alice kept her mouth firmly buttoned when she was asked.

In fact, Maurice looked far more presentable, in a blue check shirt and nicely pressed grey pants. He and the Pol girl seemed to be getting on like a house on fire. They'd been laughing together on the settee for almost an hour.

Cora's lips bared in a snarl when Fionnuala came into the room with a plate of sandwiches. She'd very much like to know what favours Fion Lacey had done for Horace Flynn so that he'd seen fit to leave her his lovely big house, yet hadn't thought to let *her* have a penny.

Billy was there! Billy had come into the parlour supping a can of beer. Her own husband had been invited to Alice's party and hadn't said a word – not that they normally exchanged many words. There'd just been those weeks while John was living with them. Since then the usual silence had prevailed.

John!

She hadn't cried much in her life, but she still cried when she thought about John and the future that had been denied them – the future *together*. It would always remain a mystery why he'd left Garibaldi Road so suddenly. That morning she'd woken up, felt for him, but he wasn't there! After Billy had gone to work she'd rushed around to the yard. But it was already on fire, blazing away, throwing sparks into the sky. Someone must have called the fire engine, because it arrived almost straight away. She had stayed for hours, watching the building fall to pieces, watching the flames gradually subside, watching the firemen carry out something on a stretcher.

There didn't look to be much left of John under the tarpaulin. She longed to snatch it off and kiss the burnt remains of the only man she had ever loved. Cora clenched her fists and her nails bit into the soft flesh of her palms.

A burst of laughter came from inside the house whose occupants interested her so greatly. Billy, of all people, had made a puppet out of his hand and was making it talk. She couldn't hear what it was saying, but everyone was falling about.

Fion suddenly leapt to her feet and closed the curtains, and Cora was left desolate, with nothing to see.

In the parlour Fion shuddered and said to nobody in particular, 'It's funny, but I felt as if there was someone watching us from outside.'

Chapter 14

It was April Fool's Day and the baby had taken it into its head to fool them by arriving early, though Pol had always been vague about the date. Cormac opened the window, put a tape of soothing music in the tape recorder and lit a fresh joss stick.

'Take deep breaths, Pol. Really deep now,' he instructed when the labour appeared to be reaching a climax. He sat on the edge of the bed and took several deep breaths himself to demonstrate how. 'Sing your song. "Here we go round the mulberry bush, the mulberry bush, the mulberry bush. Here we . . ."' he warbled very much out of tune.

Pol screamed.

'I didn't think it was all that bad,' Cormac joked.

Pol screamed again. There was a veil of perspiration on her brow and her body was rigid with fear.

'Push,' he commanded, determined to stay calm. 'No, don't push. Oh, where's that bloody instruction book?'

'On the table,' Pol yelled. 'Cormac, I think I need to go to hospital.'

'But we were going to do this by ourselves!'

'No, Cormac. *I* was going to do it by myself. *You* were going to help and you're not helping a bit. Ooh!' she groaned. 'I never knew you could be in such pain. Fetch your Fion. She might know what to do.'

'She's gone to a coffee morning.' Cormac felt a stir of panic. 'I'll ring for the ambulance.'

'Do it quickly, Cormac. Please!'

Two hours later Pol was delivered of a perfect baby girl weighing six pounds, two ounces. Mother and baby seemed unharmed after what had turned out to be an unexpected ordeal.

'Who does she look like?' Pol asked Cormac when he was allowed in to see her and the new baby. 'Wally, Frank the Yank, or you?'

Cormac had thought he wouldn't care, but when he stared at the little, round, scrunched-up face discovered, somewhat surprisingly, that he did. 'Me. She looks like me,' he claimed, despite the fact that the baby had red hair exactly the same shade as Frank the Yank's.

Pol touched her on her tiny ball of a chin. 'Say hello to mummy and daddy, Skylark.'

Cormac groaned. 'Oh, no, Pol. Not Skylark.' He thought they'd dispensed with Skylark. It had been Buttercup for a girl the last time they'd discussed names.

'It's a lovely name, Skylark.'

'Except this is Liverpool. It isn't full of flower people like San Francisco. Everyone will poke fun at her at school. I suggest we call her something else as well, say . . .' He said the first name that came into his head: 'Sharon! Skylark can be her second name.'

'All right, Cormac,' Pol said, easygoing to a fault.

'That girl of Cormac's, she had her baby this morning,' Billy told his son when he called in Lacey's Tyres at teatime, 'TYRES FITTED ON THE PREMISES' it said on the newly painted board outside.

Maurice drew in a quick intake of breath. 'What did she have?'

'A girl. A pretty little thing, according to Alice. Going to call her Sharon.'

'That's nice.'

'Business good today?' The plan was for Billy to continue going out to work until the firm was doing well enough to keep them both busy.

'Not exactly.' Maurice pulled a face. 'Two cars, that's all, and only three tyres between them.'

'Things'll improve, son,' Billy said stoutly. 'Once word gets around how cheap we are.'

'It takes time for word to get around, Dad. We need to advertise now.'

'Can't afford it, Maurice, lad. We've used up all the bank loan to buy stock and do up the yard. They're expecting us to start paying the loan back in the not too distant future.'

'I know, Dad.' Maurice glanced fearfully around the yard that had once housed B.E.D.S. The cheap retreads from Hungary were stacked in neat heaps around the wall – it hadn't exactly been cheap to buy so many. Then there was the smart hut that had been erected in place of the burnt-out building because it was essential to have an office of some sort; the telephone; the sign; the second-hand van, bought when John's old van proved beyond repair; the chicken-wire roof they'd had put up when they discovered two boys fishing over the wall for tyres with a giant hook.

He wasn't making enough to live on, let alone pay back the loan. Dad didn't realise you could go to prison for defaulting on a loan – it was *him* who'd go, not Maurice, because it was taken out in his name. He'd been getting on well with his dad since Uncle John's funeral. There hadn't been the opportunity when he was growing up to discover how kind Billy was – and he'd worked like a Trojan getting the yard ready. Over the last few months Billy's support for his son had been rock solid.

Maurice felt nausea rise, like a ball, in his throat. Everything was his fault. He'd thought all you had to do to start a business was find the premises, stock them with whatever you wanted to sell and that was it. You were made; the customers would come flocking in. Perhaps they would have if there'd been adverts in the press, or the site weren't so much out of the way. As it was, hardly anyone knew they were there. Every day Maurice felt more desperate and the feeling of nausea was never far away.

'Which hospital is Pol in?' he asked when Billy emerged from the hut with two mugs of tea.

'Liverpool Maternity. Why? Are you thinking of going to see her?'

'I might,' Maurice muttered. It was another thing that added to his misery, thinking about Pol. Maurice wasn't sure, but he had a feeling he was in love with her. They'd first met at Alice's party on Christmas Eve and he'd been unable to stop thinking about her since. He'd started going round to the house in Stanley Road on the pretence of seeing Fion, but in reality to see Pol. Something about her childish fragility struck a chord in his heart. He wanted to look after her, cherish her, keep her warm at night. He had stupid visions of them growing old together, stupid because she belonged to his cousin, Cormac. There was a saying, 'All's fair in love and war', but Maurice was fond of Cormac and couldn't bring himself to steal his girl from behind his back, always assuming Pol was willing to be stolen in the first place.

Mind you, Cormac was no longer the person he used to be. He looked a proper ponce in those daft clothes and had made no attempt to get a job. Although he hadn't been successful, at least Maurice had tried to find work. These days he didn't feel as inferior to his cousin as he used to.

'I think I'll close early tonight, Dad.' Lacey's Tyres was open twelve hours a day, from seven in the morning till seven at night.

'No,' Billy said stubbornly. 'I'd sooner we stuck to the hours it ses on the board. You sod off, son. I'll lock up.'

Alice and her daughters were just leaving the hospital when Maurice arrived bearing a meagre bunch of flowers that was all he could afford. Cormac had gone in search of tea, he was told, and baby Sharon was in the nursery.

'You can keep Pol company till the new dad comes back,' Alice suggested.

'Hello, Pol. Congratulations.' Her eyes lit up as he approached the bed, but Pol's eyes lit up for everyone. She wore a faded cotton nightie that hadn't been ironed. He wished he could have bought her something rich and silky, trimmed with lace, but not only did he not have the money, it wasn't done for men to buy nighties for other men's girls.

'Thank you, Maurice. Are those for me?' She gasped, as if he'd presented her with a magnificent bouquet of roses. 'They're lovely. What are they?'

'Dunno.'

'They're very pretty, whatever they are. I'll ask the nurse to put them in water after you've gone. How's business?'

Pol was one of the few people in whom Maurice had confided the true state of Lacey's Tyres. If anyone else asked he would reply modestly, 'Not bad.'

'Bloody awful,' he said gloomily. 'I'm worried sick, if you must know.'

'Oh, you poor thing,' she said, her blue, doll-like eyes

343

so full of sympathy that Maurice easily could have cried. He longed to bury his head in her small breasts and sob his heart out. 'Things will buck up soon, Maurice. They're bound to.'

'I hope so.' He explained about not earning enough to pay back the loan. 'It's me dad who worries me. He's the one who'll get into trouble, not me.'

'Perhaps you should expand, Maurice, sell more than tyres.' She waved her arm vaguely. 'Other bits for motor cars, fr'instance: brakes and stuff.' She patted his hand, when it should have been *him* patting *her* hand, her being the one in hospital, like.

'Gosh, Pol, I hadn't thought of that.' It was a good idea, but he hadn't the cash to buy so much as a tyre gauge. Still, she meant well. 'You're very clever, Pol,' he said admiringly.

'Me!' She laughed. 'What a lovely thing to say. Everyone usually thinks I'm very stupid.'

'You're anything but stupid,' Maurice said, meaning it sincerely.

Cormac was about to enter the ward when, through the glass panel in the swing door, he saw his cousin, Maurice, sitting beside Pol's bed. He always felt uncomfortable with Maurice, as if he had stolen from him something of incalculable value. One of these days, when Alice was dead, he might tell Maurice the truth about their parentage, something that was out of the question while Alice remained alive. He, Cormac, had lived twenty-one enjoyable years of Maurice's life, while Maurice had endured twenty-one years on *his* behalf with Cora.

Once again Cormac went to push open the door and once again he paused. Maurice was leaning on the bed, arms crossed, laughing at something Pol had said.

344

Unaware he was being watched, his face was naked, showing everything, hiding nothing, and Cormac realised with a shock that his cousin was head over heels in love with Pol.

Was he jealous? No, Cormac decided calmly, standing aside to let a nurse into the ward. What was the point of being jealous over something that couldn't be helped?

Did he mind? Cormac wasn't sure. He was in love with Pol himself. He had assumed that one day they would get married, have more children and spend the rest of their lives together, that they would be happy. It wasn't until now that it came to him that something was lacking, because he had never looked at Pol the way Maurice looked at her now, so *absolutely*. Cormac felt almost envious. Would he ever look at a woman like that?

And Pol? Sometimes he wondered if Pol would have gone just as willingly with Wally or Frank the Yank, had they asked. Pol loved everybody. She was like a kitten, happy any place where she was warm, comfortable and petted. She could just as easily be in love with Maurice as with Cormac.

He owed his cousin so much. Justice would be partially done if Maurice were allowed to steal Cormac's girl, just as Cormac had, inadvertently, stolen Maurice's mother.

A man came out of the ward and nearly hit him with the door. 'Sorry, mate,' he muttered and rolled his eyes in disgust when he noticed Cormac's rainbow knitted jumper, full of snags, his green flared trousers, dirty feet, his sandals. For the first time since he left Amber Street Cormac felt slightly ashamed of his clothes. He smiled ruefully. Alice used to keep him so neat!

It was time for another cup of tea. He'd return to the ward five minutes before the bell went to indicate visiting time was over. And from now on he'd give his girlfriend and his cousin every encouragement. He'd invite Maurice round to Fion's, then make excuses to go out, leaving him and Pol together.

After all, it was only fair.

It didn't *feel* very fair, not right now, not to Cormac. In fact, he felt quite depressed. Sniffing audibly, he wished Maurice hadn't come to the hospital, that he'd never discovered he was in love with Pol.

Lord, he'd give anything for a spliff to blunt the rawness of his misery. He had been looking forward to life with Pol and his daughter. Well, there was a one-in-three chance she was his daughter and probably no chance at all if you took into account the red hair.

The debt to Maurice had to be paid some time.

'Christ, Mam, you're not half bad-tempered lately,' Lulu said acidly. 'Every time anyone opens their mouth you bite their head off.'

'Don't you dare swear in this house!' Orla screeched.

'I hate you, Mam.' Maisie's lip curled.

'So, hate me. I don't care.'

'I hate you too.' Paul's lip wobbled. He was the most sensitive of the Lavin children.

'Join the club,' Orla snarled.

'I'm leaving home,' announced Gary. 'I'm going to live with Nana Lacey.'

'Well, don't let me stop you. Shall I pack a suitcase?'

Orla and her four children glared at each other across the breakfast table. Then Orla's face collapsed and she held out her arms. 'Oh, come here. I love you! I adore you! You are the most beautiful children in the world and I am the most horrible mother. I don't deserve you. I truly don't deserve you. I'm sorry. I'm sorry, sorry,

sorry.' She kissed their heads one by one. 'So sorry,' she whispered.

'Are you in the club, Mam?' Lulu asked. 'Nana Lavin said you might be.'

'No, luv.' Orla sobbed. 'I'm not in anything as far as I know.'

'Is it an early mennypause?' enquired Gary. 'Granny Lavin thought it might be that as well.'

'It can't be both, luv. It can only be one or the other and it's neither. It's just that your mother's been in a state with herself lately.'

'What sort of state?'

'An upside down, inside out, up in the air, down in the dumps, topsy-turvy sort of state.'

'Wow!' said Gary, impressed.

'I promise not to be bad-tempered again, least not till tonight, then you'll just have to excuse me and tell yourselves I don't mean it.'

The children went to school. Orla washed the dishes, dried them, made the beds, dusted, threw herself on to the settee in the parlour, burst into tears, cursed her husband . . .

'I *hate* you Micky Lavin,' she said aloud.

No, she didn't. She loved him. But she wished he'd try to understand just how *unhappy* she was, how unutterably and stultifyingly bored she was with life. The trouble was, putting it bluntly, Micky was too thick to understand. Micky felt exactly the opposite and was so lacking in imagination that he couldn't understand anyone feeling different. He was as happy as a sandboy. He enjoyed his lousy job without a future, he was perfectly content living in this grotty little house. Going to see Liverpool or Everton play football at weekends was the ultimate joy, particularly if they won. Micky didn't want a car, holidays abroad, flash clothes, posh furniture. He didn't mind seeing the occasional film as long as lots of people in it got killed, but as for the theatre, it belonged in an alien world, as did books that contained words of more than one syllable, anything intellectual on television, politics and newspapers that weren't littered with pictures of naked girls.

It meant they had nothing to talk about. Even sex had lost its thrall and become a tiny bit tedious with someone who was essentially a moron.

Micky had refused to let Mam buy them a house somewhere nicer with a garden for the children to play.

'Why not?' Orla screeched. She seemed to screech an awful lot these days.

'I've got my pride,' Micky said huffily.

'You weren't too proud to fill this house with stuff that had fallen off the back of a hundred bloody lorries.'

'That's different.'

'In what way is it different?'

He shuffled his feet. 'I dunno, it just is.'

She'd grown past him. He wanted to spend his life standing still, but she wanted to go forward. She would have got a proper job, but it would mean giving up the newspaper and the extra money wouldn't have been enough to make a difference. Besides, although she would have denied it till she was blue in the face, she got a thrill out of attending various pathetic functions and announcing, 'I'm from the press,' and occasionally seeing her name under the headline of a news item she'd sent in. She kept hoping the *Crosby Star* would take her back in the office so she'd be a real reporter, but there hadn't been a vacancy in ages.

This afternoon, she was interviewing some stupid ex-Everton footballer – anyone willing to take up kicking a ball up and down a field as a career *had* to be stupid. She'd only been asked because Dominic Reilly came from Pearl Street. His parents still lived in the house opposite. His mam, Sheila, had had twelve children. Orla shuddered delicately: *twelve*! Dominic, who at thirty-two was the same age as herself, had come back from Spain for the wedding of one of his numerous brothers and was returning that night. She had no idea what he'd been doing in Spain, but it was the first on the list of questions she'd prepared. At least it broke up the tedium of the day.

She went out and bought the *Guardian*, and read everything except the sport. Would that great intellectual Micky Lavin be interested in the fact that the war in Vietnam was escalating? No, he bloody wouldn't. Nor would he care that Mrs Gandhi had become Prime Minister of India, or that Great Britain had just elected a Labour government led by the vaguely dishy Harold Wilson. Orla had sent him out to vote, but he'd met a mate and gone for a game of billiards instead.

Seething, Orla rolled the paper into a ball and flung it across the room. It was time she got ready for the interview.

It was also time she had some new clothes, she thought irritably when she examined the miserly contents of her wardrobe. Except there wasn't the money.

'You'd look lovely dressed in rags,' Micky insisted when she complained.

In that case she was bound to look lovely, because there was nothing but rags hanging on the rail. Orla sulkily removed a black skirt and a white blouse that mightn't look so bad if they were ironed. She didn't just need new clothes, but a new house, a new husband, a new life.

She left her long brown hair loose, made her face up carefully and, promptly at three o'clock, knocked on the Reillys' front door. Sheila Reilly opened it. She was a pleasantly pretty woman, lumpily overweight, though anyone would be overweight if they'd had twelve children. Sheila was as old as her mother, but had children younger than Orla's. Two toddlers hung silently to her skirt who, unless Sheila had had more babies when no one was looking, were grandchildren – she had hordes.

'Hello, Orla, luv. I suppose you've come to see our Dominic.'

'If he's available, Sheila. I'm from the press.'

'I know, luv. He's expecting you, though where you'll find the quiet to talk I don't know. I've half a dozen of the grandkids here to see their Uncle Dominic.'

'We can go over to our house if you like.'

'I'm sure he'd appreciate that, if only for a bit of peace.'

Dominic came into the hall. He was casually dressed in pale blue linen slacks, a white, short-sleeved shirt and white canvas shoes. 'Hi, there. I've seen you around, but I don't think we've ever spoken before. I vaguely remember you from school.'

'We didn't move in till you'd left home. I vaguely remember you from school too.'

They shook hands. Orla hadn't realised he was quite so good-looking, quite so tall, quite so tanned. He reminded her a bit of Robert Redford, with his dark-blond wavy hair and broad build, his dazzlingly warm smile.

'Orla said you can use her house for the interview, luv.'

'That's a relief, otherwise I won't be able to hear meself think.'

They crossed the street to the Lavins'. Orla felt super conscious of Dominic's arm brushing against hers when she showed him into the parlour. She asked if he'd like a cup of tea. 'Or sherry?' There was sherry over from Christmas.

'Tea would be grand, ta.'

When she returned he was sitting on the settee, arms stretched along the back, legs crossed. A gold watch glinted on his brown wrist, muscles bulged in his arms, his waist was very slim.

Orla swallowed and looked away. She settled in a hard chair, pad on her knee, pencil poised, coughed importantly and asked her first question: 'What were you doing in Spain?'

For some reason Dominic choked on the tea. She hoped it wasn't too hot. 'Playing football,' he replied.

'They play football in Spain? I didn't realise. What part of Spain?'

'Barcelona.' His face had gone very red.

'They have stadiums there, just like in Liverpool?'

'Just like in Liverpool.' He nodded and she wondered why his brown eyes were glinting with amusement.

'And what made you go to Spain in the first place? Couldn't you get a job playing football in this country?'

He regarded her silently for several seconds. 'That's right,' he said eventually. 'I was on me uppers, if the truth be known. The offer from Barcelona was a lifeline.'

'You poor thing,' Orla said sympathetically, making a note in her pad. She glanced at him surreptitiously. He looked very odd, as if he was about to bust a gut. Perhaps he was dying to use the lavatory.

'Is this for publication?' Dominic asked.

'Of course.' Orla tossed her head importantly.

'In that case I think we'd better start the interview again, otherwise you're going to make a right fool of yourself.'

'Am I, now!' she said huffily. 'In exactly what way?'

'For one, you clearly know nothing about football.

351

Barcelona is one of the leading clubs in the world, with a stadium every bit as good as those in this country, if not better. For another, I was offered a hundred quid a week to play there, twice as much as I was getting with Everton. I live in a flat overlooking the Mediterranean, I drive a sports car, I have a beautiful girlfriend – though she's not as beautiful as you. All in all, I live the life of Reilly – appropriately, considering me name.' He burst out laughing and didn't stop till tears ran down his cheeks. 'Oh, Gawd!' he gasped, wiping them away with the flat of his hands. 'I haven't enjoyed meself so much in a long time. It makes a change to have a reporter feel sorry for me; they're usually so sycophantic it makes me want to puke.'

Orla felt dizzy with shame and embarrassment. If only she had condescended to tell Micky about the interview he would have filled her in on Dominic's background. 'Jaysus!' she muttered, unable to meet his eyes. 'I wish the floor would open up and swallow me.'

'I don't, because then I wouldn't be able to look at you any more.'

She found herself blushing on top of everything else and remembered he'd said something about his girlfriend not being as beautiful as she was. There was silence in the world for a while as Orla stared at her shoes and Dominic Reilly stared at *her*, and her stomach trembled in the way it had done in the early days with Micky. Then Dominic gave her a challenging look and patted the cushion beside him and Orla knew that if she responded to the challenge everything would change, even if it appeared nothing whatsoever had altered when the children came home from school and Micky from work.

The notebook and pencil fell to the floor as Orla got up and moved into Dominic's welcoming arms. After a while they went upstairs to the bed where she'd lain with Micky for almost fifteen years.

She was sorry afterwards – deeply, wholeheartedly, wretchedly sorry. Perhaps she wouldn't have felt like that if it hadn't been so wonderful. For half an hour, an hour, she'd glimpsed another world, a world of blue seas and golden sands, of beautiful clothes, good times, parties, a world in which every day was different from the day before, where exciting, unexpected things happened, as opposed to the drab, colourless world she occupied now, in which every day was the same as the next, counting Sundays when she went to church and to tea with Mam or one of her sisters, or they came to tea at hers.

Then Dominic rose from the bed, kissed her gently and went home, and the wonderful world came crashing down around her ears.

After a few minutes she went and soaked in the old-fashioned bath that had fallen off the back of a lorry, using the last of the bath salts Micky had bought her for Christmas. At the time she'd thought how little imagination he showed: he gave her bath salts, talc, cheap perfume, every year, usually Boots' own brand. She noticed a scratch on her wrist from Dominic's watch. He'd had to take it off. She'd put disinfectant on it when she got out.

The events of the afternoon hadn't made her love Micky more, she wasn't suddenly counting her blessings, appreciating what she already had. On the contrary, she would much sooner not have glimpsed that other magical world. It made the one in which she lived seem drabber, even more colourless than it had been when she woke up. There were so many things she would never know, never do, sights she would never see if she lived to be a hundred.

She was gentle with the children when they came home. Nothing that happened would ever make her love them less. Lulu was the reason she'd been stuck with Micky, but that wasn't Lulu's fault but her own.

'What's the matter?' Micky asked that night when they were watching telly – least he was watching. Orla was miles away.

'Nothing.'

'You're very quiet. It's not like you.'

'Isn't it?' She looked at him and noticed his hair was receding slightly at the temples, that he had a small paunch. He also had a hole in his sock that needed mending. 'Shall we go to bed early tonight?'

'I wouldn't say no.' He grinned and, for a moment, she saw the teenager who'd charmed her all those years ago. Perhaps if she could lose herself in him, recapture the magic of those days . . .

They went upstairs. There was a time when they would have leapt naked into bed, but now Orla put on her nightdress, Micky his pyjamas. He went to put out the light, stopped and said in a voice she'd never heard before, 'Who does this fuckin' watch belong to, Orla? And what's it doing beside our bed?'

Orla turned up in Amber Street late one Sunday night just as Alice was thinking about going to bed. Unusually for Orla, who was inclined to arrive in a flaming temper over something, she appeared pale and listless.

Alice sat her down and made her a cup of cocoa. 'What's wrong, luv?' she asked sympathetically.

Orla didn't look at her mother but stared at her shoes. 'Mam, don't get mad at me, but I've done something awful.' There was a pause. 'I've slept with someone and Micky found out.'

'Jaysus, Orla!' Alice's sympathy vanished, to be

354

replaced with anger and alarm. 'You stupid girl,' she snapped. 'Who was it?'

'It doesn't matter who it was, Mam.'

'Then why are you here? What d'you expect me to do about it?'

'Nothing, Mam,' Orla said in a subdued voice. 'I just wanted to tell someone, that's all. Micky's making me life hell.'

'I'm not surprised. Most men would if they found their wife had been sleeping around.' Alice frowned. 'He's not hit you, has he?'

'No, Mam. He just won't talk to me, that's all.'

'You can hardly blame him, luv.' Alice thought what a perfect world it could be if only human beings, including herself, could bring themselves to behave sensibly. 'When did this happen?'

'Last Monday. Micky hasn't spoken to me since. Not that I mind, to be frank, but there's a terrible atmosphere at home. The children have noticed and it's making them dead miserable.'

Alice remembered Sheila Reilly had been in Lacey's the Saturday before last having her hair done for her son, Niall's, wedding. She'd mentioned Orla was seeing Dominic, her eldest, before he went back to Spain. Alice immediately put two and two together. Micky Lavin was a nice, hard-working lad, but as dull as ditchwater and without an ounce of Dominic Reilly's glamour. She didn't approve of what her daughter had done, but could understand Orla being bowled over by a man so entirely different from her husband.

'I should never have married Micky, Mam,' Orla cried tragically. 'I wish things had been different then, the way they are now. No one's nagging our Cormac and Pol to get married.'

'No one nagged *you* to get married,' Alice reminded her.

'No, but it wasn't on in those days to have a baby out of wedlock. I felt obliged to marry Micky for Lulu's sake. If I had me time over again, I wouldn't go anywhere near an altar.' She buried her face in her hands and began to cry. 'I'm ever so unhappy, Mam. I have been for years. All those dreams I used to have are dead and I feel all dried up inside. I ache for something nice to happen, something interesting or unusual or enjoyable. I long to go out and have a good time or go on holiday abroad, somewhere like Spain. I wish we had a car so I could learn to drive, and I'd just drive and drive and drive till I came to the end of the rainbow. I wish – oh, Mam,' she sobbed. 'I wish all sorts of things.'

'I know, luv.' Alice patted her daughter's knee. She was like a beautiful wild animal trapped inside a cage, the exact opposite of her mother who gave the slightest opportunity of excitement a wide berth. 'I'll buy you a car if you like. As long as Micky doesn't mind.' She knew she was being too generous, too indulgent. After all, Orla shouldn't be rewarded for her bad behaviour. But a car would make things better for the whole family.

'Oh, *would* you, Mam?' There was something terribly pathetic about Orla's excited reaction, as if Alice had opened the door of the cage a few enticing inches. 'It would help with me job as a reporter. I could go further afield, not just stick to Bootle. And I could take the kids out weekends, to Southport and Chester and places. I'd take them on the train, except I can never afford the fares. As for Micky, I don't give a fig if he minds or not.'

'Sweetheart, I don't want to make things worse between you two.' She remembered Micky had ada-mantly refused to let her buy them a house and wasn't likely to take kindly to a car – he had more character than people gave him credit for.

'Oh, you won't, Mam. A car will make me happy and if I'm happy then so is Micky.'

Alice thought this an exaggeration. No doubt Orla had been happy making love with Dominic Reilly, but it hadn't exactly sent her husband into paroxysms of delight. Her main concern, though, was her daughter, who'd arrived wan and pale, and now looked happy and excited, as if she'd just been handed a million pounds.

Chapter 15
1970

The air on Easter Saturday was as heady as wine: pure and sparkling, with that exceptional clarity only evident in spring. When the Nuptial Mass was over and the bride and groom posed for photographs in St James's churchyard the sharp, fresh aroma of recently cut grass combined with the earthy smell of upturned soil, adding to the flavour of the day.

Lulu Lavin made an exceptionally pretty bride. There were appreciative murmurs from the waiting crowd when she stepped out of the grey limousine in her simple white voile frock with short sleeves and a drawstring neck. Calf-length, the hem hung in points, each decorated with a tiny rosebud. More rosebuds were threaded through her dark hair arranged earlier that morning in Grecian style by her Nana Lacey. Her shoes were white satin, flat, like a ballerina's. She looked for all the world like a nymph, as did the bridesmaids, in the palest of green: her sister, Maisie, her cousin, Bonnie, and Ruth Mitchell, great-grandpa's daughter, who was Lulu's great-aunt, though three years her junior.

From across the churchyard Orla Lavin, fiercely proud, watched her daughter while the photographs were being taken. Lulu was about to escape the narrow, suffocating streets of Bootle. In two weeks' time, after their honeymoon in Jersey – a present from Alice – Lulu and Gareth would live in his tiny one-bedroomed flat in an unfashionable part of London and Gareth would continue with his ambition to make a living as an artist, though he hadn't so far sold a single painting. The people who had seen his strange, incomprehensible pictures anticipated he never would. The couple had met on a demonstration in London that Lulu had gone to with her Aunt Fion.

Everyone, except Orla, considered it a most inauspicious start to married life: the husband not earning a bean and reliant on his eighteen-year-old wife to put food on the table.

But Orla had given her daughter every encouragement. 'Go for it, girl,' she whispered, more than once. 'Even if things fail, you've given it a try. You've had your fling. You won't spend your life thinking that you've wasted every minute, that there's a million things out there to do and you haven't done a single one.'

'Things won't fail, Mum,' Lulu had assured her, clear-eyed and full of confidence. 'I love Gareth and he loves me. I can't wait for us to be together.'

And now it was done. Lulu was Mrs Gareth Jackson and would shortly be starting on a great adventure.

'Can I have the parents of the bride and groom?' the photographer shouted.

Micky nodded curtly at Orla and they posed for several photographs with the newly married couple; with the bridesmaids; with each other; and with Gareth's widowed mother, Susan, a feisty, bizarrely dressed woman, something of an artist herself, according to Fion, with whom she'd immediately become friends.

Orla was making awkward conversation with Susan, hoping she hadn't noticed the tension between the bride's parents, when she saw the middle-aged, strikingly good-looking man lurking just round the corner of the church. He grinned when their eyes met, then stepped back, out of sight. What one earth was he doing here? she wondered fearfully. How did he know about the wedding? How the hell was she going to get rid of him, not just from the church, but from out of her life?

'I want a photie with Great-grandpa,' Lulu announced.

'Go on, luv.' Bernadette pushed Danny forward. 'It's you she wants, not me,' she insisted when Danny tried to pull her with him.

Bernadette watched the erect, silver-haired figure of her husband stand stiffly between the bride and groom. It was obvious he was making a determined effort to hold himself together and her heart filled with aching sadness. In the not too distant future she was going to lose him. He hadn't told her what was wrong. She hadn't asked. But for the last two months he'd eaten like a bird and hadn't touched the ale he'd always been so fond of. In bed at night he held her tightly in his arms, as if worried he might never hold her that way again.

Alice came up. She nodded at the wedding group. 'How is he?'

'Not so good, Ally. He was sick again this morning. I thought he'd never stop vomiting.'

'It still might not be too late for him to see a doctor.' It had become a bone of contention between the women, whether Danny should, or should not, seek medical attention.

Bernadette shook her head firmly. 'Danny's the most intelligent man I've ever known. He knows where the doctor lives, but when it comes down to it, he'd sooner die in his own way, luv, quickly and as painlessly as possible, not have long-drawn-out treatment and operations. He'd hate me and the children to see him an invalid.'

'Whatever you say, Bernie.' Alice tried not to sound

cold. She had no more wish to lose Danny than did Bernadette and she longed to interfere. She felt an outsider in the relationship between her father and her best friend.

'Your Cormac's girlfriend looks very studious,' Bernie remarked, changing the subject. 'What's her name?'

'Vicky. She's not a girlfriend, just a colleague from work. She's the one he's starting the business with.' Alice's gaze drifted from her son towards Pol and Maurice Lacey. Pol was expecting her third baby. Alice still found it shocking the way Pol had transferred her affections from Cormac to Maurice not long after baby Sharon was born, though Cormac had taken it incredibly well and there was a surprising lack of animosity between the cousins. Of course, the switch had caused no end of gossip at the time. It was hard for people of her age to get used to the way some young people behaved these days. Morals seemed to have gone out the window during the Sixties. In Alice's opinion it had started with rock'n'roll, and men growing their hair long and wearing earrings.

'As soon as they've finished the photographs I'll show you the three Lacey salons,' Cormac said to Vicky. 'We're lucky, starting off with an outlet, even though it's only small.'

'Have you discussed it with your mother yet?' Vicky enquired. She was a serious young woman wearing an ill-fitting brown costume, flat shoes and round, horn-rimmed glasses. Her dark, crisp hair was boyishly cut.

'Alice was all for it. We're an entrepreneurial family, Vic. My father had his own business. So does my cousin, Maurice. Mind you, his is just ticking over.' At that moment a beaming Maurice didn't appear concerned that he just managed to scrape a living from Lacey's Tyres.

'Why do you call your mother Alice?'

'It's just a habit I've got into,' Cormac explained.

'I've not long turned me house into a refuge for battered women,' Fion was informing Susan Jackson, the bridgegroom's mother. 'Why don't you come and take a look after the reception? You can stay the night if you like. It's a big house and there's plenty of room.'

'Don't the neighbours mind, about the refuge, that is?' Susan asked.

'Oh, yes. They're forever complaining, to me and to the corpy. I just don't take any notice.'

'Good for you. I'd love to stay the night, save rushing home on a late train. And next time you're in London you must stay with me.'

So many children, thought Maeve Adams as she watched them bent like birds searching for confetti, swinging on the railings, getting their new clothes dirty. The older children tried to look grown-up in the new gear bought specially for the wedding. By this time next year Orla could be a grandmother, yet her . . . She was thirty-five, getting on. But there were still so many things needed for the house – a bigger freezer for one – and she and Martin had always promised themselves they'd have a garage built on the side. And Martin didn't like driving a car that was more than a few years old, worried it might be unreliable. And the kitchen was getting a bit old-fashioned – she'd like plain white units for a change – and while the workmen were there, they might as well have the floor retiled; terracotta would look nice.

But none of these things would be possible if she stopped work to have babies.

Martin came over and took her hand. 'Penny for them, darling.'

'I was watching the children,' Maeve said wistfully. All

362

of a sudden the kitchen and a new freezer didn't seem to matter.

'We don't need children when we've got each other.'

'Don't we?'

'No, we jolly well don't,' Martin said. Perhaps he didn't mean to sound so irritable. 'I hope you're not getting broody on me, Maeve. Our lifestyle would have to change drastically if we only had my salary to live on. We'd have to go without all sorts of things.'

Maeve sighed and supposed that, to keep Martin happy, she'd have to go without children.

Orla managed to escape the guests and make her way round to the side of the church where Vernon Matthews was leaning against the wall, smoking. He threw the cigarette away when she approached and tried to take her in his arms.

She pushed him away and said angrily, 'Don't you dare touch me!'

'Worried your hubby might see?' His smile was almost a sneer.

'Naturally, but I wouldn't want you touching me if we were stranded alone together on a desert island.'

'You didn't always feel like that.'

'Well, I feel like that now.' She had been mad to sleep with him. It had happened two years after the incident with Dominic Reilly. In all that time Micky hadn't touched her – he still hadn't, though Orla had got used to it by now. But this was before she'd got used to it, when she used to drive the second-hand Mini Mam had bought deep into the countryside, singing to herself, feeling liberated. Mixed with this was a sense of gut-wrenching frustration, a longing for something even faintly interesting to happen.

After a while she got into the habit of stopping at out-of-the-way pubs for a drink of lemonade or orange juice.

It made her feel sophisticated, a woman of the world. She would get out her reporter's notebook and pretend to make notes, so people would think she was a businesswoman on her way to an important meeting.

The second time she stopped a man approached and asked to buy her a drink. Orla told him politely to get lost. A few weeks later, when she was approached again, she accepted the drink. The man turned out to be a commercial traveller who'd been on the stage in his youth. He was interesting to talk to and asked if he could see her again. Orla refused, though she had quite enjoyed the illicit excitement of the occasion. She hadn't felt like herself, but a different person altogether.

The next man who bought her a drink asked if she'd like to come upstairs with him to his room.

'You mean, you're staying here?'

'No, but I very quickly could be.'

'I'd sooner not.' Orla was beginning to feel like a character in a novel. She called herself unusual, romantic names whenever she met a man, which was happening regularly: Estella, Isabella, Madeleine, Dawn.

Micky wanted to know where she took herself every day in the car. 'Nowhere in particular,' Orla said vaguely. 'Just around. Sometimes I interview people for the paper.'

'I suppose anywhere's better than home,' Micky said nastily.

'You said it first,' Orla snapped.

They were nasty to each other most of the time. They slept in the same bed, their backs to each other. They got dressed and undressed in the bathroom.

She told Vernon Matthews her name was Greta. They met just before Christmas in a little thatched pub in Rainford that did bed and breakfasts. There were silver decorations and a lighted tree in the lounge. He was about fifty, with dark hair and dark eyes, and a Clark Gable moustache. He told her he was a representative for an engineering company and always used the pub as a base when he was in the north-west.

He also told her she was one of the most beautiful women he'd ever met. His dark eyes glistened with admiration when he said this and Orla's stomach twisted pleasantly. She felt very strange, almost drunk, though she'd only had orange juice. Afterwards, she felt convinced he'd slipped something in her drink.

Orla couldn't remember agreeing to go upstairs, but she must have, because the next thing she knew she and Vernon were lying naked on a bed together, making love. Her first thought was how to escape, but she knew it was no use trying to push away the heavy body on top of hers. She thought about screaming, but if someone came they might call the police and it could get in the papers – it was the sort of situation she was always on the lookout for herself in her role as a reporter.

Eventually, Vernon reached a noisy, gasping climax and collapsed on top of her. Orla slipped wordlessly from beneath, got partially dressed and went into the bathroom where she washed herself from tip to toe. When she came out, Vernon Matthews had emptied her bag on the bed and was going through the contents.

'How dare you!' she expostulated.

He merely laughed and picked up her driving licence. 'Orla Lavin, 11 Pearl Street, Bootle,' he read aloud. 'So you're not Greta, after all. And according to this, you're married. Does your hubbie know you spend your afternoons playing the whore?'

'I don't think that's any of your business.' She snatched the licence out of his hand.

'I could make it my business pretty damn quick.'

Orla began to push the things back in her bag. She said

threateningly, 'If you say anything to me husband he'll kill you. He might kill me first, but then he'll kill you, I promise you that.'

Vernon laughed again. 'Oh, I'm shaking in my shoes, I really am.'

He lay on the bed and watched her leave, and Orla drove back to Bootle like a maniac. It was weeks before she could bring herself to use the car again, and then it was to do some genuine reporting for the *Crosby Star*.

She thought the whole horrible experience was over and done with until three months later, when she got the first phone call.

'Hello, it's me, Vernon. Love in the afternoon, remember?'

Orla was alone in the house and the hairs prickled on her neck. 'What do you want?'

'To see you. I keep thinking of those happy hours we spent together. I can't wait for a repeat.'

'Then I'm afraid you'll have to wait for ever,' Orla said shortly. She put the phone down.

It rang again almost immediately. She left the receiver off the hook until the children came home from school.

The phone calls continued for ten days, usually in the mornings. Perhaps he had too much sense to ring when Micky was home. They stopped for three months and Orla thought she was rid of him, until they started again. He must call when he was in the Liverpool area and he only called to torment her, have some fun. Orla would be reminded of their afternoon together, which Vernon would describe in sickening detail if she held on and tried to plead with him to stop.

Sometimes he wrote letters: horrible, explicit letters that she burnt immediately, without opening, once she realised who they were from. It was awkward when

Micky was home and he picked up the post before she could get to it.

'Aren't you going to read it?' he would ask when she stuck the letter on the sideboard, unopened, waiting to be burnt.

'I'll read it later. It doesn't look important.'

One day, not long ago, she'd driven to Crosby to deliver some reports, wondering why a grey Marina stuck to her tail the whole way. When she came out, Vernon had been waiting, smiling, holding out his arms.

'You're crazy,' Orla had shrieked hysterically. 'Haven't you got a job to go to? Why won't you leave me alone? I never want to see you again.' She'd got in the Mini and driven away before he could reply, terrified, knowing she was trapped in a situation entirely of her own making and unable to think of a way out.

Now he'd had the brass cheek to turn up at her daughter's wedding, to spoil everything, at least for her. He must have seen the announcement in the *Bootle Times*.

'I'd like you to go,' she said shakily.

'And I'd like to stay.' She could tell he enjoyed getting under her skin, hearing her voice shake. 'I was wondering if I could inveigle my way into the reception.'

'I'd stop wondering if I were you. I'm not the only person who knows exactly who's been invited.'

His mouth twisted. 'That's a pity.'

'You're the one who needs the pity. You're crazy. Anybody sane would have better things to do with their time. Perhaps it wouldn't be a bad idea if I found out where you lived and told your wife what you were up to.'

'I haven't got a wife.' His eyes flickered and she knew he was lying. She felt she had got one up on him for a change, but it was useless knowing he was married. There was no way she could discover where he lived.

'Orla!' Bernadette came round the corner of the church. 'They're going to take a photie of everyone together.' She smiled at Vernon. 'Hello.'

'Hello, there,' he said charmingly. ''Bye, Orla. See you again one day soon.'

Cormac and Vicky managed a quick tour of the three Lacey's salons before sitting down to a ham salad in Hilton's Restaurant, where the reception was being held and where Cormac had celebrated his twenty-first.

'The salon in Opal Street is a bit off the beaten track, but the other two on main roads will make wonderful showcases for our products,' Vicky enthused.

Cormac grinned. 'Our products! That sounds very grand and businesslike, Vic.'

Vicky went pink, something she was apt to do very easily, particularly if Cormac was around. 'I suppose it does, for a business about to be started in my parents' garage. Still, I think grand and businesslike is what we should aim for, Cormac.'

'I think so too. And "Lacey's of Liverpool" sounds very grand indeed. You don't mind your name being left out, do you?' Cormac said anxiously.

'Not under the circumstances – and I've never liked the name Weatherspoon. If our products are associated with an already long-established hairdresser's it will help get them off the ground.'

'You talk like a business manual, Vic.'

Vicky tried to discern if there was the faintest hint of flirtatiousness in Cormac's tone, but decided there wasn't. She was nearly thirty and Cormac was the first man she had fallen in love with. Not that he knew. Not that he would *ever* know, because she would never tell him. She might have done had she been as remotely pretty as any one of his three sisters. Even his mother looked gorgeous in a lacy lilac dress and little matching hat. Vicky sighed. If Cormac so much as suspected she was in love with him he'd probably run a mile.

They'd met three years before when Cormac had started work in the research department of Brooker & Sons, a large company in St Helens where Victoria Weatherspoon had worked since she finished university with a degree in chemistry. Brooker's, a household name, were primarily the manufacturers of domestic cleansing agents: washing-up liquid, washing powder, scourer, bleach, soap. They were also famous for their baby products and produced a small range of cosmetics, including shampoos and conditioners.

For most of the three years Cormac and Vicky had done no more than pass the time of day. They had never been involved in the same research project. While Vicky concentrated on ways of making the washing-up liquid more bubbly or the scourer more ruthless, Cormac was involved in different experiments which could lead to the world being rid of every speck of dirt and every known germ.

Two and a half months ago – Vicky remembered the day precisely, it was January the fourteenth – she and Cormac happened to be working late together. He was sitting on a stool at a table at the far end of the laboratory, writing, presumably a report on his current project. Vicky was using the shaker, a piece of machinery that gripped containers and tossed them about crazily for two minutes so that the contents were thoroughly mixed.

'What's that you're doing, Vic?' Cormac enquired.

'Mixing shampoo for my mother. Sorry, is the noise getting on your nerves?'

'No. I was wondering what the smell was, that's all.'
Cormac sniffed appreciatively. 'It's very nice. What is it?'

'Geranium oil.'

'Do we make geranium oil shampoo?' He put down his pen and came towards her.

Vicky felt her heart quicken. 'No. This is Brooker's basic mixture before the perfume's added. I didn't steal it, Cormac. It's been paid for, I can assure you.'

'Gracious, Vic. I wouldn't give a damn if you pinched a ten-ton container. I'm just interested in what you're doing, that's all.' He looked with surprise at the row of plastic bottles on the worktop. 'There must be enough there to last your mother the rest of her life. Sorry, Vic,' he said apologetically, putting his hand on her arm. 'I'm being dead nosy. It's just that I'm bored witless writing up a report. I was looking for a diversion, that's all. Even so, I wouldn't mind knowing what your mother's going to do with so much shampoo.'

'She sells it, Cormac. She belongs to the Women's Institute and they have a sale of work every month to raise money for charity. Aromatherapy oils have a heavenly smell. The shampoos go like hot cakes. I usually make a couple of dozen a month, using different fragrances. This time I'm using geranium, lavender, lemongrass and rosemary.' Vicky wondered if her dull, monosyllabic tone was as evident to him as it was to herself. She sounded as if she was reading the lesson at a funeral.

'Aromatherapy oils?'

'The Egyptians first used them, possibly as long ago as 3000 BC. They can be used for massage and, oh, for all sorts of things, as well as making cosmetics.'

'Hmm! Interesting.' Cormac rocked back on his heels. 'Fancy a drink when you've finished, Vic?'

Over the next few weeks they went for several more

drinks after work. Vicky could hardly believe it when he told her about his life on the road belonging to a group called the Nobodys.

'I must have smoked every known substance. We didn't know where we were most of the time.'

'I would never have guessed.' His neat good looks didn't fit in with the life he'd just described.

'What about you, Vic? What have you been up to since you left university?'

'Working in Brooker's,' she confessed, slightly ashamed.

'Ah, an upright, conscientious member of society, unlike myself.'

'I wish I'd been a bit more adventurous, if only in my job. Brooker's is so . . . so . . .'

'Mindnumbingly dull?' Cormac suggested, making a face, and she laughed. The more they saw each other, the more relaxed she became.

'I suppose so. I once had visions of doing something as spectacular as splitting the atom.'

'Or discovering penicillin. I know, Vic, me too.'

A few days later Cormac said, 'Is there anything unique about Brooker's shampoos, Vic?'

'No. Most shampoos contain the same basic substances: aqua, sodium laureth sulfate, cocamide, hydroxypropyltrimonium, glycerine.'

'Wow!' Cormac looked impressed. 'Could we mix all those various chemicals ourselves?'

'I beg your pardon?'

'Could we buy the cocamide and the glycerine and the other unpronouncable chemicals and make our own shampoo?'

'Of course, Cormac.' She looked at him wonderingly. 'You mean you and me? But why should we want to?'

He answered her question with another. 'Do you want to stay at Brooker's for the rest of your life, Vic?'

'Well, no.' She had always hoped to get married and have children, and Cormac was the person she'd like to achieve this ambition with. Fortunately, they were both Catholics, so religion wouldn't be an obstacle. The only obstacle was the fact he hadn't shown the slightest interest in her as a lifelong companion. 'No, I definitely don't want to stay at Brooker's.'

'Neither do I,' he said with a heartfelt groan. 'I'll never get the sort of job I wanted when I was at Cambridge because I didn't finish the course. I was lucky Brooker's took me on, but I want more than a career trying to make bleach thicker and whites whiter. I thought we could go into business together making aromatherapy shampoo and conditioner. I was virtually brought up in a hairdresser's, so I suppose it's only natural I feel drawn to the idea. I'm not suggesting we give up work. That can wait till things catch on, which might be months or years.' He wrinkled his nose. 'It could even be never.'

Had it been anyone else but him, Vicky would have pronounced him mad and walked away. But it *was* Cormac, whom she loved and who had actually suggested they do something together. She would have preferred it to be something other than starting their own business, but it was better than nothing at all.

As the weeks went by, however, she began to catch some of his enthusiasm. They would start off with a thousand bottles each of shampoo and conditioner of several different fragrances. His mother was thrilled to bits at the idea and had promised to use them in her salons – providing they were satisfactory – and display them for sale. Vicky still lived at home in Warrington with her parents and her own mother was equally thrilled. She had offered the garage to use as a workshop.

'Daddy won't mind. He can leave the car outside,' Mrs Weatherspoon said dismissively – her mother had always worn the trousers in the Weatherspoon household.

They only needed a small amount of equipment, which was fortunate as they only had a small amount of money between them, a few hundred pounds of savings. Initially there would be a lot of tedious work to do by hand. It should be a simple matter to obtain the formula for Brooker's shampoo and conditioner, and they would change a few of the basic elements so theirs would be different.

Sample bottles were ordered, a brand name decided upon: Lacey's of Liverpool.

'It has a ring to it,' Cormac mused. 'A few years ago Liverpool was the most famous city in the galaxy. Lacey's and Liverpool go perfectly together. It's not exactly gimmicky, but it's unusual.'

'We still haven't decided what colour bottles,' Cormac reminded her at the wedding as a waitress removed their plates. The best man, a friend of Gareth's, was nervously studying the speech he had written beforehand.

'I like the opaque white ones best. White with gold lettering.'

'I'm not sure if I don't prefer the black.'

'Black's showy, white's tasteful,' Vicky said stubbornly. It wasn't often she got her own way in the enterprise.

'We could have black bottles for the man's shampoo, the sage.'

'That's a great idea.'

He smiled broadly and put his hand over hers. 'We make great business partners, don't we, Vic?'

'Oh, yes, Cormac. Great.'

★

If you ask me, Sarge,' the driver of the police car said out of the corner of his mouth, 'women whose blokes have given them a good hiding have almost certainly asked for it.'

'Shush, Morgan.'

'She can't hear, Sarge, not with that howling baby and the screaming kids.'

'D'you think they asked for it too, the children?'

'Possibly. I've boxed me own kids' ears before now. Sometimes kids – and wives – need to be shown who's boss.'

Sergeant Jerry McKeown glanced over his shoulder at the woman on the back seat who was trying to quieten the baby and soothe two small children at the same time. Her face was covered in blood. 'Have you ever blacked your wife's eye and split her lip?' he asked sarcastically.

'Well, no, Sarge. 'Course not.'

'That's what's happened to Connie Mulligan in the back. So, get a move on, Morgan. She needs a doctor quick and afterwards a place to sleep, out of danger, like.'

'The woman who runs this women's refuge is probably a right ould cow,' Morgan said derisively. 'One of them feminists, I bet, and a lesbian too. All they do is run men down and that's only because they're too ugly to catch one for their selves.'

'You're full of worldly wisdom, Morgan. That's the place, over there. I think it might be a good idea to stop and deliver our passengers safely, not just speed past and chuck 'em on to the pavement.'

'Whatever you say, Sarge.'

The car stopped. Jerry McKeown jumped out and tenderly helped the injured woman and her terrified children out of the back. 'You'll be safe here,' he assured them. The woman recoiled from his touch and didn't speak.

374

He vaulted up the stone steps and knocked on the front door. It was opened almost immediately by a tall women in black jeans and T-shirt. Her bountiful hair was knotted on top of her head, cascading around her face and neck in feathery tendrils. She had large, beautiful eyes, a strong nose and mouth, and he had never seen anyone look so kind, so concerned, as the woman enfolded Connie Mulligan in her lovely long arms and drew her into the house. 'Come on, luv. I've been expecting you. The police phoned to say you were on your way. There's tea made and a nice, warm room ready for you. The doctor will be here soon – it's a woman.'

She glanced at Jerry McKeown and made to close the door. 'Thank you, officer,' she said briefly.

'Can I come in, make sure she's settled?' It hadn't been his intention to go inside, but he'd quite like to get to know this woman more.

'I'm sorry, but men aren't allowed on the premises. It's a rule. I had to put me own brother out not long ago and he was forced to find a bedsit near where he works.' Another woman had appeared and was taking the injured woman and her children to the back of the house. The tall woman made to close the door again, but Jerry put his foot in the way.

'Can I have your name, please? For the records, like.'

'I thought you already had me name on your records, but never mind. It's Mrs Littlemore. Mrs Fionnuala Littlemore.'

'Ta.' Jerry McKeown returned to the car.

'You might like to know, Morgan, that the woman who runs the place isn't old, isn't a cow and definitely isn't ugly. I wasn't there long enough to establish whether or not she's a feminist.' As for Fionnuala Lacey being a lesbian, he very much hoped not.

He went back to the house early next morning wearing plain clothes. A boy of about ten, with a grave, grown-up expression, opened the door.

'I thought Mrs Lacey said men weren't allowed on the property,' Jerry remarked with a smile.

'I'm her son, so she makes an exception.' The boy didn't smile back.

'What's your name?'

'Colin.'

'Well, Colin, does your mum make an exception for your dad as well as you?'

'Me dad's dead.'

'I'm sorry about that, Colin.' Jerry had never been so pleased about anything in his whole life.

'Who is it, luv?' Fionnuala Littlemore came into the hall wearing the same clothes as the night before. 'What do you want?' she asked abruptly when she saw the policeman on the step. 'Connie's in no position to make a statement yet. Anyroad, she'll only talk to a women police officer, so you're wasting your time if you come again.'

She was looking at him, but not *at* him. She wasn't seeing him properly. If they met in the street tomorrow, she wouldn't recognise him from Adam. But Jerry had come prepared to make her notice him.

'I've brought some toys for Connie's kids. I got them last night in Tesco's. They close late Fridays.' He held out a plastic bag. 'I hope they like them.'

'I'm sure they will. Thank you very much, officer.'

'The name's Jerry.'

'Thank you, Jerry. Connie will be pleased. Well, tara. It was nice of you to come.'

'Also . . .' He stuck his foot in the door before she could close it. The bloody woman still hadn't *seen* him. 'I'd like to make a contribution towards the refuge.

You're doing a great job. I admire you. I hope you'll find this ten quid a help.'

'Oh, we will. Thank you, er, Jerry.' She took the note and tucked it in the pocket of her jeans.

'Also,' Jerry continued desperately. 'I wondered, do you ever have fund-raising events, jumble sales, like? If so, I'd be willing to give a hand.'

'Well, there's nothing planned at the moment.'

'In that case, when the bloody hell can I see you again, other than on this bloody doorstep?'

'Oh!' She blinked and took a step backwards.

She'd seen him at last!

Fion saw a very tall, broad-shouldered, rugged man in his thirties, smartly dressed in a navy-blue suit. The skin on his face was weather-beaten and his nose was slightly crooked, as if it had been broken. His lips were scarred – he either boxed or played rugby. Very short brown hair stuck up in little spikes around his crown. He was anything but handsome, but he wasn't ugly either. In fact, taking in the quirky smile and the warm brown eyes, she thought him very attractive and liked his air of dependability. She could trust this man.

'Are you married?' she asked.

It was his turn to blink. 'Divorced, no children.'

'I never go out with married men.'

'Does that mean you will, go out with me, I mean?' He couldn't believe his luck.

'Mondays are supposed to be me day off.'

'Then I'll pick you up Monday at half-seven. OK?' He removed his foot and Fionnuala Littlemore closed the door.

'I'm meeting Sammy tonight and going straight from work to the pictures, Mum,' Maisie said as she was leaving. 'Don't do me any tea.'

'And when are we going to meet this Sammy?' Orla enquired.

'I dunno, Mum. It's not as if it's serious. I'm not going to be like our Lulu and get married at eighteen. I want to have a good time first. By the way, what's wrong with Dad? He was coughing and sneezing all night long.'

'He's got a cold, luv. One of those terrible summer ones. It doesn't help working in a foundry and he wouldn't dream of taking a day off. Anyroad, have a nice time tonight.'

Gary left not long afterwards. She was glad he'd managed to avoid manual work, not that there was much future in a shoe shop, but at least it was clean. Paul, her baby, left it right till the very last minute before leaving for school where he was in his final term.

Orla breathed a sigh of relief and made a fresh pot of tea. She took it into the yard to drink because it was such a lovely July morning and wished for the millionth time they had a proper garden. It was good to be alone at last and think about the phone call she'd had last night from Cormac.

'Hey, sis. Me and Vic have just decided you'd be perfect.'

'What for?'

'For selling Lacey's of Liverpool hair products. You've got a car, you've got the personality and you wouldn't have to give up your job with the paper.'

'I might be interested, Cormac. What sort of salary are we talking about?' There was something about the tone of his voice that made her anticipate what the answer would be.

'We weren't thinking in terms of salary, Orl, just commission,' he said sweetly. 'Twenty per cent, same as Mam gets, plus your expenses, i.e. the cost of petrol.'

'Make it twenty-five per cent,' Orla said promptly.

'I'll be putting meself out a bit more than Mam. But I'm only doing it because you're me brother and I expect to be given a high-powered job one day when you're successful.'

'You'll be head of international sales, sis,' Cormac said with a chuckle. 'It's a promise.'

She would be the only sales rep because, although he and Vic were working flat out, they couldn't produce enough bottles to cater for a larger market. 'It's a bit of a chicken-and-egg situation,' Cormac said. 'We can't take orders until we turn out more and we can't turn out more till we've got the capacity to do it, though we'll have to bite the bullet soon and get some proper equipment. Me and Vic are working ourselves to a standstill turning out stuff by hand.'

A few Liverpool shops had ordered, and since reordered, quite large supplies. Mam usually sold out within days of fresh stock being delivered. An advert in *The Lady* had produced dozens of orders in the post.

Orla would be supplied with leaflets and samples. She would start with Lancashire and Cheshire, and go further afield when they'd been covered. Chemists and small supermarkets would be her main target. Big supermarkets ordered centrally and would be approached when the company felt able to cope with a large amount. 'I don't suppose expenses would cover the cost of a nice business suit?' she asked wistfully. 'I don't possess anything remotely smart, Cormac.'

'Sorry, Orl. Anyroad, you always look nice, whatever you wear.'

'Oh, yeah! That was a typical man talking.'

She would start on Monday and was already looking forward to it. Tonight she'd tell Micky, not that he'd be interested. It might prove difficult when she went far enough away to have to stay overnight, but she'd cross that bridge when she came to it. She finished the tea and went to check the pathetic contents of her wardrobe in case anything needed washing. On her way downstairs with a denim skirt and two white blouses she heard the backyard door open and footsteps in the yard. Micky must have come home, which didn't surprise her, as his cold was really bad.

To her horror, when she entered the living room by one door, Vernon Matthews was coming in by the other. He must have waited for Micky and the children to leave. He looked overdressed for the warmness of the day, in a dark suit, collar and tie, black, highly polished shoes.

'Thought I'd give you a surprise.' He smirked.

'Get out of this house immediately!' She could hardly control her rage, which was mixed with panic and a feeling of fear. There was no one in the houses on either side.

She might as well not have spoken. 'I thought we could have a little chat.' He sat in Micky's chair under the window and, although he must have known he was less than welcome, he had the air of a man who felt entirely at home in the strange surroundings. Orla, disorientated and confused, could almost believe he belonged there.

'I don't want to talk to you – *ever*!' But she had already learnt it was a waste of time trying to reason with him. He didn't listen, or he didn't want to know, or perhaps it was just another way of tormenting her, taking not a blind bit of notice of what she said.

'Oh, come on, Orla. We had a lovely talk that first time, didn't we? Followed by an experience I shall never forget. I'd very much like to do it again, in fact. Now seems an appropriate time, when there's no one around.'

Orla leant limply against the sideboard, wondering

what to do. If she ran down the hall and out of the front door, she could scream for help. Or she could dial 999 and ask for the police. Except what would she tell people: the police, whoever came to help if she screamed?

He was watching her through lowered lids, still smirking, as if he recognised her predicament. 'Have you met this man before?' was the first question she'd be asked and it would all come out, the details of the afternoon they'd spent together in the pub in Rainford. Even if she tried to deny it, how could she explain how he knew where she lived? She had no idea what would happen then, whether he would be arrested, charged. Birds' wings of panic fluttered in her chest.

'Oh, come on, Orla. What harm would it do?'

He was actually getting up, coming towards her, smiling. Orla seized a large statue of Our Lady off the sideboard, ready to strike if he so much as touched her.

'Let's go upstairs. Just for a little minute, eh?'

'I'll swing for you first.' She raised the statue but he easily caught her wrist in his hand. The statue dropped to the floor but didn't break. The birds' wings were beating madly now, painfully. He slid his other arm around her waist and tried to pull her against him, groaning. 'I've been waiting too long for this.'

Orla tried to raise her knee and thrust it in his stomach, but her legs, her body, were trapped by his weight against the sideboard. She spat in his face instead.

'What's going on here?'

Micky! Feverishly red, face glistening with perspiration, eyes black with anger and tinged with incomprehension. He must have felt too ill for work after all.

'Just trying to renew my acquaintanceship with your wife,' Vernon said lightly.

'Out!' Micky seized his collar, flung him through the

kitchen, into the yard, into the entry that ran along the back, as if Vernon had only the strength and weight of a small child. Orla had never dreamt her husband was so strong, though she realised it was a strength born of uncontrollable rage.

Micky slammed the yard door and slid the bolt. He returned inside and Orla shrank back in the face of his anger. 'How long's he been coming round?'

'He's never been before, Micky, honest,' she stammered, more terrified of him than she'd been of Vernon. Micky looked as if he could easily kill her. 'He came when I was upstairs, just walked in.'

'Then what was that about renewing his acquaintance-ship with me wife?' Micky snarled.

'I met him once, more than a year ago. He's been pestering me ever since.'

'Why didn't you tell me?'

'Because . . . because . . . oh, I don't know, Micky.' She had no idea about anything any more.

'You slept with him, didn't you?' His eyes had narrowed to slits.

She hadn't the strength to deny it. She nodded.

All Micky's rage subsided in a slow hiss of breath. He sank into the chair Vernon had recently vacated and buried his face in his hands. 'I used to love you once, Orla,' he whispered.

'I *still* love you, Micky.' She had never felt such total love as she did now, staring at him, hunched in the chair in his shabby working clothes. He had started to shiver. In a minute she'd make tea, get him aspirin, put him to bed. She wouldn't take the job Cormac had offered. And she'd give up reporting, find an ordinary job in an office not far away. The car could be sold. She'd never feel fed up or bored again. Somehow, in some way, she would talk Micky round into them starting again. She had been sorry about Dominic Reilly, but at the same time was too annoyed with Micky to care that they hardly ever spoke, never made love. This time she would work on him, *make* him love her again. She felt a surge of excitement at the idea of them recovering the feelings they'd had for each other when they were teenagers, when they'd first moved to Pearl Street.

'I'll just pack a bag,' Micky said, easing himself out of the chair.

'Why?' she asked, bewildered.

'I'm leaving, that's why. Surely you don't expect me to stay after what happened today?'

'But I love you, Micky!'

He looked almost amused. 'You have a funny way of showing it, Orla.'

'I've been a terrible wife, Micky. But I learnt me lesson today.' She took hold of his hands. 'Let's start again. Remember what it used to be like? Remember the first time in the entry behind our house in Amber Street?'

He removed his hands from hers, none too gently 'I remember. You made me life hell and you've been making me life hell ever since. You always thought yourself too good for me, didn't you?' He looked at her thoughtfully, head on one side. 'Perhaps you were, still are. All I know is, luv, that I've had enough of you. I was going to hang on till the children were a bit older, till Paul reached eighteen. Under the circumstances I'll be off today. We'll sort out the divorce later.'

Orla felt herself go cold. 'You mean there's someone else?'

'There's been someone else for two years.' He smiled gently. 'If you hadn't been so wrapped in yourself you might have noticed.'

'Who is she?'

'Just an ordinary woman without your airs and graces who makes me feel good about meself for a change.'

Orla's voice rose. 'Who is she, Micky?'

'I hope you're not going to lose your temper, luv.' Micky's voice was mild. 'It doesn't sit well, considering what's just happened. If you must know, it's Caitlin Reilly from Garnet Street who used to live across the road. Her husband was killed in an accident on the docks when they'd hardly been married a year. She's got a lad the same age as our Paul.'

'She was in our Maeve's class at school. She used to come round to our house sometimes. Her married name is Mahon.' Caitlin was a pretty, round woman, the image of Sheila, her mother. 'You've got a nerve, Micky Lavin,' Orla said hotly, 'going on about what happened today when you've been having an affair for two whole years.'

'We've both done wrong, Orla, though don't forget you were the first. I was bloody mad earlier, I admit it, but what man wouldn't be if he came home and found a strange bloke trying to rape his wife?'

Wordlessly, Orla went into the kitchen and put the kettle on. Over the years, despite the contempt she felt for Micky, the impatience, deep inside she still loved him. The fact that he no longer loved her shook her to the core. There had always been an unshaken conviction in her heart that, no matter what she did, no matter how much she riled or offended him, Micky would remain steadfastly loyal through thick and thin. She considered pleading with him to stay, coaxing him to bed so that she could show him how much she cared.

But common sense prevailed. If Micky stayed, in a few weeks' time, when she'd got over her fright that morning, she would feel discontented again and start nagging him to do things she knew he never would.

The kettle had boiled. Orla made the tea, found the aspirin and took both into the living room, where Micky was leaning against the mantelpiece, staring into the empty grate.

'I'd like you to stay,' she said. When he opened his mouth to argue, she said quickly, 'I'll leave instead. Ask Caitlin and her son to come and live here. It'll set a lot of old tongues wagging, but who cares?'

Micky's jaw dropped. 'It'd break the kids' hearts if you left, luv.'

'They'd be just as upset to lose you. Anyroad, I won't be far away. I'll find somewhere nearby to live – Mam'll put me up for now.'

'But what will you do with yourself all on your own?'

'Our Cormac's offered me a job. I was going to tell you about it tonight. I'll do me best to make something of it.'

She would put her heart and soul into the job with Lacey's of Liverpool, drive all over the country, stay away for as long as she liked, knowing her children would be safe with Caitlin Reilly.

Orla's spirits soared. She was free to do the sort of things she'd planned on doing twenty years ago before she'd met Micky Lavin.

Chapter 16

'Where are you off to today, luv?' Alice enquired.

'Bury, Rochdale, Bolton,' Orla said briskly. She wore a smart black costume and was thrusting the new leaflets Cormac had brought the night before into a briefcase, checking she had enough samples. 'I'll probably be home dead late, Mam, so don't wait up.'

'I wouldn't dream of waiting up, luv, considering the hours you keep. I don't know how you keep going to be frank.'

'Enthusiasm keeps me going, Mam: commitment, ambition. The things you felt when you started Lacey's.'

'I didn't feel any of them things, Orla. I just wanted to get out the house away from your dad.' Alice smiled. 'I'm glad you're happy, though. I thought you'd be dead miserable, breaking up with Micky, though you never stopped complaining about the poor lad since the day you married him — and before, if I remember right.'

Orla closed the briefcase with a snap. 'I miss the kids,' she said soberly. 'I miss them coming in for their tea, making cocoa at bedtime. I even miss — only a bit — doing their washing. Still, Lulu's gone and I think our Maisie's more serious about this Sammy than she'll admit. Gary was talking about joining the Navy. Soon, there'll only be Paul left.'

'And he'll have Caitlin's lad, Calum, for company.' Alice always made a point of not sounding as shocked as she felt by all this switching around, as if marriage, relationships, were just a game of musical chairs. Pol had left Cormac for Maurice Lacey, Orla had walked out on Micky and, before you could blink, Caitlin Reilly had moved in and there was talk of divorce. She knew of other respectable women whose children were divorced or living in sin. That policeman, Jerry McKeown, that Fion had taken up with, had been married before, leaving Maeve the only one of Alice's children who led a conventional married life. At least, so far!

'Are you off now, luv?'

'Yes, Mam.' Orla kissed her. 'I'll see you when I see you. D'you realise what time it is? You'll be late for work.'

'I'm taking the morning off.' Alice flushed. 'I'm having another driving lesson.'

'Good for you, Mam,' Orla sang as she slammed the door.

An increasing number of cars were appearing in Amber Street, so Alice didn't feel too ostentatious buying one herself. It was only a little car, a Citroen Ami, though she was beginning to wonder if she'd ever get the hang of the damn thing.

She was on edge, waiting for the instructor to arrive in his own car, when the telephone rang.

'Mrs Alice Lacey?' a male voice enquired.

'Speaking.'

'I'm calling regarding a Mrs Cora Lacey. She's your sister-in-law, so I understand.'

'That's right. Is something wrong?'

'You could say that, Madam. We would be obliged if you would come to Bootle Police Station straight away.'

'Why?' Alice asked irritably and immediately regretted it. Cora might have had a bad accident.

'Because the lady concerned has been apprehended and gave your name as her closest relative.'

'Apprehended! Why?'

'That will be explained at the station, Madam.'

Cora was in a cell, hunched in her camel coat as if it were a blanket, her small, sallow face expressionless. She'd been caught shoplifting, according to the desk sergeant, trying to nick two woollen vests from a shop in Strand Road. It was a first offence, so charges wouldn't be pressed, but Cora had better keep her hands to herself in future, he said warningly, else she'd find herself behind bars.

'Cora!' Alice said reproachfully when the women were alone. 'What on earth possessed you?'

'Needed vests for the winter, didn't I?' Cora shrugged her shoulders churlishly. 'Me old ones were in shreds. It must be twenty years since I last bought some.'

'I would have bought you vests, Cora.'

Cora snorted. 'Oh, you would, would you?'

'Rather than see you steal them, yes. Look, can we go home? I feel uncomfortable here.' Alice glanced at the barred window, the hard bench on which prisoners were supposed to sleep. 'I've come in a car, not mine, the driving school's. The instructor turned up for me lesson just as I was leaving. I'll just have to forget about this week's lesson.' Lord knows what the instructor would think, being asked to take her to the police station – such a nice young man too.

Cora didn't speak on the way home. Alice got out of the car when she stopped in Garibaldi Road – Cora had given her name to the police, and she felt obliged to see her safely home and find out why she had been driven to steal.

Inside the house, Cora seemed to sag. 'I'm going to the lavvy,' she mumbled.

Alice realised she was far more affected by the events of the morning than she pretended. She went into the scrubbed kitchen to make tea and was shocked to find the cupboards bare: no tea, no sugar and not a drop of milk on the premises. Was Cora so skint she couldn't afford even basic food? Later, she'd buy the woman some groceries. It was years since she'd given a thought to Cora – someone had mentioned seeing her outside the church at Lulu's wedding, but that was all.

Cora came in, looking more composed. 'You can go now,' she said belligerently. 'There was no need to have come in the first place.'

Alice had no intention of going. 'Why are you so short of money that you need to go thieving? I always thought you had private means – and Billy's working.'

'The "private means", as you call them, dried up a while ago. And Billy's never given me more than a few bob a week in years.'

'Why not ask for more?'

The yellow face twisted in a scowl. 'He's hardly ever here to ask. These days, Billy spends most of his time in Browning Street with Maurice and his family. 'Stead of the ale, most of his wages go on propping up that useless business of Maurice's.'

'Then what on earth are you living on?' Alice asked, alarmed. Now that she had removed her ancient coat, Cora, always thin, looked no more than skin and bone.

'Nothing, if you must know.'

'But a person can't live on nothing, Cora,' Alice cried.

Cora turned on her angrily. 'Look, I'd appreciate it if you got out me house and minded your own business. How I manage is nowt to do with you.'

'Then why did you give the police my name?'

'Yours was the only name I could think of. I didn't want Billy or Maurice knowing, did I?' Cora swayed and would have fallen had not Alice leapt forward and caught her.

'Have you had anything to eat this morning? Come on, let's go into the other room and sit you down.'

Alice settled her sister-in-law in an armchair and fetched a glass of water. 'What you need is a cup of hot, sweet tea, but all you've got is the water. How long has this being going on, luv?'

The near-collapse seemed to have broken Cora's spirit. 'Since earlier this year, when I turned sixty,' she said in a hoarse, frightened voice. 'Apart from the few bob I get off Billy, which pays the rent, I haven't had a penny piece. The 'leccy bill's not paid, nor the gas. I can't remember when I last ate.' She looked at Alice, her strange eyes terrified. 'When they stopped me outside that shop I nearly died, imagining me name in the papers, everyone knowing.'

'There, there,' Alice soothed, but there was something not quite right about what Cora had just said. 'I thought women were entitled to a pension at sixty?'

'Oh, Alice.' Cora had begun to shake with fear. 'I've done something terrible, worse than a bit of shoplifting. The thing is, I'm scared to claim me pension. I've got the book, they sent it months ago, but I daren't take it to the post office.'

'Why on earth not, Cora?'

Cora was wringing her hands agitatedly; spittle drooled from the corner of her mouth. 'When we first moved here,' she said in the same hoarse voice, 'I found a Jacob's biscuit tin full of papers in the fireplace cupboard. Two spinsters used to live here, sisters, about fifty. They went to America during the war. I've no idea what happened afterwards, whether they came back or not. The tin was full of private things, birth certificates, like, insurance policies, some shares. I kept them, they weren't taking up much room, in case they wrote one day and asked for them back.

'Years later,' Cora went on, 'I got a letter from the government to say one of the sisters, the oldest, was due for her old age pension. They sent a form for her to sign.' She paused.

'Oh, Cora, you didn't sign it!' Alice gasped.

'I needed money. I was desperate for money. By then, there was nothing but Billy's wages coming in. I signed the woman's name and filled in something to say I was her niece and she'd given me authority to collect the money from the post office. Two years later a form came for the other sister, so I signed that too. And I cashed the insurance policies and sold the shares.'

'You could go to prison for a long time for that, Cora,' Alice said primly. 'It's called fraud.' She was shocked to the bone. Shoplifting was one thing, but this was far more serious.

Cora grabbed her arm. 'Do you think the police will check up on me, now they've got me name and address, like?'

'I doubt it. I take it you've stopped taking the pensions?'

'Months ago, when I heard about me own pension. I got frightened. I thought it would look suspicious, collecting three pensions from the post office, all at the same address.' The small hand tightened, claw-like, on Alice's arm. 'I'm worried I'll be asked for death certificates, seeing as the pensions aren't being taken any more. I'm worried someone from the government will wonder why I'm not taking me own.' Cora released Alice's arm and collapsed back in the chair. Her eyes had almost disappeared into their sockets. She looked like death. 'What am I going to do?'

'I have absolutely no idea, Cora,' Alice said coldly. She got to her feet. 'I'll be off now and buy some groceries. I'll not see you starve. And I'll give you a few bob to be getting on with.' She emptied the contents of her purse on to the coffee table. 'There's nearly three pounds there. When I come back, let's have the electricity and gas bills and I'll see they're paid. But that's as far as I'm prepared to go. If you must know, I'm thoroughly disgusted by what you just told me. I haven't a clue what advice to give. It might help if you moved to a smaller house that's cheaper to run. And I suppose you could collect your pension from a different post office.'

Alice paused at the door. 'When you feel better, I suggest you look for a job. We need a cleaner at the salons. It's either early in the morning or late at night, whichever suits best. You can let me know if you're interested when I come back with the food.'

The door closed. Cora swivelled her head and watched Alice go down the path. She turned to shut the gate.

Cow!

She had never hated anyone as much as she hated her sister-in-law at that moment. *I'm thoroughly disgusted by what you just told me.* Oh, was she, now! What did she know about being on your beam ends, not knowing where your next meal was coming from? Alice Lacey had always had it soft.

Still, there'd been no need for her to have been so understanding, Cora thought grudgingly. Oh, she'd gone on a bit, but another person might have ranted and raved, and washed their hands of Cora altogether when they heard the criminal things she'd done. There was money on the table and food on its way. She'd even

392

offered her a job. It meant that Alice cared, even if it was done with a sickly air of being holier than thou that made Cora want to puke.

We need a cleaner at the salons.

Well, Cora had cleaned before and she'd clean again. In fact, she'd spent her whole life cleaning. She glanced round the shining, spotless room. The furniture was probably out of fashion, but it had been lovingly cared for, tenderly polished. The net curtains were the whitest in the road. Cleaning was what Cora was good at. She'd take the job because she had to live. Anyroad, soft-girl Alice would almost certainly pay more than most employers.

Cora enjoyed cleaning the three hairdressers. So there would be less chance of being seen by the neighbours she started early, at six o'clock. Each salon took just over half an hour, and she felt enormous satisfaction when she'd finished and the plastic surfaces shone, the mirrors sparkled, the sinks gleamed.

She didn't mind working on her own. She was used to it. Most of the time she preferred her own company and early in the morning, with few people around and hardly any traffic, it was easy to pretend she was the only person in the world, a situation Cora would very much have preferred. Sometimes she even sang as she worked.

Billy didn't know she was working. Billy knew nothing about her. He never had. Cora had been cleaning the salons for a fortnight when he came home one night at about half past seven. They hadn't spoken to each other in a long while and she was surprised when he came into the living room and asked if she'd make him a cup of tea.

She was about to tell him to make it himself, but

remembered he didn't ask for much, probably knowing he wouldn't get it.

'Is something wrong?' she asked. He looked on edge, jingling the coins in his pocket as if he needed something to do with his hands. His face was hot and red, and she noticed his mouth kept twitching. 'Is Maurice all right?'

He didn't answer. Cora made the tea sweet and strong, the way Alice had wanted to make it for her the day she'd been arrested for shoplifting.

'What's the matter, Billy?' she asked, putting the tea beside him on the coffee table.

'I've done something dead wicked, Cora.' Tears trickled down his fleshy cheeks. At sixty-three, he was still a good-looking man, with thick, iron-grey hair and a clear complexion. His paunch had almost disappeared since he'd come off the ale. 'I've set fire to the yard.'

Cora gasped. 'You've *what*?'

He was looking at her with round, scared eyes, like a little boy, the way Maurice had done many years ago. 'I've set fire to the yard. I suppose I must have got the idea from our John, though in his case it wasn't intentional.'

'But *why*?'

'Because it was the only way out. He was losing money hand over fist, our Maurice. He's no business-man, Cora. He was making scarcely enough to feed his family, while the overdraft got bigger and bigger, and I was the one paying it back.' He swallowed nervously. 'The writing's been on the wall a long time. Six months ago I pumped up the insurance on the premises, so now Maurice can claim he's lost his livelihood. As I said, it seemed the only way out.'

'You mean you've been planning this for six months?' Cora was impressed.

'I reckon I must have.'

'Had the fire properly taken by the time you left?'

Billy nodded. 'The smoke was black. I could see it rising over the rooftops. The fire engines came, I heard them.'

'What happens if they blame our Maurice?' Cora frowned.

'There's something happening at Sharon's school, a concert. I deliberately waited till a night when he'd have – what d'you call it, luv?'

'An alibi.'

'That's right, an alibi.'

'And what about you, Billy? Have you got an alibi?'

Billy looked at her pleadingly. 'Only if you swear I've been home with you for the last few hours.'

'Of course I will,' Cora said instantly. It was the first time Billy had done something she admired. He was smarter than she'd given him credit for. She regarded the slumped figure in the chair and gave the shoulder a little squeeze. 'Come on, Billy, cheer up. Everything's going to be all right, I can feel it. In fact, it's going to be better than before, with Maurice out of trouble and you without an overdraft to pay.' She stood. 'Shall I make you something nice for your tea, luv? Fish and chips? Or there's bacon and eggs if you prefer it. Afterwards, we can watch telly. There's some good programmes on tonight.'

'Fish and chips would go down a treat, luv.' Billy sat up and squared his shoulders. He smiled. 'I never thought you'd take it so well. You're a good sort, Cora.'

At the end of September Danny Mitchell died quietly in his sleep. Bernadette woke and found him by her side, his body as cold as ice, smiling peacefully. She allowed herself a little cry before telling Ian and Ruth. If only she'd been awake to kiss him goodbye, so that he would have felt her arms around him as he slipped from this world to the next, and she could have kept him warm for a little while longer.

Then she woke up the children and rang Alice.

At the funeral there was a stiffness between the wife of the deceased and his daughter. Alice was convinced she'd been sidelined during her father's last few months on earth, prevented from seeing him as much as she would have liked.

Bernadette had thought Alice too interfering. Danny didn't want to be nagged to see a doctor, brought tonics, asked in a maudlin voice how he felt. They had played a game between them, she, Danny and their children. The game was that he was temporarily out of sorts but would get better very soon. It meant that even when he was on his deathbed they could laugh when otherwise they might have wept. The game had continued until the night Danny died. But Alice was a spoilsport and refused to play along with them.

'He's asleep,' Bernadette would claim whenever his daughter came to see him. 'I'd sooner he wasn't disturbed.'

She didn't like doing it. Alice was her best friend, but Danny was her husband. He came first.

'We're a rapidly expanding company,' Orla informed the middle-aged, impeccably dressed manager of the small, exclusive Brighton department store. At first he'd been slightly irritated at being interrupted, but she'd soon brought him round. 'We've recently moved to a new factory in Lancashire with the very latest equipment.' This wasn't strictly true. The new factory was a dilapidated building on a run-down trading estate near St Helens and the equipment was second-hand. However, it was the case that the company was rapidly expanding. In a few weeks' time, at Christmas, two new lines were being introduced: skin freshener and cleansing lotion. Perfume was on the cards for next summer.

'I like the look of it,' the manager said. 'And I like the name too: Lacey's of Liverpool. It has a nice ring to it.'

'That's what everybody says.' Orla smiled her most dazzling smile. 'I use it meself.' She ran her fingers through her shining brown hair. 'I'm a walking advertisement for our products.'

'And an excellent advertisement, I must say.'

'Would you like me to leave some samples?' She smiled again.

'I'd sooner place an order.' The manager's answering smile was more speculative than dazzling. 'Are you free for dinner tonight?'

Orla giggled. 'Depends on how much you're going to order.'

'How about a hundred bottles of each?'

'Then I'm free for dinner.'

Cormac and Vicky would be pleased: another two hundred bottles on top of the order for two hundred and fifty she'd taken that morning, making over a thousand she'd sold during her two days on the south coast.

Orla was a first-class sales representative for Lacey's of Liverpool. Within the space of six months she had sold the company's products in virtually every city and major town in the country, charming the male managers and buyers, and flattering the women. 'You've found your niche,' Cormac had declared appreciatively. He and Vicky had taken the plunge and were working out their notices with Brooker's.

Life sometimes got a little lonely on the road, staying in shabby hotels with nothing much to do at night-time. There was always the pictures, but Orla felt even more lonely in a cinema by herself when the rest of the audience were in couples. She missed her children. Occasionally she even missed Micky, particularly his warm presence in bed beside her. But next morning she always woke up refreshed, looking forward to the day ahead and the feeling of achievement when she took a big order.

When Lacey's of Liverpool became properly established, Orla would become Head of Sales and have her own office, a secretary. She visualised having charts on the wall showing the movements of reps all over the country. And when the company became more successful still, there would be no more need for reps. Orders would automatically come flooding in on reputation alone, or so everyone hoped, and it would then be Orla's job to seek markets abroad, in Europe and the States, all over the world.

She hugged herself when she thought about travelling to America to introduce Lacey's of Liverpool's products to discerning customers there. She wasn't doing exactly what she'd planned all those years ago when she was a teenager, interviewing famous people, but this was even better. One of these days a reporter might want to interview *her*.

The manager of the Brighton department store sat unnecessarily close throughout dinner. He kept putting his hand on her thigh, or grasping her arm, and she could feel his knuckles press into her breast. Orla didn't particularly mind. In its way, it was rather thrilling. She'd let him kiss her when the evening ended, but that was all. After Vernon Matthews, kissing was as far as Orla was prepared to go.

'Would you like something to eat, Maeve?' Fion enquired.

'No, thank you.'

'Well, it's time I made the kids' tea. I'm starving meself, as it happens.'

'I'll come and help.'

The sisters went into the big shabby kitchen of Fion's house in Stanley Road. A woman was already there, furiously mashing potatoes. Sausages sizzled on the stove. A small boy was squirting washing-up liquid on the floor.

'Don't do that, Tommy, luv,' Fion said mildly. 'It'll make people slip over.'

The woman turned and slapped the child's ear, hard. 'I'm sorry, Fion. I didn't realise what the little bugger was up to.' Maeve gasped and the little boy started to howl.

Fion said, not quite so mildly, 'Olga, don't you dare let me see you hit Tommy again. You're only here because someone did the same to you. This is a refuge, for children as well as their mothers.'

'I don't know how you stand it,' Maeve said when a sullen Olga and a sobbing Tommy had gone.

'I feel as if I'm doing a bit of good.' Fion was wiping off the fat Olga had splashed all over the stove. She took a big packet of fish fingers out of the fridge.

'Doesn't your nice policeman mind?'

'Jerry? Oh, he minds a lot. He wants us to get married. I said I'd marry him as soon as I found someone to take over the refuge.'

'I couldn't stand it meself. I'd feel as if me house wasn't me own. And Martin . . .' Maeve paused.

'And Martin what?'

'Martin couldn't stand it either.'

'Speaking of Martin, won't he be home from work by now and wanting something to eat?'

'Possibly.'

'Is something wrong, Maeve?' Fion regarded her small, neat sister searchingly. Maeve hadn't been to work that day. She'd arrived at one o'clock and they'd sat talking about nothing in particular ever since. Fion had expected her to go home ages ago to make Martin's tea, but Maeve had stuck to the chair and continued with the conversation that was rapidly running out of steam, mainly because she seemed unable to concentrate on one subject for more than a few minutes. She looked on edge, kept glancing at her watch, couldn't keep still.

'Everything's fine,' Maeve said in the sort of voice that indicated everything was nothing of the sort.

The telephone rang and Maeve said, 'If that's Martin, don't tell him I'm here.'

'Why ever not, sis?'

'Just don't, that's all.'

Fion went to answer the phone and came back a few minutes later. 'It wasn't Martin, it was Mam. Martin's just phoned to ask if you were there. She said he sounded worried. I didn't say you were with me.'

Maeve didn't answer. The phone rang again. When Fion returned she said, '*That* was Martin. He sounds even more worried. What's up, sis?'

'I'm pregnant!' Maeve burst into tears. 'I had a test this morning and it was confirmed.'

'That's marvellous, luv.' Fion flung her arms round her sister. 'I'm so happy for you.'

'So am I.' Maeve wept. 'But Martin won't be happy, he'll be livid. Oh, Fion! He'll be so cross. Can I come and live with you?'

'Of course, but surely it won't come to that? Martin will be thrilled to pieces. After all, how long is it you've been married? Going on thirteen years.'

Maeve shook her head wildly. 'I told you, Martin will

be livid. He doesn't want children. He wants holidays and garages and new fridges, new cars.'

'Then it's about time he grew up and lived in the real world,' Fion said crisply. 'How did it happen? Did you forget to take your pill or something?'

'No. I *stopped* taking the pill.' Maeve sniffed and managed a tiny smile. 'I haven't taken it since Lulu's wedding. I decided I wanted a baby more than I wanted Martin.'

'Then why are you so worried about him finding out?'

'Because I still love him.' Maeve started to cry again. 'Least, I think I do.'

The phone went. It was Mam. Martin had rung a second time and was about to contact the police. 'I told him she's only a couple of hours late, but he said she hasn't been in work today. He's climbing the walls, Fion, and I'm getting a bit worried meself. This isn't a bit like our Maeve. I mean, where on earth can she be?'

'Actually, Mam, she's with me,' Fion confessed and explained the circumstances.

Mam listened in silence, then said, 'I'm pleased about the baby, but I never realised it was mainly Martin's idea they didn't have children. It'll do him good to climb the walls for a while longer. He might have come to his senses by the time he discovers where she is.'

Fion replaced the receiver soberly. How peculiar fate was, so topsy-turvy! She recalled Maeve's engagement party when she'd been stuck with Horace Flynn and everyone else seemed to be having a whale of a time. She'd felt so grateful that Neil Greene had condescended to talk to her. Yet, years later, when she'd met Neil in London he'd looked as miserable as sin and she'd wondered what she'd seen in him. Now Maeve was in a state because she was pregnant when by rights she should be on top of the world. And Orla! Gosh, she used to be so envious of Orla, who had married Micky Lavin and was everything Fion herself wanted to be. Now Orla was wandering the country like a lost soul selling crappy make-up, trying to pretend it was fantastically adventurous, when it was in fact a desperately pathetic life for a thirty-six-year-old woman to lead. Poor Orla. Poor Maeve. And poor Neil.

I never thought I'd feel sorry for a single one of them, Fion mused, let alone all three. She felt very lucky, totally fulfilled. There was hardly another thing she wanted that she could think of. Colin had been a wonderful husband and Jerry would make another.

She resolved that tonight she would suggest she and Jerry got married straight away, because it seemed silly to waste time living apart. Anyroad, there *was* something she wanted – more children. But she wasn't prepared to move into his modern flat in Litherland. It would be too cramped. Besides, she loved this house that had been bequeathed to her by Horace Flynn. She'd been the only person who'd liked him, except when he pinched her bum. Another house would have to be found for the refuge. It would be her next project and she'd put everything she had into it. Fion mentally ticked off all the things she'd have to do: badger the council for an empty property, bring the local MP on board, start fund-raising, contact the press and get them on her side.

She returned to the kitchen. Maeve had made a cup of tea and started to fry the fish fingers.

'These look nice,' she said. 'Me and Martin have never had fish fingers.'

'They're lovely with beans and tinned tomatoes. Jerry's mad on them.'

'We always have posh, three-course dinners. They take ages to cook.'

'Well, that'll stop once you've got a baby to look after.' Fion grinned.

Maeve pulled a face. 'Martin will do his nut.'

'Stuff Martin. Any man who prefers three-course meals to babies wants his bumps feeling.'

'Hmm. If I have one of these fish fingers, will it make you short?'

'Have as many as you like. There's another packet in the fridge.'

The evening wore on. There were more phone calls from a frantic Martin. The police had refused to take action. Mam phoned to say she was beginning to feel sorry for him and could Fion persuade Maeve to go home, put the poor chap out of his misery?

Fion agreed that mightn't be a bad idea. 'I think our Maeve might welcome it by now. She's a bundle of nerves. It's best to get the confrontation over and done with.'

At eight o'clock Jerry McKeown arrived – the rule 'no men on the premises' had been relaxed on his behalf. He offered to fetch Martin in a police car with the blue light flashing.

'Can I go with you?' Bonnie demanded eagerly.

'Perhaps it would be best if Maeve went,' said Fion. 'How about it, sis?'

Maeve considered this silently for a while. 'Will Jerry wait outside the house until after I've told him? Just in case I have to come back here to live if he chucks me out.'

'If there's any such suggestion as chucking out, it'll be Martin out on his ear, not you,' Jerry said darkly.

Maeve Adams had never created a fuss during her entire neat and tidy life, had never given her mam and dad, or her husband, a moment's worry. She would have been embarrassed to think she had. Maeve strongly disapproved of the way her sister, Orla, behaved – though she wouldn't have dreamt of saying so – throwing herself all over the place and complaining loudly over just about everything in sight. She had thought it dead selfish of Fion to run away to London and give her family so much heartache. Even Cormac, whom everyone considered an eminently sensible person, had had a brainstorm and refused to finish university, then gone wild for several years.

Now, not only had Maeve missed a day's work at the hospital without phoning in an excuse, but she had disappeared for several hours, causing her husband a great deal of grief. In Maeve's eyes this behaviour was on a par with that of her sisters and brother.

She didn't want to lose Martin, who would be angry when he discovered she'd stopped taking the pill without discussing it with him first. But she'd only not discussed it because she knew he wouldn't agree. Martin's priorities didn't allow for children. They were still saving to have a garage built and only the other day he had complained that the car was getting old.

'*I'm* getting old,' Maeve said to herself as the police car – without its blue light flashing – made its way to Crosby through the evening traffic. Jerry thoughtfully remained silent. 'In a few years' time I'll be too old to have babies. And I'm not prepared to go without children just so Martin can have the latest car and a garage to put it in.'

He could be as angry as he liked. Maeve folded her small hands protectively over her stomach. She would have the baby with him or without him, it was up to him to decide.

Jerry stopped outside the Adamses' immaculate modern semi, though it looked entirely different from the house Maeve had left that morning. All the lights were on, including the coach lamp outside. The front door was wide open, the car was idling in the path, headlamps on, white smoke pumping from the exhaust. Martin was about to get in the car, leaving the house open and brightly lit for any passing burglars to help themselves. Normally as neat as his wife, his hair was on end, he was tieless and had forgotten to put a coat on, despite it being a bitingly cold November night.

He turned when the police car drew up and his face seemed to collapse with horror, which turned to relief when Maeve climbed out of the passenger seat.

'Darling! Oh, my darling Maeve. I thought you were dead. I thought you'd had an accident. Are you all right? Tell me you're all right.' He stroked her arms and neck, as if expecting to find broken bones. 'Where have you been?' He suddenly frowned when he noticed the driver of the car. 'Is that Jerry? Why is he bringing you home? Maeve, what's going on?'

Maeve decided not to beat about the bush. 'I'm having a baby, Martin. If you want, I'll go straight back to our Fion's with Jerry once I've collected some clothes – that's where I've been all day.'

'You've been at Fion's! Oh, Maeve,' he said reproachfully. 'I've been out of my mind with worry.' His jaw dropped. 'Did you just say you're having a baby? How on earth did that happen?'

'The same way it happens with everyone,' Maeve said cheerfully. 'I stopped taking the pill months ago and if you don't like it, Martin, then you'll just have to lump it. As I said, I'll live with Fion.'

'Can't we discuss this indoors?'

'There's nothing to discuss.' Maeve smiled sweetly. 'I'm having a baby and that's all there is to it. Once you accept that fact and promise not to complain about the age of the car, our lack of a garage, how much you fancy a colour telly and an even more expensive holiday next year than we had last, then I'll stay. Otherwise, I'll collect me clothes and be on me way.'

Martin's relief had turned to cold annoyance. 'I never dreamt you could be so deceitful, Maeve. Having a baby should be a mutual decision, not one the wife takes for herself. I'm very disappointed with you.'

'Not half as disappointed as I am with you, Martin Adams. Mind out me way while I go and collect a few things. I'll come back for the rest tomorrow while you're at work.'

'No!' Martin grabbed her shoulder. Jerry McKeown got out of the police car and leant against it, folding his arms. He watched the couple intently. Martin gasped and let go of his wife when he realised Jerry was concerned he might hurt her. He said quietly, 'The last thing on earth I want is for you to leave, Maeve. Come inside. We can talk there.'

'I'll come, but there's nothing to talk about. I'm having a baby and the sooner you get used to the fact the better.' Maeve marched up the path.

Jerry McKeown watched them go inside. They had forgotten all about him. He got out, switched off the engine of Martin's car, locked the doors and put the keys through the letter box. He then drove back to Stanley Road and, for the umpteenth time, asked Fion to marry him and was delighted, though slightly taken aback, when she accepted straight away.

Orla was the first person Lulu and Gareth had had to dinner in their tiny London flat. Orla watched her daughter fondly as she set the little round table in the window. It reminded her of when she was little and she'd played house with Fion and Maeve. The young couple hadn't enough dishes and the ones they had were cracked. None of the cutlery matched. The chairs were odd. The room smelt of oil paints and there was a half-finished painting on an easel in the corner – Gareth couldn't afford a studio. So far, the painting consisted of several dead fish pegged, like washing, on a line.

'What will you call it?' she asked him.

'I haven't thought of a name yet.'

They sat down to a tasty chicken and mushroom casserole followed by trifle. Orla had brought a bottle of wine.

'I'd've done something more ambitious, Mum, but the cooker's useless.'

'This is lovely, Lulu,' Orla said sincerely. A candle stuck in an old wine bottle flickered in the draught. The window of the fourth-floor room overlooked a landscape of Camden roofs glistening icily in the moonlight. It was December and painfully cold. 'I never realised roofs were so many different colours,' she remarked.

'I shall paint that scene before we leave,' Gareth remarked. '*If* we leave.'

Orla looked from her daughter to her son-in-law. 'Are you thinking of moving?'

Lulu wrinkled her nose. 'We *might*, but not till after Christmas. Last week we met this chap who owns an art gallery in New York, only a titchy place, badly run-down. He thinks the Americans would go for Gareth's paintings and has promised to show half a dozen on a regular basis – you wouldn't believe the price he suggested asking, Mum.'

'I don't want to compromise my integrity,' Gareth growled.

'Painters only paint paintings in order to sell them, surely,' Orla said. 'The money you earn merely proves their worth. There's no point otherwise, unless it's just a hobby and you don't mind giving them away.'

'See,' Lulu said triumphantly. 'I knew Mum would be all for it. Gareth's worried that if he earns money he'll have sold out.'

'I'm probably more scared no one will buy my work,' Gareth confessed glumly.

Orla tried to convince him he was talking rubbish. At Lulu's age – at any age – she would have gone to New York like a shot. She didn't want her daughter to miss out on what sounded a wonderful opportunity.

After dinner, quite a few friends dropped in, bringing more wine: artists mainly, male and female, not all of them young. The lights were turned off, leaving the flickering candle and the brilliant silver moon to illuminate the shabby room, and they talked about a myriad things – art mainly, politics, the latest films, the latest shows . . .

God, how I would have loved this, Orla thought longingly. I've missed so much. I've missed everything.

It was midnight when she returned to the small hotel in Victoria. To her surprise, there were half a dozen men in the lounge and the tiny bar was still open. She bought a double whisky and the men suggested she join them. Orla thought of her small, cold room with its small, cold bed and agreed. Five of the men were reps like herself, much older. Their clothes were cheap, their laughter false, their voices much too loud. They exuded an air of faint desperation as if this wasn't the life they had envisaged twenty or thirty years before. By now, they had expected an office with their name and title on the door, their own staff, respect.

The sixth man was very different. Better dressed than the others, quietly spoken, he exuded confidence rather than desperation. Orla gathered he was an engineer working for a French tool company, calling on firms by invitation to quote for new, highly expensive machinery.

He said very little in a quiet voice with only the suggestion of an accent. The other men called him Louis. Orla was particularly intrigued because, unlike his friends, he completely ignored her. He was a small, slender man, dark-haired, thin-lipped, with a tight, unsmiling face. She hadn't felt so immediately attracted to someone since she'd first met Micky. She kept looking at him in the hope of catching his eye, but he never once glanced in her direction.

An hour and two more whiskies later, she announced she was off to bed. The other men bade her a noisy goodnight, but Louis merely stared at his highly polished shoes and didn't speak.

Chapter 17

'This room is like a fridge,' Vicky Weatherspoon muttered. 'If I were a pint of milk, I'd keep for weeks.' She glared at the ice on the metal-framed windows, wondering if it was inside or out, and rubbed her numb hands together, but they had lost all feeling.

It was useless trying to write. She threw the pen on to the desk and tucked her hands inside the sleeves of her jumper. They felt only slightly warmer.

A plumber was coming to install second-hand central heating at the end of December. He was a very cheap, highly sought-after plumber, which meant they'd had to wait months until he was free. It hadn't been so bad in October when they'd first moved in and had spent most of their time decorating the shabby, run-down building inside and out, while Mary Gregory and Robin Hughes, both eighteen and with A levels in Chemistry, were in the workshop turning out thousands of bottles of Lacey's of Liverpool shampoo and conditioner. A business had never been started on so short a shoestring, Cormac had said, laughing.

Lucky Cormac! Vicky made a face. Cormac was at that moment in a nice warm restaurant in Liverpool, lunching with a girl called Andrea Pryce, a model, who would become the face of Lacey's of Liverpool in an advertising campaign in the press, starting January. It would swallow up all the profit the company had made so far, but hopefully be worth it in the end. Andrea was startlingly pretty and ten years younger than Vicky, who wasn't only envious of Cormac being warm. Say if he fell in love with Andrea! Say if she tried to seduce him!

Vicky tried to imagine how a woman went about seducing a man, but her imagination wouldn't stretch that far. She thought miserably that Cormac was no more attracted to her now than a year ago when they'd gone into partnership. They couldn't possibly have got on better. They were friends, they went to dinner together, had even gone to a hotel in Yorkshire on a weekend business course; they sometimes shared quite intimate thoughts. The only thing missing was romance. Cormac had shown not the slightest sign of wanting to kiss her – she didn't count the triumphant kisses he planted on her cheek when they received a big order, or the hugs he gave her for the same reason. It was a sad fact that Cormac didn't regard her as a woman, but as a mate, a business partner. He would have been just as fond of her had she been a man.

Yet with each day they spent together, Vicky only loved him more. She'd tried to make herself attractive by growing her short, crisp hair longer, but was forced to cut it off when it became a halo of wire wool. Her mother warned her she looked like a clown when she tried using make-up. 'Stick to lipstick, Victoria, and then make it pale. You've got too big a mouth for such a bright red.'

Vicky blushed at the memory and wondered if Cormac had noticed her turning up for a whole week looking as if she was about to join a circus. Did he ever notice anything about her?

The new clothes had also proved a disaster. She was short and dumpy. She didn't suit flowing frocks and pleated skirts. And, 'Your legs are too sporty for high heels,' claimed her mother. By sporty, Vicky assumed she meant her overdeveloped calves. She would never know why she had acquired such heavily muscled legs when she'd been useless at games at school.

Then she'd spent a fortune on contact lenses so she could dispense with her glasses but, try as she might, she couldn't get used to the damn things.

Still, on New Year's Day Cormac's sister, Fionnuala, was getting married and Vicky had been invited to the wedding. Naturally, she and Cormac would go together. If they spent enough time in each other's company, she thought hopefully, he might get so used to her that he'd want them to get married because he couldn't visualise another woman in his life.

Cora and Billy Lacey had also received an invitation to Fion's wedding. Cora breathed a sigh of relief that she'd been accepted back into the Lacey fold. She'd buy herself a new coat and wear that diamanté brooch in the lapel that she'd nicked from Owen Owen's a long time ago. It wouldn't hurt Billy to have a new suit – he'd lost so much weight that his best one hung round him like a tent. Perhaps they could go to town on Saturday, have a meal afterwards.

There was an odd sensation in Cora's breast when she thought about going shopping with Billy. Another person would have recognised it as happiness, but Cora wasn't used to being happy and couldn't have explained what the sensation was.

After forty years of ignoring each other, she and Billy had suddenly started to get along. Billy had more or less given up the ale and most nights they spent watching telly. One night they'd even gone to the pictures to see *The Sound of Music* and enjoyed it no end – that girl, Julie something, had a lovely voice.

Money was no longer a problem since the yard had burnt down and Billy was able to keep all his wages. As expected, Alice paid far over the odds for cleaning the salons and Cora had started collecting her pension from the post office in Marsh Lane. Maurice and Billy between them had settled all Lacey's Tyres' outstanding debts with the money off the insurance and Maurice seemed much happier working as a driver for Bootle Corporation. He'd come to tea last Sunday, bringing Pol and the kids, and Cora realised she was quite fond of the lad even if he was a loser, unlike her real son who was very much on the up and up. The kids got on her nerves a bit with their noise, but she felt like a proper grandma and had actually bought them some odds and ends of clothes.

In a few weeks' time they'd be even better off. Alice Lacey was looking to buy a house and would be leaving Amber Street for ever once she'd found one. It was Billy who'd suggested him and Cora take over Amber Street from Alice who'd had the place done up dead smart. The rent was thirty bob a week cheaper than Garibaldi Road.

Cora was surprised to find she didn't mind, not much, living in the house of the woman she'd always hated. Nowadays, there wasn't all that much room for hatred in her heart.

Fionnuala Littlemore married Sergeant Jerry McKeown on the first day of January 1971. It was snowing and Fion wore a cream fitted coat over a matching dress – Jerry had offered to buy her a fur coat as a wedding present, but Fion didn't approve of animals being slaughtered for their skins.

Over ninety guests had been invited to the reception at Hilton's Restaurant. It wasn't until six o'clock that the newly married couple left for their honeymoon in London.

Alice waved them off tearfully, though she wondered why young people bothered with honeymoons any more. In her day a honeymoon was the time you got to know each other properly. There used to be all sorts of jokes about the first night. She remembered feeling dead nervous herself, but John had been a gentle, tender lover right from the start. Nowadays, the first night happened long before the honeymoon and people knew each other far better than God had intended by the time they condescended to get wed.

She returned upstairs to where the air was fuggy with cigarette smoke and several couples were dancing to a recording of 'A Whiter Shade of Pale', which was being played loud enough to be heard several streets away.

Orla came up. 'You look dead miserable, Mam. Have a drink. What would you like, sherry?'

'Just a little one, luv.'

Orla looked as if she'd already had too much to drink herself and there were four more hours to go before the reception ended. She also looked much too thin, Alice thought worriedly. Her eyes were unnaturally bright. She seemed to laugh a lot at things that weren't remotely funny. It was an unnatural life she led, particularly for a woman: on the road, staying in strange hotels in strange places. Still, it would all change in a few months' time, when she would be based in her own office in St Helens: Head of Sales.

Alice wondered if the time would ever come when she would stop worrying about her children. At least Fion was happy, the one she'd least expected to be, and Maeve was like the cat that ate the cream since she'd fallen pregnant, though Martin didn't exactly look too pleased.

Her son appeared on top of the world, the business doing so amazingly well, but Cormac had turned thirty a week ago and it was time he got married, started a family. Of course, he already had a daughter, Sharon, Pol's eldest girl, but Alice wasn't the only one who suspected Cormac had had nothing to do with the lovely red-haired child who resembled neither her mother nor her supposed father. She'd always hoped things would get serious between Cormac and Vicky, but he'd brought that model, Andrea Pryce, to the wedding. She was a nice girl, if a trifle empty-headed.

She looked for Vicky, saw her sitting alone on a chair, looking rather downcast, and went to sit beside her. 'Would you like a piece of wedding cake to take home for your mam and dad, luv?'

'That's very kind of you, thanks.'

'I'd have sent an invitation for two if I'd known you were coming on your own. You could have brought someone with you.'

'There's no one I could have brought. I thought . . .' She paused and said no more.

'Thought what, luv?'

'Nothing.' There were tears in the girl's eyes.

Alice realised that she'd thought she'd be coming with Cormac. The poor thing was almost certainly in love with him – he chose to dance past at that moment with Andrea in his arms, clearly more impressed with beauty than brains, stupid lad. 'Would you mind helping me make everyone a cup of tea, luv?'

Vicky jumped to her feet with alacrity, obviously glad to be rescued from her lonely chair.

In the kitchen, Cora was finishing washing a mountain of dishes. 'I've just put that urn thing on to make a cup of tea,' she said when she saw Alice.

'Thanks, Cora. I was about to do the same thing

meself. I think I'll use them cardboard cups, save more washing.' Alice and Vicky began to spread the cups into rows.

'I've sent Billy out to buy some sugar 'case we run short.'

Cora looked very smart in a tweed costume with a white jumper underneath. Her hair had been set that morning in the Stanley Road Lacey's. That shoplifting incident, dreadful though it was at the time, had done her the world of good, brought her to her senses. She was much more friendly nowadays, almost human.

'I was wondering,' Cora said, 'if you'll be leaving the carpets behind when you move. We've carpets of our own, naturally,' she added hurriedly, 'all fitted, but it seems daft to take them up and cut them down.'

'I'm leaving all the fixtures and fittings, curtains included.' Alice sighed. She was dreading leaving Amber Street, but circumstances and her children were forcing her out. The circumstances were that the salons were making a mint, not just from hairdressing, but she was the only stockist in Bootle of Lacey's of Liverpool products and they sold like hot cakes. She had never been so flush, yet nearly every one of her neighbours had to struggle to keep their heads above water, which made her feel dead uncomfortable.

As for the children, they'd been nagging her to buy a place of her own for years: Southport, or near the sands, Ainsdale or Formby way. When they were little she'd taken for granted she knew better than her kids, but since they'd grown up they seemed to think they knew better than *her*. Perhaps it was only natural. After all, she'd constantly tried to rearrange her dad's life, much to the chagrin of Bernadette.

It reminded her for the umpteenth time that she hadn't seen much of her friend since Danny died. There remained a stiffness between them. Bernadette was at the wedding, naturally, a pale, rather sad figure, surprisingly old, Alice thought when she'd come into the church with the children. This was the first big occasion that she'd attended as a widow.

'Excuse me, Vicky. I won't be a minute.' Impulsively, Alice went back into the reception. Bernadette was standing with a group, yet somehow looking very much alone, watching Ian and Ruth dance together. Alice was struck by how closely seventeen-year-old Ian resembled his father. Tall and lithe, he had the same appealingly wicked smile. She touched Bernadette's hand. 'He's going to be a heartbreaker one of these days, just like me dad.'

'I think he already is. I'm not sure if it's a good thing or a bad one that he looks so much like Danny.' Bernadette gave a rueful smile. 'It means I'm reminded of him a hundred times a day.'

'I reckon it's good.'

'I suppose so.'

They looked at each other. Alice wrinkled her nose. 'I'm sorry, Bernie.'

'For what?'

'For barging in when me dad was ill, trying to take control, insisting he see a doctor.'

'You only had his best interests at heart, luv. Trouble was it wasn't what Danny wanted. Perhaps I should have been a bit more tactful meself.'

Alice linked her friend's arm. 'Why don't we go to the pictures next week? We can have a meal beforehand. *Butch Cassidy and the Sundance Kid* is on at the Forum. I've been dying to see it for ages.'

'So've I.' There was an expression of relief on Bernadette's face. 'I'd love that. Ally. I'll pop in the salon and we'll arrange a time.'

'Come to tea tomorrer and we can do it then. Bring Ian and Ruth, except they'd probably find it dead boring. None of me grandchildren want to come to tea any more, not even Bonnie and she's only nine. I'll be glad when our Maeve has her baby and I'll have a little 'un again.'

Sheffield in January! Anywhere in January when it was snowing hard and freezing cold made you yearn to be somewhere else, like the South of France.

Or Spain.

Orla thought about Dominic Reilly, living in Barcelona. He'd married the girlfriend he'd said wasn't as beautiful as she was – it had been on the front page of all the papers. As soon as she could afford it she'd go on holiday to Spain. Perhaps Mam would come with her. She didn't fancy going on her own. In fact, she was fed up to the bloody teeth with being on her own and couldn't wait for April when Cormac had announced the company would go through a sort of minor relaunch and she would be working permanently in St Helens. A lot depended on how well the press campaign went with that model. If it went well, there would be no more need for her to roam the country, thank the Lord.

She trudged through the slush towards the hotel. At least it had a more-or-less decent lounge and she could sit in comfort until it was time to go to bed in an icy room with icy sheets.

The hotel also had a bar. By the end of the evening other reps would arrive, some of whom she'd be bound to know and she'd have people to talk to, make her laugh.

What a lousy day! The weather was vile, the street lamps a depressing sickly yellow, the traffic horrendous, and her car was parked miles away. Even worse, half the places she'd called in, mainly chemists, had refused to see her, even the ones where she'd made a prior appointment: people were off with colds and flu, and they were too busy.

She was beginning to hate this job. This wasn't adventure. It was no longer the least bit exciting. Maybe she was a bit run down because she seemed to have lost all her initial enthusiasm.

The hotel at last! The usual seedy establishment that looked as if it hadn't seen a lick of paint in years. Lots of plastic flowers and oatmeal paintwork. Orla hung her heavy trenchcoat on a rack in the hall. Underneath, she wore a smart black suit which no one had seen all day because this was the first chance she'd had to remove the mac. She went into the empty lounge with her briefcase. There was no fire, but an elderly radiator emitted moderate heat. The bar was in the corner and there was no one behind the tiny counter. Orla rang the bell, a woman appeared and she ordered a whisky.

'Sit down and I'll bring it over.'

'Ta.' Orla chose the armchair closest to the radiator and tucked her legs against it. The woman brought the whisky. As soon as she'd gone, Orla drank it in a single gulp. She felt in the briefcase for the half–bottle she'd bought on impulse on her walk back, the first time she'd ever done such a thing, but tonight, for some reason, she felt exceptionally depressed, what with the weather and a completely wasted day.

Refilling the glass, she drank the contents, slower now, before filling up the glass again. She wasn't trying to avoid the bar prices, just the embarrassment of reordering so quickly.

It had become a habit, starting off the evening with a couple of whiskies. They helped her forget about the present and think about the future, which looked particularly rosy when she'd had a few drinks, though she'd never had three before in such a short space of time. She drained the glass, closed her eyes and felt a pleasant warmth swill round her stomach, which reminded her how empty it was because she'd forgotten to have dinner. She'd eaten nothing since she'd left another hotel that morning – where had it been? Rotherham.

'Good evening.'

Her eyes shot open to find the sombre figure of Louis Bernet staring down at her. He wore a grey suit and a very white shirt that contrasted agreeably with his brown skin and smooth black hair. This was the second time they'd met since the night in London when she'd had dinner with Lulu and Gareth. On the last occasion they'd chatted amicably, only about trivial things. He wasn't as unfriendly as he had first seemed, more reserved, a bit shy.

'Hello.' She tried to smile.

He nodded at her empty glass. 'Would you like a drink?'

'Yes, ta.' Another drink wouldn't hurt. Not tonight, when she felt so unusually miserable.

'Whisky?'

'Please.' He'd remembered what she drank, her 'tipple', as Grandad used to say. He went over to the bar and for some reason Orla's eyes filled with tears. It must be thinking about Grandad, which made her think of Bernadette, Mam, her sisters, her children. And Micky.

Bootle seemed worlds away from this cold, crummy hotel. In Pearl Street there'd be a roaring fire in the grate, the telly would be on, the kids would be home from work desperate for their tea – and Caitlin Reilly, or whatever her name was now, would be bustling in and out of Orla's kitchen getting food ready.

Jaysus! 'What am I doing here?' Orla asked herself. 'Why did I leave?' At that moment. Pearl Street with her husband and children seemed the most desirable place on earth. 'I must be mad. I'm searching for rainbows, but you can only *see* a rainbow. You can't touch it.'

Louis Bernet returned with the drinks. He sat in the armchair next to hers. 'We seem to be the first here.'

Orla nodded and pulled herself together. She reminded herself that she was with a devastatingly attractive man. The first minute she'd set eyes on him, she'd sensed a magnetism about him. Now they were alone together and it was her opportunity to . . . to do what?

To make eyes at him over the whisky, flutter her lashes, lick her lips and pretend she was a scarlet woman? Except she wasn't a scarlet woman. She was Orla Lavin from Bootle, married, with four children whom she badly missed.

'What company do you work for?' Louis asked. He had the faintest of French accents. 'I didn't ask the time we met before.'

'Lacey's of Liverpool. It's my brother's firm. We make cosmetics. As from April, I'll have me own office back home. Would you like some samples? You can give them to your wife.'

'I haven't got a wife. Do you have a husband?'

'Sort of.' Orla paused. 'We're separated.'

'He must be mad, this husband, allowing himself to be separated from a woman like you.' His narrow lips twisted in a smile.

Orla forgot the house in Pearl Street and its occupants. She traced the rim of her glass with her finger as she'd once seen an actress do in a film, someone like Ava Gardner or Elizabeth Taylor. 'I'm not very nice,' she said seductively. 'That's why me and me husband parted.'

'I don't believe that.'

'It's true.'

'You seem exceptionally nice to me.' He moved his legs so that their knees were touching.

Orla's flesh felt as if it was on fire. A pulse throbbed in her throat. She was trying to think of an answer, when Louis said, 'Have you eaten yet?'

'I forgot to eat.'

'Would you join me for dinner here?'

'They serve meals?'

He shrugged and spread his hands, a very foreign gesture. 'Not very good meals, but edible. There aren't any restaurants nearby and it's too awful a night to go searching for one.'

'In that case I'll be pleased to join you for dinner.'

Louis was right. The meal was just about edible: badly cooked lamb, very dry roast potatoes, frozen peas. He ordered a bottle of wine to make the food go down more smoothly.

On top of the whisky, it also made Orla more than a little light-headed. She began to see the romance of the situation: two virtual strangers, stranded in a third-rate hotel, snow whipping against the windows. All that was needed was some haunting music.

During the meal he told her about himself. He'd been born in a little village north of Paris. His parents had a smallholding. The village was very dull, nothing ever happened. He'd been taken on by a local engineering firm to train as a draughtsman. At twenty-one, he'd gone to work in Paris. He kissed his fingers and threw the kiss into the air. 'Ah, Paris!' He pronounced it Paree. 'Paris is *très* beautiful. Very, very beautiful. And so full of life. It has everything a man – or woman – can possibly want.'

'I'd love to go there,' Orla breathed.

His brown eyes smiled into hers. 'I'll show it to you if you like.'

'I *would* like.'

'In the spring?'

She felt dizzy. 'Yes, in the spring.' She'd never met anyone like him before. He seemed so grown-up and sophisticated compared with the other men she'd known, particularly Micky, who was a child by comparison.

No one else had come into the dining room by the time they finished the meal. They returned to the lounge where an elderly couple had bagged their armchairs by the radiator. Otherwise the room was empty. The other reps must have wisely stayed in town and found bars with a bit more life in them. The clock showed half past nine – the last few hours had raced by.

Louis took her elbow. 'Would you like another drink?'

'A whisky and soda,' she replied, though she'd already drunk far too much. 'Just a little one.' She swayed and almost fell into an armchair.

'One more drink and I think we should go to bed.' He regarded her challengingly, eyebrows raised.

'If you say so,' she said demurely. Every nerve in her body felt alive. She couldn't possibly sleep on her own after tonight. A memory returned, of the night in a Bootle entry when she'd first made love with Micky. She had the same feeling now, of wanting to be touched all over, but this time by Louis Bernet.

Orla quickly drank the whisky. Louis held out his hand and helped her to her feet. She wondered if he felt the same pounding excitement as she did. She could hardly stand and it wasn't all to do with the amount of alcohol she'd drunk.

Her room was on the third floor. They took the lift,

where they kissed for the first time and Orla felt a rush of raw desire when she felt him pressed against her.

In the corridor she stumbled and Louis grabbed her arm. He supported her as far as her room where, to her surprise, he paused. There was a look of what might have been irritation on his face. 'I didn't realise you'd drunk enough to get in this state and I find drunken women rather unappealing. Tonight you'd go to bed with any man who asked.'

'That's not true!' Orla cried. She didn't want to be alone. She couldn't stand it, not tonight. 'I don't usually make a habit of this sort of thing. I'm only doing it because it's you.' There was a sob in her voice. She unlocked the door, put her hands round his neck and drew him into the chilly room. Snow was whirling crazily against the windows and the traffic outside was muted. 'I'm more tired than drunk, but not too tired to . . .' She paused, blushing. '. . . To make love with you.'

Perhaps it was the blush that convinced him she was, at least partially, telling the truth. He sighed and said huskily, 'You're also extremely beautiful – and very hard to resist.'

'Please don't try.' She removed the jacket of her black suit. The blouse underneath was blue and very frilly.

He came over and took her in his arms, buried his head in her shoulder. She could feel his lips through the thin material of the blouse. Then he began to undo the buttons, so slowly and deliberately that she wanted to scream at him to hurry. He slid the blouse off her shoulders, his hands warm on her skin as he pushed her down on to the bed and her head swam. He took off his jacket and kissed between her breasts, then pulled down the straps of her underskirt and bra so that she was exposed to him. She felt both vulnerable and wanton as she took his head in her hands and directed his lips on to her right nipple. He sucked greedily, kneading the flesh around with his fingers. Then he transferred to the other breast and Orla moaned.

Suddenly he released her and lay back on the pillow, all passion apparently spent.

'What's the matter?' Orla asked, bewildered.

'Nothing. Let me hold you, come here.' He slid an arm round her shoulders and put the other across her waist.

Orla began to touch him, but he caught her hand and held it tightly. 'Let us lie still a minute, *chérie*,' he said softly.

'But why?' What had she done wrong? It can't have been anything all that bad, because he was being so gentle with her. But it was very mysterious all the same.

'Because there are times when it is good to stop and think, just stay quiet for a while.'

She began to catch his mood, her own passion having vanished with his, and relaxed against him. He was still almost fully dressed and he felt warm and comfortable.

'Do you ever get lonely, Orla?' His voice was little more than a whisper.

'Lately I feel lonely all the time,' she said with a sigh.

'Me, also. All the time. But unlike you, I have no family to return to.'

'You poor thing!'

'I am very much a poor thing. I have spent the last ten years travelling across Europe, searching for something I have yet to find.'

'Love?'

He nodded. 'Love, possibly. Happiness, maybe. Who knows what? It might be God. And what are you searching for, *chérie*?'

'I'm not searching for anything. I'm just doing me job.'

'No, you're searching, like me. I could see it in your eyes.' He laughed quietly. 'I've seen the same expression in my own, that's how I know. You weren't satisfied with what you had. It's why you left your husband and children. After a while, the searching can become very tedious.'

'I suppose it can.' She wondered what he was getting at. Was he leading up to something? He had turned out to be a very strange man. She liked him more now than she did before, even if she couldn't understand him.

The hotel was exceptionally silent and it would have been easy to believe they were the only two people in it. Apart from the traffic, there wasn't another sound to be heard.

'You are a lovely woman, Orla.' He caressed her face and touched her hair with his lips. 'I like you very much. I think I could very easily fall in love with you if given half a chance. You pretend to be so sophisticated, but you're not. You're vulnerable, like a child. I shouldn't have asked you to come to bed with me. I was taking advantage of your need, not for sex, but for something else: romance perhaps, which is a very different thing. I feel ashamed, but I only did it because, like you, I didn't want to spend the night alone.'

'Why are you saying all this, Louis?' Orla whispered. 'Why didn't you take advantage? What stopped you? Was it something I did?'

'No, I just wanted to say these things before I told you. I want you to realise how hopeless your search is, so you'll understand you're not missing anything when you go back home to your family.'

'Told me what? And I can't go home till Saturday, and then it's only for the weekend.'

'I think you should go now. You see, *chérie*, you have a lump in your left breast, a large one. Now is the time for you to return to the people you love – and the people who love you.'

All she wanted was for him to leave. She appreciated being told so kindly, if rather strangely, about the lump – another man might have noticed, made love and said nothing. But now she knew and all she wanted was to be with her mam.

Louis understood how she felt. He helped her pack and took her in his car to where hers was parked. It was still snowing.

'I meant it about Paris,' he said when he had put her things in the boot and came round to the driver's side to say goodbye. Orla rolled down the window. 'I hope and pray it might still happen. Here's my card in case you feel like getting in touch when you're better.'

'Thank you. Thank you for everything, Louis.'

As she was driving out of the car park, Orla threw the card out of the window, then closed it.

The journey to Liverpool was a nightmare. Snow kept sticking to the windscreen. The wipers were useless. Lorries thundered past, spraying her with slush. She couldn't see. The car kept skidding on the icy surface, but she managed to steady it. She wasn't sure if she cared if the car crashed or not. Would her children, her family, find it easier to cope with her death in an accident rather than a long, slow death from cancer? She reminded herself that the lump might be benign and, even if it wasn't, you could have treatment. Patsy O'Leary, who worked for mam, had had breast cancer and recovered. She'd had a breast removed. But Patsy was nearly sixty. Orla was only thirty-seven and to lose a breast would be the end of everything.

'This is a funny time to come home, luv,' Mam said

when Orla came in just as she was making the first cup of tea of the day. 'It's only just gone seven and I'm not long up. Don't tell me you've driven all night in this weather? No wonder you look exhausted.'

Mam looked so welcoming and comfortable in her candlewick dressing gown, her greying hair all mussed. Orla burst into tears. 'Will you come to the doctor's with me later, Mam. I'm too frightened to go on me own.'

A week later and tests showed that the lump was malignant. And there was a smaller lump in the right breast that was malignant too. Orla was advised to have a double mastectomy.

'Oh, Mam!' she screamed in the hospital when the doctor conveyed the terrible news.

'I wish it was me, luv,' Alice whispered. 'Oh, dear God, I wish it was me.'

'You can wear a padded bra,' Fion said practically later that night when the family gathered together in Amber Street for a conference. 'No one will know.'

'*I'll* know,' Orla yelled. 'I'll be deformed for the rest of me life.'

'Orla, you'll still be as beautiful as ever,' Cormac assured her. 'After the operation you can carry on with the job exactly as planned, with your own office in St Helens.'

'I'll be as ugly as sin. And you can stuff the job, Cormac. I don't want it.'

'I'll pray for you, Sis,' Maeve said softly. 'I'll pray every minute of every day, I promise.'

'It's too late for prayers.' Orla wept. 'It's happened. Anyroad, I don't believe in prayers. They don't work. I used to pray for all sorts of things, but I never got them.'

Instead, she'd got a husband in a million and four lovely children, Alice thought sadly. Enough to make most women happy, but Orla had always wanted the impossible.

'I imagined one day I'd get married again, but no man will ever want me now.'

Cormac shuddered and turned away. How would he feel about Andrea if both her breasts had been removed?

Alice glanced at her other daughters. Fion made a face and Maeve shrugged. No one quite knew what to say.

'Jerry, I want a baby. I want to conceive tonight,' Fion told her new husband when they got into bed.

'I'll do me best, darling. I'm already trying hard, but I'll try twice as hard if you like. Anyroad, why the urgency all of a sudden?'

'I'm not sure.' It was something to do with Orla, something stupid, as if a new life growing inside her would act as protection against what was happening to her sister. Or perhaps it was a wish to grab at things that mattered before it was too late. 'Just a minute.'

'Where are you off to?' Jerry enquired patiently when Fion got out of bed.

'I'm going to kneel the way we used to do when we were little and say a proper prayer for our Orla.' At the end of the prayer, Fion slipped in a little one for herself. 'Please God, please make me conceive tonight.'

'How's Orla?' Martin enquired stiffly when Maeve came home. He was sitting in the lounge with a typed letter on his knee.

'In a state, as you can imagine. I'd be in a state meself if I was in the same position. She's having an operation next week.'

'I'm sorry to hear that. Oh, by the way . . .' He waved the letter, 'This is from that double-glazing firm who contacted us last year. Remember we said we might be interested in the spring? I rang and told them it's off because my wife has given up work. Another thing, I think the clutch might be going on the car. We really need a new one – car, that is – but I suppose we'll just have to do with a new clutch instead.' He sniffed disdainfully.

'Did you tell the double-glazing firm exactly why I'd given up work?' Maeve enquired. 'That I'm having a baby in three months' time?'

'It was none of their business.'

'Nor is the fact I've given up work. I suspect you didn't tell them that at all. It's just another little dig at me for getting pregnant without your permission. You'd sooner have double glazing and a new car than a baby.' Maeve's usually serene face darkened with anger. Normally she was patient with him, but tonight, thinking about Orla, she wasn't in the mood. Her voice rose. 'You've got your priorities all wrong, Martin.' If he didn't buck up his ideas, there'd soon be another divorce in the Lacey family.

Orla opened her eyes. A familiar face was bending over the hospital bed. A kiss brushed against her lips. 'Micky!'

'Hello, sweetheart. How are you feeling?'

'Still a bit dopey. You look well.' She'd forgotten how handsome he was, even if his dark hair was slightly thinner and his face had filled out somewhat.

'You probably won't believe me, but so do you. A bit pale, that's all.' He stroked her cheek. 'Do you mind me coming to see you?'

'Of course not. For a moment I thought you were here because I'd had a baby. Doesn't Caitlin what's-her-name mind you coming?'

'Caitlin left a while ago, Orla. She couldn't compete.'

'Against who?'

'You, luv. She said I still loved you and always would. I couldn't help but agree.'

'What about the divorce? I've kept expecting to get a solicitor's letter.'

He looked sheepish. 'I never got round to seeing a solicitor.'

'Micky.' She took a long, shuddering breath. 'Has me mam told you?'

'Yes and I want you to come home with me. I'll do everything for you, wait on you hand and foot. I've already arranged it with work. I've got leave of absence until . . .' He bit his lip.

'Until I die?'

'Sorry, luv. I didn't mean to put it like that.' He began to weep. His tears stung her face and she left them there to mingle with her own. 'Don't die, Orla,' he pleaded. 'The kids are going crazy back home. Lulu keeps ringing up from New York. She's ready to get on a plane at the drop of a hat.'

'It's going to happen, Micky. The lumps have been removed, but the cancer's everywhere. I'm too far gone to operate. They're going to try something called radiotherapy, but they don't hold out much hope.' She was amazed that she could speak so sanely and sensibly when she knew that she was going to die in the not too distant future.

'Will you come back to Pearl Street with me and the kids, luv?' His good-natured face was screwed up anxiously, as if nothing before had mattered to him as much as her reply.

'Have you discussed it with Mam?'

'She says it's up to you. You must do as you think best.'

'I'm in an awful mess on top, Micky,' she whispered.

'Lord knows what I'll look like when the dressings come off.'

He began to cry again. 'Oh, Orla. I know it's terrible for you, but it doesn't bother me. You're still the best-looking woman I've ever known.'

'And you're the best-looking man.' To her amazment, she managed a dazzling smile. 'I'll come back to Pearl Street and be with you and our children, Micky.'

It was still surprising, the things that could fall off the back of a lorry: an electric blanket, for instance; a lovely, spongy Dunlopillo cushion to lean against in the armchair; delectable items of food; pretty little bits of jewellery; perfume; filmy scarves; a lovely nylon bed jacket – things that Mrs Lavin, her mother-in-law, brought round frequently, to 'cheer you up, like'.

She hadn't realised how much she had come to love her in-laws, who bore her no ill will for having walked out on their son, only returning because she was dying. Neither did Micky, nor her children.

In the past, Orla had been too wrapped up in herself, in her own needs and desires, to notice how nice people were. But now there was no future to think about and she was able to see things in a less self-centred way. She had never before been in receipt of so many hugs and kisses from her children, no doubt because they knew they would have been impatiently shrugged away in the past. Now Orla wanted to be hugged and kissed as much as possible because there was so little time left – six months, maybe a year.

Lulu came home from New York for a week to see her mother. Gareth's paintings were selling like hot cakes, she announced, and they were buying an apartment in Greenwich Village. She also announced that she was expecting a baby late in October. 'You'll be at the christening, won't you, Mum?' She squeezed her mother's wrist, as if daring her to say no.

'In New York, luv?'

'It costs the earth to have a baby in America. I'll have it here, in Liverpool.'

'Then I'll be at the christening, luv. I promise.'

The house was besieged by visitors: family, friends, neighbours. Orla had passed the point of thinking she would get better, that there was hope. It made things easier for the visitors, not having to pretend. She imagined being the star of a terribly moving drama that would make a fantastic film – Vanessa Redgrave would be marvellous in her part.

Once she had got over the trauma of the operation, she felt well enough to go out, though she tired easily. She bought a stiff padded bra and filled it with cotton wool, so no one would guess she had no breasts when she went with Micky to the pictures and to the theatre when a couple of tickets managed to flutter off a lorry. After two visits to the hospital for radiotherapy, she decided not to go again. It made her feel washed out and she knew it was a waste of time.

The actual act of dying Orla tried not to think about. Only in the dead of night, lying in the double bed with Micky asleep beside her and the glimmer of the street lamps peeping through the gap in the curtains, would she let herself visualise closing her eyes for the very last time on the people she loved most dearly. She would never see them again. She would be gone from their lives for ever. They would miss her, grieve for her, but after a while they would have no alternative but to get on with their own lives and it would be as if she had never existed.

Sometimes she would start to cry, waking up Micky, who would take her in his arms and she would sob that

433

she didn't want to die, to leave him and the children. But what could Micky say except, 'Shush, luv. There, there, sweetheart, don't cry.' He never said, 'Everything's going to be all right,' because they both knew it wasn't.

Micky was a saint for taking her back. When she thought about her moods and tantrums in the past, the bad-tempered scenes that were all her fault, she felt ashamed and embarrassed.

'I was horrible to you, wasn't I?' she said one night when the children had gone to bed and they were sitting on the settee in the parlour having just watched an old Humphrey Bogart film on television.

'You certainly were,' he agreed.

'I'm sorry,' she said penitently. 'I decided the other night that you're a saint for putting up with me for so long.'

He smiled ruefully. 'I'd sooner have married you, luv, than any other woman on earth. I just wish I'd been able to make you happy.'

'No one could have made me happy. I wanted too much.' She linked his arm. 'But you're making me happy now, Micky. I feel wonderful, being home. I remember thinking, it was the night in Sheffield, just before I came back, about how much I was missing Pearl Street and me family. I longed so much to be here I felt an ache in me heart.' The encounter with Louis Bernet she kept to herself. She'd told everyone she'd noticed the lump when she was having a bath. 'Though I'm worried about the children. It's not good for them, watching their mother die in front of their eyes. Our Maisie hardly ever goes out these days – I remember I used to nag her for never being in – and Gary's put off joining the Navy until . . . well, you know. Poor Paul's forever on the verge of tears. He's more sensitive than the others. As for

Lulu, I daren't think what her phone bill will be like. She calls every other day.'

'We can't shield them from reality, Orla, luv.'

'I suppose not.' She chuckled. 'I'll be a grandma, won't I? If I live long enough. It's strange, because our Fion, who's a year older than me, has just announced she's in the club and Maeve's only got another six weeks to go. I wish . . .'

'Wish what, luv?'

'Oh, nothing.'

Later, in bed, Orla said, 'I've been thinking, Micky.'

'I thought as much, you've been dead quiet.'

'I'd like a baby too.'

Micky gasped. 'Don't talk daft, luv. You can't guarantee . . . That's a stupid idea, Orla.'

'You were going to say I can't guarantee I'll be alive in nine months' time, but I will be, Micky, I swear it. I'll *keep* meself alive to see Maeve's and Fion's babies born, as well as me granddaughter and me own baby.'

'That would be dead irresponsible,' Micky said, outraged. 'Who'd look after it, for one thing?'

'Everybody,' Orla said promptly. 'Mam would and me sisters would, and your mam and dad would. And you would, Micky, as well as our children. It would be the dearest loved baby in the world.'

Orla coaxed and cajoled for the next half-hour, but Micky remained implacable. But still Orla persisted, giving all the positive reasons she could think of for having a baby. 'It would make me so happy, Micky. I wouldn't feel as if I was dying if I had a baby growing inside me. It would be like knowing me soul would be passed on to me child.'

'That's nonsense, Orla.'

After another half-hour of persuasion, Micky said reluctantly, 'Let's see what the doctor has to say.'

'No. The doctor will advise against it. I know he will.'

'There!' Micky said triumphantly, as if this proved his point.

'The doctor can't do anything else. If he said "go ahead" and things went wrong, he'd be open to blame.'

'So, you concede things can go wrong.'

'Things won't go wrong, but the doctor can't be sure of that. He'll advise against it to protect his back.'

'You might not conceive.'

'If I don't, I don't. But I'd like to try.' She began to touch him. 'Please, Micky,' she whispered. 'Anyroad, I'm not the delicate invalid you seem to think, not yet, and I feel like making love.'

'All right,' he said in a choked voice, 'we'll make love tomorrer – after I've bought some French letters. As for a baby, I'd prefer you thought about it for a bit longer than a few hours. We'll talk about it again next week. Oh, don't stop, luv. Don't stop. I've been dying for you to do that ever since you came home.'

Chapter 18

Bernadette Mitchell looked up in surprise one morning when her best friend came storming through the backyard into kitchen.

'You'll never guess what our Orla's gone and done,' Alice raged. 'She's only got herself pregnant. I've never known anything so irresponsible in all me life. If circumstances were different, I've have torn her off a strip a mile wide. As it was, I felt obliged to keep me mouth shut.'

'You'd think Micky would have been more careful,' Bernadette gasped, equally shocked.

'Orla wouldn't have let herself get in the club if she hadn't have wanted to – she learnt birth control the hard way, didn't she? She could always wrap poor Micky twice around her little finger. I'd like to bet it's all her idea.'

'It's a funny idea to have, Ally.'

'Well, you know Orla. She always has to be different. *She* can't just die like ordinary people.' Alice clapped her hand to her mouth. 'Jaysus, Bernie, that was a terrible thing to say. It's just that I'm so upset. And you know what she said, our Orla? "It will be like being born and dying at the same time, Mam." Oh!' Alice burst into tears. 'It's so sad, I could cry for the rest of me life.'

'What does the doctor at the hospital have to say?'

'She hasn't told him yet. I reckon he'll have a blue fit.'

'They might make her get rid of it.'

'Over my dead body, they will. It's a daft thing Orla's done, but it's done, and that's all there is to it. There's no going back. Is that kettle on for tea, Bernie? If I don't have a cuppa soon, I'll faint. Kids!' Alice sniffed and dried her eyes. 'They worry you sick when they're little and you think it'll stop when they grow up, except it gets worse. There's something dead funny going on between our Maeve and Martin, and Cormac's been moping around like a lovesick rabbit ever since that Andrea girl went back to London. Then there's Orla . . . I sometimes wish I'd never had children, I really do.'

'No, you don't, Ally. We women would be lost without our kids. Here's your tea. Let's take it into the other room. Shouldn't you be at the salon?'

'No, I should be at me new house in Birkdale measuring for curtains. I'm signing the final contract on Friday.' Alice sighed. 'Oh, Bernie. I hate signing things. Remember that bloody agreement Cora had me sign? Ever since, when I've signed anything I've been worried what I'm letting meself in for.'

'I wish it were me signing for a lovely bungalow overlooking Birkdale golf course,' Bernadette said wistfully.

'I wish it were you too. I'm dreading it, me. Anyroad, only toffs play golf. I'd sooner look out over Anfield football ground or Goodison Park.' Orla's news had put her in a bad mood and she was exaggerating. The bungalow was beautiful, with large, luscious gardens front and back, a lounge big enough to hold a dance in, two bedrooms and a dream kitchen. Alice had gasped in admiration when she saw the cream fitted units, matching tiled walls, the plum-coloured floor. There was a pine table almost as big as her present kitchen. The fridge, cooker and automatic washing machine were being left by the vendors, an elderly couple off to live in Spain.

Mind you, she still felt as if she had been badgered into moving by the children. It didn't help, either, when she casually mentioned to Billy Lacey she was only *thinking* of moving and he'd leapt on the idea of taking over her old house. In a weak moment she'd agreed it would be a good idea, though she felt certain Cora wouldn't. Unfortunately, Cora had, and both her and Billy had been in and out of the place like yo-yos ever since wanting to know what she was leaving behind. She wouldn't need a van to move. The few things Cora and Billy hadn't collared would fit in the boot of the car.

'Have you ever been in love, Vic?'

'Yes, Cormac. Very deeply in love.'

'Was it reciprocated?'

Vicky shook her head. 'No.'

'The chap must be a fool.'

'He's a complete idiot.'

'You're a prize, Vic. You'd make some man a wonderful wife.'

'You're drunk, Cormac. In your present state you'd make some woman a lousy husband.'

Cormac stared gloomily into his beer. He wasn't drunk, just mildly inebriated, but Vicky was still fed up with him. They'd come for a drink after work because he claimed he couldn't bear to be alone and all he'd done, for the umpteenth time, was ask questions about Andrea. Why hadn't she phoned? Why was she never in when he phoned her?

How was Vicky supposed to know? She was glad the affair had ground to a halt when Andrea had gone back to London – she took it for granted it had been a *proper* affair from the sickening way they mauled each other when they thought no one was looking. Now there was talk of using Andrea again when they promoted their perfume, Tender, in the spring. After all, Andrea was the face of Lacey's of Liverpool. It would be daft to have a different face, or so Cormac claimed, sensibly as it happened.

Vicky was dreading it because she knew the affair would start all over again. She had no idea whether Andrea was as smitten with Cormac as he was with her, but she was the sort of girl who probably liked having a man dancing constantly in attendance. No doubt she'd been thrilled to bits to find a good-looking single male available when she'd come to Liverpool for the press campaign.

'Do you think I should go down to London and look for her?' Cormac asked.

'Whatever you like, Cormac. I can't possibly pass an opinion.'

'Why not?'

'Because it's none of my business, is it? You must do what you think is best.'

'You're a lot of help, I must say. I haven't a clue what's best.'

Vicky scowled and quickly changed it to a smile – she looked plain at the best of times. She'd look hideous if she scowled. 'If I were in your position, I'd go to London.'

'There!' Cormac looked delighted. 'I knew you'd come up with an answer. I'll go tomorrow after we've seen that rep about the boxes.' They were contemplating selling their products in sets, covered with cellophane in pretty cardboard boxes.

'Glad to be of help,' Vicky said and immediately regretted sounding so sour.

He turned up next morning in his only suit to go to

see Andrea: light-grey flannel with a blue shirt and navy tie. At midday, after they'd placed an order for boxes and the rep had gone, they went together out to his car.

'Will you be able to manage on your own?' he asked cheerfully and Vicky wondered if he'd give up the idea of Andrea and London if she said she couldn't.

She preferred not to find out. Anyway, she'd been left by herself loads of times before. 'I won't be on my own, will I?' Since Christmas, Lacey's of Liverpool had taken on four more staff. There was a secretary, to type the letters and answer the phone, in an elegant reception office by the door; a young man for the newly formed packaging department; two women for the large room now referred to as the workshop. 'I thought I might go and see your Orla tonight, take her some samples of Tender.'

He kissed her chastely on the forehead. 'Give her my love if you do.'

'I will, Cormac. Have a nice time.'

She watched him leave with tears in her eyes. In a few hours' time he might well be holding Andrea in his arms. Tonight, they would go to bed together. It hurt so much, just thinking about it, that she got a pain in her chest and wondered if her heart was breaking into a million little pieces.

While Cormac was driving down to London, his sister, Orla, was being examined by an astounded doctor who had just been informed that she was pregnant. Across the room a nurse glared at her, shocked and angry.

'An accident, I assume,' the doctor said coldly. 'You should have been more careful in your condition. I'll arrange for a termination straight away.'

'It wasn't an accident,' Orla said cheerfully. 'It was

deliberate. And I don't want a termination, I want the baby, if that's all right with you.'

The doctor gasped, the nurse snorted. 'Since you ask, it's not all right,' the doctor snapped. 'It's one of the most stupid things I've ever heard. To be blunt, Mrs Lavin, you're dying. You might not live long enough to bring the baby to full term. Having a child in your condition is quite mad.'

'I *am* mad,' Orla agreed. 'And I will live long enough for me baby to be born. I *will*. I swear it.' She grinned. 'Though I might not breastfeed.'

The nurse rudely butted in, 'And who'll look after it?'

'The whole of Bootle.'

'What brought this on, pray?' the doctor enquired while the nurse tut-tutted. 'The wish to have a child under such dire circumstances.'

'Well, both me sisters are expecting, as well as me eldest daughter. I didn't want to be left out. Besides . . .' Orla paused.

'Besides what?' the doctor prompted.

'Normally, I wouldn't have dreamt of having another baby. But things aren't normal, are they? I'll be bringing a child into the world that wouldn't have been born otherwise. It seems to be a fruitful thing to do with me last few months on earth.'

The doctor's face broke into an unexpected smile. 'That's rather tortured reasoning, Mrs Lavin. Even so, I admire your spirit. I'll have your notes transferred to the maternity hospital straight away where my friend, Dr Abrahams, will look after you from now on. I'll ask him to keep me informed of your progress. You can be assured he will do all he can to see you have a healthy baby.' He went over to the desk and behind his back Orla stuck out her tongue at the nurse.

*

Alice opened the door to the house in Pearl Street in answer to Vicky's knock. 'Hello, luv. Come in. Orla will be pleased to see you.'

Vicky gasped when she was ushered into the parlour. 'I didn't realise you were having a party.' Every chair was occupied and there were people sitting on the floor. The light was switched off and dozens of candles and night lights burnt steadily on the mantelpiece. The flames flickered wildly from a sudden draught. There was music, very subdued, from a record player in the corner: Frank Sinatra singing 'Pennies from Heaven'. Voices came from the living room, the rattle of dishes from the kitchen.

'It's not a party,' Alice said. 'It's often like this. You must come more, luv. The world and his wife are welcome as far as Orla is concerned.'

'Vicky!' Orla shouted from across the room. Her cheeks were flushed, her eyes brighter than the candles. She looked more alive than anyone else in the room, in a white satin kimono, vividly patterned, and high-heeled red shoes. Her face was heavily made up and she wore too much jewellery. 'Give us a kiss. Everyone who comes has to give me a kiss. What would you like to drink? Micky, someone, get Vicky a drink.'

'I'd like a glass of white wine, please,' Vicky said to the young man who was Cormac's cousin. His name was Maurice, she remembered. She went over and kissed Orla on the cheek. 'I've brought you some samples of our new perfume. It's called Tender.'

'Tender is the night,' Orla crooned. 'Let's try some.' She unscrewed the tiny bottle and dabbed behind her ears. The heady scent of spring flowers mingled with the smell of melting wax. 'Oh, it's the gear. You and Cormac will be millionaires one day.'

'You've given me an idea for our next one. It's going

to be more musky than this, for evenings. We could call this one Tender Mornings and the other Tender Nights. It would probably be best if we brought them out together.'

As was her way, Vicky melted into the background and found Maurice by the door with her wine. Fion was smiling up at her from the settee. She patted the arm. 'Sit down, Vic.'

'Thank you,' Vicky whispered. 'Who are all these people?'

'Laceys, mostly. Don't forget, there's fourteen of us altogether, seventeen with Bernadette and her kids, and twenty-five if you include Uncle Billy's lot. Some people are neighbours, some are friends from school.' Fion laughed. 'When I was young I could never understand why our Orla was so popular. She was horrible to everyone as far as I could see, yet they all liked her. I used to be as nice as pie, but no one liked me a bit.'

'I'm sure that's not true.'

'It is. It might still be true for all I know. The thing is, I don't care any more.'

'You'd never think Orla was . . .' Vicky blushed. She'd been about to say something very tactless.

'Dying?' Fion supplied. 'Oh, it's all right. You can say it quite openly. We all do. Orla doesn't mind. You've heard of people who make a drama out of a crisis, well that's what Orla's doing with knobs on. The sicker she gets, the more dramatic the crisis will get. She's even got her stage make-up on, see! In a few months' time we'll all be gathered round her bed waving candles and singing hymns, and she'll be smiling at us angelically from the pillow. She's enjoying herself no end.' Fion's voice changed, became softer. 'I don't half admire her. I didn't realise how much I loved her till the last few weeks. She's got more character in her little finger than most people have in their whole body. Did you know she's expecting a baby?'

'Yes, Cormac said. It's incredible news. And you are too – congratulations.'

'Ta. Can you feel it?'

'The baby?'

'No, the atmosphere. The whole house is throbbing with emotion. It's almost tangible. Every now and then I have to catch me breath.'

'Yes, I think I can, feel it, that is.' But she wasn't part of it. Vicky felt more like an observer than a participant in the tragic, enchanted events taking place in the tiny house in Pearl Street. She wished with all her heart she were a Lacey and these people would belong to her and she to them.

Cormac stared up at the third-floor window of the house in Camden. It was an elegant house, slightly shabby, situated on a busy road full of traffic on its way to and from the centre of London. The curtains on the window that so attracted his attention were tightly drawn against the brilliant sunshine of a lovely May morning. Perhaps Andrea was still asleep after her night out with her brute of a boyfriend. Perhaps they were *both* still asleep.

He'd looked like a brute to Cormac. His name was Alex and he had a remarkably heavy build for a banker, as well as a coarse face, a rasping voice and a plummy accent. He'd hated him on the spot.

Worst of all, Andrea hadn't been the least bit pleased to see him. She'd actually been reluctant to let him in, turning her face away when he tried to kiss her – he'd arrived in London late afternoon the day before and had driven straight to her flat. Alex had yet to make an appearance.

'I didn't answer your letters because I didn't want to,'

she said coldly. She wore tight black trousers and a long silky blouse. Her perfect feet were bare, the toenails painted crimson. 'Anyway, I've been away for most of the time since Christmas, in the States doing a fashion shoot. We went all over the place. I didn't find your letters till I got back last week. Did you need to send so many?'

'I thought we were in love,' Cormac stammered. 'I thought . . .' He stared at her lovely cold face. 'Weren't we?'

'You may have been, darling. I certainly wasn't.'

'But you said . . .'

'People say all sorts of things in the heat of passion. They don't have to mean them.'

'*I* did.'

Her expression softened slightly. 'I'm afraid *I* didn't, Cormac. I thought we were just having a nice little affair to pass the time. I won't deny that I enjoyed it. But it meant nothing.' Her smooth brow puckered in a frown. 'I could have sworn you felt the same, darling. You didn't give the impression of being madly in love.'

A key had turned in the door, and a figure in a pinstriped suit carrying a bowler hat, a brolly, and a briefcase lumbered in: Alex.

'Who's this?' he said suspiciously – and rudely, Cormac thought.

'Remember that little job I did a few months ago for a company called Lacey's of Liverpool?' Andrea trilled. 'Well, this is Cormac Lacey. Cormac, meet my boy-friend, Alex Everett.'

'How do you do,' Cormac said courteously as he shook hands with a reluctant Alex who didn't speak. 'Let me know, won't you, Andrea, if you'd like to do the job again? As I said, we're launching the perfume in June.'

'I'm sure I would, Cormac.'

'Why doesn't he get in touch with the agency?' Alex growled.

'Don't be such a sourpuss, darling. It's only natural he should approach me personally. I was best friends with Cormac and his partner, Vicky. Wasn't I, Cormac?'

'The very best,' Cormac agreed.

He'd left the flat, thought about driving back to Liverpool straight away, but felt too tired, so booked into a hotel nearby. He lay in bed for ages, staring impassively at the ceiling, feeling curiously empty, trying to discern what was wrong with him. Dawn was breaking by the time he fell asleep. Even so, he woke little more than an hour later, too early for breakfast. He left immediately to come and stare at Andrea's window.

Something in him was missing, a chemical in his brain maybe, because Andrea was right. He hadn't been in love with her. He'd realised almost straight away, as soon as he'd left the flat, expecting to be heartbroken, but finding he didn't care. He'd *thought* he was in love. He'd badly wanted to be. It was what men and women did: fall in love, get married, have children. The same thing had happened with Pol with whom he'd expected to spend the rest of his life, yet hadn't minded too much handing over to his cousin, Maurice.

Andrea was a shallow human being, he told himself, and if he hadn't been so anxiously looking for a soulmate he wouldn't have allowed himself to be so easily taken in.

Why was he gazing at the window of this shallow human being who could well appear any minute accompanied by her brutish banker boyfriend in his bowler hat?

Cormac had no idea. It was as if he expected the window, glinting so brightly in the sunshine, to send him back an answer, tell him what was missing.

The thing had gone, the link that was missing, the night of his twenty-first when Aunt Cora had informed him Alice wasn't his mam. He hadn't been able to love anyone since then. There was a coldness in his heart. He wasn't sure who he was any more, where he came from, precisely where he stood in the world.

If only Vicky were there and he could tell her how he felt. He could talk to Vicky about anything on earth in a way he'd never talked to anyone else. He'd never discussed what Aunt Cora had told him because he'd never felt the need. But he felt the need now. Vicky would tell him what was was wrong with him. She had answers, solutions, for every problem on earth. He urgently wanted Vicky and it would take hours to get back to St Helens when they could speak. In which case he'd telephone. There was a call box in the lobby of the hotel where he'd stayed.

Cormac ran like the wind back to the hotel. In the lobby he emptied his pockets of change and arranged the coins in little piles on the box: pennies, sixpences, shillings. He was about to dial the factory when he remembered it wasn't yet eight o'clock and Vicky would still be at home.

'Hello.' Her voice was quietly efficient when she answered.

'Vicky, it's Cormac.' The words tumbled over each other. 'I need to talk. I'm in a terrible state, Vic. There's something wrong.'

'Cormac! Have you had an accident or something? Is Andrea all right? Are you still in London?'

'No to the first question, yes to the others. Oh, damn! This thing needs more coins already. Hold on a mo.'

'Give me the number and I'll ring back,' Vicky said crisply. 'A long-distance call will eat money as fast as you speak.'

Cormac shoved a pile of pennies in the box, reeled off the number, put down the receiver and snatched it up again a few seconds later when it rang.

'You know you asked once why I called Alice Alice?' he said immediately, sinking down on to a black plastic chair. The long leaves of a pot plant brushed against his cheek.

'I remember, Cormac. And you're calling now, a whole year later, all the way from London, to tell me why?'

'Because she isn't me mother. Aunt Cora is. I was born the same night as Maurice and she swapped us over in the hospital.' His voice rose to a wail. 'Oh, Vic! I don't know who I am. Least I do, but I'm not the person I want to be, the person I always thought I was. I'm someone else entirely.'

There was silence from the other end of the line for quite a while as Vicky took in this startling fact. 'Don't be silly, Cormac,' she said eventually. 'You're Cormac Lacey and you always have been. You belong to Alice. They put you in her arms in the hospital and she took you home and brought you up. As far as Alice is concerned, you're her son.'

'And as far as Auntie Cora is concerned I'm *her* son.'

There was another pause, then Vicky said in a strangely puzzled voice, 'But you can't be.'

'Yes, I can, Vic. Somehow, I believed Cora when she said she switched me and Maurice around. It's the sort of thing she would do.' Cormac shuddered. 'She's evil.' And she was his mother!

Then Vicky said in what Cormac called her 'school-mistressy' voice, 'I'm surprised at you, Cormac. You're supposed to be so clever. How could you not know such a basic fact?'

'What are you talking about? What basic fact?'

'That a brown-eyed couple can't have blue-eyed children. It's something to do with genes. I thought it was something everyone knew. Your Uncle Billy has brown eyes and so does your Aunt Cora – I remember noticing what a strange brown they were at your Fion's wedding.'

'Not everyone's got a mind like an encyclopaedia, Vic,' Cormac snapped. 'People can't be expected to know everything.' He gulped. 'Does that mean . . .?'

'It means that if it's true your aunt swapped you round with Maurice, you weren't actually her baby to swap in the first place.'

'Then whose baby am I?' Cormac shrieked. A man had come into the lobby with a suitcase and was staring at him strangely.

'Maybe the nurses got confused and put the two Lacey babies in the wrong cots in the first place,' Vicky said sensibly. 'Cora merely put you back in the right one.'

'I'd love to believe that, Vic. Except – Mam told us this loads of times – it was hell on earth in the hospital the night I was born. There was an air raid and everyone was moved down into the cellar and back again. A woman was brought in who'd been found in the wreckage of her house about to give birth. I could belong to any bloody one.'

The man with the suitcase clearly thought he was sharing the lobby with a lunatic. He hurried into the dining room.

'Oh, Cormac, don't think about it now. Come home. But drive carefully. We'll talk about it tonight over dinner.'

'All right, Vic.' His voice trembled. 'I can't wait to see you.'

'Nor me you, Cormac.'

He replaced the receiver. Vicky had created more

questions than answers, but he felt better after talking to her. In fact, he felt better all round. He sniffed. The smell of fried bacon came from the dining room and he suddenly felt very hungry. Mistakes had been made when he was born, but what did it matter after such a long time? And perhaps, you never knew, Cora had put him in the right cot after all. If so, he had much to thank her for. After he'd eaten he'd give Mam a ring; he still had plenty of change. They'd hardly spoken since she'd gone to live in Birkdale in her posh new house. Then he'd go home to Vicky.

It made Alice feel dead peculiar to get out of bed, pull back the curtains, and be met with nothing but the sight of her own back garden and miles and miles of sky. Apart from the birds, there wasn't a sound to be heard. She'd been used to coming face to face with a row of tightly packed houses across the street, hearing the clink of milk bottles, cars, voices as people went to work.

Every morning she found herself leaving earlier and earlier for the hairdresser's, coming home later and later. Pretty soon she'd be sleeping there! What would it be like in the winter? She dreaded to think.

She missed having friends in the same street or the next one, the library and the post office being just round the corner, as well as every sort of shop a person could possibly need. Instead, she had to drive everywhere, even to Mass.

Bernadette claimed she wasn't giving the bungalow a chance. She came to visit and ran her fingers along the cream worktop, looked out of the window at the pretty garden where Ruth and Ian were playing, and said, 'It's beautiful here, Ally. You'll soon get used to it.'

'I suppose so, Bernie. I'm trying hard.' She sniffed. Bernadette was the only person who knew she hadn't settled in. 'What have Cora and Billy done to me old house?'

'I don't know, luv, and I'm not likely to, am I? I can't see them asking me inside.' She regarded Alice sternly. 'The trouble with you, Alice Lacey, is you've made a ton of money but don't know how to enjoy it.'

Alice sighed. 'I'd give it away, except no one will take it. Only Orla let me buy her a car.'

'Talking of Orla, how is she? I haven't seen her for a day or so.'

'Driving everybody mad, including Micky, though he loves it. I wouldn't have thought it possible for a woman in Orla's state to get on so many people's nerves.'

Maeve Adams felt the first twinge of what might have been a contraction soon after breakfast. Martin had just gone to work. She glanced at her watch, calmly made a cup of tea and waited for the next twinge. It came half an hour later and was stronger than the first. The baby was on its way!

Glancing at her watch again, she washed the dishes and was just making the beds when a wave of pain passed through her tummy that couldn't possibly be described as a twinge.

She cautiously made her way downstairs, took the suitcase, already packed, out of the understairs cupboard and, in quick succession, rang for a taxi, the hospital in Southport to say she was coming, Martin at work to tell him he was about to become a father – should he be interested, that was – then her mother at the hairdresser's. Finally she rang her sisters to let them know that the first of the four Lacey babies due to arrive that year was already on its way.

'Good luck, sis,' Orla sang. 'As for me, I do believe me bump's starting to show a bit.'

In the taxi, she took deep breaths all the way. The driver assured her he'd once delivered a baby on the back seat, so there was no need to worry if it came early. Maeve worried all the same. The contractions were getting closer and more painful with each mile.

'You look very calm.' The nurse smiled when she walked into the hospital, the taxi driver coming behind with her case.

'Well, I don't like to make a fuss.'

The labour was swift and very painful, but still Maeve didn't make a fuss. She just gritted her teeth, took more deep breaths and got on with it. Her little boy was born within the hour. He weighed eight pounds, three ounces.

'He's beautiful,' said the midwife.

'All babies are beautiful,' Maeve said serenely. 'Can I hold him? I've been waiting nearly thirty-six years for this.'

'Only for a minute, dear. We've got to get you sewn up. You need at least three stitches.'

Maeve was propped against the pillow, her baby wrapped in a sheet and placed in her arms. He felt big and warm. He was real. He was a real, live baby, with real hands and feet and perfect little fingers, a snub nose, a tiny rosebud mouth, hardly any hair and sleepy blue eyes. And he could move. He could wave his hands and wriggle his body. He could make a noise, the sweetest sound she had ever heard, a squeaky croak. And he was hers! Maeve Adams was a mother at last. Her calm deserted her and she burst into tears, just as Martin walked into the delivery room, slightly dishevelled, his tie crooked and his usually neat hair on end.

He stood at the foot of the bed, looked at her, then at the baby. 'So, you've done it,' he said in a voice devoid of expression.

'Yes, I've done it, Martin. This is our son. I thought we might call him Christopher.' Maeve wiped her eyes with the corner of the baby's sheet. 'Isn't he beautiful?'

Martin edged closer. 'He's got no hair.'

'Lots of babies are born without hair. It'll soon grow. Would you like to hold him?'

'I'm not sure. I might drop him.' He came closer still. 'He doesn't look like either of us.'

'There's plenty of time,' Maeve said placidly. 'I thought he looked a little bit like Grandad.'

'He's got my mother's mouth.' Martin suddenly sat on the edge of the bed and gathered his wife and his new son in his arms. 'Oh, Maeve, I'm so *scared*,' he said hoarsely. 'I'm scared you'll love him more than me, that he'll take my place in your heart. I'm scared to love him myself in case he dies, babies do sometimes. What if he's unhappy at school, gets bullied? What if he goes off the rails when he gets older, the way your cousin, Maurice, did? Or he runs away like Fion? How must your mother feel about Orla? We're going to worry about him for the rest of our lives and I don't think I can cope.' He began to cry. 'We were so happy before, darling. Why did you have to spoil everything by having a baby?'

'*I* wasn't happy, Martin, and I suspect you weren't either. No, don't argue.' She put her hand over his mouth when he opened it to speak. 'We cared about such trivial things. Our baby's *real*. Oh, yes, he'll be a worry, but the world would come to an end if everyone stopped having babies because they were scared of the future. If your parents and mine had felt like that, neither of us would have been born. As to loving him more than you, I'll love him differently, that's all. You'll find the same.'

The door opened, the midwife came in and clapped her hands. 'Would you mind waiting outside, Mr

Adams. I'm about to sew your wife back together. I'll take baby into the nursery and you can admire him through the window. There are more visitors outside who can't wait to see this lovely little chap.'

Alice was in the corridor with Bernadette and Fion. A few minutes later Orla and Micky arrived, Orla proudly displaying her bump. Then Martin's parents, and later on his sister and his niece. Cormac came with Vicky. By then, Maeve had been wheeled into a ward, exhausted but extremely pleased with herself.

Martin felt dazed as he was hugged and kissed, his hand was shaken, his shoulder punched, and he was congratulated so many times he felt as if he must have done something uniquely remarkable to deserve such approbation.

The men decided there was just time enough to wet the baby's head before the pubs closed. On the way out, they passed the nursery, where Martin paused and looked at his son lying wide awake in his cot. By God, he was a magnificent baby, far superior to every other one there. He longed to pick him up and cuddle him. He caught his breath. In another week's time, Maeve would bring him home and he could pick up his son whenever he pleased.

'What it is to be a Lacey!' Vicky remarked to Cormac on the way back to St Helens in his car. 'There's always something going on. If there isn't a new baby, or several new babies, in the pipeline, then someone's getting married or a party's thrown for no reason at all as far as I can see. All my family's ever celebrated is my parents' silver wedding. We merely went to dinner on my twenty-first because there weren't enough people to make a party.'

'We have funerals too,' Cormac said soberly. 'I think there's one on the cards in the not too distant future.'

'I hope not. Your Orla looks as if she could live for ever. What's coming next? Whose baby is due first, Fion's or Orla's?'

'Neither. Lulu's due in October. At least that's when she's coming back to England. The other two are expected to make an appearance about a month later. By the way,' he said, changing gear, 'you forgot about the wedding.'

'I didn't know there was a wedding. Who's getting married?'

'I can't tell you yet because the woman hasn't agreed.'

'You mean, there might not be a wedding?'

'Not if the woman doesn't agree.'

'You're talking in circles, Cormac,' Vicky said patiently. 'Is she having trouble making up her mind?'

'No, it's more a matter of her not having been asked.'

She laughed. 'Then why doesn't the man ask her?'

'D'you think he should?'

'Of course he should, if he wants to marry her.'

'In that case, Vicky Weatherspoon, will you marry me?'

'I beg your pardon!'

'You heard, Vic.' He grabbed her knee, removing his hand immediately when they had to turn a corner. 'I want you to be my wife and I desperately hope you want me for a husband, because I can't live without you.' He looked at her sideways. 'What do you say?'

'Yes, I'll marry you, Cormac.' She was amazed her voice sounded so sensible when she really wanted to scream with delight. It was the question she'd been aching for since the day, years ago, that they'd first met. In her wildest dreams she never thought he'd ask. Now he had and she would savour the words for the rest of her life. She would have preferred the surroundings to be more romantic: a candlelit restaurant, champagne and for Cormac to have gone down on one knee. Maybe in real life that didn't often happen.

'When?' he demanded. He was grinning. He looked incredibly happy and all because Vicky Weatherspoon had said 'yes'.

'Before all the babies are due so everyone's sure to be there. Say September.'

'September it is. We'll buy an engagement ring on Saturday. What sort would you like?'

A round one, she wanted to say. Any sort of stone. In fact, a piece of string would do. 'A diamond solitaire,' she said dazedly.

'What will your folks have to say?'

'Oh, they'll be thrilled. *I'm* thrilled.' She turned to him to explain exactly how thrilled she was that they were getting married, to tell him how much she loved him, always had, always would, but something prevented her. She merely pressed her shoulder against his and said nothing. Theirs would be an unequal partnership. He looked happy, but there'd been something casual about his proposal, as if he had taken for granted what her answer would be. They were comfortable together and, on his side, there wasn't the passion he'd clearly felt for Andrea. He hadn't told her that he loved her. There was still time for that, but Vicky knew he would never love her as much as she loved him — it might embarrass him to know how much. She would have to hold back a little, stay calm, be cool, match his emotion with her own.

Despite this, Vicky's heart throbbed with a dazed, exultant happiness. Before the year was out she would be Mrs Cormac Lacey and, whatever the circumstances were, she couldn't wait.

Chapter 19

The three sisters had never been so close. Every afternoon Fion and Maeve, with baby Christopher, would arrive in Pearl Street to sit with Orla and gossip, play cards for pennies, swap jokes – Orla had learnt some that were very near the knuckle during her time on the road. Fion laughed heartily and Maeve winced.

Micky had given the backyard a fresh coat of paint and a set of white plastic garden furniture had fallen off the inevitable lorry accompanied by a red and white striped umbrella. Baskets of flowers hung on the walls. There was a tub of hydrangeas in each corner. On sunny days the women sat outside – it was like a pavement café in Paris, Orla said once. Micky grinned foolishly before escaping to the pub for a drink, as he was inclined to do when the house was taken over by three women and a baby.

'I bet it's not a bit like Paris,' Orla said after he'd gone. 'But it pleases Micky no end to hear me say it. I'm learning to be nice, though it's a bit late in the day.'

Alice usually managed to join them for an hour and when Cormac discovered his family met every day, he came over from St Helens whenever he could, so that the five Laceys could be together – after all, time was precious. In a matter of months there would be only four of them left. They talked about the years when they'd only had each other, before husbands and children had appeared on the scene. They talked about John. Alice found it upsetting that they could remember so little of the time when everything had been perfect in the house in Amber Street, before their father had had the accident and everything had changed.

'In my mind, there was always a horrible atmosphere,' Fion claimed.

'Same here.' Maeve nodded.

'I remember hating him so much,' said Orla.

'I loved him.' Cormac made a rueful face. 'Trouble was, I always had the feeling he didn't love me back.'

'He had other things on his mind.'

'What do you mean, Mam?' asked Cormac. 'What other things?'

Alice hesitated before deciding they were old enough to know the truth, old enough for it not to hurt them any more. She told them about the day Lulu was born when she'd gone round to B.E.D.S. and found John with a new young family.

'You mean he dumped us for another lot?' Orla gasped, outraged.

'No, it wasn't you, his children, that he dumped, it was me, his wife. He found a girl as damaged as himself. But she got better and he began to treat her the same way as he'd done me, and she left him.'

'Poor dad,' Cormac said, always the softest. She was glad he was engaged to Vicky who she felt sure would never hurt him as his father had done.

It was strange that Fion, thirty-eight, but a strapping, healthy woman, was the one who suffered most during the early months of pregnancy. She was often sick, her legs swelled, she had dizzy spells, went off her food. Whereas Orla, the invalid, bloomed. Her hair was thick and glossy, her eyes star bright. Her skin had the texture of the thinnest, finest china and she had never smiled so much. The baby was growing well in her womb.

'She's a blessed baby,' Orla cooed. 'She's charmed.'

'She?' said Micky.

'Oh, it's a girl. She's another me. She's coming to take my place after I've gone.'

'No one can ever take your place, sweetheart.' Micky knelt in front of the chair and laid his face against her stomach. He felt the sharp bones of her hips under his hands and could have sworn he could hear his baby's heart beating. He wondered how he would manage to get through the next few months without completely breaking down. It was a tremendous effort always to appear composed, to look after the endless guests, engage in conversation, when he was being torn apart inside.

Orla was the only woman he'd ever wanted. He'd loved her since they were fourteen and they'd been in the same class together at school. But this love, burning, wholehearted and totally committed, hadn't been enough to make her happy. She had slept with other men. She had walked out on him. If it weren't for the cancer, she would be in an office in St Helens dreaming of even better things. She'd only returned to him and their children because she was dying.

It made him feel guilty for being so glad that she was back. For Micky, a dying Orla was better than no Orla at all and there would be nothing left for him after she had gone.

She ran her fingers through his hair. 'Cheer up, luv. Life is for enjoying, not enduring.'

'Don't say things like that.'

'Why not? It's true.' She lifted up his head, rather painfully, by the ears, and slid into his arms. 'If I'd had a bit more sense, I would have enjoyed meself more when I had the opportunity. And I'd like to think you've got a lot of years left to enjoy. I'll be keeping me eye on you, Micky Lavin, from up in heaven.'

He kissed her. 'They'll never take you in heaven, Orla. You'll be keeping an eye on me from a place much warmer than that.'

Lacey's of Liverpool perfumes were proving a great success. Tender Nights and Tender Mornings came on to the market in June. The lovely face of Andrea Pryce featured prominently in a press and television advertising campaign carried out from London. Andrea and Cormac never met again.

All the big Liverpool stores had extensive displays of the local products: Lewis's, Owen Owen's, George Henry Lee's. Cormac and Vicky were looking for a bigger factory so they could expand their range to include lipstick and face powder.

'In a few years' time we'll do an entire range of make-up,' Cormac boasted.

'How can you have aromatherapy mascara and eye-brow pencil?' Orla wanted to know.

'Don't ask awkward questions, sis. We're working on it.'

'Do you wish you were part of it, luv?' Micky asked when Cormac had gone.

'I'm having a baby, Micky, which is far more important.'

Cora Lacey helped herself to a couple of perfumes while she was cleaning the Strand Road salon, the morning one and the night one, though personally she couldn't tell the difference. They would do as a birthday present for Pol, save buying something.

Alice noticed, but tactfully kept her mouth shut. Cora

was an excellent cleaner and as long as she didn't make off with one of the dryers she didn't care.

At the end of August, six months into her pregnancy, Fion started to feel better. The feeling of constant nausea went away, along with the dizziness and the swollen legs. She ate like a horse and developed a passion for apples, which were at least healthy.

Fion, though, would have preferred to remain sick, or indeed feel much worse, if it could have prevented her sister's sudden deterioration.

Orla was rapidly losing weight, getting thinner and thinner, almost daily it seemed to concerned onlookers. She was having pain more severe than she had known humanly possible. Every nerve in her body shrieked in raw agony. It was the cancer, not the baby.

The baby was all right. The baby was fine. Dr Abrahams, who had adopted her as his special project, confirmed that her child was coming along well when Orla went to see him at the hospital.

'Would you like some painkillers?' he asked for the fourth week running.

'No, doctor.' Orla shook her head violently. 'I'll not forget what Thalidomide did to unborn babies. There's no way I'm taking so much as an aspirin in case it harms me little girl. I'd sooner have pains than tablets, any day.'

'You're a very brave woman, Mrs Lavin.'

'No, I'm not, doctor. I'm a realist. Anyroad, I've learnt that, if I notch meself up a gear, the pain goes away and I can't feel it any more.'

The doctor looked at the starry eyes in the thin face. 'You're a very remarkable woman then, Mrs Lavin. Will you allow me to say that?'

'I've always wanted to be remarkable at something, doctor. I'm glad to have managed it at last.'

★

Micky's sole reason for existing was to take care of Orla. The children felt the same. They came straight home from work every night to sit with their mam and hold her hand, to fetch and carry, to bring her anything on earth she wanted.

To please them, to make them feel needed, to make up for the hurt that she had caused them, she asked for a daily newspaper and made a show of reading it, requested cups of tea and glasses of lemonade she didn't feel like drinking. Maisie massaged her feet which she found extremely irritating. She pretended an interest in football, which she loathed, but Micky and the boys were passionate about it. It meant they could watch the − far too many − matches on the telly without feeling they should be watching something on another channel that Orla would in fact have found ten times more interesting.

September, and the weather was sunny, gently warm. The trees in North Park began to shed their russet leaves and the flowers in the Lavins' backyard bent their heads and died. The big petal balls on the hydrangeas turned brown. Pretty soon they would become brittle. Next spring they would have to be pruned to make way for new blossoms.

Orla sat on a white plastic chair, knowing she would never see this happen. But her baby would. She laid her hands on her stomach. The baby had been very still this morning. She felt a moment of fear, closed her eyes, concentrated hard and directed all the goodness left in her emaciated body on to the baby, now fully formed in her womb. Her little daughter gave her an almighty kick. Orla gasped with pain and relief.

The other pain she'd learnt to live with. It didn't matter any more. She'd stepped outside it.

★

Alice woke up every morning in the silent bedroom of her silent house with a deep sense of foreboding. The next few months would be nightmarish. What would Christmas be like with one of her children gone for ever? She also felt unreasonably depressed that Cormac, her baby, was getting married, which she might not have done if it hadn't been for Orla. There was a saying: 'A daughter is a daughter for the rest of her life. A son is a son until he takes a wife.' She was losing two children. She wouldn't be needed any more. It only emphasised the fact that she was on her own. The future seemed very bleak.

Then she would get up, pull herself together and prepare for the day ahead. She never let anyone, not even Bernadette, know how low she felt.

Lulu Jackson came back from America a few days before the wedding. Gareth was to fly over nearer the time the baby − Alice's first great-grandchild − was expected the following month. Alice picked her up from Manchester airport, took her to Pearl Street to see her mother, then to the bungalow where she was to stay. There was plenty of room and she was glad of the company.

'I like your frock, luv,' she remarked. Lulu wore a spectacular yellow garment lavishly trimmed with lace with its own little lace bolero.

'It's Indian and it's not really a maternity dress. I can wear it afterwards. I brought one for Mum in cream. I thought she might like to wear it to the wedding. Oh, and I've got you a scarf, Gran. There's this lovely Indian shop right by where we live in Greenwich Village.'

As soon as they'd eaten, Lulu asked if she'd mind if she returned straight to Pearl Street. 'I'd like to spend the evening with Mum. She looks well, doesn't she? Far better than I expected. A bit thin, that's all.'

'Your mam always manages to put on a show, Lulu. And I wouldn't build up your hopes too much that she'll be at the wedding. It's not exactly close, way over the other side of Warrington. Apart from the hospital, she hasn't been outside the house in months.'

Lulu's pretty blue eyes filled with tears. 'She was always bursting with life, me mum. She was the only person who encouraged me to marry Gareth. Everyone else thought marrying an artist was daft. And she thought going to New York was a great idea.'

'She saw you doing the things she'd wanted to do herself,' Alice said sadly. 'Anyroad, luv, come on. I was intending to spend the evening at Pearl Street meself. You'll find the house bursting at the seams.'

It was raining steadily on the Saturday of the wedding. The sky was a miserable grey, heavy with clouds, and there wasn't the faintest sign of blue.

Lulu emerged from her room in an even more magnificent frock than the one she'd arrived in: tangerine silk with an embroidered bodice and long, loose sleeves. Her hat was merely a circle of velvet trimmed with net.

'You make me feel very drab,' Alice remarked as she glanced in the hall mirror at her plain blue suit and conventional flowered hat.

'You look lovely, Gran. But then I can never remember a time when you didn't.'

The young woman and the much older one kissed lovingly. Alice smiled. 'That's a nice thing to say, but I can't help noticing me hair's as grey as the sky outside.'

'You *still* look lovely. I hope I look as beautiful when I've got grey hair.'

'Flattery will get you everywhere, Lulu. I'll be changing me will in your favour as soon as I get back.

We'd better be off. The coach is due in Marsh Lane at half past ten and I've promised to show meself in the hairdresser's before we leave.'

A coach had been hired for the bridegroom's guests. The men were pleased. They wouldn't need their cars so could drink as much as they liked.

Alice parked outside the Lavins', where the door was wide open, despite the rain. She waved at Fion and Jerry who were just about to go inside – Fion looked big enough to be carrying half a dozen babies.

'Tell your mam I've nipped round Opal Street. I'll be back in a minute,' she said to Lulu. 'Pass us that umbrella out the glove compartment, there's a luv.'

'My, don't you look a sight for sore eyes,' Patsy O'Leary gushed when Alice entered the salon. Patsy was silver-haired now. Her daughter, Daisy, with the long, gleaming ringlets, had never gone near the stage when she grew up. Nowadays Patsy boasted endlessly about her grandchildren, all of whom were exceptionally talented in their various ways, or so she claimed. She had never ceased to get on Alice's nerves, but she had grown fond of the woman who had worked for her for more than a quarter of a century.

She nodded at her other staff and promised to bring them a piece of wedding cake on Monday. They were mostly new. How many staff had she had over the years? How many customers? How many heads of hair had been permed, shampooed and set, trimmed, dyed a different colour?

'Oh, someone rang about the upstairs flat,' Patsy said. 'A man. I don't know where he heard about it. I told him it wasn't available yet. It had to be decorated.'

'I must get someone in to do it,' Alice murmured. 'I've been meaning to for ages.' Since the last tenant left in July.

'Well, you've had other things on your mind, haven't you?'

'Actually, in here could do with a coat of paint at the same time.' She glanced at the walls, where the paint was peeling off in places. 'I hadn't noticed before. I'm usually too busy working.' It worried her that she was letting the place fall to pieces around her ears, the way Myrtle Rimmer had done, and another, younger woman would end up taking it over, bringing it back to scratch. She suddenly laughed.

'What's so funny?' asked one of the customers.

'Nothing. I was just having a flight of fancy, rather a morbid one.'

'This is no time to be morbid,' Patsy admonished. 'Your only son's getting married today.'

'So he is. I'd better be going.'

Orla was wearing the cream dress Lulu had brought from America. The thin material lay over the bulge in her stomach and Alice felt concern for the tiny child curled up inside the tissue flesh, the fragile bones.

For once, Orla looked very down. Apart from Micky, Alice was the only other person there. Everyone else must be waiting in the coach. 'I wish I was coming, Mam.'

'So do I, Orla, luv.'

'We're going to have a fine ould time,' Micky said heartily, though Alice sensed a strain of desperation in his voice. 'On our own for a change, nice and quiet. There's a match on the telly this avvy.'

'Did you see the children, Mam? *Our* children. Didn't our Lulu look a treat in that frock? It's funny to think I'll be a grandma soon. And Maisie's wearing a mini-dress – I hope Vicky's family aren't too disgusted. It hardly covers her behind.' Orla's mouth twisted and Alice realised she was trying to laugh. 'It's just the sort of frock

467

I'd have worn meself at her age. And the lads, they had new suits – I bet you can guess where they came from. They looked dead handsome. Oh, I'm so proud of me kids, Mam.'

'And I'm proud of mine, particularly this one.' She stroked her daughter's face. 'You know Cormac and Vicky are coming to say goodbye before they leave for their honeymoon, don't you? Vicky's keeping her wedding dress on so you can see her in all her glory – are you listening, luv?'

Orla's eyes seemed to be floating backwards into her head. Alice touched her arm, frightened, and the eyes flickered and fixed on her mother's face. 'Yes, Vicky's coming. Have a nice time, Mam. I'll see you later.'

'She's been doing that all morning,' Micky said worriedly as he showed Alice out. 'Drifting away, as it were, not hearing.'

Alice hesitated by the door. 'Perhaps it would be best if I stayed.'

'Cormac will only cancel the wedding if you don't turn up. Go and have a nice time, like Orla said.'

She managed to stay dry-eyed throughout the entire ceremony, mainly because Mrs Weatherspoon, who looked so fierce and capable when she marched into church, made a desperate show of herself, sobbing helplessly, getting louder and louder, until the noise resembled a banshee's wail. The guests on the bride-groom's side began to smile, the children giggled and the noise woke up six-month-old Christopher, who started to howl. Cormac could hardly keep a straight face and the bride's shoulders heaved.

Alice was glad that what she had expected to be a touching occasion had turned into something resembling a pantomime or farce. She wasn't exactly in the mood for tears, particularly her own.

The light mood continued throughout the afternoon at the reception, held in a modern, rather featureless hotel. Even a shamefaced Mrs Weatherspoon was able to see the funny side of things. 'I don't know what came over me,' she said to Alice. 'I really hadn't expected to cry.'

'I expected to cry buckets, but I think it's the first wedding I've been to when I haven't shed a tear.'

The best man, Maurice Lacey, made a far better speech than anyone thought him capable of.

Cora watched him, feeling unexpectedly proud. Maurice would never be a success like Cormac, but he'd become a solid citizen, with a lovely family, a nice house in Browning Street and a reasonably well-paid job with prospects of promotion. Pol had obviously decided a long while ago that he was a better bet than Cormac, and Pol was prettier than that Vicky by a mile. Vicky had a face like the back of a bus. It was said that all brides managed to look beautiful on their wedding day, but Vicky proved an exception to the rule. Cora wouldn't have fancied having her for a daughter-in-law.

Alice was pleased to see Orla's children enjoying themselves. It would do them good to have a break, forget the tragedy they had been witnessing for so many months.

At five o'clock, Cormac came over. 'Vicky and I are leaving in a minute, Mam. We're going to Orla's first. Vicky will get changed upstairs, then we'll be off to the airport and Majorca.'

'I'll come with you, if you don't mind,' Alice said with alacrity – she was pleased that Cormac had begun to address her as 'Mam' again lately. She could never understand why he'd stopped.

'Why don't you stay and enjoy the reception? It's going on till all hours and everyone's having a whale of a time.'

'I think Micky might like some company back in Pearl Street. Orla didn't seem quite herself this morning. I'll just say goodbye to Mr and Mrs Weatherspoon.'

On the way to Bootle, Vicky sat in the back of the car, where her massive brocade crinoline dress with long puffed sleeves could be more easily accommodated. Personally, Alice thought she would have suited something much plainer so she didn't look too much like the cake but, naturally, no one had asked for her opinion.

It was still raining steadily when the car drew up in Pearl Street – it hadn't stopped all day. Alice jumped out and knocked on the door of number eleven and was surprised when no one answered. She was about to go round the back when Sheila Reilly came out of her house across the street.

'Alice. I've been keeping a lookout for you. I'm sorry, luv, but your Orla went into a coma early this avvy. Micky rang for an ambulance and she was taken to the maternity hospital. He said to tell you the minute you came back.'

'Ta, Sheila. I'll go straight away.' Alice was already on her way to her own car, which she had left parked outside the house that morning.

'Would you like a cup of tea first?' Sheila called. 'Steady your nerves, like.'

'No, thank you.'

Cormac was standing on the pavement. 'What's up, Mam?'

In a trembling voice she explained the situation. 'You go off on your honeymoon, luv. Vicky will just have to get changed in the Ladies at the airport.'

'I'll do no such thing,' Vicky said. She had rolled

down the car window and was listening. 'Cormac, drive Alice to the hospital. It doesn't matter about us.'

'Get in, Mam,' Cormac said in a voice that brooked no argument and Alice did as she was told.

Micky was walking up and down the hospital corridor like a wild man. He looked as if he had, quite literally, been trying to tear out his hair. His eyes were mad with grief and Alice wondered if he'd lost his reason.

Mr and Mrs Lavin were there, Mrs Lavin sobbing uncontrollably. Alice immediately assumed the worst. Her body seemed to seize up, she could hardly speak.

'What's happened?' she croaked.

'Orla's having a Caesarean at this very minute,' Micky said raggedly. 'They don't hold out much hope for the baby. As for Orla, they think this is the end.'

'Aah!' The cry came from her very soul. Orla had invested every shred of herself into this baby. If it died, it would all have been in vain.

Cormac had been searching for somewhere to park. He came rushing up with Vicky, still in her bridal gown. Mr Lavin explained the situation and went to fetch everyone cups of tea.

They had to wait over an hour for news, though it felt more like twenty. No one spoke. It was almost seven o'clock before a nurse appeared. Alice searched her face, trying to discern from her expression if the news was good or bad. She didn't look particularly grave.

'The baby has arrived safely,' she announced and there was a concerted sigh of relief. 'It's a girl and she appears to be in surprisingly good shape, though she's only tiny, barely three pounds. She's gone straight into an incubator. Her dad can see her later on, but no one else, I'm afraid. As far as the mother is concerned, I'm sorry to say there's no change.'

471

Micky made no sound. He hid his face in his hands for several seconds. When he removed them his face was pale, but he was himself again. His eyes were normal. 'Orla will be pleased about the baby,' he said. For the first time he seemed to notice Cormac and Vicky. 'Isn't it time you two were on your way?'

'We'd sooner stay.' Vicky's dress rustled as she went over and embraced him and Alice thought she'd make a fine Lacey. She was pleased and proud the girl was now a member of the family.

'And I'd sooner you went,' Micky growled. 'If Orla was asked for her opinion, she'd say the same.'

'I think so too,' Alice put in. 'There's enough of us here.'

'Would you like me to ring the reception, tell the children?' Cormac asked.

'No, leave the kids be.' Micky shook his head. 'Let them enjoy themselves as long as possible. They'll know soon enough. Tara, Cormac. Tara, Vicky. Good luck.'

The newly married couple left, albeit reluctantly. Cormac said he'd telephone as soon as they reached Majorca.

Mr Lavin left to fetch more tea. A young woman walked past in a dressing gown, heavily pregnant. 'I'm just going for a walk,' she said, 'to try and bring it on. It stopped coming the minute we got here.'

Another nurse arrived and said Micky could see his new daughter. He came back after only a few minutes. 'She's so tiny,' he said gruffly, holding out his hands about twelve inches apart. 'Pretty, like a doll, with lots of fair hair.'

Mrs Lavin began to cry again. Voices and footsteps could be heard approaching and Orla's children came hurrying round the corner, their faces anxious, their eyes bright with fear.

'How's Mum?'

'Can we see her?'

'Has she had the baby?'

'Are you all right, Dad? You should have told us.'

They crowded round their father. Micky hugged them one by one and tried to answer their questions. It seemed to Alice that he'd aged since morning, when she could have sworn he didn't have a stoop. His features were blurred. He looked middle-aged. For some reason she remembered the desperate young man who'd called at the house in Amber Street all those years ago asking for Orla who was hiding upstairs and Alice was obliged to tell him lies, send him packing, though she'd tried to do it kindly.

She left the group, feeling in the way. No one had taken a blind bit of notice of her, which she found quite understandable. No doubt Fion and Maeve would arrive shortly – they'd probably taken the children home first. She found a padded bench in a quiet corridor by the closed X-ray department where she sat, feeling extremely alone, wondering how John would have felt if he were there, knowing his favourite daughter was dying. Well, once she'd been his favourite. Perhaps another daughter had taken her place, just as another woman had taken hers.

'Alice! We've been looking for you everywhere.'

It was Billy Lacey accompanied by Cora. He sat beside her and put his arm round her shoulders. 'Are you all right, luv? You look dead lonely all by yourself.'

'I'm fine.' Alice sniffed. 'Just felt like a bit of peace and quiet.'

'I don't blame you. That Mrs Lavin doesn't half go on.'

Cora sat opposite. She saw Alice grit her teeth, as if determined not to cry, unlike that other woman, Micky's mam, who was making a terrible scene, not helping things a bit. It struck her that Alice had never made a scene, not even when John had left. She'd just gritted her teeth, like she'd done now, and got on with things. When you thought about it, John Lacey hadn't been much of a catch, not compared with Billy who'd stuck by his wife through thick and thin. It had taken a long time for the penny to drop, but Cora realised she'd married the right brother after all. As for Cormac, Alice was welcome to him and his ugly missus. She'd prefer Maurice and Pol any day.

Thinking about it, Cora couldn't remember anything that Alice had done to spite her. In fact, she'd only tried to help. It was Alice who'd collected her from the police station that time, then given her a job even after she'd heard about the pensions Cora had been fraudulently collecting all them years.

There was a funny sensation in her stomach as she leaned over and patted Alice on the knee. 'Everything's going to be all right, luv,' she said consolingly, even though she knew, and Alice and Billy knew, that it wasn't.

Then Billy stood up and slapped his thigh. 'Come on, ould girl. We'd better start making tracks. It's still raining cats and dogs outside and I don't know if there's any buses running at this time of night.'

Cora stood up and linked his arm, and they went home together to Bootle.

During the long night that followed the relatives were allowed to see the patient once, a few at a time. Alice went in with Fion and Maeve.

Orla was lying peacefully still, long, dark lashes resting on her white cheeks, lips curved in a slight smile. Fion gasped. 'I've never seen her look so beautiful!'

474

'She looks about sixteen,' Maeve whispered.

Alice said nothing. She bent and kissed the cold, smiling lips, and wondered if she would ever kiss them again.

In a hotel room in Majorca, which smelt of strangely scented blossoms and chloride from the pool below, and where the blue, luminous water of the Mediterranean could be seen from the balcony, Cormac put down the phone. 'No change.' He sighed. 'There are times when I wish I smoked. I have a feeling a cigarette would be a great help at the moment.'

'It would also be very bad for you,' Vicky said primly.

'I've heard there are people around who say the same thing about sex.'

'Oh!' Vicky looked nonplussed. She was sitting up in bed with nothing on, a sheet chastely covering her breasts – she'd only been a married woman for a matter of hours and nudity took some getting used to. 'Oh, they can't possibly be right about sex.'

Cormac grinned. 'If those people are so very wrong – about sex, that is – then I assume it would be OK if we did it again.'

She blushed. 'It would be OK as far as I'm concerned.'

'As we are the only two people whose opinion matters, I suggest we do it immediately, though it will be necessary for you to remove that sheet.'

Vicky removed the sheet.

The hospital was very quiet. Occasionally a baby cried, there were footsteps in other corridors far away. Outside the room where Orla lay, her husband, her children, her sisters and her mother hardly spoke, and when they did it was in subdued murmurs. Mr and Mrs Lavin had gone home long ago.

Fion felt ashamed of how much she longed to be at home, under her own roof, with Jerry's warm body in bed beside her and the kids safely asleep not far away. They weren't the sort of couple who lived in each other's pockets, but she badly missed her husband right now. She squeezed the hand of Maeve, sitting beside her.

Maeve must have been having the same thoughts. 'You really appreciate your own family in situations like this,' she whispered. 'I shall never feel irritated again if Martin changes Christopher's nappy wrongly or complains about the car.' He still did occasionally.

'We're ever so lucky, sis.' Fion sighed. 'We've got everything.'

'I know, but it's a pity it takes a tragedy to make us realise it.'

Sunday afternoon, and Micky and Alice were persuaded to go home and rest. Jerry drove them. It was still raining heavily and the clouds were even greyer than they'd been the day before. Jerry stopped at the end of Pearl Street, where Micky got out, and Alice said quickly, 'I think I'll go and see Bernadette before she leaves for the hospital. She sent a message to say she was going this avvy.'

'Are you sure? I'll take you home if you prefer. It's no trouble.'

'It's kind of you, Jerry, luv. But I prefer Bootle to Birkdale at the moment. Anyroad, me own car's around here somewhere.' She couldn't possibly go back to her smart bungalow at a time like this, even though she would have liked to get rid of her hat, collect a mac and change her suit for something more comfortable. She got out of the car, kissed Micky and almost ran, not to Bernadette's, but to the dark, silent salon in Opal Street,

476

where she let herself in and sat under the middle dryer – something she hadn't done in years.

She hadn't realised she was quite so tired. Almost immediately, she fell awkwardly asleep, a sleep full of horrible dreams, which she couldn't remember when she woke up, but she knew her mind had been preoccupied with things unpleasant.

Jaysus! Would the rain never stop! She could see nothing, not even her watch, because by now it was completely dark, but the downpour sounded even heavier, as if the rain was bouncing off the pavements.

It would have been better to have gone to Bernadette's, where she could have slept in a proper bed, had something decent to eat, not be stuck here with nothing but her own miserable thoughts to keep her company.

Mind you, what other thoughts could you expect to have at a time like this? Alice found herself dredging up every single memory she could of Orla. Orla being born, walking for the first time, saying her first word, her first day at school – she'd come home and informed her mother she was the prettiest in the class, as well as the cleverest.

'Arrogant little madam.' Danny chuckled when he was told – she'd been her grandad's favourite, as well as John's. Alice had never had a favourite. She loved all her children the same and would have felt just as devastated had any one of them been in hospital in a coma.

'Oh, I feel so *sad*!' The sadness rolled up into a ball at the back of her throat. In a minute she'd make a cup of tea – except there'd be no milk. At weekends Patsy usually took home what was over in case it went sour.

Perhaps it wouldn't be a bad idea to turn the light on, go round to Bernie's who might be home again by now. She was only making it worse, sitting by herself in the pitch dark, longing for a drink. She was about to heave herself out of the chair when the key turned in the lock and someone came in. She held her breath. It was a man, she could just make out his bulky form against the window.

He reached for the light, turned it on and uttered a startled cry when he saw her. 'Alice! I am feeling a definite sense of déjà vu.'

'Who are you?' For some reason, she didn't feel the least bit frightened.

'Have I changed so much?' the man said dejectedly.

She stared at him. He wore a well-cut tweed suit and looked about fifty. Once he had been handsome, still was in a way, but his face was deeply lined, his expression careworn. Iron-grey hair, slightly receding and wet from the rain, was combed back from his forehead in little waves. He was smiling and it was a nice smile that involved his entire face, including his very blue eyes, which were dancing merrily in her direction. Despite everything that was happening in her life, despite the fact that she didn't recognise the man from Adam and he had just walked uninvited into her salon, that somehow he had a key, Alice smiled back.

'I remember doing precisely the same thing,' the man said. 'Coming in, finding you in the dark – oh, it must be twenty years ago. You gave me a fright then. Mind you, this time I deserve it.'

'Neil!' She stared at him in disbelief. Suddenly he looked achingly familiar and she couldn't understand why she hadn't known him straight away.

'Whew! Recognition at last. How are you, my dear Alice? If you knew how many times I have longed for this moment you would be deeply flattered.' He came and sat beside her.

'How did you get in?' she stammered. 'Well, I know

how you got in. I mean, how did you get the key? No one's supposed to have it.'

He dangled the key in front of her eyes. It was attached to a St Christopher medal keyring that she remembered well. 'This is my original key. I forgot to give it back and have kept it all these years. I was hoping it would fit, that you hadn't had the lock changed, because I wanted to see the flat. I intended sneaking in and out so no one would know I'd been, but you seem to make a habit of sitting under a dryer in the dark.'

'What if there'd been someone living upstairs?'

'I knew there wasn't,' he said surprisingly. 'I heard from a friend in Bootle that the flat was vacant, but when I phoned I was told it was badly in need of decoration. I wanted to see exactly how bad it was in case I could manage it myself.'

'Patsy said someone had phoned.' Alice frowned. 'Have you taken up painting and decorating?'

'Only of the upstairs flat.' His smile faded. 'Things haven't gone exactly well for me over the last few years, Alice. In fact, nothing's gone well since I left Liverpool all those years ago. I suddenly decided I'd like a little bolt-hole to hide in when I felt particularly low. And what better place than the one where I spent the happiest years of my life.'

They'd been happy years for her too. Looking back, the time they'd spent together seemed unreal. The flat had also been her bolt-hole, a place where she'd felt able to leave all her troubles outside and relax in Neil's arms. It felt like a million years ago.

'Would you mind having me as your upstairs tenant a second time?' he was saying. 'It would only be for occasional weekends.'

'I don't think I would mind that at all, Neil,' she said, and wondered if she was still dreaming and, if so, how much of the past had been a dream and how much had actually happened. At what point in her life would she wake up?

He smiled at her delightedly. 'Well, now that's settled, enough about me. What about you, Alice. How are Cormac and the girls and your multitude of grandchildren? How many do you have now?'

'Seven,' she said automatically. 'No, eight.' She'd forgotten about the tiny girl who'd been born the night before. Her eyes filled with tears when she thought about Orla, whom, incredibly, she'd almost forgotten since Neil had arrived. Just as she had done the other time he found her in the dark, Alice started to cry. She told him about Orla, the baby in the incubator, the wedding yesterday. Time fell away, the years merged to nothing, as he held her hand, patted her cheek and agreed that it was all quite unbearably sad, but that one day, a long time off, it would be bearable again, incredible though that might seem right now.

'God works in mysterious ways that I don't pretend to understand,' he said.

'Me neither.' She sighed. 'What time is it?'

'Just gone nine.'

She must have been asleep for hours. Her neck ached from having been in an uncomfortable position and she had pins and needles in her legs. 'I'd better be getting back to the hospital.'

'Can I come with you?'

'Oh, yes, please'. She didn't care if it sounded too eager, she just wanted him there. She didn't care about anything much at the moment. It didn't matter that she was fifty-seven and he was ten years younger. It didn't matter if they got back together again though she had a feeling it was what he wanted. Nor did it matter if they didn't. It would be nice to have him in the upstairs flat again, but if it all fell through, that didn't matter either.

Nothing mattered except the moment, now, when she was about to return to the hospital to see her child who would shortly die.

She got tiredly to her feet and went over to the window. The street lights were reflected, wobbling slightly, in the wet pavements. 'It's stopped raining,' she remarked. 'The stars are out.' She noticed that Neil's bones creaked as he came to stand beside her. Together, they watched the stars.

Then one star, more vivid than the others, left its mates and shot across the sky. Alice turned off the light so she could observe more clearly the bright, twinkling point passing over the earth, soaring silently towards who knew where. She pointed. 'See that one! It must be a shooting star.'

'I can't see anything.' Neil shook his head.

Alice knew then that Orla was dead and, for the Laceys, nothing would ever be the same again. The star had been her daughter's final flamboyant gesture to the world.

She held her breath. One day, very soon, she would go abroad, to a place that Orla would have enjoyed. She would go by herself, but she wouldn't feel lonely, because Orla would be with her in her heart. She'd like that.

'I hope Micky was with her when she passed away,' she murmured softly. 'Or at least I hope he saw the star.'

MAUREEN LEE

MAUREEN LEE IS ONE OF THE BEST-LOVED SAGA WRITERS AROUND. All her novels are set in Liverpool and the world she evokes is always peopled with characters you'll never forget. Her familiarity with Liverpool and its people brings the terraced streets and tight-knit communities vividly to life in her books. Maureen is a born story-teller and her many fans love her for her powerful tales of love and life, tragedy and joy in Liverpool.

The Girl from Bootle

Born into a working-class family in Bootle, Liverpool, Maureen Lee spent her early years in a terraced house near the docks – an area that was relentlessly bombed during the Second World War. As a child she was bombed out of the house in Bootle and the family were forced to move.

Maureen left her convent school at 15 and wanted to become an actress. However, her shocked mother, who said that it was 'as bad as selling your body on the streets', put her foot down and Maureen had to give up her dreams and go to secretarial college instead.

As a child, Maureen was bombed out of her terraced house in Bootle

Family Life

A regular theme in her books is the fact that apparently happy homes often conceal pain and resentment and she sometimes draws on her own early life for inspiration. 'My mother always seemed to disapprove of me – she never said "well done" to me. My brother was the favourite,' Maureen says.

> I know she would never have approved of my books

As she and her brother grew up they grew apart. 'We just see things differently in every way,' says Maureen. This, and a falling out during the difficult time when her mother was dying, led to an estrangement that has lasted 24 years. 'Despite the fact that I didn't see eye-to-eye with my mum, I loved her very much. I deserted my family and lived in her flat in Liverpool after she went into hospital for the final time. My brother, who she thought the world of, never went near. Towards the end when she was fading she kept asking where he was. To comfort her, I had to pretend that he'd been to see her the day before, which was awful. I found it hard to get past that.'

Freedom – Moving on to a Family of Her Own

Maureen is well known for writing with realism about subjects like motherhood: 'I had a painful time giving birth to my children – the middle one was born in the back of a two-door car. So I know things don't always go as planned.'

My middle son was born in the back of a car

The twists and turns of Maureen's life have been as interesting as the plots of her books. When she met her husband, Richard, he was getting divorced, and despite falling instantly in love and getting engaged after only two weeks, the pair couldn't marry. Keen that Maureen should escape her strict family home, they moved to London and lived together before marrying. 'Had she known, my mother would never have forgiven me. She never knew that Richard had been married before.' The Lees had to pretend they were married even to their landlord. Of course, they did marry as soon as possible and have had a very happy family life.

Success at Last

Despite leaving school at fifteen, Maureen was determined to succeed as a writer. Like Kitty in *Kitty and Her Sisters* and Millie in *Dancing in the Dark*, she went to night school and ended up getting two A levels. 'I think it's good to "better yourself". It gives you confidence,' she says. After her sons grew up she had the time to pursue her dream, but it took several years and a lot of disappointment before she was successful. 'I was *determined* to succeed. My husband was one hundred per cent supportive. I wrote

'I think it's good to "better yourself". It gives you confidence'

lots of articles and short stories. I also started a saga which was eventually called *Stepping Stones*. Then Orion commissioned me to finish it, it was published – and you know the rest.'

What are your memories of your early years in Bootle?

Of being poor, but not poverty-stricken. Of women wearing shawls instead of coats. Of knowing everybody in the street. Of crowds gathering outside houses in the case of a funeral or a wedding, or if an ambulance came to collect a patient, who was carried out in a red blanket. I longed to be such a patient, but when I had diptheria and an ambulance came for me, I was too sick to be aware of the crowds. There were street parties, swings on lamp-posts, hardly any traffic, loads of children playing in the street, dogs without leads. Even though we didn't have much money, Christmas as a child was fun. I'm sure we appreciated our few presents more than children do now.

What was it like being young in Liverpool in the 1950s?

The late fifties were a wonderful time for my friends and me. We had so many places to go: numerous dance halls, The Philharmonic Hall, The Cavern Club, theatres, including The Playhouse where you could buy tickets for ninepence. We were crushed together on benches at the very back. As a teenager I loved the theatre – I was in a dramatic society. I also used to make my own clothes, which meant I could have the latest fashions in just the right sizes, which I loved. Sometimes we'd go on boat trips across the water to New Brighton or on the train to Southport. We'd go for the day and visit the fairground and then go to the dance hall in the evening.

We clicked instantly and got engaged two weeks later

I met Richard at a dance when he asked my friend Margaret up. When she came back she said 'Oh, he was nice.' And then somebody else asked her to dance – she was very glamorous, with blonde hair – still is, as it happens. So Richard asked me to dance because she had gone! We clicked instantly and got engaged two weeks later. I'm not impulsive generally, but I just knew that he was the one.

Do you consider yourself independent and adventurous like Annemarie in The Leaving of Liverpool *or Kitty* in Kitty and her Sisters?

In some ways. In the late fifties, when I was 16, Margaret and I hitchhiked to the Continent. It was really, really exciting. We got a lift from London to Dover on the back of a lorry. We sat on top of stacks of beer crates – we didn't half get cold! We ended up sleeping on the side of the road in Calais because we hadn't found a hotel. We travelled on to Switzerland and got jobs in the United Nations in Geneva as secretaries. It was a great way to see the world. I've no idea what inspired us to go. I think we just wanted some adventure, like lots of my heroines.

Your books often look at the difficult side of family relationships. What experiences do you draw on when you write about that?

I didn't always find it easy to get on with my mother because she held very rigid views. She was terribly ashamed when I went to Europe. She said 'If you leave this house you're not coming back!' But when we got to Switzerland we got fantastic wages at the United Nations – about four times as much as we got at home. When I wrote and told her she suddenly forgave me and went around telling everybody, 'Our Maureen's working at the United Nations in Geneva.'

> 'If you leave this house you're not coming back!'

She was very much the kind of woman who worried what the neighbours would think. When we moved to Kirby, our neighbours were a bit posher than us and at first she even hung our curtains round the wrong way, so it was the neighbours who would see the pattern and we just had the inside to look at. It seems unbelievable now, but it wasn't unusual then – my mother-in-law was even worse. When she bought a new three-piece she covered every bit of it with odd bits of curtaining so it wouldn't wear out – it looked horrible.

My mother-in-law was a strange woman. She hated the world and everyone in it. We had a wary sort of relationship. She gave Richard's brother an awful life – she was very controlling and he never left home. She died in the early nineties and for the next few years my kind, gentle brother-in-law had a relationship with a wonderful woman who ran an animal sanctuary. People tend to keep their family problems private but you don't have to look further than your immediate neighbours to see how things really are and I try to reflect that in my books.

You don't have to look further than your immediate neighbours to see how things really are

Is there anything you'd change about your life?

I don't feel nostalgic for my youth, but I do feel nostalgic for the years when I was a young mum. I didn't anticipate how I'd feel when the boys left home. I just couldn't believe they'd gone and I still miss them being around although I'm very happy that they're happy.

Are friendships important to you?

Vastly important. I always stay with Margaret when I visit Liverpool and we email each other two or three times a week. Old friends are the best sort as you have shared with them the ups and downs of your life. I have other friends in Liverpool that I have known all my adult life. I have also made many new ones who send me things that they think will be useful when I write my books.

Have you ever shared an experience with one of your characters?

Richard's son from his first marriage recently got in touch with us. It was quite a shock as he's been in Australia for most of his life and we've never known him. He turned out to be a charming person with a lovely family. I've written about long-lost family members returning in *Kitty and Her Sisters* and *The Leaving of Liverpool* so it was strange for me to find my life reflecting the plot of one of my books.

....

Describe an average writing day for you.

Wake up, Richard brings me tea in bed and I watch breakfast television for a bit. Go downstairs at around 8 a.m. with the intention of doing housework. Sit and argue with Richard about politics until it's midday and time to go to my shed and start writing. Come in from time to time to make drinks and do the crossword. If I'm stuck, we might drive to Sainsbury's for a coffee and read all the newspapers we refuse to have in the house. Back in my shed, I stay till about half seven and return to the house in time to see *EastEnders*.

Don't miss Maureen's bestselling novels:

Stepping Stones
Lights Out Liverpool
Put Out the Fires
Through the Storm
Liverpool Annie
Dancing in the Dark
The Girl from Barefoot House
Laceys of Liverpool
The House by Princes Park
Lime Street Blues
Queen of the Mersey
The Old House on the Corner
The September Girls
Kitty and Her Sisters
The Leaving of Liverpool

Mother of Pearl

1939. Amy was just eighteen when she met Barney and they fell deeply in love. Their romantic, passionate marriage was a match made in heaven – and then war came. Barney volunteered to fight, and when he returned to Liverpool after VE Day, everything began to change. But what was it that made Amy kill her adored husband – and what happened to their five-year-old daughter, Pearl?

1971. Amy has been released from prison. But her freedom changes the lives of everyone – not least Pearl. Now twenty-five, she was brought up in a very happy home by her aunt, and has no idea of the terrible secret hidden in her past. As the truth unravels, both Amy and Pearl are caught up in the shocking fall-out of one family's tragedy.

£6.99

ISBN: 978-0-7528-9381-5

All Orion/Phoenix titles are available at your local bookshop or from the following address:

Mail Order Department
Littlehampton Book Services
FREEPOST BR535
Worthing, West Sussex, BN13 3BR
telephone 01903 828503, *facsimile* 01903 828802
e-mail MailOrders@lbsltd.co.uk
(Please ensure that you include full postal address details)

Payment can be made either by credit/debit card (Visa, Mastercard, Access and Switch accepted) or by sending a £ Sterling cheque or postal order made payable to *Littlehampton Book Services*.
DO NOT SEND CASH OR CURRENCY.

Please add the following to cover postage and packing

UK and BFPO:
£1.50 for the first book, and 50p for each additional book to a maximum of £3.50

Overseas and Eire:
£2.50 for the first book plus £1.00 for the second book and 50p for each additional book ordered

---

BLOCK CAPITALS PLEASE

name of cardholder ....   *delivery address*
                      ....   *(if different from cardholder)*
address of cardholder ....

....

....

....

          postcode ....   *postcode* ....

☐ I enclose my remittance for £...........................

☐ please debit my Mastercard/Visa/Access/Switch (delete as appropriate)

card number ☐☐☐☐☐☐☐☐☐☐☐☐☐☐☐☐

expiry date ☐☐☐☐   Switch issue no. ☐☐